USA TODAY & WSJ BESTSELLING AUTHOR
giana darling

The Fallen Men Series. Book Five.

LICENSE NOTES

To everyone who has known the exquisite agony of unrequited love.

*"**The best people** possess a feeling for beauty, the courage to take risks, the discipline to tell the truth, the capacity for sacrifice. Ironically, their virtues make them vulnerable; they are often wounded, sometimes destroyed."*
— Ernest Hemmingway

PLAYLIST

"Dark Night" —The Blasters
"Bad Company" — Bad Company
"Holdin on" — Flume
"The One That Got Away" — The Civil Wars
"Hurts"— Emeli Sande
"Bury a Friend" — Billie Eilish
"Free Fallin'"—Tom Petty
"Watch Me"—The Phantoms
"Lie"—NF
"I Hate U I Love U"—gnash feat. Olivia O'Brien
"Sex on Fire" —Kings of Leon
"Tattooed on My Heart"—Bishop Briggs
"Beat the Devil's Tattoo"—Black Rebel Motorcycle Club
"Closer"—Nine Inch Nails
"Not Above Love"—Aluna George
"Gypsy Woman" —Jonathon Tyler & The Northern Lights
"Mixed Signals"—Ruth B.
"Four Walls"—Broods
"River"—Bishop Briggs
"Bounce"—Timabland ft. Missy Elliot
"Kisses Down Low"—Kelly Rowland

"Closure"—Vancouver Sleep Clinic ft. Drew Love
"If You Want Love"—NF
"Dark Night"—The Blasters
"No Good"—KALEO
"You Shook Me All Night Long"—AC/DC
"What Have I Done"—Dermot Kennedy
"Last Resort"—Papa Roach
"Miracle Love"—Matt Corby

CHAPTER ONE

Lila

THE GREATEST LOVE AND GREATEST LOSS OF MY ENTIRE LIFE moved into the house next door when I was five years old. I was only a kid, so it might be hard to understand exactly how profound my underdeveloped brain understood that moment to be, that moment when Jonathon Booth unfolded his long, lean teenage form from his family's minivan and stepped onto the lawn fifteen yards from where I sat playing in the grass with my brother, Dane.

But I got it.

Even then, I knew the absurdly pretty man with a thatch of perfectly tousled golden-brown hair and a gait so fluid he moved like water even in his gangly teens would become the epicentre of my life.

I believed every relationship could be distilled down to a handful of moments.

My complicated friendship with the man who would come to be known as Nova began the very same day he moved in.

Dane was trying to entertain me and failing. I didn't like doing childish things like playing with the cheap, permanently stained toys he bought me from Value Village or reading from any of the books we checked out from the library.

Not even half a decade of life under my belt and I was already an adventurer, eager to drag my older brother from exploration to exploration. We walked through the woods at the back of our property discovering abandoned fox dens and families of deer grazing in meadows between the seams of the trees. I liked to dive into the icy waters that pooled beneath the craggy rocks of the mountains, running down the middle of the province from tip to toe like one great, boney spine and collect the wild flowers that bloomed on the grassy hills until I was coated in pollen and fragrant as wine.

But that day, Dane didn't want to explore.

He usually gave into my whims, especially because exploring meant we didn't have to stay in the small cracker box house with our father and his cast of criminal friends.

But that day, one I remember vividly from the exact cerulean blue of the sky overhead to the feel of the silken blades of grass tickling my bare thighs, something was happening in that house that I didn't understand.

Dane did, and therefore, he'd decided we should stay close.

I wasn't worried like he was about the sketchy man with the twitch and the leer, pockets bulging with cash and waistband distorted by the press of a gun who was inside with our papá, 'doing business.' I didn't remember that he'd been by before, that he owed Papá a lot of money, and even the bulge of bills in his pockets wouldn't have been enough to repay him. I wasn't old enough to notice, as my brother did, that Papá, Ignacio, was the kind of man who exacted payment in the flesh.

Dane barely noticed when the grey minivan rolled to the curb across the street carting a U-Haul nearly as big as our house.

But I did.

All at once, as soon as the engine stopped, the car exploded with activity. An older man pushed open the driver's side door while the rear automatically pulled back to reveal three adolescent boys who almost tumbled over each other in their quest to get out of the vehicle.

There was loud chatter, the sharp yip of young male laughter, and a lone female voice raised in motherly warning from the other side of the van.

Instantly, I wanted to go over to them.

Especially when the last occupant unraveled his long form from the interior and emerged into the mid-afternoon sunlight.

He had none of the tattoos he would come to be famous for, or the signature five o'clock shadow that perpetually dusted his angular jaw later, but he was still heart stoppingly beautiful, even at seventeen.

Even through the eyes of a five-year-old.

"Dane," I whispered, about to impart the first secret I'd ever cultivated. A secret that had instantly formed in my untried heart. "Dane, do you see those people?"

It was as if they were too good to be true, and in that neighborhood, they were. We lived in a ramshackle house on the edge of the invisible line that delineated the 'good' neighborhoods of Entrance, BC, from the seedier part of town. The house across the street was nice, with a massive wrap-around porch and large picture windows, even though the paint was peeling and the yard hadn't been maintained in years.

The family looked nicer than our surroundings, every single one of the four boys beautiful, the father strong and strapping, the wife, when she rounded the car, young and sweet like one of my kindergarten teachers.

I think I wondered at the time if they were actually real or a product of my often-overactive imagination.

"Quiet, Li," Dane hushed me, his eyes narrowed, lean torso torqued awkwardly as he strained to hear something.

Immediately, I quieted, my gaze moving to my brother, my protector.

He was twelve years older than me, tall and already stronger than our papá because he spent a lot of time working out to be so. He was smart, too, like a whip, one of his teacher's had said even though I didn't understand what that meant.

If he told me to be quiet, I was silent and still as a tree trunk.

Then, faintly, I heard it.

The tinkling crash of glass from inside the house and the low boom like a bass from a blown speaker as my father yelled at someone.

He yelled a lot.

So I didn't understand why Dane was being so cautious.

I opened my mouth to say so when there was another noise, this one so loud even the neighbors across the street stopped their antics and froze with their eyes on our urine yellow house.

A loud crack like a heavy tree limb breaking off.

A gunshot.

Dane flew into motion, crouched as he jogged across the yard to peer into the kitchen window.

"Stay here, and do *not* come inside, Li, you hear me?" he ordered.

I nodded mutely, watching with my heart in my throat as Dane slowly opened the screen then the front door and disappeared inside.

This was not the first time we had heard a gunshot from our house.

When your father was a popular drug dealer, the noise was only one of a collection of abrasive sounds in the musical soundtrack of your life with him.

A little scream leaked from my mouth when a throat cleared behind me. Instinctively, I spun around, my fist wrapped around the stupid, stained, plastic bucket filled with flowers I'd picked in the meadow behind our house, I threw it at the person behind me.

The cute teenager I'd been eyeing blinked down at his dirt and petal covered denim shirt then peered up at me through the flop of wavy hair over his forehead. I noticed his eyes, so deep a brown they seemed as rich as the brushed suede jacket my mother wore on special occasions.

I held my breath, my primary fear forgotten in the face of this new, immediate situation.

He was going to hate me, beat me at the very least, or yell in my face for throwing dirt at him, I was certain.

My father had done more for less to Dane over the years.

Instead, his mouth thinned as a hoarse shout sounded from inside our house, and then he bent into a crouch so that we were eye level. His forearms braced on his jean-clad thighs, hands dangling in the gap between his knees so I could see the carefully drawn lines of a Sharpie splitting his skin with illustrations. There was a lone flower striking up from the dirt, but it was what he'd drawn beneath the earth as it edged up one wrist that drew my focus. Little creatures with sharp teeth burrowing deeper, a broken skull crumbling to dust at the edge of an eye socket. It was graphic and as horrible as it was alluring.

"You doin' okay over here?" he asked, pulling my attention back to his somber eyes.

My voice was locked in its box, shored up under sand like it was buried in the ocean floor beneath leagues of sea water.

The nice-looking woman, the mother, appeared over his shoulder and smiled down at me too.

"Hey, sunshine, why don't you come on over to our house for a beat? Seems your family is having some trouble, and we don't want you to be any part of that, do we?"

She had a voice like sun-warmed velvet, worn and smooth. I wanted to listen to her speak all day.

Still, I said nothing.

At that point in my life, kindness was more suspicious than cruelty.

I didn't understand their angle, and I wished Dane would come out to help me.

Instead, he was inside with our father and a gun.

The neighbor's dad walked across the street toward us, his cell phone to his ear, his voice low and angry as he spoke into it.

"Yes, Pine Crescent, Entrance," he confirmed as he stopped before us and immediately took his wife's hand. He looked down at me, and his voice went soft as he asked, "Hey girl, you think you can give me your name?"

My name.

He was a stranger, and my school teacher had said not to speak to strangers, but I'd already spent the first half decade of my life with strangers coming in and out of my home.

Strangers were the cornerstone of my father's business.

The teenager smiled at me encouragingly when my eyes fell to him.

"Lila," I told them. "Lila Davalos."

"Hi, Lila," the father said to me, a big smile in his thick beard. "I'm Diogo Booth. This is my wife, Molly, and our oldest, Jonathon. Why don't you come on over and meet the rest of my boys? I got one about your age."

"My brother's inside," I muttered, finally driven to speak because there was no way I was going to move an inch without knowing Dane was okay.

Diogo cursed under his breath as he shared a tense look with Molly, but the teenager named Jonathon distracted me by reaching out to finger a yellow petal of the sunflower I still clutched too hard in my small, sweaty palm.

"You like flowers?" he asked, low and intimate like he was sharing a secret with me.

I didn't have friends. Most of the kids at Entrance Elementary School had nicer clothes, nicer homes, and nicer lives than I did, so they didn't like me much. Some of them pulled my hair or spit on the scuffed patent leather shoes my mother liked me to wear. My Papá said it was because I was different, not just poor. There weren't many mixed kids at school, but there were a lot of international students, so I thought it had more to do with the holes in my clothes than the colour of my skin.

So I wasn't used to this attention, to the quality of a kind gaze searching my face in order to know me, in order not to scare me.

It was novel and truthfully, uncomfortable.

I squirmed. "Who doesn't like flowers?"

Jonathon titled his head, the silken strands of his hair sliding over his tanned forehead into those warm eyes, tangling with his lashes. "Is that why you like 'em?"

Diogo moved away, rounding our little group to go to the house. I opened my mouth to protest because Papá did *not* like noisy neighbors, but Molly gave me an encouraging smile that shut me up.

"No," I said quietly. "I like flowers because they're wild and beautiful." I twirled the mangled stem in my hand. "They're free."

It was the reason I had flowers all over the room I shared with Dane even though he was a boy, and boys weren't really supposed to like flowers. But Dane was okay with it, with me and all my petals, because he said they were pretty just like me.

I wasn't pretty, everyone told me so, from the kids at school to Mamá and Papá, but it still made me happy to think Dane thought so. Especially because *he* was pretty. He had a different mum than me, so he was darker than I was, taking after his African Canadian mother with her flawless skin and fine, dark curls. But he had our Papá's eyes. Light and bright like the sky just after dawn when it's newly blue.

I loved his eyes.

"I need to go inside now," I decided, thinking of Dane alone in there.

Papá didn't like anyone, not really. But he liked me, and he'd try not to hurt or kill anyone if I was in the house with him.

"I don't think so, honey," Molly argued, stepping forward so she was in line with Jonathon then crouching too. "Why don't you stay out here with us until the police come and check on things?"

"Papá doesn't like the police," I told her solemnly. "Most people on this block don't like them either."

Molly rolled her lips between her teeth as I fed her the first indication that their family had not moved to a good place.

"Get the fuck off my front doorstep, motherfucker," Ignacio demanded as he opened the front door at Diogo's incessant knocking, immediately drawing all of our eyes.

Unfortunately, Ignacio was an attractive man. He had the rich colouring of his Mexican mother and the muscled build of a man who works with his hands. Ostensibly, he was a construction foreman and made good money doing it too.

In reality, he was Entrance's biggest hard drug supplier.

We didn't live large. Mostly because it would have drawn even more notice from the cops, but also because Ignacio had a plan.

Make bank then cut and run back to Mexico to live like a king.

My mother didn't like the heat. She didn't like drugs, and she didn't care much about money.

But she loved Ignacio.

So she stayed with him.

I was five years old. I shouldn't have understood their complicated dynamic, but growing up in an unsafe environment makes kids smart before their time.

I understood.

I also understood Molly's shocked frown at my father.

He was too beautiful, too well dressed to be the owner of such a rundown house, to be the one to discharge a gun in his home with his kids outside in the yard.

This was Ignacio's magic as a criminal.

People don't expect beauty to be bad.

"Is Lila your daughter?" Diogo asked, completely unfazed by Ignacio.

Diogo was taller, built thick and heavy like he could wrangle a bull.

I thought maybe Ignacio should be the one to look afraid, but, of course, he didn't.

"She done something?" Ignacio questioned, shooting me a look and a wink.

He wouldn't mind if he had.

In his own way, he loved me. Called me his *abejita*, little bee, because I always had pollen dust on my nose.

If Diogo had a serious problem with me, Papá would put a bullet in his head rather than chastise me.

Family meant everything.

"No, but we were concerned when we heard a gunshot," Diogo said calmly as he crossed his big arms over his chest. "Everything okay in there?"

Ignacio's face tightened, features sharpening, his smile a slick spill of evil between his cheeks. "You a cop or something?"

"No, but I did call them."

Ignacio leaned a hip against the doorframe and crossed his bulky forearms over his chest. He appraised Diogo as if he had all the time in the world and not a single care about the police coming.

I was five, but I knew better.

"You some big shot from Vancouver, think you can roll into my town and stick your nose where it don't belong?" Ignacio mused, coiled and still like a snake before the strike.

I wanted to warn Diogo, but when I went to move closer, Jonathon held me still with a hand on my shoulder. When I looked up at him, he whispered, "You've got a scary dad."

I nodded like *duh*.

He winked, and on his kind face it was an entirely different expression than on my father's. "So's mine."

"Just a common fisherman," Diogo replied, and I noticed he had a slight accent, the spice of a foreign land like the kind I'd always wanted to visit. "But even a common man can sense evil when it comes around. Whatever you got going on in there, think about hitting pause while your kids are around, yeah?"

Quick as a lightning strike, amicable Ignacio was gone, and the drug lord was in his place. He lurched off the doorframe before Diogo could blink and was in his face, a knife suddenly pressed to his throat.

When he spoke, spittle flew into the taller man's beard, trapped like bugs in a web.

"Let's get one thing straight before you and your Brady bunch get any ideas. This is my house. My territory. You want friendly neighbors, I suggest getting another postal code. And, *blanquito*? Next time you think to fuck with me or mine, remember that I know where you live, and I gotta helluva lot more friends in this town than you." Abruptly, he stepped away from the Diogo with a wide, almost manic grin. He backed up into the doorframe, whistled at me with a jerk of his head to join him, then addressed the family gathered on our lawn as I made my way to him. "Welcome to the neighborhood, *amigos*."

He laughed as he turned on his heel and disappeared into the dark, dank interior of our home.

I hesitated.

Truthfully, I thought the Booth family was foolish.

Even I knew you didn't just move into a new, seedy neighborhood and insert yourself into someone's conflict. If Ignacio had taught me anything, it was to mind your own business because no one else was going to mind it properly for you.

I couldn't understand why they'd come over to check on me, and it was mostly curiosity that made me stick my head back out the front door before I closed it.

Jonathon and Molly had joined Diogo on our cracked concrete path. Across the street, the three other boys waited patiently in the front yard playing a game together.

They were so fascinating. I felt their strange, new beauty like an ache in my chest, an echo in a hollow place that I didn't know back then should have been full.

Full with love and support and laughter.

Instead, I watched with empty eyes as Molly lifted a hand to me as if she wanted to reach out and touch me.

"Be safe," she whispered, unshed tears thick in her voice.

"You come get me if you need me," Jonathon said, voice strong, brow angled fiercely over those velvet brown eyes.

It seemed like something a father would say, yet he was only a boy.

"You need anything, you know where we live," Diogo echoed.

"I'm good," I lied easily, because I'd been lying all my life, and it was all I knew, sunk so deeply in my DNA it felt part of my very flesh. "I'm with my family. We're all good here."

And then I closed the door.

Dammit.

I could still remember just how much it hurt to do that, to close the door on the first people to give me a taste of hope.

It was still sweet in my mouth as I turned the two locks and slid the deadbolt home.

But it turned to ash when I moved down the dark hall, listening to Dane whisper furiously at Ignacio.

"I can't believe you. I seriously *cannot* believe you would do this right now. With Lila in the front fucking yard!"

"She's not a kid anymore," Ignacio argued with a shrug. "She should know the family business."

"She's fucking *five*," Dane argued.

This was true, but even at five, I knew there was some truth to what Ignacio said.

I didn't feel very much like a kid.

And whatever childish inclinations I might have secretly harboured in the deepest hollows of my soul died a swift death by decapitation when I rounded the corner to the living room and saw exactly what had happened to the gunshot.

It had pierced a man right through the center of his chest.

Ignacio flipped his Zippo open to light his cigarette then regarded me curiously over a plume of smoke. "Just a dead body, *abejita*, nothing to cry about, okay?"

I nodded woodenly. I didn't want to cry, but the fact that I didn't made my stomach curdle like bad milk. It wasn't the first time I'd seen blood, but this was different.

Or at least, it should have been.

Instead, I stood there as silent and dead inside as the body Dane was tidying on the ground.

He stopped mopping up the blood on the hardwood and leaned back on his haunches to regard me. "Go to our room and stay there, okay, Li?"

"No, no, she's here. She might as well learn the facts of life and death." Ignacio laughed lightly and moved forward to clasp my shoulder warmly. "This is the family business, Lila, and just like our family, no one fucks with our business. You get me?"

My tongue was buried in the ashes of my combusted hope, so I nodded, mutely, dumbly.

He didn't like my lack of passion.

Ignacio sighed heavily, smoke swirling into my hair as he bent to one knee to look me in the eye.

He regarded me then, like a scientist with a microscope.

"You listen to me good here, Lila. Family is *everything*. You earn, you fight, you *die* for family. This man here? He died for our family because he threatened our family. *Tienes que defender tu honor. Y a tu familia*. It's as simple as that."

You defend your honour. And your family.

Ignacio lived and died by that mandate.

He paused then moved so quickly I flinched when he jerked the gun from the back of his waistband. Grabbing my hands, he fitted them to the gun, his meaty hands clasped on top so that I could bear the awful, awkward weight.

"You feel this? This is the weight of a life. I took it with one squeeze of the trigger."

"Ignacio," Dane argued, standing up and lunging toward us. "Don't put a gun in her hands. *Fuck*. What is wrong with you?"

Ignacio moved our hands easily, swiveling the gun so it pointed at my brother. My arms locked, breath a wheezing pant as I tried to pull away from the gun, from my papá and his evil intent.

Ignacio raised a brow at Dane, making a silent point I didn't understand, but my brother seemed to get it because his lips thinned, and he held up his hands in surrender.

Satisfied, Ignacio turned back to me and smiled softly, his expression tender against the hard sight of the gun held between us. "You're a sweet girl, *abejita*, but you must grow strong. You cannot be soft if you want to survive, *si*?"

"*Sí, Papá*," I murmured, but my voice was a single thread

pulled from a complicated tapestry of emotion clogging up my chest.

I was scared of the gun and angry with my father for putting it in my hands as if it was a disease that would seep through my skin and infect me for life.

I was horrified that I'd leveled a weapon at Dane for even a second, even forced to do it as I had been. For the first time in as long as I could remember, I felt like crying.

The tears lodged in my throat and made my eyes hot and glazed over like fired pottery.

Ignacio smiled as he dropped the gun from my grasp, easily taking it in one hand and tucking it back into his pants. I swallowed thickly when he took my face in his rough hands and brought me close to kiss my forehead.

"You are my sweet girl, but don't worry, I will see you strong before you are grown," he promised.

I wasn't sure why, not at the time, why that sounded so much like a curse.

The only thing I understood with absolutely clarity as I helped my father and brother roll the body up in an old sheet was that I didn't want to be there doing that. I didn't want to be wiping blood up with a white towel, watching it turn thick with blood and red as paint. I didn't want to watch Dane's jaw clench and his eyes smolder as he glared at our father the entire time we helped him out.

I didn't want to be there when the police came, suspicious but resigned because they didn't have a warrant and couldn't enter our home without one. They questioned Ignacio who lied and Dane who lied, and even me, little Lila with the flowers in her hair who Officer Hutchinson often gave candies to whenever he was called out to check us out (which was often) lied too.

As I said, lying was second nature to me by then, even at five.

There is a saying my mother taught me.

El que con lobos anda, a aullar se enseña.

He who runs with wolves learns to howl.

You are the company you keep.

I had been born to liars, raised by liars.

It never occurred to me to tell the policemen the truth. I wasn't hardwired that way.

All I knew after that day was that I didn't want to be *there* anymore.

In a house with a father who scared me even though he loved me.

In a house with a mother who tried to be gone as often as she could to avoid the monster of Ignacio under all our beds.

I didn't want to be there.

And my yearning heart had finally found a beautiful flower to land on.

If you had asked me the next morning what I wanted to be when I grew up, I would have told you with absolutely certainty, excitement in my eyes and resolve in my voice...

"I want to be a Booth."

CHAPTER TWO

Lila

FROM THAT DAY ON, I WAS WITH THE BOOTHS MORE OFTEN
than not.

For Dane and I, the Booth family was a godsend. Jonathon
and Dane were the same age. Milo was four years older than
me, Oliver two, and Hudson one year younger.

We fit.

More than that, Diogo and Molly Booth were more than
happy to *make* us fit. It was clear they were not the kind of
people that could live across the street from neglected children
and do nothing.

So almost every night, we joined them at their massive,
hand carved oak table for dinner. Diogo was a fisherman, a
good one, so we had seafood nearly every night from the leftovers brought in on his commercial boat. He liked to cook
dishes from his native Portugal, rich stews that used the entire

fish carcass and rustic bread he made using his big, rough hands. Molly was good at sewing, a necessity with four overactive boys, and she took to making me clothes too. She even forced Dane and I to shower more than our usual once a week.

It took me three days to love Molly.

Maybe three weeks to love Milo, Oliver, and Hudson.

A few months to love the quiet, somewhat rough and blunt Diogo.

And, of course, my little heart had loved Jonathon from the moment I saw him wearing the sunlight like a crown on his pretty head the day they moved in.

I'd never before in my life felt so cared for.

I knew my mother loved us, because she tried as well as she could to show us in little ways that she cared, even if she avoided the house as often as she could. She worked long hours at the diner off the Sea to Sky highway outside town, and the rest she spent at the bar. She drank too much, but the scent of it was sweet in my nose when she returned home late at night and checked on me in bed. She liked wine and sweet coolers that smelled of peaches and pears. I didn't care that she drank because she was a nice drunk, even affectionate sometimes.

Ignacio loved Dane, and looking back, it was obvious he would have taken a bullet for his son, but he had a poor way of showing it. He was grooming Dane more than raising him. Preparing him to 'be a man' the only way he knew how. Being a man meant being ruthless, being loyal enough to kill or die for your brethren. It didn't mean hugs or praise or shared mealtimes.

He was raising Dane to be a man, but he straight up loved me. I looked like him, for one. Even though I was an ugly child, there was the promise of his carved features in my plump, childish face, the lingering sense despite my mismatched features that they would somehow rearrange themselves as I grew into something appealing.

At least, that was what Ignacio told me. He cared about beauty because it was one of his most effective tools, and I could tell he was excited to see how I might make use of it when I came into my own.

He liked to keep me close, tucked under his arm, perched on his knee, a mini-me doll to draw compliments from his business associates. He liked to play the good papá, the family man drug dealer who was just trying to provide for his family. And he was, trying to provide for me, at least, his *abejita*, but barely for the son he viewed as a soldier and certainly not for the wife he didn't love.

Outside our parents, before the Booths, we had no one.

Ignacio's family was still in the Yucatan and Mamá's family were originally from Puerto Rico, but her immigrant parents had died years ago.

So Dane and I had each other.

We were more than siblings. More than best friends.

Dane was everything to me, and even though I was only five, I tried to take care of him as much as he took care of me.

It was nice when Molly and Diogo stepped up to help us, though. If anything, it made Dane and I closer because we were happier.

Laughter became a daily occurrence in our lives, and I discovered for the first time that Dane had a belly laugh, deep and low like water rucked up from an old well.

I loved it, and I loved the people that gave that to us.

I should have known that it wouldn't last long.

Nothing good ever did for the Davalos family.

I was six years old when my mother died.

Memory is a funny thing because I couldn't remember her ever being much of a mother before her death, but as soon as she was killed, I could suddenly recall half a dozen ways she'd been good to me.

The way she worked oil through my thick brown hair then plaited it into braids that made me feel almost cute.

The way she collected cans and jars for me to use as vases for the many flowers I picked in the spring and summer.

The way she made *maduros* that tasted sweeter than candy, and how she let us eat them straight out of the hot pan, still dripping with oil.

How one time she had crawled into bed with me and Dane after a really bad fight with Papá and held us all night, singing sweetly and telling us stories of her own life when she was a girl.

I hadn't known much about Ellie Davalos except that she was gorgeous like no one I'd ever seen before. Exotic and curvy and so unique I could pick her out of a crowd just catching sight of her almond eyes or big curls.

I hadn't known much about my mother, but I remembered every single thing about the night she was murdered.

Because I was there.

I saw who did it.

And then, when she fell to the ground in her sullied yellow summer dress stained with blood, I was the one to catch her.

But first, I woke up to yelling.

Any child in an angry home has their own barometer for domestic disputes.

A low, thudding bassline of shouts meant I should try to go back to sleep.

The shrill wail of my mother passionately defending herself meant I should try to stop Dane from getting involved because one or the both of my parents might turn their anger on him.

My mother was known to hit as well, pretty yet mean as a rattlesnake when she went up against Ignacio.

That night the house filled with static, the air buzzing, thick and hot with summer heat and deep, vibrating anger.

"You're a filthy cunt, you know that, Ellie?" Ignacio demanded coldly. "Only a fuckin' bitch would sleep with a man for money."

"It wasn't for money," she shrieked. "It was for one ounce of affection! When was the last time you touched me?"

"When was the last time you deserved it, hmm? When was the last time you made dinner for the family? The last time you played with Lila or even asked Dane how he's been doing?"

I could hear them as clear as if they were in my cramped bedroom at the back of the bungalow with me, and no amount of layering my pillow, blanket, and stuffed rabbit over my head would muffle their fury.

"You sleep around like a goddamn whore," Ignacio fumed. "And what do I do? I fucking let you because hey, I don't wanna touch that snatch, and it keeps you away from the house, away from our kids, so I'm fine with it. What I am *not* fine with, *puta*, is you selling information about my fucking business."

"You're scum," Mamá screamed, high and shrill like the whistle of our rusting tea kettle. "You're fucking scum, and you think you're king of this place, but you know what you are? You are king of shit all, Ignacio. Shit all!"

There was a whoomphing thump, and I winced in bed, wishing more than anything that Dane was there to comfort me.

But he wasn't.

It was a Thursday, and on Thursdays, Dane snuck out to see his secret girlfriend, Anne Munn.

So I was alone amid the wilting blooms in my bedroom, the air hot and stale because it was mid-summer and so hot the Okanogan Valley was alive with wildfires. I was sweating, so thirsty my tongue peeled like Velcro off the roof of my mouth, but I didn't dare to venture to the kitchen for water.

That was their battleground.

I curled tighter beneath my blanket, listing off flower varieties in my head to distract myself from the chaos in the kitchen.

I always started with sunflowers because they were my favourite, their bright, smiling faces such a marvelous contrast to the grit and grime of my reality.

Little Becka, Soraya, American Giant.

"I'll take the kids and *run!*" Mamá screamed over the clang of falling pans.

"Over my dead fucking body," Ignacio roared.

Pacino, Zohar, Baby Bear, and Elegance.

"You can't keep an eye on them all day long, Ignacio, and I swear, I'm taking them with me."

"No one takes *my* kids. You think they'd wanna go with you anyway? You're practically a stranger to them, Ellie. They'd be more likely to go with the fucking ice cream truck driver."

A female war cry and then a series of thumps.

Mamá always ended up hitting Ignacio when she was in a rage.

Bashful, Frilly, Suntastic Yellow.

"I'm taking them, I'm taking them, I'm taking them—"

Mamá chanted, high and clanging, an alarm I wished I could shut off.

There was a sharp rap against my bedroom window that startled me so badly it broke the seal on my lips and a bright, high sob burst through. I peered under my blanket through the low light at the window, heart beating so hard in my chest it felt like a hammer strike.

Some of Ignacio's friends had come by before and peered through the window after a deal or on their way to the back porch where Papá held court. Luckily, they hadn't done anything but look and leave streaks of greasy fingermarks against the window pane.

It wasn't one of Ignacio's friends there now.

It was mine.

Jonathon's face was cut into harsh angles by the grimy yellow light of the street lamps, but I recognized him in the dark, even in the midst of my own personal hell.

It wasn't strange to find him at my window either.

He was an insomniac, which he'd told me meant he couldn't sleep. Embarrassingly, I'd followed that up by asking if he was a vampire.

He hadn't laughed in a mean way, which was one of the many reasons I loved him. He never made fun of people who were inferior to him in any way. He was more handsome, funnier, and more charismatic at seventeen years old than most people ever were, but he was also kind, his endearing smile authentic.

It wasn't until a few years later that the smile I'd once loved turned brittle at the corners and cracked like an ill-fitting mask.

But right then, in the midst of my terror, I'd never seen anything so lovely as Jonathon Booth's smile through the yellow glint of the window pane.

He jerked his chin at me then worked his fingers under the ledge to jimmy the window up its tacky seams.

"Come here," he whispered, his hand snaking through the gap, fingers unfurled, a pen drawn image of a lotus flower in the center of his palm. "You come stay with me tonight."

I bit my lip as there was a crash of breaking porcelain in the kitchen. Sometimes, when Dane wasn't home, I thought Jonathon made a special effort to check in on me. And sometimes, if I needed him, he would arrive at the window and pull me free of the stinking wrath boiling up the walls of my house before it could scald me.

But sometimes, when I was too terrified to leave Mamá alone with Ignacio or Ignacio alone with Mamá, worried their fury would raze the house to the ground, I begged Jonathon to stay.

I unpeeled my sticky tongue from the roof of my mouth to do just that when he sighed gustily and heaved the window open even farther so he could swing himself through it. He landed nimbly on his scuffed black converse and made his way to my bed. When he sat, I felt the ugliness in my chest, the knotted mass of emotions residing there, loosen.

He smelled like tobacco and something spicy that itched my nose in a good way.

Instantly, my hand snapped out of the covers to clutch at his.

His wavy hair fell across his brow as he stared down at our cinched hands, and for one moment, almost scarier than the minutes before that, I was worried he'd reject me.

But then he gave my small hand a firm squeeze and tipped his chin up so I could see the depthless brown of his shadowed eyes.

"I'll stay 'til Dane gets back, yeah?" he whispered.

I nodded, scooting back on the bed so that he would have some room to lay beside me on the lumpy mattress. He hesitated for a second before swinging his shoes up on the covers as he settled on his back.

I closed my eyes and dragged a deep lungful of his familiar

scent. His big body was effectively between me and the door, me and my fighting parents, me and the raw brutality of my life. Tucked away in the floral, humid air of my bedroom amid the pots and plants, rucked up against the wall with a boy I trusted almost as much as my brother, I finally let myself relax.

We were quiet for a long time, long enough for the fight to die down, the front door to slam as one of my parents left in a huff, and silence to descend.

I thought maybe Jonathon was asleep until he shifted his head on my purple pillow and looked at me with wide, alert eyes.

"Not sleepy, huh?" he asked softly, his voice barely audible above the rasp and texture of his head sliding over the pillow. When I shook my head, the left side of his full mouth curled up. "Yeah, me either. Whaddya do when you can't sleep?"

I shrugged, feeling heat in my cheeks as I fiddled with the edge of my comforter.

He nudged me with an elbow then winked when I looked at him. "C'mon, you can tell me. You know I won't make fun. Hell, maybe I can even steal some'a your tricks. I could use the sleep."

"I make lists of flowers," I admitted. "I was on Suntastic Yellow Sunflowers when you came in."

His lips twitched, but true to his promise, he didn't laugh.

"Suntastic, hey? Well, I'm pretty fuckin' sure I can't name varieties of sunflowers, but I could do other flowers good enough. You wanna do it with me?"

I stared so hard at him my eyes burned, and then when that didn't work, I reached out to touch the warm skin over the hard curve of his tricep.

He quirked an eyebrow at me in question, but I surprised myself by admitting the truth of my action.

"Sometimes, Dane and I don't think you're real," I confessed on a breath, horrified that tears started to well at the backs of my hot eyes. "You and Molly and Diogo and your brothers. We never met anyone like you."

Something shifted in the planes of his face, like tectonic plates beneath the crust of the earth. Whatever emotion passed through him was too deep for me to decipher, I only knew it left his eyes so dark they looked black as he blinked at me.

"You know what, Li? You're gonna grow up and meet tons more people who treat you well, and then my family and me won't seem so weird to you."

"Not weird," I corrected harshly, nails digging into the arm I still held. "Beautiful."

I watched his mouth soften, thinking it was too red for a man but that I liked it anyway.

"Okay, not weird. But I mean it, this…" he gestured to the cramped room, the lingering memories of the argument in the kitchen haunting the space like a silent spectre, "is only temporary. Dane's almost eighteen, and he's gonna take care of you. He's gotta plan."

I knew Dane had a plan. He'd been hatching plans to get us out and away from our parents since I could remember. He was smart, but it was hard to do well at school when you had a part time job as a drug dealer's protégé combined with the stress of raising a little girl because your parents couldn't be bothered to do it well themselves. He was noble and strong with a sense of heroism that we both shared. I knew he wanted to be a cop or a soldier or something *important* where he could fix broken lives like he swore he was going to fix ours. But that kind of job took education, and education took money that we didn't have and time we couldn't spare. So he figured he'd get into some sort of trade, and we'd get a little apartment, just us two.

But something about the plan made me sad and in the confessional silence we'd created in my bedroom, I was brave enough to admit that much.

"I wish he didn't have to plan," I murmured. "I wish he only ever had to dream."

Jonathon made a sound at the back of his throat, an involuntary grunt like my words had socked him in the stomach.

"Do you have any dreams, Flower Child?" he asked me, trying to lighten the mood with one of his sideways smirks. "You wanna open a flower store or something?"

I frowned because I didn't have any dreams, not really. I clung to Dane's plans for us like a dream, because I was hopeful but suspicious of our ability to succeed.

But for myself?

No.

I hadn't been given the tools to even know how to build one.

Instead of answering, I turned my head on the pillow to offer Jonathon my shining eyes in reply.

His lips twisted, a smile deformed by pity. "We'll find you a dream. Don't worry. There's plenty'a time yet for you."

"I bet you have dreams," I said, because Jonathon was always moving and shaking, meeting new people, trying new things. Almost like his good life bothered him, always searching for something new to test his edges against.

He exhaled deeply and looked up at the ceiling like it held all the answers. "Yeah, I got dreams."

"I can keep a secret really good," I rushed to say, then blushed at my eagerness and shrugged lamely. "I mean, if you wanna tell me."

I traced his slightly smiling profile with my eyes and felt warmed by his ease with me. He was loose and relaxed, still in a way I rarely saw him. I liked that. I liked that he could be at rest in my small room wrapped in the hot green scent of leaves on my cramped twin bed.

"My dreams don't line up real well with my family's dreams for me. So I think I'll keep 'em to myself for a while longer. But you'll be the first person I tell, yeah?"

That was somehow even better than being told right away.

"Okay," I agreed easily, the last syllable warbled by a mammoth yawn.

Jonathon chuckled. "Okay, Li, why don't we try your flower game, huh? We can get some sleep before Dane comes home. You start us off."

I snuggled deeper into the warm bedclothes, turning on my side so I could face him and tuck my knees up to my chest to hug while I slept.

"Anemone."

"Baby's Breath," he countered, reaching over to gently flick my nose.

I scrunched it up. "I'm not a baby."

"No, but it's gotta be said, I wish you were. You're eyes are too damn old for six years'a life."

I pressed them closed so he couldn't read anything else I had written in my hazel eyes and stubbornly continued.

"Carnation."

"Daisy."

"Evening Primrose," I murmured because it was already working.

An hour ago, sleep had been out of the question, but enclosed in my room with Jonathon like a sentry at my side, I trusted him enough to reach for the hand of sleep and be led into the dark.

"Flower Child," I heard him murmur distantly as I sank into slumber. "I hope you find some dreams tonight."

I WOKE UP BECAUSE I COULDN'T BREATHE.

There was a hand over my mouth, fingers pressed up under my nostrils so I couldn't drag air through my nose. Instantly, I froze. It was a conditioned response. The history of abuse in my family had taught me that the only course of action in a crisis was to be still and be calm or else face an escalation of violence.

So I tried to focus my eyes on the figure looming over me.

My mamá.

The whites of her eyes glowed in the dark, her irises pools of depthless black. She looked haunted. No, not haunted, because I always imagined ghosts as sad beings.

She looked demented.

Driven by some crazed force that was telling her to steal my air.

I blinked hard to clear the fuzz at the corners of my thoughts and tried not to panic.

"Hey *nena*, come with your mamá now, okay?" Mamá swooped lower over me, and I realized she was at the end of the bed, being careful not to disturb Jonathon who was still passed out beside me.

Jonathon.

I tried to kick his leg somewhere to the right of me, but Mamá's hand clamped down viciously on my struggling limb, and her eyes glowed even whiter.

"Listen to me, *nena*, I need you to do exactly what I say. Get up quietly, and come with me. We don't want your papá to hear, do you?"

I didn't.

Mamá didn't care that there was a teenage boy in her six-year old's bed, but I knew Ignacio would kill Jonathon as soon as he discovered him there.

So I nodded as much as I could under the force of Mamá's hand, breathing deeply when she released me.

Before I scooted off the bed, I shot a look at Jonathon.

He looked more peaceful than I'd ever seen him, one arm flung over his head, the other low on his stomach, mouth lax, lashes long fans over his cheeks.

My stomach cramped at the thought of him hurting, at the thought of the Booth family hurting if Ignacio discovered him there when all they'd ever done was help Dane and me.

I sucked in another deep breath and crawled off the bed even though I didn't want to go anywhere with Mamá.

Ignacio had been cruel earlier when he'd said she was a stranger to us.

But he wasn't incorrect.

I bit my lip as she took my hand and started to cart me from the room. We walked swiftly and silently down the short hall to the kitchen where the broken detritus of their fight lay scattered across the floor. A small wedge of glass jabbed through my heel, but I didn't make a sound, and I didn't stop.

Ignacio was a light sleeper.

We were at the front door when I noticed the small suitcase beside the frame and a chill bit viciously into my spine.

I was no longer worried about where we were going.

I was worried about how long it would last.

With a grunt, I wrenched my hand away from Mamá. The force sent me hurtling to the ground where I landed in a pile of glass that shredded my palms and the backs of my thighs where they were exposed by my sleep shorts.

A short wail worked itself free of my throat before I could choke it back.

But it was too late.

Mamá stared at me in abject horror for a moment before she cursed and flung the door open.

I caught a glimpse of a man in a leather jacket with a thick beard and a big tummy standing in front of a truck before the roar of a familiar voice echoed down the mouth of the hall.

"*ELLIE!*"

I shifted to get up off the floor and out of the way of the ensuing argument, but the long, sharp teeth of a broken glass cut deeper into my thighs. Wetness sluiced between my legs, and when I looked down, the previously yellow-tinged linoleum was red with blood.

I blinked, my mind disassociating from my body.

There was a loud crash. A door flung against a wall.

Then the stomp of heavy, angry feet over the old, creaking floor.

Even his breath was audible, like a great, terrifying dragon disturbed from his sleep and furious for it.

Ignacio appeared in the dark mouth of the hall, his fists balled, face twisted with all-consuming rage. His gaze swept over me, and his mouth twisted up small and tight, a poor attempt to cap the emotions I knew were bubbling in his chest.

The second his gaze hit Mamá in the doorway, he blew.

"Are you trying to take my kid?" he asked, low and loud, more growl than words.

Mamá stood frozen like cornered prey even though the door was open at her back.

I was six years old, but I was still smart enough to know she should have *run*.

Instead, she called for backup.

To this day, the details are blurred.

But I remembered a few things, murky memories bleeding and faded like old tattoos inked into my mind.

The biker waiting by the car appeared behind Mamá with a gun.

Ignacio had one in his hand suddenly, and he was yelling.

But Mamá? She was screaming, and then suddenly she was diving toward me, tugging my hand to drag me over broken glass toward the door.

Screaming that I was hers.

Hers!

Ignacio warned her.

God, he warned her.

Let go, or else.

Touch her again, you're dead.

I mean it, Ellie, you take one more step, I'll shoot.

You know I will, Ellie. And you know I never miss.

Let Lila go.

The biker had his gun raised, and when Mamá got close enough, he stepped slightly in front of her.

Maybe to protect her.

Maybe he saw this as an opening in the drug trade and decided to take advantage.

They said the man shot first.

It would have hit Papá, they said, the police afterward who had crawled over the scene like ants on their hill, if Jonathon Booth hadn't chosen that moment to shove Ignacio to the ground.

The man's bullet missed them both cleanly.

But Ignacio's fired too.

In the millisecond before Jonathon tackled him.

He pulled the trigger on his revolver, and the bullet found its way straight into Mamá.

She was holding my hand tight one moment.

And the next, it was limp.

I let go to stare up at her, my vision blurred with tears, throat raw because I'd been screaming for them to stop and hadn't even known it.

Her expression was blank in that moment before death. Pale as a sheet of untouched paper, empty of thought as shock overtook her and blood poured from a circular entry wound in her cheek.

And then she fell.

I guess I tried to catch her because her torso landed

awkwardly on my folded legs, and something inside my left knee *snapped* on impact.

I cried out, but I didn't really feel the pain.

I could only feel Mamá, so heavy in my arms.

In the movies, people always die right away.

Pop. Thunk. Dead.

But Mamá didn't die so quick.

She lay looking up at me like a fish out of water, mouth working slightly, blood pooling on her tongue, eyes glassy.

I didn't know how to help her, and I didn't try.

I just held her.

I held her as Ignacio lurched up from the floor and launched himself at the biker.

They fought brutally, guns abandoned, hands their weapons because passion called for physical blows, and both of them were passionate about Mamá.

Ignacio carved a massive gash into the biker's chest with a piece of glass, but it was the biker who knocked Papá out by shoving him into the edge of our dining room table.

The biker disappeared after that, and no one was ever sure who he was.

But I didn't notice any of that.

I only noticed Mamá, and then when he crawled through the glass over to me, Jonathon.

He sat behind me and curled around my small form so that I was cocooned by him.

Protecting me.

It was only then that I noted I was trembling fiercely and keening like a wounded animal as I looked down at Mamá.

As she died in my arms.

It didn't take long, but it was long enough.

When Mamá took her last breath, Ignacio was out cold on the floor, and the biker was gone.

It was just the boy next door and me, sitting on glass, sticky with drying blood, holding a dead body.

The Booths had called 9-1-1, and they were already on their way.

That was how they found us, Diogo racing in just as the cop cars pulled up with their flashing lights cutting coloured shapes across the yard.

He stood in the doorway, staring blankly at his son and me on the floor in the middle of a war-torn home, and he started to cry.

I'd never seen a grown man cry before, and it shocked me out of my stupor enough to notice that I was crying too.

And so was Jonathon.

His cheek was wet against mine as he curled me closer and then carefully stood up with me in his arms, my legs over one arm and my neck braced by his other.

I stared mutely up into his brown eyes, caught like an insect in wet amber.

"You're comin' with me," he said in a voice as raw as an open wound. Involuntarily, his hands squeezed me tighter to his chest, and I hissed as he pressed into the open cuts filled with glass on the backs of my legs. "You're comin' home with me."

Diogo was there then, too, his hulking, inelegant form shading us from the blue, the red, and the white lights splashing through the house. He slowly lifted a big hand, watching me as he did it, then he carefully, gentle as a petal landing on grass, placed it on my head and ran a rough thumb over my brow.

It felt like an anointment.

"You're coming home with us," he echoed.

And it was funny.

Not in a laugh out loud kind of way because nothing about the nightmare of my life in that moment was worthy of laughter.

It was funny as in ironic, though, I didn't know how to explain the emotion until many years later.

Ellie had been fighting for me to be *hers*.

Then she was dead.

Ignacio had claimed I was *his*.

Then, after an open and shut trial, he was incarcerated for life for manslaughter.

And then, I was no one's.

But the Booths... the Booths tried to make me theirs.

CHAPTER THREE

Nova

I'D BEEN AWAKE FOR HOURS, BUT THEN AGAIN, I COULDN'T ever sleep for shit. Insomnia had plagued me since I was fresh outta the womb. Though lately, I had real reasons not to sleep. The loss of Dane and Lila hovered over the Booth home like a mushroom cloud of toxicity. We moved slower, talked lower, smiled less. After the calamity of Ellie Davalos's murder, social services had pried them right outta our hands and placed them separately in cities hours apart from each other by car. They were away from us and away from each other in a way not one'a us could stand.

In the short seven months since we'd moved to Entrance and met the kids next door, we'd fallen hook, line, and fuckin' sinker for Dane and Lila Davalos.

Dane was my boy, the best friend I'd ever had. I was the kinda guy who'd always had lots'a friends, but I was also the kid who didn't *feel* for anyone, not much and not really.

My parents and brothers were good people, salt of the earth kinda people, or maybe more fittingly, salt of the sea. They had love and affection to give stray cats, lost kids, family and friends galore.

I wasn't born that way. Easy with a smile, free with a laugh, I could entertain the best of 'em, but I didn't get in for bondin'. People didn't interest me much because most people were *easy*. I could see their needs and desires like florescent lights at the back'a their eyes, and it was borin'.

Dane wasn't borin'. He was the farthest fuckin' thing from borin', and not only because he was the son'a Entrance's premier drug dealer, but because he was cut from bad cloth yet somehow constructed into a good man. He was stand-up, the guy who stuck by your side through thick and thin. He didn't judge, and he couldn't be swayed from his own ethical standards.

Between the two'a us, I was the fuck up. The one who got arrested graffitiin' the side'a Evergreen Gas Station for the seventh time, the one that got chased off a property by a father and his shot gun for sleepin' with both his daughters. The one that didn't give a fuck about anythin' unless it was fun or interestin', unless it would push me to feel more alive.

And Dane was there through it all, drivin' his shit ass Honda Civic as the getaway car, takin' a punch that was meant for me straight to the gut and then dishin' out his own to beat down the motherfucker who was jealous of me flirtin' with his girl.

We were opposites, you get me? Me from good stock, kind, solid people, but I was skewed, wrong and rebel in a way I could never ignore. And Dane? He was good straight through, even if his blood shoulda made him mean.

So at first, takin' an interest in Lila was purely for Dane. There was nothin' he loved more in the world than his sister. He was knighted to her, a champion to the death. I reasoned, if Dane was my boy, Lila was just as much my responsibility. We were brothers, so she was my sister.

I had three brothers already, and truth be told, they were all varyin' degrees of fuckin' annoyin', so I wasn't into babysittin' a girl.

But Lila was different.

She followed Dane around without complaint, doin' everythin' he did and doin' it with a smile because she was with her brother, and that was her favourite place to be.

When Dane decided to try his hand at skateboardin' 'cause of me, Lila did too, and honest to Christ, she took to it like a duck to water. It made sense to get her a pink, child-sized skateboard of her own for her sixth birthday, and I pretended that big smile on her awkwardly constructed face didn't hit me right in the chest.

When Dane started fuckin' Anne Munn, the hottest girl in our grade at Entrance High, I looked out for Lila so he could sneak out to be with her. Didn't think anythin' of it, just kept an eye on the front door of the Davalos house from my bedroom window. Creeps and fuckin' pervs were in and outta that house like gnats, and none of us liked the fact that Lila had to live under that roof.

There was nothin' we could do, my parents or me, but watch out for them. Dad even looked into it, reportin' them to Child Protective Services, but the odds'a them bein' split up and sent away were huge, and we didn't have anythin' concrete.

That night, Ellie Davalos dead on the floor between Lila's spindly legs, we got somethin' concrete.

So, I didn't get what the fuckin' hold up was on getting' the two of them back where they belonged.

With us.

It haunted me. The thought'a them alone and apart, achin' with loss and fear. I tried to chase the ghosts away with alcohol and sex—God knew there was enough high school pussy available to me—but nothin' worked. Not even the sweet heat of a woman or the tight grip of my fingers around a pen.

The pen I was holdin' exploded in my hand, the second one that night. I flexed my fingers to work the tension outta them, ignorin' the wet, black stain sinkin' into my fingers.

I liked the ink. Always had. It reminded me that I could change the way people viewed me. That I could construct my self-image into somethin' I could be proud of, and maybe one day, help others do the same.

"You should be asleep."

I looked up from the kitchen table where I'd been inkin' new words into the wood grain to see my mum standin' at the mouth of the stairs, wrapped loosely in her blue linen robe. She was sleep rumpled, but those eye— the only blue ones in the family—were alert.

Molly Booth didn't miss anythin'.

I tossed the ruined pen on the table and smeared my inked hand against my black sweats as I leaned back in the chair. "So should you."

"I'm the mother here, Jonathon," she noted mildly as she went to the kettle and filled it at the sink. "Sometimes, you forget that."

I shrugged a shoulder, tryin' not to be moved by the fact that my mother was alive and so beautiful in the anemic moonlight filterin' through the big window over the sink she nearly took my breath away. It was a stark reminder that Dane and Lila's mum was dead. That they'd never have their mother's comfort again.

"Nearly eighteen now," I reasoned.

She snorted softly as she set the kettle over the burner and took the wooden chair across from me. "Honey, you've been raising yourself since you could cogitate."

This was true. There was a disconnect between me and

my folks, between me my brothers too. It was complicated, but easy to summarize: they were better people than me.

I liked chaos and askin' hard questions that created discomfort.

I liked fuckin' with authority because it was fun, and I was arrogant enough to think I was better than my teachers and the cops, that what I wanted to do was in the spirit'a fun and growth, so if it didn't hurt anyone who the fuck should care?

I'd stopped goin' to my parent's church when I was seven, tyin' myself to the tree in our old backyard with lengths of my dad's fishin' line so I wouldn't have to leave with them. It had taken hours for Dad to cut me free of the transparent fibres with his pocket knife.

The apple didn't just fall far from the fuckin' tree.

In my case, it wasn't an apple at all.

But I was blessed because they got it. They got that I was painted in different strokes and contrary colours, and they just let me *be*.

My heart burned in my chest as I thought of Dane and Lila again, parentless and so fuckin' alone.

"We gotta do somethin' about this, Mum."

She sighed gustily, restin' her head in her hands as she stared at me. My fingers itched to draw the curve of her cheek and the three lines fannin' out delicately from her wide eyes. "I know you're feeling this hard. I know..." She struggled to find the words, reachin' for my ink stained hand to hold even though it was still streaked with black. "I know witnessing what happened isn't something you're ever going to get over, even with Dr. Canterbury's help."

I tried not to flinch at the mention of Meredith's name. She was helpin' plenty, just not in the way Mum mighta thought.

"But we have four kids on a fisherman's salary," she continued, face twisted with shame. "I'm sorry to say it, but we have to be frugal as it is. How would we possibly care for two more kids?"

"You and dad always say money doesn't matter. Love and family do," I reminded her, my voice as hard as the edge of a blade.

I was bein' an asshole. If anyone would want to take in the less fortunate, it was my mum. But the painful weight of my privilege compared to Dane and Lila ached like a lance struck through my ribcage.

Mum winced and looked down at my hand in hers, tracin' her thumbnail through the black pigment until it formed a misshapen heart. "I know what we said, and we meant it. You know, your dad's parents disowned him for marrying me? I was pregnant out of wedlock, Canadian, and disrespectful of their customs." Her laugh was uncharacteristically hard, chewed off, and discordant. "I thought for sure Diogo would stay in the Algarve, and I'd go home to Ontario to raise you by myself, nineteen and alone."

"But Dad wouldn't let that happen."

Her smile was small and tender, an expression of some memory I couldn't see. "No, he wouldn't."

"So he won't let this happen now," I surmised. "He won't abandon them. Because, Mum, you can bet sure as fuck I'm not goin' to."

She laughed lightly as she studied me, eyes gentle against my face. When she cupped my cheek, I let her, because I was too old for affection like that, but I knew she needed it then.

And maybe I did too.

"My dark horse," she whispered. "So unique and brave and *wild*. I didn't doubt for one second that you would. I don't know how, but we'll find a way to make it work, honey. We always do."

THREE WEEKS LATER AND THE PAPERWORK WAS MOVIN' through the ranks of government like molasses in the cold. There was a permanent itch under my skin, a restlessness I couldn't fuckin' curb.

I needed to *do* somethin'.

I was seventeen, man enough to take action myself.

Dad was workin' harder than ever tryin' to expand the business to bring in more money just in case they got approved to foster Dane and Lila. I'd seen Mum at the computer in the den, clickin' at the keyboard with each pointer finger as she searched for part time jobs online.

Why did it have to fall to them?

Short answer? It fuckin' didn't.

Which was why I was walkin' away from the parkin' lot of Entrance Bay High instead of goin' to class, searchin' down Main Street for job postin's in windows. There was somethin' in the kitchen at Stella's Diner, but I wasn't hot on the idea of washin' dishes until my hands were too raw and red to draw.

Still, I'd gone in and convinced Stella to give me a trial right then and there. If she wasn't satisfied, she didn't have to hire me. If she was, she didn't have to go through the hassle of interviews.

She'd agreed.

Mostly, I thought, because a group of college girls had trailed in behind me and stayed the whole time I worked in the back just so one'a them could snag my number.

So I got a job that would go a long way to help payin' the

bills for a family of six gone to eight soon as we got Dane and Lila back. Like hell I'd tell my parents I quit school to help out, though, and I wouldn't have to as long as mum kept lettin' me do the books. She hated numbers somethin' fierce and had put me in charge at thirteen when I kinda showed a penchant for math.

When I finished my shift four hours later, my hands were singed from the steaming water and hard, industrial soap, my skin burnin' like a low-grade buzz of electricity. I hissed as I exited at the back of the diner the handle pokin' the new blister on my palm as I pushed into the cool night air. Stella'd hire me so I shoulda felt some sense of satisfaction. Instead, I flipped open my phone and stared at the photo of the dirty alleyway Dane had captured in Vancouver outside his foster home, then the cluster of indigo berries Lila had sent from her blueberry farm in the Okanagan.

It'd been a few days since I'd sent them anythin' myself, and I knew they lived for the glimpses of home. So even though I was tired as fuck and my hands ached, I hefted my backpack over my shoulder and headed out of downtown Entrance to find somethin' to tag with graffiti.

I was thinkin' they'd like a mock-up of *The Three Caballeros* because it was one'a the only movies they'd had growin' up, and Lila liked to call us that sometimes, like we were some kinda boxset.

Who woulda thought, two seventeen-year-old guys and a six-year-old girl they both woulda died for.

It was weird as fuck, somethin' I never mentioned at school to the friends there who didn't matter because they'd never get what family meant to me or mine.

But they were mine.

My life, my choice, my family.

I didn't give a fuck that I'd known them for less than a year or that they were hours away from me now.

I could still show them that someone cared about them when it seemed like they didn't have fuck-all left.

So I trekked the twenty minutes out of town to get to the industrial neighborhood north on the Sea to Sky Highway where I could graffiti without threat of Entrance PD cruisin' by. There was a bar I'd been meanin' to hit up, a long, low, one story buildin' painted turquoise with a bright pink neon sign that read *Eugene's*. There were rows of Harley's outside and a lot filled with dirt-filmed trucks. A rough man's hangout.

I doubted they'd mind more graffiti bein' added to the edifice, and I was hot shit with a spray can.

Dumpin' my bag on the ground, I stepped back with an aerosol can of black and studied the empty left corner of the wall on the far side of the back entrance before gettin' to work. I wore a bandana over my mouth to keep my throat from gettin' too raw from the chemical spray and my hood pulled up to obscure my face from any nosy fuckers passin' by. When I finished, night had settled a dark cloak over the lot, and my design was lit only by the harsh yellow glare of the artificial lights installed at the base of the roof.

My arms ached from holdin' them up, and my eyes burned with exhaustion, but I finally felt good, at peace for the first time in a long time.

I dug my phone out from the back pocket of my jeans and snapped a photo of *The Three Caballeros*.

"'S not bad," a gruff voice said from my left, startlin' me so bad I dropped my phone to the asphalt, wincin' as I watched it crack.

Anger on my tongue, I whipped around to deliver a scathin' fuckin' beat down to whoever the hell thought it was a good idea to sneak up on a guy with spray paint in one hand and his phone in the other.

"You wanna face full'a chemicals, ass—" I choked off the curse when I caught sight of the man who'd spoken.

Because he was huge.

As in, fuckin' mammoth.

Tatted, bearded, clad in a leather cut with badges sewn onto the left breast, the top one of which read '*VP*'.

I recognized him because I'd seen the fleet of bikes roll through town on a rumble of manmade thunder and had taken note. And I'd taken note because somethin' in their way, the independence, the flagrant refusal to fit in and toe the line, stirred my blood and called to me like a howl from fellow wolves.

He was a member of The Fallen MC.

The most notorious outlaw motorcycle gang in Canada, not to mention their factions in the States and across the Pacific in Europe.

They were no joke and trust me, this guy didn't look it either.

I swallowed hard past the fear lodged in my throat, not because I was uncomfortable, but because I lived for this.

The edge.

One steep enough I might not survive a fall off of.

I picked up my phone, shoved it in my pocket, and affected a lean against the brick wall. Jerkin' my chin up at him, I asked, "Not bad? Clearly, you're no art lover."

It coulda been my imagination, but I thought I caught a twitch of a smile in his dark beard.

"Nah, don't think I've ever set foot in a museum or gallery. Doesn't take an art lover to appreciate sheer beauty, though, does it?"

His praise burned in my gut like a straight shot of whiskey. "It's just some Disney shit."

He stalked forward, his gait a threat because of his sheer size even if he didn't mean to be intimidatin'. He stopped at my side and tipped his head back to take in the art from close up.

"Don't care what it is, it's fuckin' good."

"Yeah," I agreed easily. "I've got natural born fuckin' talent."

He slanted me a look, thick brows arched. "Just a kid and you already got an ego the size'a the Pacific."

This time, I cocked a brow. "You've seen my work, it's good shit. Don't see any point in bein' humble if it's just for show."

He made a noise that was half-laughter, half-grumble. "Gotta fuckuva lotta confidence for a kid so young."

I eyed him critically. "You're what, thirty?"

He had the permanent tan and crow's feet of a man who spent too long outdoors in the sun without protection and the kinda lived-in ease that said he'd been a self-assured man for a long fuckin' time, but he wasn't *old*, that much was obvious.

"Nail on the head," he confirmed. "And you're what, twelve?"

The need to lie burned through me even though I knew he'd call me on my shit. "Nineteen."

Amusement flared in his pale, eerie, silver eyes, but he didn't argue with me. Instead, he slapped a ham-sized hand on my back and squeezed my shoulder. "You're lucky Eugene's a fan'a the can. He'll like the addition, but you best come in and meet 'im. He doesn't take too kindly to random punks taggin' his building."

"This is his art?" I asked, shocked because the designs on the sides'a the building were nearly as good as mine. "He's not bad."

He chuckled and started to lead us toward the door. "Can't wait to see you say that to his fuckin' face. He's gonna lose it."

Forty minutes later, I was sittin' at a red leather booth in the dim, neon-punctuated light of Eugene's kickass bar. It was one'a those places that played like a dive bar but was infinitely cooler, racked with personality from the graffiti and neon signs, to the collection of straight-up characters litterin' the stools and open floorplan. Bikers, off-duty strippers-off-duty, a booth fulla cops in plainclothes sharin' buckets of beer, and a sexy group of college girls titterin' behind their hands and throwin' back shots as they slid side-eyed looks at my table.

My table where Zeus Garro and his brothers sat surrondin' me.

They were all big men, huge across the shoulders, long in the limb, big hands scarred and tatted and be-ringed, layin' like discarded weapons on the table. They were rough and scowlin' when they weren't smilin', only because they had the squint'a men who'd spent too long in the sun and they gave zero fucks when most other people flapped their mouths.

They were the fuckin' *shit*.

I was seventeen, the son of an immigrant fisherman and a homemaker. My skin was inked with pen, not permanent pigment, and my swagger came from knowin' a good life, not a bad one.

But they didn't give a shit. Zeus saw me, and I mean fuckin' *saw* me. He saw somethin' in me that didn't have a voice or a name until he dragged me inside the dark bar and sat me at a table with his men.

Somethin' that yearned for brotherhood and chaos and freedom.

Somethin' The Fallen men had in spades.

"Workin' at Stella's to save money so your family can foster two neighbor kids," Zeus confirmed slowly, spinnin' a big silver skull on his finger. "Not often a teenager thinks'a someone other 'an himself, let alone two kids down on their luck with no connection to 'im."

Guilt and anger burned through me harder than the three beers I'd already consumed. Apparently, if I was with the bikers, Eugene didn't give much of a crap if I was of age.

"They're family," I said, wishin' I could burn the words into the air, into the fabric of the fuckin' universe so no one would try to take them from us again.

He tipped his head to the side and stroked his short beard with tattooed fingers. "You got an old heart and a rebel kinda mind. I'm thinkin' you didn't like school anyways, didn't feel good there with those people who smiled so fake and fuckin' nice like the world isn't a bad place and they aren't bad people." He leaned closer, forearms on the table, big, craggy face so close to mine I could see the smile lines in his cheeks and the creases beside his hard eyes. "Feel like you understand shit but no one understands you."

My knee set to bouncin' beneath the table, a jittery nervous habit I'd never been able to kick. I wasn't used to this. Lila'd once told me in her sometimes-creepy childhood wisdom, that I was like an iceberg. So many people saw the surface 10% and assumed that's all I had to offer when the real me was mostly submerged in murky depths.

I hadn't realized until that moment how horribly vulnerable it felt for a practical stranger to sense my vastness.

He smiled thinly, a memory in his eyes, stale pain stamped on his features. "Not judgin' ya, kid. Just sayin', there's no real beauty without some serious depth, yeah? It's admirable as fuck what you're doin'. Respect the hell outta it."

My heart was tappin' out a staccato beat in my chest, too fast, too outta tune with my natural rhythms. So I sucked in a quick sip of beer to steady it and plastered my signature grin between my cheeks. "Hell, man, I must be pretty as shit to get you to call me beautiful."

Zeus tipped his long-haired head back to the ceiling and shook with belly deep laughter before rightin' himself and grinnin' outright at me. For such a physically terrifyin' guy, he was kinder than most men I'd ever known. "Gotta say, man, you gotta be the cockiest motherfucker I ever met, and that's goddamn sayin' somethin'."

"It is," a man named Bat agreed with a smile that was more plastic than flesh. He had the broken and glued together look of a man who'd been through hell yet hadn't quite come back. "But he's right. Betcha think you could pull anyone of the women in here, eh?"

I slouched back in my chair, legs splayed, hand dangerously close to my junk. One'a the sexy college girls, a redhead, wet her glossed lips with the tip of her pink tongue.

"Yeah, man," I drawled, mouth curled to the left in a smirk meant for her. "I damn well can."

Zeus, Bat, and the two other guys, a huge-ass blond named Axe-Man, and a quiet, First Nations guy called Kodiak, burst into loud laughter, drawin' the eyes of all the girls at the table who basically let out a collective swoon.

Like takin' candy from a baby.

I sat up in my chair and leaned my forearms on the sticky tabletop. "Fifty bucks."

"To get the girl's number?" Kodiak grumbled.

I cocked an eyebrow. "Hey now, let's not make this too easy. Fifty bucks I'm hookin' up with her behind the bar in the next twenty minutes."

Axe-Man grunted. "Kid, you do that, I'll give ya a c-note."

I grinned at them wolfishly as I kicked my chair back. "Done."

"Hey, Casanova," Zeus called out as I started to turn. "You lose, you clean the garage free'a charge for a month."

I jerked my chin up in agreement and swaggered over to the table of girls. The redhead, blushed nearly as red as her hair, and I wondered if she'd flush the same straight down to her toes when I put my tongue on her.

I stopped beside the booth, leanin' against the edge of it with a small, wicked grin as I stared down at the women. The redhead was right beside me, so she had to crank around awkwardly in her seat to look at me.

I winked at her when she made the effort. "I'm bored."

She blinked, surprised by my approach. "Oh?"

One of her friends, a gorgeous Indian woman, spoke up

with flirty sass. "Oh yeah, what are we supposed to do about it?"

The grin spread wider between my cheeks. "I'm so glad you asked, gorgeous. See, I was sittin' over there with my buddies shootin' the shit, and all I could hear was the sweet sound of the laughter comin' from this table. So," I knocked my knuckles against the tabletop, "maybe you invite me to sit down, and I'll have a reason to laugh too."

"Wow," the sweet, auburn haired girl breathed under the rush of laughter from the rest.

"Smooth," the other girl approved. "I'm Daksha, why don't you take a seat...?"

"Nova," I offered with that smile women seemed to like, a wolf poorly disguised as a sheep. "Nova Booth."

HER TONGUE WAS SWEET IN MY MOUTH, BUT KATIE'S, THE redhead, felt even better against my neck, licking at my beating pulse. Daksha moaned as I palmed her tit through the opening in her blouse, and Katie giggled softly as I pulled her tight with an arm around her waist, hand to her ass on my other side. They were so soft, curves pressed to my edges, fragrant like desserts at a picnic in the park. There was so much to love about women, the headiness of their vulnerability when they gifted it, the darkness of their desires when they unleashed them.

I had a lotta love in my heart for every kinda girl, but

these, women confident enough to entertain their own fantasies? They made me hard as stone.

Daksha gripped my dick through my jeans while simultaneously biting into my lip. "Who do you want, Nova? Katie, me, or both on our knees?"

My hand fisted the back of her thick, silken hair and tugged so I could softy snarl into her panting mouth. "Why don't we see how you both look down there, and I'll letcha know."

Katie laughed again. "You are so fucking sexy."

"Hey," I said, catchin' the tip of her chin in my hand so I could speak against her lips. "I don't know the half'a it compared to you two."

She melted against me, droppin' to the asphalt behind the bar like butter on a stove. I braced my legs as she made quick work of my belt and fly, then sighed as her soft hands dove into the denim and fished my cock out. Daksha hummed with approval as she dropped beside her friend, and together, they started to lave me with their tongues.

I closed my eyes, leaned back against the graffitied wall, and let the pleasure soak through me.

"What the actual fuck, Katie?" A male voice barked from the side of the buildin'.

Katie froze, hand wrapped around me like a vice, mouth open and pink tongue extended. She seemed confused at first, sunk so deep in her arousal and intoxication that it took her a moment to swim to the surface of reality.

When she did, she dropped my cock like a hot coal and lurched to her feet so quickly she stumbled.

I frowned because I hadn't thought she was that drunk. Reachin' out, I steadied her while addressin' the jock who'd interrupted us. "What the fuck yourself? Give the women some goddamn privacy."

"Says the guy who's assaulting them behind a bar," he snarled, stalkin' forward. In the yellow cast of the security lights his face was florid with anger. "Get your hands off my girl."

I raised an eyebrow at Katie who gaped like a fish out of water. "You taken, sweetheart?"

Mutely, she shook her head. "He wishes, though."

Instantly, my blood went hot. "He bother you much?"

She hesitated, because the asshole was still comin' at us. "Um, yeah."

Daksha unfolded from her knees gracefully and was kind enough to tuck my now-limp dick back in my pants, givin' it a little regretful pat after she zipped my fly. "Tries all the time. He's a dickhead."

Dick Head was close enough now to lunge out and grab for Katie. I gently, firmly, moved her behind me and faced him with bared teeth.

"Seems she doesn't think you have a right to barge in here, man. Why don't you take a hike?"

He scoffed. "Why don't you fuck off, pretty boy, huh? Think you're better than me or something?"

"It's not about me," I said calmly even while I dipped casually into my jean's pocket to grasp my keys between my knuckles. "It's about the girls."

"Katie doesn't know what she wants."

"Ethan," Katie tried to protest.

"You come with me now, I won't have to beat up your pretty boyfriend," he taunted, crackin' his knuckles.

He was on the large size, obviously a gym junkie with a neck as thick as his thigh. But he lumbered as he strode across the asphalt, no agility, no grace.

And I doubted he had three brothers and a best friend who was a street fighter.

I could take him.

Bouncin' light on the balls of my feet, I grinned a little maniacally at the fucker. "Seein' how Katie is a grown woman—trust me, after feelin' those curves, I know she's *all* woman—I'm thinkin' we respect her wishes and you. Fuck. Off."

Ethan eyed me for a moment, takin' in my stance, my tall, lean form that still needed some fillin' out, but was built considerin' my age.

And then he opened his mouth and hollered, "Avery, Bruce, Leland!"

I sighed dramatically as there was a murmur of voices from the front of the bar, and then three figures rounded the shadowed corner to join us.

"That scared, huh?" I teased. "Don't see why, it'd be hard for me to fuck up your ugly mug any worse."

Easy as flashin' red before a bull, he charged. Before his friends could flank him or he could think up some better approach, the fucker was swingin' his heft in a fist aimed right at my head.

Damn, I'd been hopin' for a real fight.

I ducked, the air stirrin' over my head as he missed his mark, then I twisted on the ball of my foot, hips torqued for maximum force, and I landed a brutal uppercut straight to his lower left flank.

The air exploded from his lungs in a bleat like wounded cattle. As he doubled over, I launched to my feet, drivin' my knee into his downturned face.

I could feel the bones crunch against my limb like crumbling crackers, wincin' in sympathy despite myself.

He keeled over, droppin' to his knees where he cupped his bleeding face and started cryin' like a fuckin' baby even though he'd practically begged me for it.

But there wasn't time to relish in a job well done since his three idiot friends were approachin' at a clip, yellin' curses at me, and assurin' me I would 'feel the pain.'

I chanced a look over my shoulder and jerked my chin at the girls. "Get inside, don't need you gettin' hurt after all this."

Katie instantly moved toward the door, but Daksha waited. "Seems pretty shitty to leave you to get beaten up."

I barked out a laugh then chuckled even harder when Katie jumped back from the backdoor as it swung open from the inside and a mammoth body that was hard to forget stepped into the dark lot.

I winked at Daksha. "Dick Head isn't the only one with friends, yeah? Now get inside."

She shook her head, but there was a smile on her lips as she ran back to Katie who was waitin' for Zeus, Kodiak, Axe-Man and Bat to fit their huge ass selves through the doorframe.

They strolled slowly toward us, not in a rush even though the three assholes were in front'a me in the next heartbeat. I knelt quickly as one stepped forward and punched into his upper right knee.

He went down with a wail.

Another kicked me in the side.

I coughed, crouched on my hands and knees, allowing myself a fuckin' breath before lurchin' into the fight again. But then a massive mitt was in my face, knuckles tatted, fingers ringed with skulls and a gold ring that read 'DAD'.

Grabbin' hold of the hand, I got to my feet and smirked in the face of Zeus Garro who was shakin' his head at me.

"Why do I got the feelin' trouble follows wherever your pretty boy face goes?" he groused good-naturedly.

I winked. "I gotta feelin' you've seen your fair share'a trouble too."

Zeus grinned, a feral, wolfish expression that made him look more beast than man, but before he could respond, one of our attackers lunged forward to punch him in the gut. Zeus deflected the blow the way someone would swat aside a fly then landed a brutal, cracking punch against the man's chin.

He went down in a way I knew meant he would stay down.

"Gotta say, I'm thinkin' we're cut from the same rebel cloth," Zeus said as he wiped blood off his rings with the edge of his tee. "You wanna hang 'round with us, see how it goes, I'm thinkin' we'd be happy to welcome you into the fold."

Bat finished up with the last assailant, leavin' him on the ground and steppin' over him on heavily booted feet so he could slap me on the back. "Welcome to the club, Casanova."

And just like that, a kid who had never been lost in his whole fuckin' life felt like he'd finally been found.

CHAPTER FOUR

Lila

"THE FATHER KILLED THE MOTHER."

It was that time between sunset and twilight, when the sky bleeds from pinks and purples to a soft-edged blue. The crickets were chirping in the long grass in the field behind the old house, and fireflies were starting to sputter with light.

I sat on the concrete front stoop, legs bare against the rough stone, pebbled with goose flesh as the air cooled and the sun dropped past the horizon.

I was trying to focus on the night, on the earth as it inhaled and exhaled all around me. I tried to remember I was just a speck in the belly of the beast, nothing more or less significant than a mote of dust or a grain of sand.

But it was hard not to focus on my foster mother's conversation as she spoke on the phone in the kitchen. Her thin voice wound like a ribbon through the cracked open window over the sink and fell in my lap like an unwanted gift.

"Poor thing was there," she continued over the clang of pots as she prepared dinner. "She doesn't speak much now. I wonder if she might be a bit...dim. Or if it's just the trauma, you know?"

I peeled apart the blade of grass in my hand, pulling out the seeds and adding them to the pile beside me before I moved on to the next.

I knew the germination cycle of the grass in her back field. How long it would take to plant from seed to growth. What kind of conditions were needed for certain plants to grow. That it was stupid of her to plant hyacinth in the full shade at the side of the house when they needed sun.

I wasn't dim.

But I understood why she might think so, given I'd avoided speaking to her and her wife, Rhonda, whenever I could get away with it. It wasn't that they were bad people. It was that I found I had nothing to say, not even when someone asked me a direct question.

I thought, maybe, I had left my voice back in Entrance. That it had torn out of my throat while I was screaming for my parents to stop fighting. For my mother not to die.

"Just plays outside all day long. Obviously, her parents let her run wild! She comes home with dirty hands and skinned knees and then won't even tell me where she's been."

I didn't get why she cared. I didn't cause any trouble, didn't bother any of the other farmers in the small valley of Summerland, B.C., so why did it matter what I did?

"I'm telling you, Lisa, we've had all kinds of kids stay with us, but Lila? She...well, it's like she doesn't care about anything. She just exists. It's not as if she's a problem child, but it's concerning, and honestly, a little *creepy*. She does exactly as she's told with this blank face, and she never talks unless we ask her a direct question. I'm worried we won't be able to reach her. She's been here six weeks and no change."

No change.

I pulled the old flip phone from the back pocket of my jean shorts and opened it to read the last text message.

JONATHON: WE'RE WORKING ON IT, FLOWER CHILD. BE PATIENT AND SAFE, YEAH?

DANE: NINE WEEKS AND ELEVEN DAYS, LI. I'LL BE THERE NO MATTER WHAT IN NINE WEEKS AND ELEVEN DAYS. EVEN IF WE DON'T HAVE THE LEGAL SHIT SORTED OUT, I'LL BE THERE, AND YOU'LL COME WITH ME. I PROMISE.

I moved my thumb over the little screen, wishing I could actually see the Booths, actually touch Dane.

I felt slightly breathless without them. The crushing weight of missing them too heavy on my chest, cutting off my air flow at every inhale.

"The only time she ever gets cross is when I try to throw out her flowers," Marge continued as she ran the tap. "So I don't touch them anymore, even when they wilt and rot in the glass. Rhonda used to collect bugs, so they have something in common, but I barely know how to talk to the girl."

Done with eavesdropping, I pushed off the step and began my twilight walk of the property.

Rhonda and Marge Croft owned a blueberry farm on the edge of Summerland, and their sweeping property was my happy place. Every evening before dinner, I walked under the ponderosa pine trees, trailing my fingers through the long wheatgrass, dragging deep, clean droughts of hot, arid summer air through my open mouth so I could taste the mineral breeze off Lake Okanogan. I took pictures with my phone. The tight bunch of a blue hydrangea, the fading edge of Giant's Head Mountain against the darkening sky, the silky black back of a raven lurking in the gloomy pines.

It was our ritual.

Dane and Jonathon and me.

We took pictures of pretty things to send to each other.

Dane sent photos of Vancouver, the hard angles of blue-tinted glass buildings and the sweep of the Pacific Ocean spread out from rocky beaches.

Jonathon sent pictures of people from home, of Molly in her kitchen and Diogo coming home from work still done up in his wet canvas overalls. He sent videos of Milo and Oliver playing basketball at the hoop in their driveway and shots of Hudson making a mess everywhere he went. He walked along Main Street every week to snap shots of Mac's Grocer and Honey Bear Café and Stella's Diner.

He knew Dane and I lived for those photos.

I'd scroll through them before I fell asleep, the glare of the phone harsh beneath the covers of my bed.

My favourite were the images Jonathon sent of his graffiti.

He graffitied everything. Every inch of skin he could reach with a pen on his arms and legs, chest and feet. The entire interior of the Booth's modest farmhouse had been transformed by his art, painted onto the floors and up the walls where the designs bloomed on ceilings and around doorframes.

And now he had taken to graffitiing the town.

Dane and I both knew it was for us.

A sunflower on the black brick of Evergreen Gas Station.

A pair of blue eyes, Dane's eyes, looking out from the seawall in the bay.

He was leaving pieces of us all over the town we'd been forced to abandon.

I cried whenever he sent a freshly spray-painted design, and I laughed when he took to wearing a black skeleton bandana over his face as he crept around in the dark to do his work.

Even kilometres apart, Jonathon Booth knew how to bring joy to the Davalos kids.

But nothing could reach me that night.

It was Ignacio's birthday.

Maybe I shouldn't have felt so sad about it, that I wasn't with my father and never again would be to celebrate his birth. He'd killed my mother, after all.

But he was still my papá.

The man who let us shove his face into the *tres leches* cake while we chanted *mordida!* Who taught me how tie my shoes and patiently braided my hair in the morning before school.

The man who provided the only adult guidance I'd ever known.

There was an ache in my chest like the two sides were divided by a crater I would never be able to bridge between loving him and hating him.

It throbbed acutely as I lay down in the dirt between the rows of low blueberry bushes and stared up at the blackening bowl of the sky.

The night was so quiet in the farming valley that I heard the crunch of tires on gravel long before I would have in Entrance.

It didn't interest me at first.

Marge and Rhonda were good people, often having friends and family drop by to visit, but I wasn't in the mood to pretend I was okay around company, so I stayed in the dirt.

When my phone buzzed with an alert, I raced to flip it open to find the latest update from Dane or Jonathon. It had been two days since they'd texted.

It was a picture from Dane, the plastic black curve of a glove compartment.

Not his best effort.

I was about to flip it closed when it vibrated again.

A photo from Jonathon, this one of his knee. There was a

tear in his worn jeans and on the skin showing through the gap he had drawn a sunflower he'd labeled "*Suntastic Yellow*."

My chest warmed as I drew my thumb over the screen, pretending I could touch the petals.

Before I could reply, another image came through.

I tapped it and immediately choked on my inhalation of shocked breath.

A selfie of Dane and Jonathon pressed cheek to cheek. My brother was beaming widely, his face so dazzling to me that tears pricked the backs of my eyes and started to roll down my cheeks into the dirt. To see his face expressing genuine happiness again felt like a punch to the solar lexis. And then, Jonathon beside him. More subdued, his grin a curling of lips and the slight cocking of a single eyebrow that made him look rakish and mischievous.

Like he was keeping a secret.

Before I could even begin to wonder what it could mean that Dane and Jonathan were together again, there was a clamor of voices coming from the front of the house.

"Lila," I imagined someone called.

But then again, louder, someone did. "Lila!"

My heart stopped for one long moment, and then as if prompted by a starter gun, I took off at a sprint. I jumped from the dirt and ran through the rows of bushes, scattered blueberries bursting under my toes, arms pumping, legs churning so hard they burned after only a few steps.

I'd never run faster, propelled by the force of hope at my back.

"Lila!" Another voice called from the front as I reached the backyard. "Li, where are you?"

"Here," I panted quietly as I started to round the house. Then louder, "Here!"

I broke through the side gate and exploded into the front drive, the asphalt under my tender feet still warm from hours in the sun.

And there they were.

All of them.

Diogo and Molly.

Milo, Oliver, and Hudson.

Jonathon.

And Dane.

I couldn't breathe. There was no space for air in my lungs, they were wrung so tight with impossible joy. My mouth was open, panting, but I couldn't find my voice. My blood was pumping hard through in my body, but I found I couldn't move.

Only my eyes stirred, hot as fresh coals and wet, so wet they leaked down my cheeks, over my neck, down the slope of my chest to dampen the fabric of my t-shirt.

I stared at them so hard it hurt, and then I stared at Dane.

He looked good, healthy and happier than I'd ever seen him. His face was spilt open in a wide, white grin, his eyes sparkling the way the noon day sun did over the lake. He'd grown even taller, definitely becoming broader through the shoulders and chest in the time we'd been apart.

He looked like a man.

A whimper worked its way free of my throat like the whine of some broken engine. It seemed to breach the tension between us, and before I could blink, Dane was moving.

Then I was running too.

He dropped to his knees on the pavement the moment before I hurtled myself into his arms. The second I wrapped my arms around him and dug my face into his neck, the crisp curls behind his ear tickling me familiarly, I burst into ruckus sobs.

I couldn't control myself. I clutched at his back, gripped his shirt so tightly it warped the material, crawled up his torso so that I wound around him like a baby koala.

This was my brother.

The only person who had loved me my entire life and had always tried to put me first, even before himself.

And he was there.

Holding me.

It felt too good to be true, and my anxiety drove me to claw at him and squeeze him as tightly as my small body would allow.

Dane's husky chuckle ruffled my hair. "You still smell earthy and sweet as spring."

And that was it, the end of my composure. Sobs barrelled up my throat and tore across my tongue, a tempest of disconsolate sound.

"Shh, Li, you're going to make yourself sick," he murmured to me as he stroked a big hand down my hair and back, letting me maul him. "Quiet, now, my Li girl."

"I-I-I can't," I wailed helplessly, tossing my head back so I could look at his face, snot trailing across my cheek with the momentum of my turn. "I love you so much."

"I love you," he answered calmly, always so composed, always so ready to tether my wild soul. "I'm here now, and I love you."

I placed my chubby hands on his cheeks to feel the planes of his face, the way a beard pushed up through the skin of his jaw and abraded my palms, how his cheekbones angled so high and so steep. I delighted in recognizing the familiar shade of his dark skin and the way his left eye twitched when he was tired. I ran my thumbs over his brows and finished by tipping my forehead back against his neck, more settled by my physical examination than by his soothing words.

I had always been tactile, touch the only affirmation my mind would believe.

"There we go," Dane murmured as he picked me up and planted me on his hip like I was a baby.

I was too elated and too exhausted by my emotional waterworks to protest. Instead, I fisted a hand in his tee and rolled my head so I could look at the Booths as we walked back across the driveway to them.

Molly was the only one openly crying, but Hudson had red eyes and a serious sniffle as he clung to his mother's hand. Milo and Oliver were pressed shoulder to shoulder, taking solace from each other, and Jonathon stood beside Diogo, both men with their arms crossed and feet braced like they were ready to slay anyone who got in the way of our reunion.

My heart ached so badly it dropped a beat.

"Hi," I said, suddenly shy.

I hadn't seen them in weeks. Maybe things were different. Maybe, like my parents, they'd forgotten how to love me.

But then Molly was surging forward with Hudson, enveloping both of us in a hug. She smelled of home, of leavened bread and sun-soaked linen.

"Hey, sweet girl," she said through her tears and her smile. "Hey, sweetie."

Then Diogo was over her shoulder, his huge hand descending on my head. I was proud to wear it there like a coronet.

"Hey, girl," he said in his rumbly, lightly accented voice. "You ready to come home?"

"Are you serious?" I breathed, tears flooding my eyes again.

Dane laughed and pressed his cheek against mine. "It took a while, but they got it sorted out with the province. Molly and Diogo are going to foster us until I'm eighteen and I can take guardianship of you in nine weeks."

"And eleven days," I added, making everyone laugh in an expression that was more relief than humour.

"Or longer," Molly said as she pulled back in order to let Milo and Oliver pat my back, touch my hand, kiss my cheek.

The Booths were tactile, too, and I took every ounce of their bright affection like the sun starved hyacinth at the side of the farm house.

"You two don't have to move out until you're ready," she continued. "If you want to stay so Dane can go to school or something, we'll be happy to have you."

I could feel Dane's shift, the way his spine straightened and his shoulders locked. "We'll see."

Molly looked at him with her big, sad brown eyes, lips rolled between her teeth, and then she nodded. "Okay. For now, why don't we talk to your foster parents and get your stuff? If we hustle, we can make it back to Entrance before midnight."

"Unless you want to spend one more night here?" Jonathon teased.

He was still standing a little set apart from our group, his hands in the pockets of his baggy, distressed jeans. There was a small, easy grin stamped on his rosy mouth, but he didn't look happy, not really.

He looked worried.

Something twisted in my chest because the same vulnerability I had felt moments ago seemed to be echoed in him.

I squirmed until Dane let me down, and then I walked over to Jonathon, slowly, even though I wanted to run.

He eyed me with that fake grin affixed to his face, his eyes the only true tell of his wariness.

I didn't stop moving until I was against him, my arms wrapped around his waist as I hugged him.

It was the first time I'd ever embraced him, and it made me remember the last time he'd touched me, curled around me like a human shield amid the chaos of my mother's murder.

This time, it was me who could comfort him.

I tipped my head up to look into his eyes and found him watching me, his grin flattened into a confused grimace.

"Thank you," I said softly, just for him. "For saving Papá and trying to save my mamá."

Something worked behind his eyes, and the corner of his

mouth disappeared between his teeth. Then his hand lifted and settled on my shoulder for a brief squeeze before he leaned down to say just to me, "Wasn't tryin' to save them, Lila. Wasn't about them at all, yeah?"

I sucked a shaky breath in through my mouth and slowly nodded. "Yeah, okay. But you should know, I found a dream."

"Oh, yeah?" This time his smile was genuine.

"Yeah," I said, trying to find the courage to be bold enough to tell the truth. "I thought of it the first day when you guys moved in next door, and now, it's kind of coming true."

"What is it then?"

I scuffed my bare foot against the asphalt, took a deep breath, and said the truest thing I'd ever had to say, "I dreamed I'd be a Booth."

CHAPTER FIVE

Lila

"*FELIZ CUMPLEAÑOS!*" I SHOUTED AS I FLUNG OPEN THE DOOR to the bedroom Dane and Jonathon shared and sprinted over to my brother's sleeping form. "Happy birthday, Dane!"

Then, not waiting for the rest of the family to file in behind me, I started singing at the top of my lungs as I launched myself at Dane's bed and kneeled on his chest so I could chant into his sleepy face.

"Estas son las mañanitas,
que cantaba el Rey David,
Hoy por ser día de tu santo,
te las cantamos a ti,
Despierta, Dane, despierta,
mira que ya amaneció,
Ya los pajarillos cantan,
la luna ya se metió."

I ran through the verses of *Las Mañanitas* as I shook my big brother's shoulders and stared down at his smiling, indulgent face.

When I finished, I cocked my head to the side and beamed at him. "We made you a *tres leches* cake! Molly and me! Do you want us to shove it in your face now or later?"

Dane scowled at me in mock anger and shot up into a crunch position so he could grab me under the pits and tickle me. I snorted on my laughter and squealed as I tried to evade his hands.

"You're not going to shove cake into my face this year, right, Li?" he demanded as he tickled and tickled me.

I gasped, clutching at my middle, aware that the Booths were gathered around the bed laughing at us. "No, no, I'm not!"

He stopped and bopped me on the nose. "That's what I thought."

"She might not," Hudson called out, only five and always eager for mischief. "But I will!"

Everyone laughed, and I felt the sound score through me. I wondered if you could be scarred in a positive way, if something could sear so deeply into your skin it left a magnificent, lasting imprint.

And then I realized that must be the reason why Jonathon loved the idea of tattoos so much.

I closed my eyes for a moment and made a wish like it was my birthday instead of Dane's, hoping that this day would remain tattooed on my psyche forever.

"You ready for your birthday breakfast?" Diogo asked. "Molls made you the Booth family classic. Chocolate chip and blueberry pancakes."

"Oh, fuck yeah." Jonathon shoved up from his grey comforter, wavy brown hair all over the place like sleep had run its hands through it.

"Language," Molly chided half-heartedly.

"Mum, we know what fuck means," nine-year-old Milo said with a sage shake of his curly head.

"I'm a terrible mother," Molly bemoaned, but she was smiling.

"The worst," Oliver agreed, wrapping his arm around her waist. "You can make it up to us with those pancakes."

"Pancakes sound good," Dane agreed, but he pulled me up onto his thigh and wrapped an arm around me. "But Lila and me got something important to do real quick first."

Molly rolled her lips under her teeth, eyes suddenly wet like a pipe had burst behind her lids. I stared at her in confusion, but she smiled wanly at me and let Diogo gently usher her out the door with the rest of the crew.

"What do we have to do?" I asked Dane when it was just the two of us. "Don't you think we should spend the day with them? What if they think we don't love them and—"

"Hey, hey. Li, you've got to stop worrying so much about that. If you live your life in fear, scared that if you act against someone in any way they'll leave you, you won't ever live at all. Not really, not fully."

I stared at my hands, trying to call up the warmth of the laughter that had echoed through the room only minutes before. "I just don't want to lose them."

Dane was quiet for a long minute, just holding me, breathing into my hair. Finally, he pulled away enough to look into my eyes, his so clear a blue I thought they were the prettiest thing I'd ever see in my whole life.

"You are the fiercest, bravest, and kindest girl in the whole world. If someone chooses not to love you, they aren't worthy of you. It's really as simple as that."

There was an ache in my throat that made it difficult to speak. "What if I do something stupid that makes them angry?"

I'd seen the product of anger, how it led to violence and how violence led to death.

Not just with Mamá and Papá, but with other people in Ignacio's business.

You could love someone and still hurt them.

Still leave them.

And that was the nightmare that lived in the darkest corners of my heart.

The crippling fear that everyone I loved would leave, and I would be alone.

Dane crushed me to his chest and made a noise in his throat that meant he wanted to cry but he wouldn't. "The Booths might screw up at some point, you might fight over something or get annoyed with each other because that's natural for a family, but that doesn't mean you have to lose them. I'm not so good at this part, but if you love someone, even if they hurt you, if it's in you to forgive them, you should. Everyone makes mistakes, Li."

"Not you."

"Not yet, maybe, not with you," he agreed. "But I'm just a kid too. I've got years to go, and I'm not stupid enough to think we'll go our whole lives without hurting each other. It's just human nature." He paused, a slight smile tilting his mouth as he saw me bite my lip. "No matter what, though, Lila Mia, we'll always forgive each other, yeah?"

"Promise?"

He tipped his forehead against mine and whispered, "Promise. Now, I'm eighteen today, so that means I can legally apply to be your guardian like we talked about, but…" he studied my face. "What do you think about staying with the Booths? I want to be able to look after you properly, but even after I graduate in a few months, I won't be able to make real good money for a while. I'm working on that, but for now, what do you say?"

Something I didn't even know had been twisted up in my chest unspooled. "Yeah, I want that."

He smiled. "I thought so. It's nice having a big family, and they're good people. The best."

"The *bestest*," I added, because it was true.

"Yeah, Li, for sure. But listen, I got something drawn up for us." He moved away to lean down beside the bed and rummage in his backpack. When he came up with a stack of stapled pages, I frowned but accepted them from him. "This is paperwork to legally change our last name. I'm eighteen now, so I can do it and apply for you as well because you're a minor. I don't want us to share the same last name as Ignacio anymore. You and me? We've always been our own family, and I'm thinking we need our own name."

Our own name.

Not Davalos. Not Ignacio's or Ellie's.

Just *ours*.

"Yeah," I whispered because my voice was lost in the swirl of emotions raging through my chest. "Yeah, I want our own name."

Dane grinned, more boyish and carefree than I'd ever seen him. "Yeah, I thought so. Why don't you pick one for us?"

My eyes went round as twin coins. "Like any name I want?"

"Like any name you want," he agreed, ruffling my hair before he got out of bed and slipped sweatpants over his boxers. He'd gained weight and muscle since we moved in with the Booths, and he wasn't so gangly anymore. I liked seeing him fit and healthy; it made something in my chest bloom.

I flopped onto my back on his bed and stared at the ceiling where Jonathon had painted a black sky filled with constellations across the entire space. Name ideas ran through my mind too quickly to catch until I turned my head on the linen sheets and looked out the window at the grassy knoll to the left of the house. It was overrun with morning glory, with daisies and daffodils, and the random red burst of poppies.

My mind slowed and stilled, soothed by the sight of those flowers swaying so gently in the breeze tunneling through the streets off the ocean.

They were peaceful, steady in their life cycle, gone so quickly but always returning, just as lovely as before.

At first, I wanted a flower.

Dane and Lila Lilac.

Dane and Lila Suntastic.

Dane and Lila Clematis.

But I didn't want a name that represented just one thing, one flower, one star in Jonathon's painted-on universe.

I wanted a name that had the possibility of meaning anything and everything depending on what I wanted to plant within myself as I grew up.

So I swivelled my head on the blankets to look at Dane as he crouched beside the bed so that we were eye level and reached out my hand to touch him on the forehead the way Diogo had done with me after the murder, when he'd promised me his family.

And I anointed Dane with our new name.

"Meadows," I said softly, tattooing it on his brow with my touch and my intent. "Dane and Lila Meadows."

BREAKFAST WAS DELICIOUS. I'D NEVER EATEN PANCAKES because Mamá barely cooked, and Ignacio only made what he knew and liked, which was mostly beans, rice, and greasy, deliciously seasoned meats cooked on a grill. Dane and I both ate way more than we should have, and the Booths laughed with us as we smeared the confections in whipped cream.

Dane got presents from everyone, and he let me help him unwrap them. They were packaged so prettily in tidily folded black and silver paper that I hated ripping them apart.

But Dane loved the gifts.

A fishing rod from Diogo because all the other boys had their own.

A black toque sewn with Dane's name in silver stitching across the brow from Molly.

Milo and Oliver had pooled their money to buy him discounted Nike sneakers. They were so white they glowed, and I could tell by the way my brother touched the high tops gently with his big hands that he was afraid even his fingers would mar their beauty.

Jonathon and I had picked out a present together. It was really from Jonathon because he had the money, but I helped him design it by painting little flowers between the skulls, guns, and brass knuckles Jonathon had etched on the underside.

It was a Krooked skateboard, black on the top, trimmed in red with our designs on the bottom. I'd known it was expensive because I'd seen the number on the till when Jonathon bought it, but I was reminded again when Dane lifted his shining eyes to Jonathon, and they shared a moment so bright and fleeting it streaked between them like a shooting star.

When Dane said, "thanks, bro," it was in a hushed, choked off voice, and when Jonathon responded it was only with a jerky nod.

Boys were so silly.

We finished breakfast and immediately served the birthday cake. Hudson and me both shoved Dane's face into the soft treat while shouting '*mordida*' like I used to do with Ignacio, and even though it made my chest tight, I was happy to continue the tradition with the Booths.

It was the best morning I'd ever had.

Until Molly paused at the kitchen island with an opened letter in her hands, her auburn brow puckered and her mouth open in a gasp. When she looked up from the letter, we were all frozen, our gazes glued to her, but it was Jonathon she looked at with utter dismay.

"Jonathon," she murmured. "Please tell me this isn't true."

My head twisted so quickly, my neck cramped as I looked at her eldest son. Confusion filtered across his face before his features solidified and his shoulders stiffened.

I would never forget what he looked like in that moment, a soldier called out by his general for flagrant treason, his shame tempered by steely determination that he'd done what was right morally if not legally. He wore his hair longer back then, and it fell in his eyes as he locked them on his mother.

"It's true," he said, voice hard, but tone deceptively easy. "And I don't care if you're mad as hell. It was the right thing to do."

Tears pooled over Molly's lower lids and splashed to the flour strewn countertop. Diogo's chair screeched as he pushed it back and strode over to his wife. He took the letter and read it, brow descending over his eyes with each passing second.

When he looked up at Jonathon, his throat was working oddly, and he seemed suspended between grief and anger. "This is unacceptable."

A muscle in Jonathon's jaw ticked as he clenched his teeth. His hands, drawn with balloons and cake, party streamers and hats depicting Dane's name and age, curled into fists over the crepe paper tablecloth.

"No, what woulda been unacceptable is if we couldn't'a gotten Dane and Lila back," he ground out. "You said we didn't have the money. I made it so we did."

Hudson knocked his shoulder into me. Without looking, I tangled our hands together and squeezed.

"What the hell are you talking about?" Dane demanded,

standing suddenly so he could lean against the table on his fists and glare at his best friend. "What the fuck did you do, Jon?"

Jonathon stood up, too, both of them canted over the big round table like mountain goats about to lock horns.

"I made it so you could be here with us," he growled. "You gotta problem with that?"

"Fuck yeah, I might," Dane shouted. "Depends on what idiotic thing did you did now."

"He dropped out of school," Molly breathed from the circle of Diogo's arms. "He dropped out of school, and the part-time job he said he got, well, I'm guessing it's full time."

Jonathon's square jaw was so tight, I could read the pulse in his cheek. "You better fuckin' believe it. I don't give a shit what you think about it, you or my parents. You think you can make me feel bad about doin' somethin' to rectify the worst wrong I've ever seen? You got another thing comin', Dane."

The air in the kitchen was hot, bubbling over like a pot left too long on the stove. I wasn't sure how to turn the heat down, so I didn't say anything even though my skin itched and my breath was too warm, scorching down my throat.

I didn't want Molly or Diogo or Dane to yell at Jonathon.

Not only because yelling reminded me of the yellow house across the street I'd used to live in with Ellie and Ignacio.

But because I thought what Jonathon did was the most selfless thing I'd ever heard.

"You're a goddamn idiot," Dane finally said into that waxy hot silence. "You know that, right?"

Jonathon scoffed because he was Jonathon, and nothing fazed him. Nothing, not even his parents or his best friend could make him doubt himself for a second.

"You think I'm an idiot, I don't give a fuck. As long as you're here, you can think whatever the hell you want."

It was so romantic to my young mind, those declarations. It didn't matter that he cussed every sentence or bit off the 'g's at the end of his words. It didn't matter that his chin was cranked so high in the air we could barely see his squinting brown eyes.

He was the most beautiful man I'd ever seen, and it went beyond so much more than his pretty eyes and wavy hair.

He was beautiful like Dane was beautiful.

Because he'd committed to me the way no one else ever had.

He'd fought *for* me, not *because* of me.

I must have made a noise because suddenly both teenagers were looking at me, their faces falling simultaneously.

"You're crying," Hudson whispered to me, a hand cupped over his mouth as if that made his words less loud amid the silence. "Do you need a Kleenex or something? You've got snot running down your chin."

I hadn't realized I was crying, but I wasn't embarrassed. I was every other thing: ashamed that Jonathon had made such a sacrifice, moved that he'd wanted to make it, in love with him for thinking it was the obvious choice to make when no one else would have.

Unable to articulate any of that, I let go of Hudson's hand and slowly rounded the table. I was so filled with feelings, it cut off communication from my head to my body, my legs wobbling and my hands shaking. When I reached Molly and Diogo, I looked up at them with my heart throbbing behind my eyes, and I whispered, "Please don't be mad at him. Please don't send him away."

Molly bit off a sob and covered her mouth with her hand.

Diogo blinked as if I'd pinched him then shook his head slowly as he bent in half to look me in the eye. His large, rough hand descended as it always did, so slowly, like I was a wild animal who would run, onto my head.

"We're mad at him, Li girl, but we would *never* send him away, okay? Just like we'd never send you away."

"I'll get a job so Jonathon can go back to school and you

can be happy with him and we can all live together still because I'll have money." Saying this in such a rush, I somehow bit my tongue, and metallic blood filled my mouth.

"Honey," Molly said softly. "You're six years old. You can't get a job."

I tipped my chin into the air like Jonathon and planted my hands on my hips. "I've got skills, you know. I can plant things because I have a green thumb." I held them up for Molly and Diogo to inspect. "And people pay for pretty gardens."

"They do," she agreed, reaching out to clasp my hands so she could place kisses on my thumbs. "But kids can't work. Only adults can do that, which is why we are upset with Jonathon. It's a child's job to learn and go to school. It's an adult's job to provide."

"He did it for us," I whispered through my throat as it closed up, my nose stopped up with tears. "Please don't be mad. No one ever did something like that for me and Dane before."

There was a hand on my shoulder, and I turned slightly to see Jonathon behind me. His face was sober like at a funeral, but when he crouched in front of me, I could tell it was because he was moved, and he didn't want anyone to see it.

"You remember your dream?" he asked.

I nodded, worried it was a trick question.

"Well, it's a dream that's come true. There's no goin' back now. We're all a big family now, and even though I did some-thin' because I felt it was right, my parents are allowed to disagree with me. Because they're my parents, they're gonna worry 'cause they want what's best for me. They feel that way about me, Milo, Oliver, Hudson, and now you and Dane. They love us, and when we don't respect them, we gotta live with the consequences'a that. But those consequences will never be to send us away, okay? That dream's never gonna die for you, Li. You're here with the Booths now, and you're here to stay."

"You are," Dane agreed, his voice too loud in the hushed, confessional space the kitchen had become. He was standing too tall, his chest puffed out. "And I've been thinking about this for a while. Now that Lila has a safe place to be, I can do what I've always wanted to do, and I can do it making money for the family so we aren't a burden—"

"You are *not* a burden," Molly interjected.

Dane ignored her.

"I'm enlisting," he continued. I was old enough to know what that meant, to feel each word like an assault rifle pounding rounds into my chest. "I'm enlisting in the navy."

"Hey now, don't do something so drastic because of this," Diogo demanded, stepping forward. "We want you here, we'll make it work."

But my brother was already shaking his head, so firm, so calm. As assured in this as he was everything else.

I felt my heart sink like a stone into the soft pit of my belly.

"Always wanted to do something worthwhile. Jonathon's an idiot, but he did something worthwhile for me and Lila by quitting school. I want to do something worthwhile by making money for this family while serving my country."

"You just want to be a hero instead of someone evil like Papá," I spat at him, backing away from Jonathon, Molly, and Diogo, inching toward the front door to be as far from my brother as I could possibly be so that maybe it would lessen the assault on my heart. "You just want to prove you're better than him."

Dane stared at me for a moment with sad, wet, velvet blue eyes. "Maybe, Li, maybe you're right. But I'm going to do it anyway, and I'm going to do it for more than just that."

"You're going to *leave*!" I screeched so loudly the words ripped through my throat and exploded in the air.

Milo and Oliver flinched. Hudson started toward me then turned away, running to his parents.

"Lila," Dane started, coming for me with his big, gentle hands extended. "Come on, now."

"NO!" I screamed as loud as I could, trying to expel the poison that was pooling in my belly, swirling around my sunken heart and spilling through my veins. "NO! You just promised me. You just promised me you wouldn't leave. What are you doing? What are you doing? You're *leaving me!*"

"I'm not leaving right now," he tried to soothe, palms open to the sky as he crept closer. "I have to join up, complete training...I might not even have to go overseas right away."

"Dane, we're at war in Afghanistan," Diogo rumbled.

Molly swatted at Diogo to silence him, but it was too late.

My eyes bugged out of my head so far I thought they would fall out.

"We're at war? Why do you want to keep fighting? We just found it. We just found it!" I yelled at him, scrambling backward down the hall to the front door faster because Dane was gaining on me, and if he touched me I'd detonate, and there would be so many pieces I'd never fit back together again right.

"Found what, Li?" he asked calmly, trying to smile, trying to comfort me when he was the one ripping me apart. "You aren't losing anything. Stop backing up. Let's talk about this, okay?"

"We just found peace," I hiccoughed, the bubble of air bursting in my throat, breaking the dam on my tears. They flooded forth, pouring like fire down my cheeks as I blindly reached for the door handle and yanked it open. "We just found peace, and you want more war."

"Lila," he said sharply as I turned on my heel and ran into the cool autumn morning. "Lila, get *back here!*"

But I didn't go back.

I did what I'd wanted to do every day in that yellow house across the street. I did what I hadn't wanted to do any of the days since I'd moved in with the Booths until now.

I ran away.

THE SKATE PARK WAS NEARLY ABANDONED SO EARLY ON A Sunday morning. I sat in one of the sloping bowls of graffitied concrete, letting the sun warm my face, eyes unseeing as they stared up at the clotted clouds blowing like overwhipped cream across the blue sky.

My tears had dried, leaving tight, salty tracks down to my ears, but at least I felt emptied. Purged. Thoughts filtered in and out of my heads thin as gauze. There was a lingering ache in my chest, but it had dulled and deepened. I knew it would be there forever, a crater carved beneath my breastbone where fear and abandonment had nearly sundered me in two.

It was only a matter of time before someone found me.

I thought maybe it would be Milo and Oliver because they always knew how to make me smile, but in the end, it was Jonathon.

It irritated me to see his face in my line of sight, his features in shadow, the sun an aura behind his head. He'd been busy since we moved in, working, and I'd thought, doing school work. In that time, he'd also changed in some indecipherable way. His smiles felt like secrets pressed between his lips. I wanted to part the pages and read what was written there, but I was too young to understand how to ask the right questions to unlock his mysteries. We hadn't spent much time together, and as a result, I was annoyed with him for being the one to find me. It felt insincere somehow.

He stared down at me without saying anything for a long moment, then shifted out of view so he could lie with his head beside mine, facing the other way.

It was irrational, but I was angry with *him* too.

He was Dane's best friend. He should have said something, protested more or better. Stopped him from hatching such a stupid, selfish idea.

My heart burned in my chest, and fire boiled up my throat, so I aimed it at the only person I could.

"You're an asshole," I told him. "You *and* Dane."

"Hey, now, what the hell did I do? And you shouldn't be swearin', Li, it's not right for little girls."

"I'm not a little girl," I said stubbornly even though I was acutely aware of that reality.

If I was an adult I could work, and Dane wouldn't have to work for the both of us. Jonathon wouldn't have had to drop out of school, and Dane wouldn't have to leave.

My age felt like an albatross around my neck, and I was furious over my helplessness to remove it.

"Okay," Jonathon agreed easily, shifting his head so soft strands of his hair brushed my cheek. "Okay, Li, you're not a little girl, but neither is Dane. He's a man now. You don't get this, maybe 'cause you're a woman, but probably 'cause you're young and you're his little sister, but a man's gotta do somethin' to prove he's a man." I opened my mouth to protest, but he continued. "He's got nothin' to prove to you, to me, or the rest of the family. It's about provin' somethin' to himself, you get me? He's a man, and he needs to test himself against his dreams. Against the real world."

"But we're finally happy," I argued then felt sudden, crushing doubt.

Was Dane happy?

Had I ever really asked him?

Before, with Ignacio, it was a given that we were just surviving. There'd been no room for personal growth or desires or happy dreams.

But now, with the Booths, there was so much room, a veritable field to frolic through and cultivate every beautiful dream we might have ever entertained.

Had Dane discovered his own dreams in that field?

It hadn't occurred to me that he could, that we were two separate people. We had always shared the same vision: survive our childhood and get away.

Together.

But we had, survived that is, and now what?

For Dane, that obviously meant it was time for him to abandon me.

"I can hear you thinkin', the whirr of that mind is drownin' out the bird song," Jonathon joked with me. "Listen to me, okay?"

I scowled at the sky because I didn't want to listen to him. I wanted to be left alone to stew in my self-righteous self-pity.

Instead, drawn by the intensity of his eyes on the side of my head like a magnetic force, I turned my head so that I could face him. Up close like we were, his eyes weren't merely brown. They shone like sunlight through maple syrup, rimmed by black and streaked through with spikes of onyx. I blinked as I looked in those eyes and felt instant contrition for being angry with him when all he had ever offered me was a safe place to be.

Like Dane.

"Okay," I agreed softly.

"I told you to find a dream, yeah? Well, I said the same thing to our boy, Dane. You know him better than anyone, right? So what do you think he would dream about?"

I cracked my knuckles as I thought, because for some reason, I was nervous.

What if Dane's dreams didn't match my own?

I wanted to live with the Booths and my brother forever. For us all to be happy and whole.

But Dane?

Of course, I knew what he wanted. He was the best person I knew, and all he had ever wanted to do was help people. As a girl, heroism was defined by my brother, not by knights in silly storybooks Papá didn't buy, or in Disney movies we couldn't watch because Mamá didn't like TV.

It was Dane who had always and forever ridden to my rescue, and I guess I'd always imagined that he would remain the same.

"He wants to save people," I muttered petulantly. "Like he saved me."

"Yeah," Nova agreed, his red, almost purplish mouth curling on the left in that way it did when he was teasing. "Dane's a white knight in old denim, and he's always wanted to do more. You don't think enlistin' would give him that? A real way to change lives?"

"It would change mine," I blurted, a flush behind my tanned skin even though I knew it wouldn't show. My anger burned and boiled under the surface like something ugly and toxic. I just kept thinking *it's not fair, it's not fair*. And it wasn't, not really, for a six-year-old to be faced with losing a brother after she'd lost the rest of her family. But it wasn't fair, too, that I should chain Dane to me just because I was too traumatized for a teddy bear replacement.

I knew there were real monsters in the world. I'd been born of one.

And I needed a real knight to face them for me.

"Flower Child," Nova called, flicking the end of my nose just to irritate me. "You with me?"

"Yeah, I guess. You think he meant it? That he won't have to leave right away?" I ventured, taking solace in the prettiness of the dark stubble sweeping over his jaw.

Without thinking, my fingers reached out to test the

texture, finding it sharp and thick where Dane's was softer, tufted in places.

Nova grinned and snapped at my fingers so I jerked them away. "Yeah, he'll be around for a while. In fact, I gotta feelin' he'll never stay away too long, and even if he does, he's always gonna write or text or email. He's always gonna be thinkin' of his little sister with the flowers in her hair."

I blushed, this one warm and electric, as he plucked a daisy from my hair and twirled it between his big fingers. My stomach fluttered like a jar of butterflies had toppled over and opened inside my gut.

"You want Dane to have a dream just like you do. It's important that you let him know that, okay? You keep any animal leashed for too long, they start to resent the hand that keeps them there, Li, and I know you don't wanna be that restraint. Not when you love him like you do."

"No one deserves a dream more than my big brother," I said, because it was true.

He was the best person I knew, and even his potential abandonment couldn't change that.

"And you gotta know," Jonathon continued, the sparkle back in his thickly lashed eyes. "If Dane goes away, he's leavin' you with us, and there'll never be a time you aren't wanted in our house, yeah?"

"What if you move out, too?" I asked, suddenly rocked by the idea of losing them both.

Why hadn't I thought of that inevitability?

They were eighteen. They could go out into the world by themselves.

And what were the *los tres Caballeros* without two of its members?

"Hey," Jonathon said sharply, drawing me back to his sombre face. "I'm not goin' anywhere. I've found my home, just gotta find my place in it. And I'll tell you a secret, if you promise not to breath a word'a it to anyone."

"Not even Dane?" I breathed, because we'd never had a secret, just us two.

"Not even," he repeated with faux sobriety. "I found'a place that feels like home. With even more family—brothers, uncles, and friends—that could be yours as well as mine."

"You mean," I sucked in a deep breath, hope alive like fire in my throat, "You'd share with me?"

His lips twitched, but he didn't laugh. "Yeah, Li, I'm happy to share with you. The way I see it, the more family the better, yeah?"

"Yeah," I agreed instantly, rolling to my knees with my hands braced on the hot pavement. "Can I meet them?"

"What?" he asked laughingly. "Right now?"

I nodded enthusiastically, and a flower, an iris, fell out of my hair. Jonathon grinned at me as he picked it up from the pavement and tucked it behind my ear before getting to his feet.

"Alright, Flower Child, let's call Dane and my folks to let them know we're okay and then we'll go meet some new friends."

THE FALLEN MEN COMPOUND SPRAWLED LIKE AN INSOLENT giant from the Faversham Inlet to the Sea to Sky Highway in the industrial neighborhood of Entrance. When we pulled up to the chain link fence at the huge gates that separated the world from the club, I was already awed by the sprawl of buildings behind the metal. There was a low-slung brick building to the right down by the water, a big garage and parking lot labelled Hephaestus Auto in ragged, cut-out sheet metal hung over the multi-garage bays. Surprisingly, there was also a pretty garden and a hangout area with picnic tables and some children's playground things tucked away amid it all.

"What is this?" I asked Jonathon from the passenger seat of Molly's blue minivan

Jonathon should have looked ridiculous driving such a sedated 'mom' vehicle, but he was cool enough to pull it off. The way he rested his left forearm on the window, his right wrist leaning casually over the steering wheel, dark eyes obscured by pitch black Ray Bans I wasn't sure where he'd gotten the money to buy. He was the epitome of a nonchalant bad boy from tip to toe.

"This is the home of The Fallen MC, Li, and it's gonna be my home soon as they let me fully patch-in. And what'd I say before?"

"*Mi casa es tu casa*," I replied hesitantly.

"Better believe it," he agreed before the gates slid open and we started to roll onto the property.

We pulled into a spot beside the garage, and when I opened the door, the scent of hot asphalt and motor oil hit my nose, undercut by the briny tang from the ocean flowing beyond the lot. I could feel the heat of the concrete beneath my purple flipflops as they slapped back to my heels, and the air was waxy against my skin as I moved through it.

It was hot for autumn, the lingering summer unwilling to yield to the impending winter winds and frozen rains. But I loved the feel of the sun on my skin, so I tipped my head to the sky and didn't complain even when Jonathon tugged my hand to lead me toward the playground area.

There was a girl there, hidden among the greenery, sitting on a green slide with a monster painted on it, tongue extended the length of the plastic. She had bright, streaky blond hair tangled and matted by the breeze. It was so shiny, so blonde, I wanted to touch it and see if it was real.

"Who's that?" I whispered to Jonathon.

He followed my gaze to the girl and grinned. "Hey, Harleigh Rose, you wanna come meet my girl, Lila?"

The girl stirred from her half-lounge on the slide and popped a headphone out of her ear. She studied me for a long moment, eyes squinted but obviously a true blue even from a distance.

"She cool?" she yelled back. "'Cause I don't got time for nonsense. You know?"

Jonathon chuckled under his breath, leading me to the edge of the garden. "I think she's pretty fuckin' cool, but why don't I let you be the judge'a that while I go find your Dad."

She nodded somberly, eyes scraping over my jean shorts and lavender peasant blouse. Molly let me pick out my own clothes, and I found I liked vintage stuff best, so we'd go just us girls to find cool treasures at the second-hand shops in town.

I worried that compared to Harleigh Rose's Guns N Roses tee, leather boots, and black, torn jean shorts, I looked like a prissy little girl in comparison, but she only pursed her lips and nodded.

"Yeah, I'm good at judgin'," she agreed, waving Jonathon off. "I'll suss her out while you do your thing with Dad."

"Much obliged," Jonathon said with mock seriousness. But he squeezed my hand and dropped to his haunches before leaving me. "You gonna be okay, Flower Child? H.R.'s a good kid. It'll probably be good for you to have a friend who's a girl, yeah?"

"Girls are stupid," I said, echoing what Miles, Oliver, and Hudson had said for years.

His magenta mouth twitched. "Lotsa stupid people in the world, but they aren't defined by their gender, I can tell you that much. I'll only be a minute, but you need me, you holler, okay?"

I nodded, nervously cracking my knuckles as I shot a look at the girl who was still studying us.

Jonathon cupped my fidgeting hands in one of his and plucked a spring of lavender from the flower box beside us to place behind me ear.

"There you go, all set," he determined with a wink, then he got to his feet, saluted Harleigh Rose who inclined her chin regally in response, and then took off for the brick building.

I stood two yards away from Harleigh Rose and blinked at her.

"Hi," I said.

"Hi," she replied.

We both stared at each other for another moment, engaged in some kind of stand-off with rules I wasn't aware of.

Finally, she smiled slightly. "You don't have many friends, do you?"

I shrugged, my stomach cramping with anxiety. "Not really. Just my family."

"Is that how you know Nova?" she asked. "He's your brother?"

"Who's Nova?"

She frowned and jerked her thumb at the door Jonathon had retreated behind. "Nova. The guy that was just holding your hand?"

"Oh," I said, feeling dumb. "I didn't know that was his nickname. We call him Jonathon."

Harleigh Rose snorted, but her eyes were smiling as she shot up from the slide and moved toward me. "Nova is short for Casanova, my dad said. He also told me he's never seen a kid get as much tail as Nova."

I didn't know what that meant, and she seemed to read it on my face.

"Tail means girls," she explained. "Jeez, I'm really gonna have to take you under my wing and teach you our ways, aren't I?"

I shrugged. "Ways of what?"

Her grin was almost evil as it split her pretty face in two. "Ways of being a biker babe. Don't worry, we're still kids, so we got lots of time."

"Okay," I nodded slowly, happy because this girl seemed to want to be friends. "I can teach you about flowers if you want, I'm really good with them."

She wrinkled up her nose, but it wasn't mean, just funny. "I'm more into music, you know? What kind do you like? Wait, let me guess," she looked at me appraisingly. "I'd take you for a country music girl."

I shook my head, thinking of the music I listened to with Jonathon—Nova—and Dane when we went driving. "No, I like rock, I think."

Harleigh Rose hooted to the sky and grabbed my hand to drag me back over to the slide and her abandoned iPod. "Nova's right, you're cool. Sit down, and I'll educate you proper on all things badass and rock'n'roll!"

That was how they found us, Jonathon and Zeus, when they came out of the clubhouse an hour later. Harleigh Rose and me with our heads pressed cheek to cheek so we could both listen to the music pumping through the little music box, nodding our heads in tandem to the beat of "Good Times Roll" by The Cars.

"You ready to go, Flower Child?" Jonathon called out with a smile in his voice.

I frowned, carefully taking the earbud out and fist bumping with Harleigh Rose when she offered me her fist.

"See you soon?" I asked, nervous suddenly.

"Oh, yeah," she agreed. "Nova's gonna be part of the club now, so we'll see each other a bunch. There's not so many kids around, so you and me? We're basically gonna be best friends."

"Oh yeah?" I asked, grinning. "I think I can manage that."

"Yeah?" Harleigh Rose asked, eyes crinkling with the force of her smile. "Done."

I nodded then walked over to Jonathon even though the man beside him looked mean enough to eat children for breakfast. I even flinched a little when he bent at the waist to put his big, craggy face level with mine.

"'Sup, girl?" he asked in a growly, monster-like voice. "You up for stayin' a while more? Nova's gonna do a project for us, and I'm thinkin' he probably needs your feminine touch."

I looked to Jonathon, eyes wide because this man was scary, but he also had a kind smile, so I didn't know what to do with him.

Those familiar brown eyes sparkled as he jerked his chin at the brick wall at the front of the building they'd emerged from then hefted up the backpack I hadn't noticed was in his left hand. "Wanna help me tag that shit up?"

My heart leapt into my throat, nearly choking on my excitement. "Seriously?" He'd never let me help him before because he said it was illegal, and I could get in trouble, but I'd always dreamed of helping him on day.

"Seriously. Zeus here wants the clubhouse tagged with the logo, and obviously, I'm the man for the job," he responded with a grin.

"Could Harleigh Rose help?" I asked, knowing I was pushing my luck but wanting my new friend to see how absolutely cool he was.

He looked to the man named Zeus who smiled. "Have at 'er, but if it's ugly as fuck, you're paintin' over it and redoin' it."

"Fuck you," Jonathon said on laugh. "We both know everythin' I produce is cool as shit."

Zeus raised an eyebrow at me, and I giggled as I shook my head.

"One time," I told them, "he made a spider that looked like a black blob."

Jonathon reached out to snag me around the neck and give me noogie. I wriggled and laughed in protest, my previous melancholy such a distant sensation it was only a tinny echo in my chest.

And as we got to work on the massive green and black skull and tattered wing logo of The Fallen MC, aprons over H.R. and me, bandanas that smelled of motor oil and leather tied around our mouths, the man they called Nova that I knew as Jonathon teaching us how to spray the can properly, I let the gift that he'd given me sink into that crater in my chest and fill up the gap.

Because no matter how long Dane was gone for, no matter where he went, Jonathon was showing me that he'd always be my family. And more, that whatever he had in spades was inherently *mine* too.

And there was no greater gift I'd ever received in my whole life than that.

CHAPTER SIX

Lila

THERE WERE A HANDFUL OF IMPACTFUL MOMENTS, POTENT memories, that founded the basis of my relationship with Jonathon 'Nova' Booth like vertebrae in a spine, holding it—*us*—together.

I was thirteen when I finally found the words for what he meant to me, even though I didn't realize it at the time. It was what he did for me that night that tattooed itself onto my heart in a way that could never be erased.

There was no moon that night, the sky spilling into the streets like an overturned ink pot coating everything in obsidian and shadow. I was in bed, but not asleep, my stomach cramped with something other than the period pains I'd been getting for a little over a year by then. I'd made a cup of dandelion tea to soothe my troubled mind and coax it to sleep, but nothing would quell that restless anxiety that seemed to turn my blood to acid.

I could have woken Hudson. He was always up for late night shenanigans, pranking his brothers or sneaking out of the house into the fields behind our house to tip cows in old lady McLintock's meadow.

I could have called H.R. who was no doubt up listening to records well past the hour she should have been asleep. She was an MC princess, so she didn't have a bedtime, but I knew she'd arrive at school the next day with deep grooves under her pretty blue eyes and a big, lopsided smile on her face because she'd just been to Old Sam's Record Shop where she'd discovered the next best thing in music.

I could have even gone to Molly, who would have woken the instant I opened the door, ushering me downstairs for a talk and some warm milk with honey.

But I didn't do anything of that because what I really wanted was to talk to Dane.

It had been three weeks since we'd heard from him, which wasn't unusual when he was deployed, but gave me anxiety all the same.

I wasn't quite an insomniac like Nova, but some nights I wouldn't sleep, wide awake thinking about my brother overseas in hostile territory with only an armoured vest and a service rifle, his wits and his brothers in arms to protect him.

This was his second deployment, and I knew he loved his job, but missing him stalked me closer than my shadow, never disappearing, a spectre even in the dark.

I curled tighter into my huddled ball on the window seat in my attic bedroom and stared out into the night, letting my melancholy spill into that inky night.

My phone buzzed on the pillow beside me, and I smiled before I could even check to see who had texted me.

There was only one person who would bother me that late at night.

Nova: You awake?
Lila: No

I smiled as the reply came in, my moroseness chased away by the light that always accompanied Nova wherever he went.

Nova: Too bad. Can't sleep, I need you to entertain me.
Lila: It's 2am, I'm a teenager, and I need my sleep.
Nova: I'm living proof that beauty rest is a lie. I sleep for shit and still look fuckin' stunnin'.
Lila: Women like humble men, you know.
Nova: Not in my extensive experience.
Lila: Barf. Please refrain from being disgusting, or when I do actually sleep, I'll have nightmares.
Nova: We both know I'm the stuff dreams are made of, not nightmares.
Lila: Okay, I'm going now.

But I was laughing as I typed, waiting for his response like it was some kind of gift.

And it was.

Nova had moved out of the house at eighteen and never moved back. He still lived in town, on Main Street over an old stationary shop that had been out of business for the last few months. I always saw him on Sundays. Diogo eschewed many things about his Portuguese heritage, but Sundays were *always* family day. But otherwise, Nova was busy working at Hephaestus Auto, apprenticing in Vancouver at a locally famous tattoo shop, and doing whatever it was The Fallen motorcycle club did for fun.

Truth be told, sometimes I missed him as much as I did Dane.

I was just about to respond when there was a knock at the door.

It was just a knock.

Three short, soft raps of knuckles against the wood.

But a violent shiver wrenched down my spine, rattling me and setting my teeth on edge.

LILA: NOVA, I THINK SOMETHING'S WRONG.

And then Molly was pushing open the door, her Irish skin pale as I'd ever seen, so white I could see through it to the blue veins in her cheek, the pulse throbbing at her neck.

I shivered again, so hard my teeth clanged.

"M-Molly?" I murmured, and I realized I was shivering, teeth chattering.

Was it cold?

No. It was late spring, and heat had settled between the mountain tops.

She had such large eyes, big irises the colour of blue hydrangeas. They weren't blinking, and I thought that was weird, so I said, "Why aren't you blinking?"

It was such a silly thing to notice.

But I focused on it. Why wasn't she blinking as she stood looking hollow and pale in my doorway at two in the morning on a school night.

"Lila," she whispered, and it was more breath than sound, wet at the edges with tears she hadn't yet shed.

And then Diogo was at the door behind her, and he wasn't blinking either as he stared at me with the same dark gaze as his sons.

"Li girl," he said in that same waterlogged tone.

And I knew.

I knew, and I realized I'd known all night. Somehow, in ways I'd never understand. Ways so metaphysical I wondered if what I'd thought as a child was true, and Dane and I shared one soul.

My phone started to ring in my hand, vibrating my suddenly hollow bones so painfully I dropped it from my numb fingers to the floor where it broke apart with a soft *pop* and scattered in pieces across the floor.

They started talking. One of them, or both, but I couldn't hear them because I was underwater. My eyes fixed on the oceanic scene Nova had painted on the wall around the door of my bedroom, on the inky depths giving way to the turquoise middle where a sea turtle swam and a school of silver fish flashed in a zig zag over the doorframe.

I wasn't breathing.

But that was okay because you had to hold your breath under water.

And I wanted to stay there, submerged, at peace in the silence and stillness under the turbulent waves on the surface.

I didn't want to hear.

I didn't want to see anything other than the deep blue ocean on my wall.

I didn't want to feel anything, not even the breath through my body or the pulse of my blood.

I wanted to die.

Because I knew, even though I was struggling so hard not to think, that Dane, my Dane, *mi hermano*, was dead.

I don't know what happened after that.

Apparently, Molly and Diogo tried to revive me from my stupor, but I couldn't be reached. I sat numb, having slumped to the floor, half propped against the window seat, my eyes blank and unblinking as I stared at the wall, my limbs as limp as cooked noodles.

I was comatose.

Shell shocked.

Molly became hysterical, and she ran out of the room to get Hudson.

He was my baby brother, and maybe he could reach me, she'd thought.

He tried.

He wrapped himself around me, ivy around a crumbling building, trying to hold me together.

He whispered in my ears, a few distorted words reaching me through the warbled depths.

Love you, we got you, you're okay.

Then Milo and Oliver were there, and they were hugging Molly who was sobbing and arguing with Diogo who was about to call an ambulance because there was something wrong with me and they didn't know what to do.

I wasn't crying.

I wasn't screaming.

I was barely even breathing.

I was nothing because I needed to be nothing, or I would shatter like my phone into small, irretrievable pieces across the floor.

My broken phone continued to ring, and finally Hudson answered it.

He spoke with someone.

Minutes later, another figure appeared in the doorway.

I knew, even underwater, who it was, and that's when I started to float up from the depths.

I *screamed*.

Like a banshee, like a demented, lost soul haunting the moors, yearning for their loved ones long dead but unable to reach them.

I screamed so loudly my throat went raw in minutes.

Hudson scrambled away from me, and released from him comforting bond, I started to thrash because it felt, literally, like my body was coming apart at the seams.

Sound shredded over my vocal chords as I flailed, and Milo, Oliver, Diogo, and Nova tried to pin me to the ground, to still me so I wouldn't hurt myself.

I'd find out later that I broke two of my fingers in the struggle.

"Lila!"

Someone was screaming, and it was a dear voice, but it wasn't Dane's voice.

A voice I would never hear again.

My screams got impossibly louder.

Outside, a dog began to bark.

Lights popped on in our neighbor's houses, and the cops were called.

"LILA!" Someone bellowed, and I could feel the word as well as hear it, the sound stuffed into my face the way we'd used to shove Dane's face into his favourite *tres leches* cake on his birthdays.

I blinked, and it felt so wrong when no one else had been blinking. When it started with Molly's big, hydrangea blue eyes staring at mine.

I blinked again because my eyes were so dry they stung, and then again because Nova was there, and I wasn't sure how that had happened.

"Nova?" I croaked, surprised that my throat hurt because I didn't remember screaming.

"Hey, Flower Child," he said softly, and I realized he was speaking in Spanish. "Come back to us, okay? We're here for you."

All I could think was when had Nova gotten so good at Spanish?

I knew Dane had tried to teach him for years, but I couldn't remember him ever saying more than a few words.

Dane.

His name reverberated around my suddenly aching skull, and reality rushed back to me with the force of a derailed train. My breath whooshed out my body on impact, and suddenly I was pitching forward into Nova, hands tearing at his shirt, at his hair, painfully pulling and ripping at cloth and scratching into flesh as I half-attacked him half-hugged him.

"Nova!" I screamed again, and I knew it wasn't my first

time because I could taste the metallic tang of blood at the back of my tongue. "Nova!"

"Hush," he demanded firmly, stroking my back with strong hands even as he let me molest him. "Quiet, Li, that's enough yellin'. Hush, I'm here. We're here. We've all got you, okay? We've all got you."

But I couldn't stop, not now that I'd started. I cried so hard I couldn't breath, and the sobs ripped through my chest so brutally they set my whole body to aching. My tears saturated Nova's shirt from collar to belly button, and I tore holes all across his back, shredding it as if I had claws.

But he held me. He cradled me in his lap and stroked me without flinching as I hurt him, and then he rocked me, soothing, humming nonsensically into my ear as I ran out of tears to shed, and my body started to crumble with exhaustion.

The yelling turned to whimpers, strange, curling mewls like a kitten in distress, lost without its mother.

"Let's get her into bed," Molly whispered at some point.

Vaguely, I was aware that Diogo had disappeared a while ago to answer a knock at the door I'd later find out was the police. Distractedly, I also realized when the sun was breaking over the crust of the horizon, spilling milky light into my bedroom, that it was hours later.

Nova didn't put me in my small twin bed in the attic.

Carefully, he gathered my overcooked limbs into his arms and descended the stairs to take me to Molly and Diogo's big bedroom. He waited beside the bed as Hudson carefully rolled thick socks over my frozen feet, as Molly gently replaced my soaked tee with a clean, dry one of Diogo's, as Milo and Oliver turned down the bed, and I crawled in.

Nova set his knees onto the bed then walked across the mattress that way until we hit the center of the mattress before he settled in, me between his long arms, inked now for real, wrapped tightly around me like the harness of a rollercoaster ride.

Him holding me close grounded me slightly, enough to start trying to breathe properly again.

Then Milo curved into me on one side and Oliver on the other, their hands twining gently with my own so that the grooves between our fingers were linked and pressed tight.

Hudson crawled onto the bed with a wet face cloth and kneeled between my legs so that he could gently mop my flushed face with the cool fabric.

Finally, Diogo and Molly got into bed after closing the blinds tightly and grabbing more pillows. They bracketed us all, their entire family tucked away in the bed around the girl they'd made their own.

I started crying again, painfully leaking out the last tears in my body as I closed my eyes and whimpered.

But these were different tears, no less painful, but oddly cleansing.

Because I knew that where Dane was now, this was what he had given me before he left.

A family that would never leave me.

A family that would protect me and love me as hard as they could for the rest of forever.

But that fact meant nothing in that moment. Nothing compared to the colossal, all-encompassing loss of the man who had been my father, my brother, my protector and best friend.

Nothing compared to losing the best man I would ever know.

The man with the curls he'd let me slot my fingers into, the one with the eyes as blue and clear as Lost Lake on a sunny summer day.

The man who had been my *everything* for so long until he'd found a way to give me even more, a whole community to love and be loved by.

But it was something I would remember and cherish for

the rest of my life, and it was enough, in that moment, to lull me into a disquieted slumber.

It took me two weeks to get out of the house. When I got older, it embarrassed me a little, as if I should have been more ashamed of my grief, hid it better, swallowed it easier. People didn't know what to do with me when they visited to pay their respects to the Booths, to me. I just sat there in the kitchen and stared at the drawings Nova had done in the wooden kitchen table, tracing my fingers over the curling slope of Hudson's name stylized in graffiti on the surface or the small version of Milo and Oliver fighting in cartoon form with boxing gloves.

I couldn't stand myself because I was a stranger in my own mind and body. Who was I without Dane?

I barely responded to questions, and even then it was mostly one-word answers. Harleigh Rose stayed over most nights, and the ones she didn't, Hudson slept in my bed, or Molly, or Milo and Oliver.

I was loved. I was *so* loved, and somehow that made me hurt worse.

Because it highlighted the way I would never be loved again by Dane who had always loved me best.

I didn't understand how I could possibly get over losing him. It consumed me, possessed me. I was turning into someone I didn't know and didn't like.

Then one day, Nova was there in the kitchen, taking my hands out of the bowl of flour and water I was churning into dough to accompany Diogo's cod fish stew. He didn't say a word as Molly questioned what he was doing, and no one tried to stop him when he wrapped a hand around one of mine and drew me out the door.

I stalled, looking at the gleaming chrome and black motorbike that rested on the curb.

"No," I asserted. "No way."

Nova stared at me as he picked up his helmet and the spare for me. Then he shrugged, ran a hand through his hair, and swung onto the bike in a smooth move that said this was not the first time he'd ridden a motorcycle.

"What's the worst that could happen?" he asked in a cold, cruel voice. "You could die? You don't seem to mind that idea much anymore."

I blinked at the design on the back of his leather jacket. The same ragged wings and skull design we'd once graffitied on the side of The Fallen MC clubhouse.

"You got patched in," I said dully.

"I did," he nodded. "The day Dane went missin'."

I nodded, cracking my knuckles as I stared at the bike.

It annoyed me that people kept saying Dane had 'gone missing.' When someone couldn't be accounted for when they were at war overseas they called it 'missing in action' as if we all didn't know they were most probably dead in a ditch somewhere blown up by an IED.

We couldn't have a funeral because it wasn't official.

I'd read in my research that sometimes it never was.

Someone just disappeared, and that was that.

"C'mon, Lila," Nova coaxed, handing me the black helmet. "Get on, and go for a ride with me."

I stared at the helmet, struggling with the onset of emotions that had broken through the careful barricade I had constructed around my mind. For some reason, tears pooled in the backs of my eyes.

"Lila," Nova called, drawing my gaze to his face to find him staring at me with his mouth so soft and his eyes so filled with love. "C'mon, gorgeous girl, get on the bike."

I sucked in a deep breath through my teeth and snatched the helmet, plunking it on my head before I swung a leg over the bike. It was surprisingly comfortable to press my groin against his ass, my chest to his back, my arms a natural latch around his narrow waist. He smelled of leather, smoke, and spice, and I pressed my nose to the leather to breathe it deeper.

"Hold on tight," he ordered before shoving down the kickstand and revving the deep, growling engine of the Harley.

When we took off down the street, I squeaked as the hair tie flew off the end of my braid, and my hair unraveled into the wind. He went fast but not dangerously so, laughing as we took low, curving corners, hollering as he gunned it down a straight stretch of road before he hit Main street.

I liked it.

The rush, the freedom, the wind's demanding fingers tugging at my hair like the kinda lover I imagined one day having for my own.

It reminded me of a part of myself that had nearly died with Dane.

I loved the wind and the earth and the rain.

I loved freedom and a smidge of chaos. I loved taking off on an adventure without any clue where I was going.

Dane hadn't liked that much, the spontaneity. He was steadfast and calm, I was reckless and wild.

We weren't the same.

I hadn't lost that part of me just because I'd lost him.

It hurt me to realize that, aching in my chest like a reviving withered organ, but by the time we pulled in front of the abandoned stationary store below Nova's apartment on Main Street I was smiling.

It was small. Lips pressed tight, mouth barely curved.

But it was there.

For the first time in two weeks.

And Nova saw it as he waited for me to swing off the bike. He grinned back at me, roguish as hell with the wind whipping through his wavy hair, his sunglasses pushed back into it, face tanned and made even more handsome by the smile printed on his bright mouth.

"Hey," he said. "Haven't seen you in a while."

I frowned at him instantly, but he only chuckled softly and slung an arm around my shoulders to usher me to the front door of the shop. He opened it with a key attached to a skull chain on his jeans then pushed me into the dark interior.

I coughed as I sucked up dust into my mouth then gasped as he flicked the lights on, and the old stationary shop came into focus.

Only, it wasn't a stationary shop anymore.

It had been transformed into a tattoo parlour.

Black walls, purple accents, silver and chrome glinting here and there. I spotted five different stations, a tall, rounded receptionist desk spray painted with a logo in silver of a skull and two crossing tattoo guns.

Street Ink Tattoo Parlour, it read.

I gaped.

"Pretty, isn't she?" Nova asked smugly, arms crossed as he surveyed the shop.

His shop.

"This is yours," I stated because there was no question.

From the art on the walls to the colours of the space and its layout, this place was all Nova Booth.

"It is," he agreed. "When I patched in, I got a loan from the club to open this place up. We've been workin' 'round the clock to get it spruced up, and now, well, it's fuckin' perfect if I do say so myself."

"It is," I agreed instantly, trailing my hands over a coy fish painted on the black half-wall behind the reception desk. "It's perfectly you."

He sighed behind me, a happy, almost relieved sound. "Needed to hear you say that more than I thought."

"What?" I looked over my shoulder at him incredulously. "Like you don't know it's perfect, you just said so yourself."

He shrugged one shoulder. "Now Dane's gone… no one knows me better than you. Woulda brought you both here, cracked a bottle'a champagne," I wrinkled my nose because I hated the sweet stuff, and he laughed. "Or maybe a beer, and we would'a made our first memory in here together. *Los tres Caballeros*."

I smiled thinly as I moved over to a station with '*Casanova*' in stylized like graffiti on the wall over the purple reclining tattoo chair.

"Your station," I murmured as I played my fingers over the sleek fabric of the chair. "Yeah, Dane would have thought it was perfect too. For what it's worth."

"It's worth everythin'," he said, voice hard bitten, eyes almost mean as he lashed out to grip my arm tightly and wrench me closer. I could see the striations of black in his warm brown eyes he was so close. "You can be sad, you can wallow, you can never get over the loss'a Dane. I don't give a fuck 'cause God knows I'm never gonna get over him either. What I do give a fuckin' colossal fuck about is *you*. You're still fuckin' *here*, Li. You're here, and Dane isn't. It sucks. It's the worst kinda thing to happen to a girl who already had tragic eyes at six. But it happened, and you. Are. Here. You wanna cherish Dane and respect his memory? You live for both of you. You like the life of freedom and joy you deserved but never got. You do it for the both of you 'cause you guys were always a package deal, and you still *are*. You can still love him and live for him just like you did before.

Don't give up, Li. Don't die with him. Don't take both of you away from mum and Dad, Milo, Oliver, Hudson, and me. Not when we fought so hard to get you both, and we've lost Dane too."

I was arrested by his speech, both because Nova wasn't the kinda guy that gave into seriousness for long, and also because it hurt to hear how selfish I'd been in my grief. Faintly, I'd been aware of Molly crying when I entered a room only to stop and force a smile onto her face. Distantly, I'd been aware of Hudson clinging to me while I slept like he was afraid to lose me too. Then a single memory of Diogo, staring blankly at his wall of tools in the garage. I'd asked him what he was doing, but he hadn't heard me. He just stood there and stared blankly at the wall, rubbing at his heart as if it pained him. I'd left him there, and when he'd finally come inside for dinner an hour later, I hadn't really noticed his eyes were shot through with red.

God, we'd all lost Dane and his considerable light.

I wasn't the only one struggling through the sudden darkness.

The sigh that left me felt like a tsunami wave of ugly, selfish mourning expelled from my lungs.

"I'm sorry," I said to him, eyes locked because I wanted him to read my sincerity there.

"You're thirteen," he replied. "You're just a girl still. I'm not mad at you. I'm tryin' to remind you that Milo, Oliver, and Hudson are just boys who lost a brother. Molly and Diogo are just parents that lost a son. I'm just a man who lost his best friend and brother, the first one I ever made by choice. We're all in it together, and we're all gonna get through it together, yeah?"

"Yeah," I agreed even though I wasn't sure exactly how to get past it. "Okay."

"Good," he nodded curtly then grinned rakishly. "Now you ready for why I really brought you here?"

As if on cue, a huge, leather clad biker opened a door toward the back of the shop and stalked through it. I recognized him because he had a daughter around H.R. and my age named Cleo.

Axe-Man trudged forward and sat down heavily on a stool at the station beside Nova's. "Sit," he ordered.

I watched as Nova moved over to his chair, peeled off his shirt, and dropped onto it. He winked at me as he raised his arms above his head and tilted his chin to the ceiling.

"Gettin' somethin' done for Dane," he explained as Axe-Man pulled over a wheeled table topped with tattooing tools to his side and started prepping. "Thought you should be here."

I nodded, struck dumb by the sight of Nova spread out over the chair like that, shirtless and easy with his half-nakedness.

He had a long torso with broad shoulders and a waist defined by hard rows of sculpted muscle I would have loved to trace with a pen. He had ink on both arms now, sleeves done up in a myriad of seemingly random art that I knew he'd drawn himself. Flowers, skulls, a pair of brass knuckles over a heavy fist, an anatomical heart shot through with an arrow fired by a demonic cupid sitting up on his shoulder. The art was beautiful and made his already extraordinary body almost sinfully handsome.

I touched my fingertips to my gaping mouth, and they came away slightly damp with drool.

Staring at him, heat rushed from the top of my scalp down to my heels as if a bucket of scalding water had been dumped over my head. My skin tingled with heat, my heart beating faster against the onslaught.

Desire. The first stirrings of it so recklessly ignited by my foster brother laid out on a table to be inked with the memory of my lost brother.

It was a foreign sensation, and I rubbed my thighs together in my jeans to try to alleviate the odd tightening I felt in my groin.

So this was it, I thought, this was what it felt like to *want* someone.

"Li?" Nova said, jerking me roughly out of my salacious daydream. "Pull up a stool, and watch a master at work. Axe-Man's almost as good as me."

The big, blond Viking of a man only grunted as he leaned forward to place a stencil at the base of Nova's throat.

"Isn't that going to hurt?" I asked, touching my own neck.

"Hell yeah," he said easily with a laugh. "But beauty is painful."

"Why don't you get it somewhere less painful?" I asked as I rolled a stool to his free side and sat down close enough to be able to count the dark hairs sprouting from his naval down into the edge of his blue jeans.

My mouth went dry as I stared at the straight, oddly erotic trail and thought about tugging it between my teeth.

Sweat beaded on my brow.

"'Cause I wanna be able to see it, to remember Dane, whenever I look in the mirror no matter what I'm wearin', and the throat is always visible," he explained.

A lump lodged in my throat, and no matter how hard I swallowed, I couldn't get it down. "You really loved him. Did you ever tell him?"

Nova's lips flatlined for a second. "Not much in the habit'a sayin' shit like that out loud. But there's lotsa ways to let someone know you love them. This is one'a mine."

He held still while Axe-Man traced the outline of the design.

"What is it?" I asked.

Instead of answering, he waited for Axe-Man to pull away

and hand him a hand-held mirror so he could see the image on his throat.

It was a lotus, bulbous and resplendent, unfolding slightly right at the base of his throat.

"A lotus," I breathed, leaning forward unconsciously to reach out for the design, my fingers hovering over it. "A symbol of overcoming obstacles, of rebirth."

"Of something beautiful created from something ugly," Nova agreed. "Dane was born in a stinkin' fuckin' mire just like you in that place with Ignacio, but he was the purest, best man I'll ever know."

"Yeah," I wheezed through the expanding mass in my throat. "Yeah, he was."

Nova nodded and leaned back to close his eyes, reaching for my hand with the one closest to me. I watched as his big hand, the back of it inked with a skull, enfolded my own.

"It's gonna take a while, but when he's done, we're gonna tag the same thing in the alleyway on the side of the shop together, yeah? That way everyone comin' to the shop'll see our tribute to Dane. What do you think'a that?"

"I think," I said, feeling something turn over in my chest. "I think that's perfect."

His big, warm hand, veined and lined with callouses, gave mine a squeeze.

And I realized what had turned over in my chest.

My heart.

Because grief had shifted the prism of the lens I used to view Nova Booth through and turned it into something more than love for a brother or a friend.

It had amplified him, multiplied him like a kaleidoscope into so much more.

And that was it, the moment when I found the words for what that man was to me and what he would always mean to me.

I loved him.

Unintentionally, but irrevocably.

And when the tattoo was finished, raw and red, white petals tinged pink at the base and sides, Dane's named scrawled in cursive beneath as a last-minute addition he'd added in my careful, somewhat shaky handwriting, I knew it for sure.

I was meant to be with him.

Despite the age difference, despite our foster family relationship, despite Dane being gone and all the other things stacked so high against us.

He was it for me.

So, when we went out back to work together on a huge depiction of a lotus blossom with Dane's name beneath on the exterior wall of the shop, I added my own small design tucked away in the folds of the flower.

JB + LM surrounded in a barbed wire heart.

Barbed because it would protect us. Because *I* would protect us, our friendship, until it could bloom like the lotus into something so much more.

Until I was grown and beautiful like the women that lingered around Nova like bees to honey, and he would notice how much he loved me too.

It was the first lie I ever inked and the last one I would ever do myself.

Nova, it turned out, would do the rest.

CHAPTER SEVEN

Lila

BY THE TIME I WAS A TEENAGER, I WAS AN EXPERT ON unrequited love, but it wasn't until I hit my mid-twenties that I truly understood how deeply the roots wrapped symbiotically around my heart could hurt me.

It would have been easy to turn brittle, for the pieces calcified by a lifetime of loving a man who would never love me back to crumble with age and crack off so I became less and less of the person I'd once been. That didn't happen because I guarded my tenderness fiercely, like a knight set to defend the crown. I didn't want to lose what made me *me* just because someone had chosen not love those things.

He was one man, one person amid a sea of others who had no qualms about showing me just how much they cared. They were mostly rough and gruff bikers, but the love they gave me was all the more miraculous and headier because of the atypical nature of their gifting it to me. I was not blood, and I was not an Old Lady. Normally, there was no place for a woman in a motorcycle club unless she was one of those two things. I was neither, and yet I had it all. Their love and respect, their championship if I needed it, and their support even when I didn't. I had brothers and fathers and uncles in leather cuts even though I'd never really done anything to deserve it.

The first person to give me that was Nova. He didn't have to, and I knew it took effort for him to weave me like that through them, so seamless no one thought to question why the young girl with no ties to the club was always hanging around. He did it because after he'd given me his own blood family, he'd found another more fitting one for himself, and he did as he had promised his best friend and my brother he would do when Dane first enlisted. He made me family in a way that would never quit.

So Nova gave me my families, even if he didn't give me his romantic love in return. How could a girl really be bitter about that? He loved me, that gorgeous Casanova, in a way more precious than he'd loved anyone else, *ever*. I knew that, and even though it was a sheer, flimsy consolation, I wrapped it tightly around myself like a bandage whenever I felt that brittleness crack through my heart.

It was enough.

Or, I convinced myself it was enough for a very, very long time.

I knew the only remedy for unrequited love was to cut off the infected limb, amputate Nova from my life in a very real way for long enough to get over him.

But how long would that take?

I'd loved him since I was five years old, and now I was twenty-one. Would it take me all of the eighteen years I'd loved him for me to *un*love him?

And what would my life consist of without him?

Because without him, there was no *his*.

No Molly and Diogo, no Hudson, Milo, and Oliver.

No Fallen MC.

No Zeus and Loulou, King and Cress…

No Harleigh Rose.

What was I left with if I uprooted Nova from my life, roots and all, so that I had hope of one day planting another garden in my heart for someone who was capable of loving me back?

Nothing.

A fallow field.

So I stayed close, and I yearned.

Over the years, that closely guarded secret I'd concealed so long in my heart took form on my flesh. With each tattoo Nova inked on my skin, it seemed more and more obvious I was deeply in love with him.

The club knew.

Even, I thought, the Booths knew.

Everyone, save Nova himself.

Then I got lazy, I guess.

No, maybe I got *daring*. Maybe I wanted him to finally know the agony of my longing so that even if he didn't return my feelings (and I knew he didn't), at least my quiet suffering would be validated with notice and perhaps then absolved.

No, I got sloppy.

Which explains why I crossed a line I never should have crossed that hot summer's night at The Fallen compound.

The club was throwing one of their epic parties, a barbeque for the families during the late afternoon that turned into a shameless, orgiastic feast of indulgences—drugs, rock, sex, and prolific drinking— at night.

The entire front lot was crisscrossed with white lights, studded with tin tubs overflowing with ice lugged in by the hang-arounds and prospects who kept it constantly stocked with domestic beer and bottles of vodka, tequila, and gin. There were speakers linked up to Harleigh Rose's iPod because she always had the best playlists, and currently

AC/DC's "You Shook Me All Night Long" was blaring through the speakers. The Fallen compound included the clubhouse, Hephaestus Auto Garage and Body Shop, and an outpost for Edge Trucking. It was in the industrial outskirts of Entrance, so there was no one around at that time of night to file a noise complaint…and even if there had been, no one would dare.

The Fallen weren't a crew you fucked with, especially over something as paltry as a club party.

It was late enough that the kids and most of the wives were gone. I was outside still, hanging with H.R., her brother, King, and his woman, Cressida on a picnic table we'd commandeered to play beer pong.

I wanted to go inside.

I wanted to go inside not because it was cold outside or I had to use the washroom.

I wanted to go inside because I'd seen Nova disappear inside half an hour ago, and we hadn't hung out all night. It was near two in the morning, I had the opening morning shift at Eugene's bar in eight hours, and I wanted to spend some of those with my best friend.

I was drunk enough that it seemed like a good idea to toss back my lukewarm Blue Buck beer and whisper to Harleigh Rose. "I'm going to find Nova."

Immediately, her face collapsed into a frown. She held up a finger for King to wait while she talked to me, but he was already making out with Cressida.

"Are you kiddin'?" she hissed, blue eyes wide with incredulity. "Bitch, you know he's probably in there with a club slut right now."

I rolled my eyes. "He's seeing Yolanda."

She was the Russian transplant new-hire at Eugene's. I'd known the second I saw her strut into the bar wearing a slinky black dress and heels higher than her IQ that Nova would be all over her the second he met her.

And I'd been right.

It was my best friend's turn to roll her eyes. "You think that's gonna stop him from banging some easily available tail tonight?"

"Why do you have to say it like that?" I asked, wrinkling my nose in disgust.

I wasn't an idiot. I knew the club called Jonathon Nova, 'Casanova', for a reason.

But he was still Molly and Diogo's son.

I didn't think he'd cheat.

"Because, babe, that's how bikers talk, and if you didn't notice yet, I was raised by them. And news flash, you've been around long enough to get how it is. You go in there," she pointed a finger at the shadowy open door to the clubhouse. "You go in expecting to find that man balls deep in club pussy."

I knew what she was trying to do. Shock me. Hurt me so that I wouldn't go in, but if I ignored her advice and did it anyway, then I'd be braced by her cruel warning.

It didn't work.

There was too much hope in my heart and liquor in my veins to allow the pain, or the potential for it, to resonate.

Instead, I checked myself out, adjusting my breasts in the low-cut, suede, tasselled crop top, hiking up the low riding, high cut jean shorts I wore. My tattoos were on full display, the bunches of peonies from the left of my waist down over my hip and thigh, my right arm sleeve, the edge of the lotus and curving scrollwork between my breasts just a tantalizing hint beneath the shifting material of my top. In the last few years, I'd finally filled out, hips and ass round, breasts large enough to capitulate to gravity just enough to give me wicked cleavage even without a bra.

I was finally a woman in a way that demanded attention.

Even Nova with his foster brother blinders had to sit up and take notice… didn't he?

I tossed my waist-length hair behind my shoulder and flashed H.R. a cocky grin I didn't feel. "It's still early, I'm sure he's just shooting the shit with the brothers. Besides, if he *is* preoccupied, what do I care? I'll just come back outside and hang with my girl, right?"

It was me asking for permission even though I didn't need it from her. It was my way of asking for validation because I knew I was being ridiculous, but I wasn't going to censure myself the way I should have.

I needed just one person to *get* me. To get how it felt to have this garden thriving and blooming in my chest just waiting for that one man to walk through it, yet knowing that he never would.

And Harleigh Rose?

She might have been prickly as a barbed rose, but she understood unrequited love more than most, and better, she got *me* more than anyone other than my brother ever had.

So she sighed dramatically, slammed the rest of her beer back, then wiped her wet mouth with the back of her hand before shoving me on my way. "Go with my blessing then, if it makes you feel better. Either way, you know I'm here."

I smacked a kiss on her cheek in thanks then turned on my heel and practically flounced up the stairs to the clubhouse, buoyed by hope.

And wasn't that the danger? Hope filled the human heart until you felt it could float, and it was so easy to forget that an overinflated balloon was that much easier to pop.

The inside of the clubhouse was dark and filled with pot smoke, sweet and cloying. The scent was familiar enough to feel homey, which was an odd thought to have as I passed by the bar where Boner and Kodiak were doing body shots off a naked stripper from The Wet Lotus strip club then down the hall where Skell was rutting into someone who was distinctly *not* his wife.

But that's how I felt there, amid the rock music and the

thick lure of smoke, in a house of depravity with a group of outlaw sinners.

Like I was at home.

I followed the hall to the end, the T-shape branching off to the left and right where the brother's rooms sprawled across the back of the building. Nova's was to the left three doors down, and I could see his door was cracked open.

Giddiness exploded like an opened jar of butterflies in my chest, their wings tickling me as they flew between my ribs.

I didn't know what I thought would happen.

Maybe I had some fantasy that I'd push open the door to find him drunk enough to be pliable, happy enough to see me after weeks of separation with me in Vancouver for university, that he'd notice me differently. That finally, he would see me independent of our historical context and view me as a sensual, grown woman.

But that was too specific. My hope was all-encompassing, so overwhelming there was no shape to it, only soft, glowing substance that spilled through every inch of me like warm water.

My heartbeat thundered in my ears, and sweat broke out over my brow as I struggled to control my anxious breathing and made my way to his door.

There was a moan, a breathy exclamation of sound that somehow beckoned me closer to the door even though it was obvious I was intruding on something.

A swathe of golden light fell from the hallway into the bedroom, illuminating a broad, tattooed back tapering into a narrow waist, the sheet clinging desperately to the hard swell of a male buttock.

I knew the play of muscles in that back.

Even in the dim light, I could trace the intricate whorls and swirls of the tattoos playing over his flesh.

My skin pebbled almost painfully as desire whooshed through me, stealing my breath, tightening my nipples to hard peaks, igniting a fire in my belly I thought would raze me to the ground.

He was fucking someone.

I should have been jealous, and I was, the taste of it metallic on the back of my palate.

But for a love-sick girl without a hope of reciprocity, the moment was too good to waste.

Seeing him like this with whoever lay beneath him was the only way I would ever get to witness all of his sexual magnetism unleashed.

Saliva pooled under my tongue.

When I pressed my thighs together, rubbing at the burn pulsing at the crown of my sex, I was slick there too.

A well for him to dip into if only he'd ever look my way to notice.

But he didn't.

He never had.

I was so convinced of my own invisibility in that moment, as I had been in many others, that I dared to do something entirely forbidden.

I leaned into the shadows of the narrowly opened door, hitched a hip against the wall, and angled my fingers down my flat belly into the crease between my jean shorts and skin.

And I touched myself while I watched my foster brother fuck another girl.

My clit was hard and burning like banked coal. I rolled my fingers over it, desperate to come after only seconds of play because the sight of Nova had lit me on fire from the inside out. When he threw the sheet back, I bit off the end of my gasp and trembled.

His ass was high and taut, twin golden moons of flesh dimpled at each side with thick muscle. I wanted to bite into that swell while I played my hand in the shadow between his thighs, trace the seam of his balls and wrap my eager fingers around his cock.

I wanted to feel the heft of him in my palm.

Sweat beaded on my crown, and a drop crawled slowly down my temple.

The woman groaned in ecstasy as he ground into her at the end of each thrust. For an awful, desperate second, I thought about grinding against the doorframe, needing to feel how he might feel against her.

Instead, I tweaked my nipple with my free hand and choked off a moan.

Nova pulled away abruptly, and I froze, fingers pressed to my clit like a stamp, chest heaving, hoping he wouldn't look my way.

He didn't.

Instead, without pulling out, he stood at the end of the bed and dragged the woman back onto his cock, shifting her legs onto his shoulders. I could see his profile then, tight with passion, flushed with leashed ferocity. He wanted to move faster, harder. He wanted to ruin her, but he didn't. Something held him back so that only a glimmer of his true dark desires could be seen in his gritted teeth and flashing brown eyes.

Watching him was intensely erotic, the infelicity of spying on a man, and not just any man but *Nova*, my foster brother, my best friend, heightened everything like a drug.

I'd never been so turned on, which wasn't surprising given that I was a virgin, waiting against all odds for the man currently fucking another woman with abandon to notice me. But I'd always possessed a vivid imagination, and it was all too easy to replace her with *me*.

My breath stuttered through my lips as my hand thrummed faster over my clit, and the moment Nova opened his mouth to speak, I knew it would be the spark to raze my self-control to the ground.

"Take it," he grunted, his hand shifting from a fist on the bed to her throat, where it wrapped firmly. "Take my cock, and make me come."

Everything in me paused for one choked moment. My hand on my clit, my breath in my lungs, my racing heartbeat. Like a stuck zipper before being released, I crashed to a brief halt and then spilled open. My pussy made obscene wet noises as I worked it through my orgasm, and my breath exploded out from my lungs. Luckily, the couple made even more sound, gasping and grunting, reduced to animals in their ecstasy.

I wrung myself dry with slow, gentle circles on my clit as I came down, leaning heavily against the doorframe. My gaze was unfocused, and I'd lost my urgency and vigilance in my post-coital haze.

That's why I wasn't expecting it when Nova finally righted himself and stared directly at me through the crack in the door.

His cock glimmered in the dim light, wet and still mostly hard, long and thick, pulsing so hard it seemed to jump slightly in the air.

Unconsciously, I licked my lips, heart still hammering, caught but too aroused to cogitate what to do about it.

And Nova?

He just stared at me.

For one long, molasses second that felt like an eternity, I looked across the sex-scented room into his handsome, sex slackened face and tried to read his reaction.

He gave me nothing.

Instead, after a moment, his gaze cut to the woman curling like a satisfied cat on the bed, and he smirked at her, giving her exposed ass a swat before he moved toward the door.

Toward me.

I held my breath but didn't move, paralyzed as prey sensing a predator.

And then he was in front of me. So close I could've counted the droplets of sweat rolling down his smooth, tattooed chest, see the flush of pink at the base of the lotus tattoo I'd watched him have inked onto his throat.

My eyes darted up to his, and my mouth opened. To say what, I had no idea.

But before I could make a sound, he closed the door.

Right in my face.

Behind the wood I could hear deep laughter and a high giggle as he rejoined the girl in bed.

Struck dumb by the experience, by his response, I removed my hand from the lip of my jean shorts and wiped the stickiness on my thigh before I went to the bathroom to clean up. The mirror showed me, grown up and out, finally developed with curves many men had told me they wanted access to.

But not Nova.

Never Nova.

Because I was his dead best friend's little sister, the girl he'd promised to protect and cherish in his stead.

I knew he would never love me just the same way I knew I would never stop wanting him. Some things were written in code, hardwired in the body. The movement of breath through the lungs, the beat of the heart in the chest. The feel of Nova in my blood was just as intrinsic. I would no sooner be rid of him, even if I could, than I would cut off my own arm.

Loving someone shouldn't be contingent on them returning that affection.

Loving someone existed apart from reciprocation.

But I knew, even as I washed my hands and slashed water on my overheated face as I tried to remind myself once again that I was good looking even if Nova didn't think it was so, that living my life loving someone like this wasn't healthy.

It wasn't what Dane would have wanted for me.

And I owed it to Dane, just like Nova had once told me, to live my life for both of us.

My love for him was more hope than substance, and it was barely enough to sustain my hungry heart.

I deserved more.

Just as Dane would have deserved more.

And Nova's reaction, his callous disregard of my obvious interest, was enough to make me want to cry because it felt like the needle that finally punctured the balloon.

I was coming to terms with it, drunkenly, slowly, when I opened the door to the bathroom and someone slammed up against me, pushing me with a hand to my chest straight back inside.

Nova.

His gorgeous mouth, pinkish purple like it was permanently berry-stained, was screwed up into a snarl, his eyes flashing.

"What the actual *fuck*, Li?" he growled, so deep and low I felt the words more than heard them.

His hand was stamped between my breasts, fingers splaying over the flesh. Unwittingly, my nipples hardened even as I fought the arousal and started to get angry.

"You ever heard of closing the door if you want privacy?" I retorted archly.

I wasn't a girl anymore.

I hadn't been in a long time.

He couldn't bully me.

"Thought the fact I was fuckin' someone was enough cause to give me some fuckin' space," he bit out

The pulse in his neck was jumping beneath his tanned, tattooed skin. The hand on my sternum flexed angrily, and he pushed me harder against the wall.

I'd never seen him so angry.

"I never would have taken you for a prude, Nova," I snapped back, getting in his face, feeling defensive because I knew I was in the wrong, but I was embarrassed he couldn't just let it go like a fucking gentleman. "What's the matter? Your dick hang a little to the left?"

His snort shot hot air over my lips. "You got a good eyeful, you tell me."

"What the hell is wrong with you?" I demanded, shoving at his immovable shoulders. "So what? Yes, I watched you, okay? For like one second. Get over yourself."

"I'm thinkin' it's you that needs to get over me," he said coldly. "The guys've been buggin' me about you lately. Sayin' you gotta thing for me, but I thought, no fuckin' way my Flower Child would think'a me like that when we're *fuckin' family*. Then there you are the other day under my gun, squirmin' like you can't get comfortable when you're always still as shit for me while I ink you. Then I realized, my hands were on your fuckin' tit. Was that it?"

He leaned closer to snarl almost up against my mouth. "Did that fuckin' turn you on, Lila?"

"Shut the fuck up," I barked, trying to shove him away, my heart kicking at my ribs like a mustang desperate to flee the barn it was trapped in. "And get out of my face and back to your slut!"

But he wouldn't get out of my face.

Instead, he stepped closer so that I wasn't just pinned to the wall by his hand on my chest, I was pressed there by the weight of his entire body plastered to mine. I could feel the absolute solidity of his chest flattening my breast, the hard muscles in his thighs pressed to mine, and his hand moving up, *up*, until it was wrapped around my throat, calloused thumb to my pulse.

My lungs were heaving, struggling to drag in air as if I had just run a race, and in a way, I kind of had. I felt like I was running for my life, from this situation, from Nova's realization that I loved him more than anyone every had or ever would, even if he couldn't love me back.

"You listen to me, Li," Nova snarled, lips curled, eyes

narrowed so I could only glimpse thin slits of molten amber. "I won't have you fillin' your head with some fairy-tale nonsense. I'm no knight in shinin' anythin', you get me? I'm a man with a bike, with blood on his hands, and some serious as fuck demons in my heart. I don't got any flowers or romance for you, and bein' honest, I never fuckin' will. Get that through your head, yeah? I don't need another pathetic girl trailin' after me lookin' for scraps."

His words pierced my chest like a hot knife through butter. No resistance, no hesitation. Just metal cut straight through muscle, skin, and bone straight to the heart of me.

"Pathetic?" I echoed, undone by his cruelty. "You're seriously calling me pathetic right now?"

This wasn't him.

This wasn't *us*.

In the years since I'd been a girl, we'd only grown closer. His best friend was gone, missing for so long he was presumed dead. So I'd become his best friend.

Not in the way of his brothers in the MC, but in the way two people move through life having each other's backs, tethered together by memories both good and bad.

He was there, holding a bouquet of wild flowers at my high school graduation.

He was there when I dropped out of university because I hated the structure of classes, and he was the one who got me the job at the bar with Eugene.

He was there when I was sick or sad, bored or lonely. He went with me on road trips down the coast and into the acrid warmth of the interior, on a two-week trip to Portugal with the Booths, and a ten-day journey just the two of us to Morocco and Egypt.

He was, in a very real way, my everything.

I couldn't remember a time he'd condescended to me, let alone insulted me.

Yet here he was, calling me *pathetic*.

I blinked slowly, trying to bank the burn at the back of my eyes that always proceeded a flood of tears. "Pathetic?" I asked again on a choked whisper. "You think I'm pathetic for loving you when you're the best man I know? You think it's pathetic to want a man like the one who has taken care of me, loved me and protected me since I was five years old? Okay, Jonathon," I said, just to watch him flinch, just because the slow softening of his mouth and eyes over the course of my speech wasn't good enough. "Okay. Then consider me pathetic."

I tried to wrench out of his hold, but even though his whole demeanor had warmed and tenderized, his body was still an immovable force against mine.

"Stop," Nova snapped, forcing his hips tighter against mine. "You think this is 'bout you? You're fuckin' wrong. This is 'bout you wastin' your life pinin' for a man who's never gonna give you a second look 'cause it's not his right to catch your eye, and it sure as fuck isn't in him to take care of a girl like you."

I didn't hear the words. My mind was still so focused on the wound gaping open in my chest, even now after he had pulled out the dagger. I felt drained and draining still, unable to plug the hole.

"Whatever," I sighed, my voice so defeated I didn't recognize it. "Let me go, and I promise, this pathetic girl will let *you* go too."

And I meant it.

I hated it so much, I felt the injustice of it roll through me on a wave of nausea.

But I meant it.

I'd been fine loving him unreciprocated, but I refused to love someone who adamantly castigated me for my feelings.

"We're gonna be fine," Nova said, an edge to his voice that could've been fear. "We're gonna be just fine, you move on from this stupid crush. You're still my girl. You'll always be my Flower Child."

My eyes were unseeing as I stared at his chin, absently noticing the slight cleft there covered in thick black stubble.

"If only we could all have our cake and eat it too," I whispered.

If I'd been looking, I might have noticed the intensity of those brown eyes under slashing, furrowed brows. I might have noticed the way the lotus flower tattoo over his throat bobbed with his rough swallow.

But that's the thing about mourning; it isolates you from the nuanced colours of the world and strips it to straight black and white.

I saw nothing but the face of the man who had refused my love.

So when he let me go with a gusty sigh that blew his yeasty breath over my face before he moved to the side, I just left.

I left without saying one more word, and though Nova might've had more to say, he didn't speak it either.

CHAPTER EIGHT

Lila

Two years later.

Jake didn't like Eugene's.

Which was crazy, because Eugene's Bar was my second home, and more than that, it was straight up, unfiltered *cool*.

It was too well-maintained to be a true dive bar, but the curated selection of neon signs, framed and signed band posters, and biker paraphernalia lining the walls was chosen by a badass through and through. You felt, when walking through the doors, that you'd entered the kind of place frequented by Hunter S. Thompson and the Rat Pack, Patsy Cline, and Allen Ginsberg.

It had ambiance and atmosphere so thick in the air it intoxicated even the straightest of laced patrons who entered.

Eugene's had a reputation for being a biker bar, a good place to grab a fancy cocktail made by the proprietor's ungainly large hands, and the best bar to discover new bands over the weekends.

I loved it.

I'd spent enough time there over the years before working there with the biker babes—Harleigh Rose, her sister-in-law, Cressida, Hannah, Maja, Cleo, and Loulou—that it had actually helped morph me into the woman I was now.

Hippie and rock.

Natural and studied.

Mellow and electric.

So the fact that my fiancé hated the place didn't just rattle me.

It irritated the fuck out of me.

Which was why we were there on date night when we really, really shouldn't have been because Jake was always such a grump at the bar.

I was trying one last attempt at acclimatizing him.

"Stop pouting," I teased him, sliding a hand down the crease of his inner thigh, wishing, not for the first time, that he'd try wearing a goddamn pair of jeans for once instead of his requisite slacks. "I'm not wearing anything under my skirt, and if you're a good boy and actually crack a smile, I might just let you fuck me in the bathroom later on."

Jake pursed his lips as he shook his head at me, but there was a small twinkle in his brown eyes that belayed his reluctant amusement. "Are you trying to get me killed? There are four men by my count in here right now that would probably have my head if they caught wind of me fucking you in the bathroom."

I bit my lower lip as I swept the bar quickly then shrugged saucily. "I count six." I winked at him. "You do have a point. The Fallen can be a teeny bit overprotective, but a little danger is kind of sexy, don't you think?"

"Lila…" he said in that way he had of drawing my name out as if he wanted to give me the time to take back what I'd said. "Sometimes, you really are too much."

Too much.

That was Jake's constant refrain when we differed on something.

I was too flirty with customers.

Too sexy in my rockabilly get-ups.

Too loud when I laughed.

Too aggressive when I initiated sex.

Too, too, too much.

I rolled my eyes at him. "It's a good thing you're gorgeous, you know? Or I wouldn't put up with the stick up your butt."

Again, his lips twitched.

It was little gestures like that that gave me hope for my fiancé. Clearly, he liked my over-the-top self enough to want to marry me, but there was something in him that wouldn't quite accept that level of life and living for himself.

He wanted to be close to the fire but not feel the burn.

I was hoping with time and patience, one day, we could burn together.

"I'm a lucky man," he said sincerely, those wide, brown eyes loving as they hooked on mine.

I hummed when he punctuated his statement with a kiss, fisting my hand in the back of his short hair, trying to hold him to me for more.

He broke off with a laugh and wiped his lips with the back of his hand. "Lila, you're getting lipstick all over me."

I grinned. "Good, lets the ladies know you're mine right off so I don't have to break their fingers if they flirt with you."

He chuckled, and it made me feel like a hundred bucks to earn that from him.

Maybe, as Harleigh Rose said, Jake wasn't perfect for me.

But not all of us could find our soulmates like she had.

After years apart, decades of loving each other in one way

or another, my girl H.R. was finally with the love of her life, Lionel Danner, a now retired cop who handled himself like an old school gentleman and looked like a young Clint Eastwood.

She was a lucky bitch.

But Jake was good to me.

He was good *for* me.

He anchored my wild heart to the and reminded me to be reasonable.

Practical.

Molly and Diogo liked him.

Hudson thought he was boring, but honestly, Huds thought everyone was boring if they had a nine-to-five job or wore a suit.

Milo liked him well enough, because they both worked in finance, but Milo wasn't the kind of guy to take umbrage with anyone.

Ares, the boy The Fallen had adopted last Christmas who lived with Zeus and Lou most of the time, King and Cress sometimes, and the Booths the rest, he didn't say anything about Jake at all. Then again, he didn't have to. I've never met anyone with more eloquent eyes than my Hispanic pseudo brother.

And those large, dark eyes were frames of gentle contempt whenever Jake was brought up. Boy was only ten, but he was being raised by a roundtable of knights in leather on chariots of chrome defined by their own very set and anti-societal set of morals.

Oliver…well, Oliver had once threatened to punch Jake because he overheard him asking me to stop with the tattoos. He was a hothead sometimes, my Oliver, but he meant well.

And the entire Booth family knew how much my tattoos meant to me.

They were all clean cut, naked of ink, but they knew and respected me, and Nova, enough not to judge us for it.

Jake just…thought I had enough.

I stared down at the rich, golden skin covered in peonies exposed at the hem of my skirt on my upper thigh and the full sleeve of flowers I wore inked into my right arm.

There was more beneath my clothes, a lotus flower between my breasts, blossoms cupped under the mounds like underwire in a bra, and a fair amount of them over my shoulders down my back.

Nova's Flower Child.

I was famous for them.

Nova had made me his muse, and in turn, he had made me nearly as famous as Street Ink Tattoo Parlour.

I knew it was nothing compared to what they received at the shop, but people wrote into my social media all the time asking for more tattoo content.

I had nearly a million followers on my Photogram account.

Street Ink and Nova had over *two* million each.

My love of tattoos had been one of the most difficult obstacles in removing my eldest foster brother from my life two years ago. How could I dissociate from a man who'd made my body into art and that art into a business?

I couldn't.

So over the years, he'd still tattooed me.

But I always brought Harleigh Rose with me.

Or Cleo, Cressida, or Loulou.

Or Milo, Oliver, Hudson, or Ares.

Once, when I was in a pinch, I even begged Bat to go with me. I'd had to promise him free babysitting for a month, but it was worth it.

Because Nova couldn't talk to me the way he wanted when other people were around.

And on every other occasion I could, I avoided him.

Sunday dinners with the Booths were the only other situation I couldn't always avoid. They didn't accept excuses unless they were ironclad. If I had to pick up a shift, maybe they'd get it, or if Nova was out of town at a tattoo convention or on a run with the club.

Otherwise, we sat at the same table Nova had inked on as a teenager and pretended everything was okay.

We laughed, we joked, we shot the shit.

But we did not *speak*.

He didn't tell me about his art. He didn't crawl into bed with me when he had insomnia the way he used to some nights. We didn't travel. We didn't hike or go on adventures.

We didn't do anything *los tres Caballeros* had done.

Just the tattoos. And never just the two of us alone.

Just that ritual I hadn't been able to kick, his hands on my skin, creating masterpieces on my flesh that sunk beneath the muscle and bone and laid deep roots in the heart of me no matter how hard I tried to weed them out.

I got one whenever it was too much.

The not loving him.

Whenever I felt missing him would tear me in two.

Just a couple hours of the two of us breathing the same air, of our voices synced with animation over the design of a new tattoo.

Of being us.

JB + LM.

I was an addict with an unhealthy fixation, but at least I had it under control.

And I'd moved on, even if my heart hadn't entirely.

I was with Jake.

As if summoned by my thoughts, there was a commotion at the door of the bar, and a group of bikers rolled in on a chorus of motorcycle boots stomping and low, smoky laughter.

Of course, as he often was, Nova was at the center of it all.

I tried only to watch from the corner of my eye as he followed Ransom, Kodiak, Boner, and Bat to the bar to catch up with Eugene, but I hadn't seen him in two weeks, and I was eager for the sight of him.

He'd cut his hair shorter, the sides and back buzzed just enough to show the tattoos inked behind his ears and up his nape, but the top was still that thick, wavy pelt of deep, glossy mink that caught the dim light in the room and reflected it like a moonbeams on a lake at midnight.

I knew I wasn't the only girl watching him strut across the space in his leather cut and old, black denim. I knew I wasn't the only one who couldn't help herself from wondering what it might feel like to shove that cut off his muscle rounded shoulders, to wrench the tight black tee over his head and discover with my tongue, teeth, and fingertips exactly how much ink he had underneath it.

"Lila," Jake said sharply, pulling my gaze to his irritated expression. "What's going on with you and Jonathon?"

He refused to call him Nova on the basis that it wasn't his given name, and he felt Nova had a big enough head already without constantly being called Casanova.

I bit the corner of my lip and cracked my fingers nervously under the table.

Jake knew all about my foster family. He often came to Sunday dinners; he'd even asked Diogo for permission to marry me before he proposed six months ago.

But he didn't know, understand, or like Nova.

"I've told you a hundred times," I said wearily. "Nothing. He hurt my feelings a while back, and we never recovered from it."

In fact, he hurt my feelings the night I'd met Jake.

After Nova had successfully eviscerated my heart, I'd stormed out of the party, Harleigh Rose following me without permission as I called Hudson to beg him to drive us down to Vancouver.

I was drunk, I was twenty-one, and I was still virgin.

That would not do.

So, armed with my fury, my best friend, and my new favourite foster brother, we'd headed downtown to one of the clubs on Davy Street to find me a hookup.

Five minutes in, I'd spotted Jake. Tall, lean, handsome and Italianate looking.

Harleigh Rose thought he looked like a clean-cut version of Nova.

I didn't care.

He was gorgeous, and when I approached him, I felt his appreciation in the way his gaze took in the flare of my hips and my hair as it swung over my exposed belly.

He'd been mine ever since.

Whether or not I was fully his....well, that was another subject.

"Seems you have unresolved business there," Jake ventured. "Maybe you should try to talk it out?"

I smiled at him, squeezing his thigh as I leaned closer to kiss his smooth-shaven cheek. "I do talk to him. He's a Booth. It would be next to impossible to avoid him," though I'd tried. "Trust me, it's nothing time won't heal."

As if sensing our conversation, Nova chose that moment to turn his back to the bar and rest his elbows on the wood behind him so he could do a visual sweep of the room. His tee stretched tight against the swell of muscles beneath, the black a perfect contrast to the bright tapestry of his ink.

It took him ten seconds to find me, and I knew the moment he did not because I could see his eyes in the dimness, but because his entire demeanor changed. The lax set of his heavy body leaning against the bar went stiff, his shoulders rolled back and up, his jaw set like stone.

I didn't smile, and neither did he.

Instead, we stared at each other for a beat that felt like a century. I could feel the roots of him tug hard around my heart, urging me to go to him.

I blinked, Boner thumped him on the shoulder, and our connection broke.

"We're fine," I repeated softly to Jake, even though nothing felt fine.

"You've been through a lot lately, if he's your family, he should support you," Jake said reasonably.

Inside, I winced. I hadn't told Jake just how much Nova *had* supported me throughout my entire life. He'd saved Ignacio from death, dropped out of high school to make money for his parents to foster Dane and I, and he'd picked up the pieces of me that had blown up when we found out Dane wasn't coming home again.

He'd done nothing but support me until that one incident in the bathroom.

Fuck me, but it was enough to make a girl feel wretched for keeping distance.

"I think he's into you."

I blinked, abruptly cut off from my reverie. "Excuse me?"

"I think he is into you," Jake enunciated. "Honestly, Lila, sometimes I don't think you see yourself properly. You're the most gorgeous girl I've ever seen, and that's even with tattoos. You're loving, loyal, funny, and kind. Just because the guy is your foster brother doesn't mean he's indifferent to you."

"He's family," I reiterated, but it felt hollow.

"He moved out when you were a kid. Yeah, maybe Milo and Oliver, definitely Hudson, see you as their sister, but this guy?" He narrowed his eyes as he peered across the busy bar at Nova who had his arms loosely crossed over the bar, leaning forward to flirt with the bartender, Olivia. "He's too far removed to have the same familial blindness the other do."

"You're just being jealous," I teased, somewhat desperately because I did *not* want to keep talking about Nova. "It's cute."

Jake scowled, but I laughed at him and kissed the corner of his pouting mouth. If I did it knowing Nova was watching, knowing he would see me happy and in love, that didn't make me a bad person, did it?

"There she is," a voice rasped from beside us, and I turned away from Jake to see Bat Stephens standing at the edge of the booth, tattooed knuckles spelling out the words 'Hell Bent' facing us as he leaned against his fists. "The girl we never see anymore."

"Hey, Bat," I said softly because I'd always had a tender regard from the man.

Arguably, he was one of the scariest Fallen men, stern faced, scarred from wars overseas, and haunted by the demons he'd collected there. He always wore his Colt M45A1 on his hip, remained taciturn at the best of times, and never, ever cracked a smile for strangers.

But his loyalty was forged first by the military and then by the brotherhood of the MC culture. I knew, as anyone did who knew him, that he would take a bullet for those he loved happily, voluntarily, while wearing a smile, because he'd do anything to save them from hurt.

He reminded me of Dane in that way, and so I let myself love him a little like my lost brother too.

It eased the ache somehow.

"Hey, man," Jake greeted with a somewhat forced grin.

He didn't like how the brothers made him feel, inadequate in his maleness, less alpha just because he wore a suit and he'd never fired a gun.

It wasn't necessarily a fair judgement, but I'd been raised the kind of girl who struggled not to feel the same.

Bat looked down at Jake, his handsome face expressionless.

Bat never gave anything away he didn't want to. I knew he wasn't happy with his wife, that she struggled to deal with their twin boys, and that she blamed a lot of things on her ex-military husband, but you'd never know it talking to him. Bat was the guy everyone in the club went to when they needed someone to listen, and even more, have their back on something.

But there was always a banked intensity in him, as if he was forcibly chaining down the demons I'd seen lurking at the backs of his dark eyes.

Once, Nova had teased that Bat was what happened when hell iced over, and the contrast suited him.

"Both've you comin' to King and Cress's engagement party," Bat said in a way that wasn't a question. "It's been too long since you dropped in."

If Jake didn't want to go, everything Bat had surmised about my fiancé would be solidified.

"Of course, we are," I said with a faux bright smile as I squeezed Jake's knee. "We wouldn't miss it for the world."

Jake stiffened beside me, but I only squeezed his thigh in a silent entreaty to go with the flow. I desperately wanted him to like the brothers, but more, I needed them to at least *respect* Jake.

Bat shot me a flat look that said otherwise, conveying with his dark eyes that he couldn't understand why I was with Jake.

I smiled thinly back at him then sucked a breath in through my teeth when Nova appeared over his shoulder, that crooked, brittle grin he'd been wearing for the last few years stamped on his stunning face.

"Hey ladies," he greeted as he dropped his mug of frothy beer to the table and grinned down at Jake and me. "Was lookin' like you were plannin' on hidin' over here all night without sayin' hey, so I thought I'd take matters into my own hands."

Bat snorted softly, but it was Jake who surprisingly responded, "We weren't planning on saying hello at all. We're here on a date."

"A date?" Nova raised a brow and looked between Jake and the bar with clear surprise. "Wouldn't take you for a man who brought his lady to Eugene's to wine and dine."

"Just as I wouldn't take you for a man who knows anything about *properly* wining and dining a beautiful, classy woman," Jake rebutted.

My eyes went wide, and I made a face at Bat who only tilted his head slightly to left as if he felt I'd brought the situation I currently found myself in. I wrinkled my nose at him, and he huffed out a small laugh before rapping his knuckles on the table.

"I'll leave you to catch up," he said before slapping Nova on the back, tilting his chin up at me, then turning back to the bar.

"Traitor," I muttered under my breath.

"You mind I take a seat?" Nova asked with a big smile as if we were all the best of the friends, and then, without waiting for a response, he sat on my side of the circular booth and scooted over until his hard thigh was pressed to mine.

I swallowed thickly as I realized I was pressed between the man I'd always wanted but couldn't have and the man I'd pledged the rest of my life to even if I wasn't sure about him.

Why did these things happen to me?

"You're lookin' good, Flower Child," Nova murmured, low and intimate as he tipped his chin to pour his warm regard down my body. Suddenly, I regretted wearing the little, frayed jean skirt and the tight, white, ribbed tank without a bra on underneath. My nipples pebbled under his hot gaze, and I nonchalantly adjusted my long hair over my shoulders so they were covered.

Nova's grin curled higher on the left side, displaying his wicked grin, his 'I'm not going to behave' tell.

He was a man of many smiles, and I knew each and every one of them.

His curled finger reached out so he could run the back of it over my un-inked arm. "You still thinkin' of sunflowers along here?"

My skin rippled with gooseflesh under the light tough, and

I shivered slightly as I moved closer to Jake who wrapped a possessive arm around my shoulders.

"Yeah," I said, then cleared my throat because my low voice was even raspier than normal. "Yeah, maybe."

"Some Suntastics," he said, eyes softening as our gazes locked.

Suntastic Yellow Sunflowers.

The blooms we'd talked about the night Ellie died.

My heart seized in my chest, and I hated him, *hated him*, for playing me so skillfully. Just because he knew me better than anyone didn't give him the right to use my vulnerabilities against me.

I hiked my chin into the air and looked down at him as he leaned into Jake. "I might wait. Jake doesn't want me getting fresh ink before the wedding."

Something ugly flashed across Nova's pretty face before he could hide it behind his affable expression. "Oh, yeah?" He looked down at his ringed hand and watched the skull flex on the back of it as he spread and fisted his fingers. "Jake doesn't want a lotta things you seem to like a helluva lot."

"And Jonathon seems to forget Lila's got a mind of her own," Jake countered, and I was relieved he could hold his own. "If she wants more ink, I have no doubt she'll get it. Maybe it's the tattoo artist she's not so hot on anymore..."

Nova's smirk was mean, sharp as a blade held to Jake's throat. It reminded me that just because he was beautiful didn't mean Nova couldn't be deadly.

"Oh, I'm a hard one to hate," Nova drawled easily. "Aren't I, *mi girasol?*"

My sunflower.

I scowled at him. "Jake doesn't speak Spanish. Don't be rude, Nova."

"Oh." He pressed his hand to his heart in mock apology. "I woulda thought your future husband would learn the language of your childhood."

"There isn't much about my childhood before you worth remembering," I snapped before I could think.

And then I paled because saying it that way—*before you*—made it seem too personal, too specific to Nova when I'd meant the Booth family as a whole.

Jake was still beside me, too quiet.

I looked up to find him glaring at Nova, his classically handsome face wrinkled with displeasure.

Across the room at the bar, Boner, Bat, Ransom, and Kodiak had all turned their backs on the cute bartenders to watch our spectacle shamelessly. I glared over at them, but Boner only shot me a thumbs up with a goofy grin.

"Nova," I said, suddenly tired, so exhausted my bones felt like they weighed a metric ton, and my heart didn't want to expend the energy it needed to beat. "Just go, would you?"

His energy, always ceaseless like the sun even behind cloud cover, ebbed as he picked up on my mood. He studied me with low lidded eyes for a moment then shifted to lean casually back against the booth.

"Nah," he said. "I'm thinkin' if you're gonna marry this guy, I better get to know him, huh?" He turned his head to snag the gaze of Olivia as she dropped beers off at a table close by. "Liv, darlin', bring us a couple rounds of whiskey shots, will you?" He turned back to us with a smooth, sly grin. "Let's do a cheers to the happy fuckin' couple, yeah? We haven't had time to celebrate the engagement, and now's a good a time as any."

I opened my mouth to protest, but Jake was rising his beer in tandem with Nova, and when he spoke, there was some kind of masculine dare in his voice I wasn't male enough to decipher.

"To Lila and me," he agreed with an indisputable edge as the two men clinked glasses.

"To the happy couple," Nova amended, and unbeknownst

to my fiancé beside me, his hand found its way to my bare thigh and squeezed the sensitive spot above my knee.

I jumped slightly, but Nova didn't relent. Instead, he patted my knee almost condescendingly as if I was a good girl, and I just didn't know it yet.

"Drink up, Li," he urged in a throaty purr.

And when Jake nudged me slightly with his elbow to obey, I did as they asked.

I tipped my mostly full glass of pale ale to my lips and drained it dry.

If there was such a thing as liquid courage, I needed it then in fucking spades.

CHAPTER NINE

Lila

TWO HOURS LATER, OUR TABLETOP WAS LITTERED WITH EMPTY glasses, spent limes collected in a dirty bowl, and salt granules stuck in the gluey stick of spilled beer.

I was laughing too loudly, too much.

But I was drunk, and Jake was drunk enough not to comment on my 'too much' nature.

Plus, Nova was there being Nova, so charming that even Jake, who hated him, was being amenable, laughing and cracking smiles for the first time in the many I'd brought him to hang out at Eugene's Bar.

That was his power, my foster brother, my ex-best friend. He could disarm even the mostly heavily defended hearts, regardless if they were male or female.

So Jake was laughing, mouth wide open, head tipped forward as if he couldn't support the weight of it while Nova regaled us with a story of the time an older woman he'd taken home had asked him to rub down with baby oil before fucking her because she liked her men oiled. Apparently, Nova had slipped on the oil and nearly taken himself out on the edge of the four-poster bed.

I was too warm with good company, copious amounts of booze, and the two bodies that pressed closer and closer at my sides. The air was alive with something underneath the sound of a local band rocking out "Sex on Fire", the smell of sweating bodies, and yeasty bear.

Alive with something dangerous.

I couldn't shake the feeling that Nova wasn't just there to charm my fiancé into liking him, that he wasn't just suddenly resolved to that fact I was getting married to a man he'd once called 'dull as a fallow field', and he wanted to try for *me* to get along with Jake.

For all he pretended to be the affable, casual pretty boy, Nova was sharp as broken glass and just as jagged.

I couldn't shake the feeling that Nova was playing a game.

Playing a game with us that I didn't understand and Jake had no hope of winning.

Nova chose that moment to flash me his white toothed grin, wide and calculating as a shark's.

"You're flushed," he murmured, swaying close to say the words against my cheek.

I touched my cheek reflexively when he pulled back. "No, I'm not. You know I don't blush." I was too dark to show the heat beneath my skin, and I was grateful for it for the layer of protection against everyone knowing what I thought.

His hand slid up my bare thigh, dangerously high, fingers curled into the soft, tender skin on the inside of my leg scant inches from my lace covered core.

"Sure feel it," he countered softly.

My breath stuttered through my open lips. I licked them unconsciously and watched his eyes follow the path. Heat scorched down my throat more potent than any of the shots we'd thrown back and pooled between my thighs. I worried, with his hand so high, he might feel the sudden warmth there, so I shut my legs closed with a snap.

Unfortunately, that trapped his hand there, stamped between my thighs like a pressed flower I was saving for later.

A bead of sweat dripped down my temple and landed on my collarbone.

With his other hand, Nova quickly swept it away with this thumb and brought it to his full, pinkish purple mouth to suck away the taste of me.

I squirmed.

"You want her," Jake said flatly from beside me.

It startled me so deeply, his voice, the fact that he was sitting beside me, pressed all along my right side, that my heart skipped a beat before shame swept over me. How had I forgotten about my fucking fiancé with him sitting right there beside me?

Because Nova Booth, the asshole, was playing serious games.

Nova tipped his head to the side, confusion set on his features as he looked at Jake. "Say again?"

Jake pressed his lips together then forged on. "You want Lila. That's what's going on between you. Whether you want to admit it or not, you want her, and you hate that she doesn't want you."

"Oh," Nova let out a quiet hoot to the ceiling as he tossed his head back to bark out a laugh before locking eyes with Jake again, his face suddenly somber. "You think?"

There was a dare there, barely imperceptible but dangerous.

Oh, so goddamn dangerous.

Because Jake, my sweet Jake, was a proud man.

A finance guy. Not as overtly alpha as Nova, but man enough not to take a threat like that lightly.

He leaned forward over me, almost as if I was forgotten, and practically bared his teeth at Nova. "I *know*."

They held eye contact for a long minute, two warriors in a stand-off I wasn't sure could end without violence. But then Nova was laughing easily, leaning back into his relaxed, slouched position across the booth as if he didn't have a care in the world.

He brought his beer to his lips and winked at me over the frosted glass.

Jake followed the interaction with narrow eyes, his pulse tattooing a strong beat in his throat.

And he did it.

He picked up the thread of Nova's carefully planted dare and bonded us to it.

To him.

"Why don't we test that theory?" Jake suggested, biting off the words, chewing through the poisoned apple Nova had been so happy to offer up. "Kiss her."

"Excuse me?" I snapped, twisting in my seat to gape at my future husband. "Jake, seriously, think about this for a second."

"I don't have to," he said, so firm I could feel his words formed in steel thrust like weapons into the heart of our relationship.

We could not do this.

We would never recover.

This I knew elementally because to do this, to kiss Nova when I'd spent years thinking of his bright, supple lips on mine, in front of the man I'd resolved to love the way a vegetarian resolves to change their diet for the better of themselves, their world, would be nothing short of catastrophic.

"Do it," Jake said to me, eyes lighter than Nova's, rounder and closer set but still so similar to my foster brother's. "If he means nothing to you beyond family, it should repulse you, right?"

"Yet you want to force me to kiss someone you think I should view as a brother?" I retorted angrily, cracking my knuckles so hard they refused to crack again. "This is insane."

"Life's a crazy bitch," Nova took the moment to intervene. "Ride her hard or die tryin', right, Li?"

Live free, die hard. The Fallen MC's motto, but also Nova's philosophy on life.

And mine.

I'd quit university because I'd hated the structure. I worked at a bar because I liked the hours, the chaos, the constant revolving door of new people and experiences.

I didn't want much out of life, not money, not power or prestige.

All I wanted out of the life was the *living*.

And this was it. A situation so fucked up it made my heart race, so dangerous I was couldn't breathe right, so edgy I couldn't think straight.

This was living.

This was what Nova did. What I did.

What we'd once loved doing together.

And in that moment, I knew I'd do it.

I'd fall on the sword Nova held out to me, just because he was selfish enough, horrible enough to want to prove what he'd known now for years.

That I was his to do with as he pleased.

If he needed to prove to himself in some machismo act of bullshit that he could have me if only he wanted me, I'd let him.

Let him feel me, my lips on his, my body on his body, the potential of me in his mouth.

And then I'd rip it away just as violently as he was now ripping away any last vestiges of our friendship.

A friend didn't sabotage.

And that was what he was doing here.

Sabotaging Jake and me.

Because we wouldn't survive the fallout.

But Nova didn't get that I was going to make sure we, him and me, didn't survive it either.

"This is your choice," I told Jake, looking him dead in the eye so he could see the gun pointed at my head, the bullet in the chamber ready to end us. "You do this, it will hurt us," I promised him.

Jake pulled me close and pressed his forehead to mine so his warm, alcohol sweet breath wafted across my face and reminded me of all the nights Ellie crawled into my bed fragrant with drink.

It reminded me of all the bad choices she'd made.

How her possessiveness had destroyed our family just as much as Ignacio's.

Jake wanted to be mine.

Nova didn't want me to be his, but he wanted to prove to everyone I *could* be.

What no one seemed capable of understanding was that I was property of *no one*.

My heart beat hard once, then slowed and grew weak as I understood the tragedy of the moment.

"I love you," Jake said, and maybe he did, but he loved himself more in that moment, needing me to prove his masculinity for him. "Nothing will change that."

Maybe for him, but not for me.

I could already feel the love leaking out of the puncture wound in my heart he'd put there.

I gave him a small, sad smile then turned to Nova who was watching me with hawk-like intensity, a predator zeroed in on his prey.

"This is your choice," I echoed to him, not even angry anymore, just tired, tired, tired.

His smile was, surprisingly, sad too. Sad, small and tight.

He nodded curtly. "I know."

Sobriety cut through my intoxication, but not enough to

quell the swell of anticipation that rose like a tide in my belly knowing what was going to happen.

Nova was going to kiss me.

I leaned back against the booth casually, as if my heart wasn't trying to break through the cage of my ribs and leap across the table. Sandwiched between the only two men I'd ever wanted, I couldn't believe it might be possible to have them both for only a second before I'd be forced to give them both up.

I couldn't breathe through the riot of emotions blooming in my chest, crawling up my throat like vines.

Nova moved closer, sinuous as a shadow moving over the seat.

The low light of the neon sign above our booth glided his exquisite features in metallic blue, making him seem other-worldly, incandescently glorious.

He was closer than he'd ever been before.

I held my breath as my man sat still beside me and the other closed the final gap between us to press his mouth over mine.

Everything faded.

The bar, the collection of bikers that had grown in number who might have been watching us, the music building to a climax, the man who put a ring on my finger sitting right beside me watching.

All of it.

And what remained was sheer, unbroken *elation*.

The feel of Nova's silken lips, the top slightly fuller, the bottom plush as it slipped between mine and lightly sucked on my upper lip.

My mouth tingled almost painfully, a thousand bee stings.

Then he growled softly, so softly, against my mouth before fisting a hand in the hair at the nape of my neck so he could tug my head back and to the side.

His lips never left mine, pressing firmly, opening my

mouth, tongue sweeping inside on a wave of heady, whiskey flavour and something lightly spiced, totally Nova.

I could smell him, that smoke and spice and leather.

I could feel him, his hard hands, one in my hair, one on my face, palming the entire side of it in one calloused palm, his knees turned into mine, thigh pressing deep into my groin so that the heat and pressure of him made me swoon.

It couldn't have lasted long.

A minute, max.

Probably less because a minute is a full sixty seconds, and I thought, truly, a minute of those lips on mine, that five o'clock shadow scratching my skin, I would have died.

So surely less.

Suddenly, Nova was pulling away, Jake's hand on his shoulder, shoving at him.

And then Nova was standing, hand locked on Jake's, which was still on his shoulder, so that my fiancé was pulled with him, up and slightly over the table, dragged halfway across me.

Nova was breathing like a stuck bull, so heated I imagined steam curling out of his nose as his chest heaved and his eyes burned into Jake.

Something passed between them that made the air flare then go flat.

Nova suddenly dropped Jake's hand and took a step out of the booth.

Jake immediately righted himself and hauled me onto his lap, both arms protectively wrapped around me.

"You want her," Jake said, each word a whip lashed at Nova. "And now you can't have her. You should have loved her while you had the chance."

Shame burned through my post-kiss haze followed swiftly by anger. I ripped Jake's arms off me and scuttled to the end of the booth, standing to face both of them.

"Go home," I ordered shakily to Jake. "I'll call you tomorrow."

"Lila—" he started, but I shook my head almost hysterically and told him the truth.

"You wanted this. You live with the consequences. And right now? I do not want to see you."

I looked at Nova who was still breathing hard, still holding himself rigid like a bull about to chase down his matador.

"And you," I said, quickly because I couldn't look for more than a moment into the intensity of his expression. "I don't want to see you either."

Without waiting on either of them, I turned on my wedged heel and hurried into the back to the women's bathroom where I instantly locked myself in a stall, put my head between my legs, and deep breathed.

Fuck, I thought.

"*Carajo,*" I swore out loud then shoved at the closed door and cursed again loudly.

"*¿Estás bien?*" a smooth, lyrical voice called to me from somewhere in the bathroom.

I froze, unused to the sound of Spanish in Entrance, B.C. There were a few speakers throughout the city, but not many. Most of the immigrants were French, Indian, Persian, or, the majority, Asian.

The female speaker repeated her question.

"Yes," I replied softly. "I'm fine, thank you."

A pause.

"You don't sound fine," she continued in Spanish. "Why don't you come out of there and I'll buy you a drink. You can unburden yourself on someone with much life experience."

I hesitated, staring down at my purple painted toenails in my kickass shoes.

"I sense it's boy trouble," she added with a smoky laugh. "This I can most certainly help with. Let me buy you a drink. Us girls must stick together, hmm?"

I sighed heavily and heaved myself off the toilet, unlocking the stall to open it, revealing the woman on the other side.

She was stunning.

So gorgeous I actually sucked in a shocked breath at the sight of her deeply curved, lush, brown body tucked into a skin-tight, white dress with a zipper that went from the bottom of her cleavage all the way down to her calves.

She smiled at me with her full, painted red mouth parted to reveal perfectly capped, white teeth, and when she moved closer, it was on a cloud of rich perfume.

But her beauty wasn't what held me arrested as she stopped a foot away from me and held out her heavily jeweled hand to shake mine.

"Hola, abejita, es bueno finalmente conocerte después de tanto tiempo," she purred.

Hello, little bee, it is good to finally meet you.

It was her name.

Irina Ventura.

Because the woman who obviously knew me, based on the fact that she'd just referred to me by the name Ignacio called me, was none other than the wife of The Fallen MC's archenemy, Javier Ventura.

Cartel boss.

Entrance's corrupt mayor.

Irina Ventura's husband.

Thankfully, she took my surprise for something else.

"Your father must have told you of me," she surmised with a little chuckle as she plucked my hand from my side and shook it warmly. "You remember, I was once his boss?"

"I remember," I said, even though I didn't.

I'd always known Ignacio worked for the Ventura Cartel, but I didn't know he reported to Irina.

She was still smiling so warmly at me, I thought she must have mistaken me for someone else. When she reached forward, I flinched slightly, but she only tucked a long strand of my dark hair behind my ear.

"So beautiful, like your father," she noted, dark eyes heavily made up and glittering like obsidian gems. "Which brings me to the reason I'm here in this…quaint place. I wonder…" She stepped even closer, so close our breasts brushed together, and her sweet breath wafted over my lips. "If you might be as helpful as him too."

CHAPTER TEN

Lila

AFTER A CHILDHOOD THAT CONSISTED OF VISITING PRISONS, you would have thought I'd be used to it by now. Twenty-four years old, and I still felt like the little girl who had been forced to visit her father every Sunday after church for two years since I was almost too young to remember. Mama had put bows in my thick, tangled brown hair, the colour always matching the frilly, second-hand dress I was forced to change into in the car. I wore glossy, patent leather shoes and white socks with furled edges that made my ankles itch.

I'd hated everything about those visits.

I didn't hate them now.

Because I wasn't visiting Ignacio Davalos.

I was visiting Zeus Garro, a man who was as close to a

father figure as I'd ever had, including the biological piece of shit who'd been in prison for almost fifteen years by that point.

There were some people you meet in life that were utterly magnetic, their gravitational force so absolute they acted like a third Pole.

Zeus Garro was one of those men.

He was a good man under all the tatts and illegal activities, and he drew good people to him with that magnetism so that the entire Fallen Motorcycle Club he was president of was filled with the same dichotomy he embodied.

Bad boys, good men.

I loved them all, even though I had none of the usual ties to the club.

No patched-in father, brother, or boyfriend.

Just one man who'd taken me in when I had no one left to give a shit about me.

One man who had given me the greatest gift I'd ever known.

The Fallen family.

And at the head of that family was Zeus, who had accepted me as his daughter's best friend and his brother's charity case easier than I ever could have imagined.

There wasn't anything I wouldn't do for Zeus.

I smiled at him as I waited for the guard to let me through the final door to the bank of telephones and glass partitions separating civilians from the incarcerated.

I didn't want to smile.

I wanted to rage. Just as I did every time I saw him behind the smeared plexiglass in a bright orange jumpsuit. He was just too big for prison, too colossal of heart and stature. His broad shoulders kissed the partitions on either side of him, and he dwarfed the plastic chair he sat in.

It made me ache to see him like that, like a great cat in a tiny cage.

"Zeus," I said as I sat down across from him and picked

up the cracked black phone. "I wish I could say orange was your colour."

He chuckled, which I'd intended for him to do, because he didn't give a crap about his colour wheel. "How's my Lila girl? Helluva sight for these poor eyes after a day'a lookin' at tatted skinheads, let me tell ya."

I beamed at him. It wasn't hard for me to admit that I'd been an unattractive child. My mother passed down her grandfather's coarse hair, but without the curls, and she died before she could teach me what to do with the mass of it, so it was always tangled despite my attempts to keep it tame. From my father, I had inherited large, almond-shaped eyes, his Hispanic olive toned skin, plus his natural inclination toward gauntness.

So, not attractive.

But that was okay because I'd developed other aspects of my personality from an early age to make up for those deficits, and when I'd met Harleigh Rose at the age of seven and she instantly fell in love with me, I finally found someone to help me cultivate my looks.

She taught me to tame my bushy hair and harness the power of my tan. She took me to the gym with one of the brothers, Bat, who taught us how to use the equipment to carve steeper curves into our girlish forms. H.R. had stuck with it for two weeks, but I'd made the gym a routine and had the results to prove it.

Still, I wasn't used to compliments, and Zeus knew it.

Which meant he was sure to let me know how lovely I was every chance he could.

He was like that. Generous with his love and attention.

I aspired to be like him, and it was exactly that character-istic that prompted me to visit him that day with a plan.

"Listen, I'm not here to shoot the shit with you, Z," I admitted, staring down at my tattooed left hand to distract myself form the sudden glower on his formidable brow. I loved the intricacy of the blooming vines as they opened their petals across the insides of my fingers and wound all the way across the backs of my hands. My other hand was luridly bare in comparison, a blank canvas as yet untouched by the kiss of ink from Nova's flourishing tattoo gun.

I resolved to go into Street Ink soon and get something done to the space, even if Jake didn't like it. Its emptiness irritated me because, in ways I was reticent to explore, it mirrored the malcontent I felt in my own life.

Hence, my plan.

I squared my shoulders as my gaze met Zeus's silver bladed eyes. "Something's got to change here. I know you've got antiquated rules about women getting involved in club shit, but that shit is up to all our ears right now, Z, and like I said, something's got to change."

He peered at me through narrowed eyes, his massive hands folding into fists on the laminate counter. "Maybe so, Li-girl, but you aren't gonna be the one to do it."

I tipped my chin into the air so I could look down my nose at him. "You got something against women I don't know about?"

He scowled.

Of course, I knew better than most that Zeus was a rare outlaw MC Prez, he valued Old Ladies and club kids—male or female—a helluva lot more than most bikers did.

I'd insulted him, but it was for a purpose.

"You wanna twist it that way when you know I'm comin' from a place'a pure love, I'll take it if it means you ditch whatever hair-brained plan you got formin'. Got a lotta respect for you, Lila, doesn't mean I'm willin' to sanction whatever heroic bullshit you're cookin' up."

"It's not dumb," I argued. "I've got a *plan*."

"Gotta daughter who had a plan'a vengeance to bring down a rival MC…don't think I need to remind you how that went for Harleigh Rose."

I winced, because I'd known he would bring up my best friend's nearly ill-fated ploy to take down the Berserkers MC in Vancouver. One of their brothers, an asshole by the name of Cricket, had raped Harleigh Rose, and my girl wasn't the kinda girl to take that shit laying down.

So she'd partnered with a local undercover cop to investigate and dismantle the organization.

In the process, she'd had to stab said cop, watch her dog die, been abducted, and had been threatened by her own mother as well as the Prez of the Berserkers.

So yeah, I had to admit, *hers* had been a hare-brained scheme.

But mine was not.

"Yeah, well, I agree H.R. went off half-cocked because she was traumatized, but I'm clear as fucking day, Z, and I gotta real plan."

He leaned back in his chair and studied me seriously as he stroked absently at his short beard. His contemplation was one of the many reasons I loved him. I was a twenty-three-year-old woman with no real affiliation to his club. I had no right to question him, to push him, to even to talk to him based on the unwritten rules of normal 1%er culture.

And here was the great and infamous Zeus Garro, listening to little old me, taking me seriously because he was just that kinda man.

"Got the feelin' I don't let you air this out, you'll go off and do some extreme shit anyway," he finally said, slanting me an exasperated look. "So I'll hear you out on the condition you relent if I tell you to fuckin' relent, yeah?"

My mouth corkscrewed to the side because I did not like those conditions.

I wanted to do what I felt I needed to do to save my family.

But I got him.

He was showing me respect, and I had to do the same.

So I tipped my chin in a gesture I'd long ago stolen from Nova and spread my hands on the table as I launched into my plan.

"The Ventura's have been fucking with our town and the club for way too long. First, they abduct Cressida and stab *nails* through her hands by proxy of their puppet MC the Nightstalkers. And then they prop up Staff Sergeant Danner's corrupt police force. Javier is coming for the club, his first step getting you locked up for a murder you absolutely did not commit," I pointed out, laying the groundwork so he would get just why we needed to take extreme measures. "I think it's past time we came for *them*."

"Oh, yeah?" Zeus asked, vaguely amused even though his eyes sparkled with something meaner, something lurking and chained in his gut that, when unleashed, would destroy everything in its path.

"Yeah." I nodded curtly. "We're going to go at Javier's Achilles Heel. We're going to go at his wife."

Zeus's amusement froze on his face. "And how the fuck do you plan to do that?"

My smile was a wide, slow spread across my face. "I'm going to offer myself up for Irina Ventura's sex trafficking and illegal pornography business."

"The hell you fuckin' are," he growled, lurching forward in his seat to snap at me, nearly pressed to the plexiglass. "You wanna head straight into the viper's den? You got suicidal intentions I don't know 'bout?"

"No," I said calmly even though my palms were sweating at the thought of what I'd have to do. "I have a family that I was lucky enough to find after I'd lost every single thing that mattered to me as a girl. I have a family that's being attacked, and I am *not* the kinda girl who is going to take that shit laying down." I took a deep breath. "And I have an in with Irina Ventura that no other person in The Fallen has.

"I'm the daughter of Ignacio Davalos. The same Ignacio

Davalos that used to run the Ventura's drug operation in Entrance before they moved operations up here. The same Ignacio Davalos who is going to vouch for me when Irina goes to him to ask if I'd make a good assistant."

"No. End of fuckin' discussion." Zeus seemed three times larger, inflated by the fury Ignacio's name always invoked in him. "You are not talkin' to that scumbag for any reason. You say he's your father? Fuck. That. You got no father. You were an orphan and then the Booth's took you and then we did. You know what Diogo'd think if he heard you spout that crap? You got no father by that name, and if you never thought 'bout him again, I'd be happy as fuck."

I let him rage. Ignacio and the club had co-existed years ago when I was a girl, but only because Z's evil uncle Crux was Prez of The Fallen back then. Of course, he and Ignacio had got along just fine.

"She came to the bar," I admitted, because Irina Ventura confronting me at Eugene's Bar had been the spark that lit the kindling of this plan in my mind. "She knew who I was, Z. She asked me straight up if I wanted the job."

Z's brows shot into his hairline. "You're fuckin' with me. In front'a Eugene?"

"She asked me in Spanish," I admitted. "But yeah."

"You said no," he stated, even though it was a question and one I couldn't give him the answer he wanted to. When I only pursed my lips, he cursed and corrected himself. "You're *gonna* say no."

"I don't want to. She doesn't know I'm part of the club. I have no official affiliation, and working at Eugene's isn't enough to mark me as yours."

"You're property of the fuckin' Fallen." Zeus slammed his fist down on the table so hard, a guard lingering at the wall behind him startled and started toward us.

I kept my cool because I needed reason to prevail here. I

needed the chance to be a hero for the men who had saved me from my youth.

I had no great love like Zeus or King or my girl, Harleigh Rose. I had nothing to lose, and so, wasn't it only fitting I be the one to take the risk?

If it didn't work.

If I died...

At least I wouldn't leave behind a love like theirs who would never recover from my death.

I'd had a fiancé, a good man, one who treated me well even though he hated The Fallen.

I thought I could've loved him one day and I *knew* he loved me.

But Jake would've recovered if something happened to me.

To be honest, after what happened at Eugene's, I wasn't even sure I could go through with the wedding, let alone give thought to what he'd feel if I died.

The kinda love Zeus, King, and H.R. shared with their partners?

That kinda loved wasn't something a person could ever get beyond.

One of them died, the other would.

So I'd do this, if they'd let me.

It would crush the Booths to lose me, but they had the rest of their sizable clan, and I knew from experience they would band together and get through alright because they'd helped me do just that when Dane passed.

Martyrdom seemed to run in the Davalos blood, and even though I was a Meadows now, that didn't mean I could shake the ache to protect.

"No, Z," I said coolly. "I'm property of no one. I came to you as a courtesy, but I've got to do this and I will, with or without you at my back."

"You're not doin' this alone," Zeus growled, and if I

hadn't known him so well, I might have trembled at the cold fury in his tone.

"Don't make me," I countered with a one-shoulder shrug.

We stared at each other, two predators locked over one prey, neither willing to concede to the other. I'd never thrown down like that with Zeus, and the strength it took to look such a powerful man in the eyes and defy him astounded me.

But I did it.

I did it shaking and nauseated, hating him and hating myself because I couldn't reconcile my need to please him with my need to save him.

"No, Lila," he said finally, softly, anger blurred at the edges with grief as he worked his mind around the problem. "Love you like my own kid, so I can't sanction this shit. I need you to get me, to hear me when I say *no*. You do this, you die. Guaranteed. Don't need another death on our hands, girl. Only been three years, we're still recoverin' from Mute. Let's keep this family whole."

"It's not whole. Not with you in here," I argued.

"Lila," he said firmly, a period punctuated on this conversation. "No."

I rolled my lips under my teeth in a struggle to accept his decision. "They won't rest until they take everything from us. You know how I know that, Z? Because they're like Ignacio. And Ignacio sure as fuck didn't stop until he'd taken everything from me in the pursuit of his own selfish agenda. Mute is *gone*, and you're *in here*. They've taken more than enough from us."

I ached with the egregious wrong of it, and I was furious because my role models—Diogo and Dane, Zeus and Nova—they'd *never* let such wrongs done to their loved ones go unchecked.

So why would I?

Just because I was a woman? Because I was softer, weaker, less pure of intention?

Hell fucking no.

I tipped my chin up and locked eyes with Zeus Garro, one of the biggest, baddest motherfuckers in North America's criminal underworld, and I threw down. "One more thing happens to us because of Javier and Irina Ventura, I'm telling you right now, I'm doing it, Zeus. And I love you, but I don't give a fuck what you say."

Zeus glowered at me, thick fingers curled into his palms, mouth a hard-set line. "'S club business, Lila. I'll say it one more time, you do somethin' half-baked, you die, you're puttin' that on me, yeah? You stay safe, and you stay sane. No. Fuckin'. Vendetta. Plan."

I stared down at my naked hand, clenched into a fist, then splayed it on the table, aware that it looked utterly bare without my engagement ring on it.

"Fine," I replied softly, not looking at him as I stood up. "But my promise still stands. One more thing, I'm going at them."

He said something else, but I was already putting the phone in the cradle and walking away. It hurt to leave him like that, a good man trying to protect me, spreading himself too thin because he had too many people to look after while behind fucking bars.

He didn't get it like I did that sometimes sacrifices had to be made.

And I was all too willing to make one myself.

THREE WEEKS LATER, ON THE EVE OF HIS WEDDING TO THE love of his life, King Kyle Garro was shot and plummeted to his death over the cliffs at Entrance Bay.

Like I'd said, the kind of love he shared with his partner, Cress?

She died, too, even while she breathed.

A walking zombie.

So we were down another two. Two souls I'd known and loved for over half my life.

Zeus wasn't surprised when I appeared before the plexiglass partition for the first time since my last visit a week after King's death.

He was already sitting there in that toxic orange jumpsuit that looked likely to split at the seams from his bulk, head tipped down, gaze in the bowl of his big, scarred hands cupped together like he was scrying the lines of his palms for answers.

He didn't look up until I was seated, the phone to my ear, waiting.

When he did, there were tears in his eyes, but they smoldered, illustrating his scalding, furious grief.

His hand shook as he reached for the plastic phone, and I thought he might break it as he white knuckled it in his fingers.

"One more thing," I whispered into the receiver.

Not an 'I told you so'.

Never.

Instead, another promise.

That I would take down the Venturas if it was the last thing I did.

I would do it for him, for Nova, for Harleigh Rose and Cressida.

For Loulou and her babies.

For the biker babes so they could be safe and their men could stay alive.

I would do it for the Booths so they wouldn't know the pain of losing a son the way Zeus did.

I would do it for me because they'd all raised me to be the kind of person who wouldn't let injustice lie like a sleeping dog.

I'd do it because I was Dane Meadow's sister, and he would have done the same.

"One more thing," I repeated, wet in my eyes, a vise around my throat robbing me of breath so my words were threadbare and weak where my intention was not. "I'm doing it, Zeus."

He blinked at me, those silver eyes so clear I felt I could fall into them like the surface of a depthless lake under clouds. The magnitude of his mourning poured over me as I continued to stare, but I bore the weight because alone in prison, he'd been bearing it too long.

"Yeah," he said, the word like air through a puncture wound, pained, breathy, explosive with relief. "Yeah, we do it together."

"You're inside," I countered.

"A caged monster is still a monster," he quipped with a raised brow. "Still got the power'a fear in my name and connections, Lila. If I'm sendin' you into that stickin', fuckin' hellhole, you best believe I'm not sendin' ya alone."

"But I'm going," I confirmed, heart thumping so hard in my chest it hurt. "It's already done. I took the job with Irina two weeks ago. Told her I needed to work out my notice at Eugene's, but I'm starting at Wet Works."

He winced. "Fuck, Li, the thought'a you there turns my fuckin' stomach." He growled under his breath as he ran a hand over his long hair.

"Does the same to me when I see you here," I told him honestly. "It's done, Z. I'm in. And I'm going to do whatever it takes to bring them down."

"Won't bring King back," he whispered hoarsely. "Lose you too? Couldn't stand it."

"I'll be careful."

"You think King wasn't?" he countered, not cruelly, but sharp, like a slap to the face so I'd wake the fuck up.

"I know he was." I leaned forward, face so close to the partition it fogged up the glass. "But they had eyes on King. He was the new Prez, the heir to Zeus Garro. Who am I? No one. They won't see me coming."

And I had to believe that was true.

Otherwise, I'd be dead.

CHAPTER ELEVEN

Nova

STREET INK TATTOO PARLOUR WAS MY HOME MORE THAN anywhere else ever I had lived. I knew every inch of motor and brick in the 1500 square foot space I'd bought with cold cash at the tender age of twenty-four. I'd known since I was five when I saw a man in the park with beauty inked into every inch of his skin from neck down to fingertips, that I wanted to be responsible for that kinda tangible, breathable art. Didn't hurt that when I picked up a pen, a crayon, or even a fuckin' stick to draw in the dirt, that I had some serious talent.

Parents were anxious about my artistic streak 'cause who the fuck made a livin' outta their passion, especially if it was creative? But then a teacher of mine in grade school who'd gone to some fancy institute in Paris called *École des Beaux-Arts* told my parents I had some serious, genius-level talent for a ten-year-old, and they'd changed their tune.

A genius in the Booth family?

We were hardy stock, fishermen from my father off the brutal shores of the Canadian west coast to our ancestors on the Algarve peninsula. We were men with large hands thick with muscle over big bones, clumsy with somethin' so delicate as a pen, but fuckin' mighty with twine, rope, and wet, dangerously edged hooks.

I say we, but I meant them.

Sure, my hands were as wide and strong as theirs, but after Mr. Larson told my parents about the potential of my art, I was saved from goin' out on the boat with the rest of my three brothers.

When they woke up before dawn to accompany Dad out on the boat, swaddled in thick layers of wool and waterproof overalls, I was sitting down at the kitchen table with a dozen blank pages and my collection of pens.

They hoped I'd be a 21st century Picasso or Bertolucci.

But I didn't like the mess of paint in oil or water.

I preferred the sharp precision of ink, the exactin' nature of its pigmentation. I loved detail, craved the tiny twists and turns of pen over paper that made a leaf seem like an entire world of topography.

It was my obsession, and soon, paper wasn't enough.

I drew on the warm wood grain of the kitchen table, down the carved legs, and up the pale oak dinin' room chairs. I painted the cabinets in elaborate Moorish patterns 'cause my father's mother had been Moorish, and I painted my mother's little parlour in an Alice in Wonderland motif 'cause she'd always been obsessed with *Through The Looking Glass*. My brothers demanded their own rooms be done, and I delivered, though, I didn't follow their directions.

For Hudson, I'd done up his ceilin' and his wooden floors in stark black, white, and red geometric shapes 'cause he was already a popular kid, a golden boy, but he had an asceticism to his personality that called to ordered and exactitude.

Miles and Oliver, only eleven months apart in age and totally inseparable, got a room cut down the middle. The same designs done on either side of the thick black line running along the center of the floor but in complimentary colours, blue and green against orange and red.

When I finished the house, I took to the streets, searchin' for anythin' ugly I could turn into art with a bottle of spray paint and my imagination.

Pretty soon, I had a reputation with the cops, even though they didn't know the identity of the boy in the purple hoodie with the hand painted, black bandana coverin' most of his face.

Unlike most graffiti artists, I didn't tag my name on my shit 'cause I wasn't stupid. I didn't need to anyway; my art was my own, and it looked it too.

When I discovered the club at seventeen, I found Axe-Man, only a handful of years older than me but already experienced, with a young daughter and ten years of tattooin' under his belt. He hooked me up with his buddy in Vancouver where I apprenticed for six years before I decided to bite the bullet and open my own place.

One could say I didn't take direction well, so it was better for everyone that I became my own boss.

My family, they'd believe in me.

Both my biological members and my club brothers.

But no one save Lila had expected my art to reach the heights it soared at now.

Millions of followers on social media.

A schedule booked a year in advantage, at least, with some spots saved permanently for celebrities who made their way north just to feel the sting of my tattoo gun.

It was more than I'd ever dreamed.

Yet lately, I'd been restless, houndin' the streets of Entrance for new adventure, pushin' Zeus then Buck then King to give me more responsibility, to send me on more and more runs, even though I'd never been so interested in them before.

My ravenous heart was fuckin' hungry, and no matter what I fed the beast, it wouldn't cease it's grumble.

After that night in the bar, Lila pressed to my front, her mouth bloomin' under mine like one'a her favourite flowers, I knew what it hungered after.

Her.

I blinked at the poster of Lila we'd hung over the reception desk near the koi fish painted up the black wall. In the shot, she was naked, the stark lightin' and a well-placed arm over her breasts hidin' her groin and tits from view while the rest of her golden-brown skin was visible. She had her head tipped back, eyes closed like she was dreamin' of somethin', and that dream was illustrated on the garden sproutin' across her skin. Peonies in bunches up her muscular thigh, high into the crease of her flared hip, a lotus peakin' out from between her breasts, vines filled with blossoms scrawled underneath those lush curves. She was breathtakin' in it, utterly mesmerizin', so none of us at the shop were surprised when new customers and old both stopped to gape at her image when they entered Street Ink.

She was my Flower Child now in ways both metaphorical and literal.

I'd tattooed each of those flowers onto that smooth skin over the years.

Still remembered the first time I'd had her in my chair, the shop empty 'cause I'd wanted, no, needed, privacy to take that virginity. We'd played our favourite rock music on low so our breath and the buzz of the gun were louder, somehow intimate.

She'd wanted the lotus first, tucked up under and between her breasts.

She was sixteen, and it was the first time I'd noticed how

much she'd fuckin' changed. No longer the scrawny little girl with dirt under her nails and pollen on her nose.

Lila was a young woman, ripenin' like fruit on a vine. Honest to Christ, I was almost afraid to put my hands on her lest she fall off into my hand like an overripe peach too succulent to toss away without taking a bite.

But my Lila? She made it easy. She had no fuckin' idea what her body could do to a man 'cause she was a virgin. That I knew 'cause she'd told me one night when I couldn't sleep and I'd crawled into bed with her like I used to. She'd had some sexy dream that had woken us both us, and she was sweaty, squirmin', obviously aroused.

I'd teased her about the man in her dream, thinkin' it was some kid at her school.

She'd cracked her knuckles, her nervous tic, and confessed there was no kid at school.

Said she was a virgin, and she planned on stayin' that way 'til she found someone worthy.

Her words had socked me in the gut in a weird way. I was pleased she was mature enough not to just bang some guy 'cause he was drunk or pushy and horny.

But my stomach flipped at the thought of her waitin' like some princess in a tower for a perfect prince that would never come.

'Cause I knew, even if she didn't, that no one would ever be good enough for her.

And if Jake Piper wasn't proof of that, nothin' was.

Motherfucker let another man kiss his woman?

That man bein' me?

The man his woman had once set her unrealistic dreams on.

The man who'd crushed those dreams beneath his boot 'cause he knew he sure as fuck would never be good enough for her.

The man who regretted it soon as it happened even

though he knew it was the right fuckin' decision.

Yeah, Jake Piper was a fuckin' dumbass.

Admittedly, so was I.

'Cause now I'd had that ripe peach in my hand, and I'd taken that first bite. I knew the taste of her burstin' fresh across my tongue, the feel of that silk mouth partin' for me to eat my fill of…

And even now, days later, after days of Lila's radio silence where she'd even missed out on Sunday family dinner, I still had that taste of her on the back of my tongue.

And despite myself, I wanted more.

Told myself it was 'cause I was a man not used to restraint.

I was a hedonist. The pursuit of pleasure was my life's refrain, and I didn't know how to pause the music, to stop and think before I fuckin' *acted* 'cause nothin' had ever been important enough to halt it before that.

"You're frowning again," Cressida said, breakin' through my broodin' with her sweet, soft voice.

I looked up to find her at my station, hands wringin' at her front, hair unwashed, eyes bloodshot over dark, near black circles.

She looked like death.

As one would, their soul mate dead before their time.

"Hey, Queenie," I murmured, instantly contrite I hadn't been payin' enough attention to notice how long she'd been standin' there. "You waited long?"

She shook her head, but there was a flicker behind the sadness in her whiskey eyes that spoke of interest. "You okay, Nova? I don't think I've ever seen you scowl like that."

I laughed easily, standin' up to fold the emaciated woman into a gentle hug. "Nah, darlin', I'm fine. Just worried about my girl, that's all."

Cress peered up at me from the circle of my arms, her gaze shrewd as it probed me.

"No," she whispered. "I think somethings happened."

My smile tried to drop but I pinned it in place and stepped away to grab my sketchbook, gesturin' for her to sit down as I did. "I'll just grab the design to show ya, but take a seat."

"Nova," she said calmly, patient as ever. "You know I'm not going away until you talk to me, right? And I mean *really* talk to me, not just the cute banter thing you do."

I gasped. "*Cute?* You think I'm cute? Really, Cress, that's fuckin' cuttin'. I expect at least adorable, maybe even enchantin'."

She rolled her eyes, but there was a little smile on her mouth that made me feel like a million bucks 'cause she didn't smile much now King was gone.

"It's Lila," she surmised in that way she had of readin' everyone even when they tried to hide. "I wondered what happened between you two. I was shocked when she agreed to marry Jake."

"Yeah, well, you and me both," I muttered, slumpin' into my stool and rollin' beside her to hand over my sketchbook. "Man's got zero balls."

She raised her eyebrow at me, and even though I knew she was playin' me so I'd spill, I ate the hook and let her reel me in.

"He was worried I was into her," I admitted with a shrug before a sly grin destroyed my look of faux innocence. "So I kissed her."

Cress's eyes went as wide as twin coins. "You're freaking kidding me?"

"I shit you not. Took her mouth, and the fucker just sat there and watched."

"I'm not shocked Jake let you kiss her, Nova. Knowing you, I'm sure you presented it like the best possible option available to him to prove you and Lila had nothing going on. What I *am* shocked by is you." She paused. "You're curious about her."

I snorted.

"Don't deny it, I can tell. The scowling, the Byronic brooding... you liked that kiss."

I stared into the eyes of one of the kindest women I'd ever known, a woman who had changed her entire life 'cause she was courageous enough to chase after somethin' better against all the odds, and I couldn't lie to her.

Not when she'd lost King a month ago, and this was the first time I'd seen her take a real interest in anythin' else.

Not when I'd loved and admired King in almost the same way I'd loved Dane, 'cause he was a good man through to his fuckin' bones, and he'd never done any body wrong unless he'd had to.

"Likin' the kiss doesn't mean anythin'," I muttered.

"Oh, Nova, honey," she breathed, teardrops poolin' on the lower trough of her lids. "It means everything."

"You love King 'cause he's worthy of that kinda love. He earned it 'cause he was whip-smart, kind to everyone, and he had a way with words that put everyone else to fuckin' shame." I smiled at her, but it felt misshapen, like plastic held too close to a flame. "You think I don't know that I have to nothin' offer someone? You think that doesn't factor into the fact I don't have an Old Lady and don't have a plan to *ever*?"

Cress reared back as if I'd slapped her then instantly bent forward to touch her cold hand to my cheek. I leaned into it unconsciously.

"Nova," she whispered, cryin' now, soft, silent tears like drops of mornin' dew tricklin' down her cheeks. "Who taught you that you have nothing to offer? Who lied to you so horribly?"

I smiled again, pressin' my lips into her hand to kiss it before I rolled closer and reached for my sketchbook on her lap, flippin' it open to a page I knew would change the topic for good.

"Here," I said, tappin' the page with my knuckles. "The

design I did up for King. All the brothers, we're gonna get it inked somewhere."

The tears moved faster, and her breath stuttered. She was beautiful even in her grief, even waxy with exhaustion and wane with hopelessness. Tragic and so lovely it made my heart throb like an open wound.

Fuck me, what I wouldn't do to take the pain away from this woman.

"It's exquisite," she whispered through her tears, delicately touchin' the pen strokes with the edge of her chewed down fingernail. "Perfect."

I'd worked on it for hours, hunched over my draft table upstairs in my apartment until my hand cramped, my back ached, and my sight had gone to shit.

But she was right.

It was exquisite.

Nothin' less for my fallen brother.

I'd watched the kid grow into a bookish preteen, to an arrogant, swaggerin' young man with a crush on his teacher, to the dynamic leader and all-round fuckin' hero he'd been before he died.

He died for us.

To get his dad, Zeus, outta jail when the Venturas and the ex-Staff Sergeant had framed him for murder.

To keep his brothers, their women, and all their families safe.

I had two tatts for fallen brothers now. Dane and Mute.

Soon I'd add King's, making it three.

Three too many.

But each of them were my best work.

And King's would take the cake.

A heavily shaded skull bearin' a tilted crown with the serpent from King's favourite book, *Paradise Lost*, comin' through one eye, curlin' down to the text that read, '*The price of freedom.*'

"Nova," Cress called to me, pullin' my gaze up to hers. "Just so you know, there is no way someone unworthy could ever have created such beauty. I'm not sure what happened to make you think so poorly of yourself, but I'm telling you, through all we've been through in the past five years, *you* are constant light and goodness. My life would be a very dark place without you. Trust me, I'm in a place now to know just how much that's true."

I blinked hard to stop the burn at the backs of my eyes then cleared my throat as I moved to my station to ready the stencil. "Thought you could be the first one to get the ink."

"You thought right," she agreed after a moment of disappointed silence, thankfully lettin' it go. "One last thing, and then I'll shut up, okay?"

"Shoot," I grunted as I collected the stencil I'd already prepped with the thermal fax, rollin' back to her side.

"Your pretty face could fade or scar, and you'd still be the handsomest man I know now," she said, her face stripped of artifice, so naked and vulnerable I almost couldn't stand the sound of her.

'Cause I knew what Cress didn't.

I wasn't worthy.

I'd learned that in therapy a long, long time ago, and it wasn't somethin' I'd soon fuckin' forget.

So I smiled at the mournin' widow, helped her roll her Great Gatsby tee up over her ribs, and stenciled the lasting reminder of her soulmate's greatness onto the side of her torso opposite a poem he'd once written for her.

I knew what greatness was, and I knew my own limitations.

Yeah, kissin' Lila had rocked my fuckin' world.

Lila was the kinda woman I'd always wanted to be with when I grew up. Only, I was thirty-five and no closer to bein' the kinda man worthy of a woman like her.

CHAPTER TWELVE

Lila

I<small>RINA</small> V<small>ENTURA RAN A SURPRISINGLY TIGHT SHIP.</small>

Wet Works was the umbrella company for her pornography and camgirl businesses, but it also provided the perfect lead-in for her more illegal ventures of prostitution and sex trafficking.

In less than a month working as her assistant, I'd seen nothing blatantly illegal take place, but I'd officially seen more cocks than I'd ever wanted to in the whole of my life.

"Oh, come on, Richard," Irina spat, throwing her clipboard at the man on set, currently getting fellatio from two red heads. "Put your ass into it! No one wants to watch a lacklustre blow job."

I grimaced as the man in question put his hands on his hips for better leverage and began to thrust wetly into the blonde's mouth while the brunette tried to keep his now swinging balls in hers.

"Better," Irina sneered, settling back in her white, leather director's chair.

She flipped her long, lush mane of black hair over her shoulder and beamed at me like we were just two girls on the couch critiquing a rom-com.

"How you doing, *chica*?" she purred to me. "You like my big, strong men?"

"They're beautiful," I agreed, even though none of them did it for me. "I'm not surprised your site is so profitable."

My boss smiled like the cat that ate the canary as she leaned over to trail her perfectly manicured nails down my floral inked arm. "Is not just the men who draw notice, mmm? A woman like you, so beautiful, would make a very nice profit."

I struggled to contain the shiver that moved through me like a ghost and affixed a coy smile to my face. "I'm shy."

Irina blinked innocently as she continued to stroke me. "*Si?* This is odd, because I have known you as the *niña de las flores*. In fact…" Her eyes narrowed and heavily made up as they were, slanted aggressively with black liner, she looked very much like a poisonous snake about to strike. "I have heard you very much like to lie naked for the man who puts these pretty flowers all over your pretty skin."

This was exactly what Zeus had been worried about.

I had no official affiliation to the club, but I was a known affiliate of Nova Booth, a long-time member of The Fallen.

Fear swarmed my throat like a hundred angry bees, but I reminded myself she was just fishing.

Any internet search would show me linked to Street Ink Tattoo Parlour. Any investigator would discover I was fostered by the Booths and still lived in their backyard.

"I love ink, what can I say?" I shrugged nonchalantly, sensually touching the sleeve of tattoos on my arm in a way that drew Irina's gaze. "How can I resist such art?"

"Indeed," she agreed, licking her lips as she followed the

path of my fingers up my shoulder and down between my breasts where the tips of the lotus blossom design could be seen. "And how can I resist using it?"

Carefully, I took a deep breath. "You hired me as your assistant."

"And you will assist me in this way, *si?*" she asked sweetly.

My gaze went to the two women on their knees blowing a guy who'd definitely taken steroids as some point in his life and a Viagra before shooting.

Was I seriously willing to give a stranger head for my family?

Acid bubbled in my stomach, and I placed a hand there as if that would help.

When I looked back at Irina she was watching me carefully behind her placid expression. Not for the first time, I wondered how many times a man had underestimated Irina Ventura because she was stunning, and therefore, they forgot just how cunning she could be.

"You have more than enough women working for you," I declared because if I'd learned anything in the last month, it was just how many people she'd roped into working for her.

So many young girls, some of them seriously suspect legally, who littered the Wet Works lot and warehouse like wraiths, zoned out, drugged up, or in tears.

They were not happy girls, for the most part.

And I couldn't blame them.

Pornography was for the desperate, or in the rare case, the seriously sexually profound.

"Fresh blood is always best," she countered, shifting in her seat so that she was fully facing me, and I could feel the full force of her energy funneled like sunlight through a magnifying glass, burning and inescapable. "You will do this for me."

I studied her idly, as if my heart wasn't in my throat beating out a staccato tune. "If I do, let's not pretend it's about money. This is about loyalty. You want me to have skin in the game so I'm less likely to betray you."

It was a ballsy move, and I wasn't sure how Irina would respond, only that she was a strong woman, and I figured she'd respect the power move.

A moment later, she laughed delightedly and clapped her hands. "*¡Qué huevos!* You are very brave, Lila. This I admire."

"Then maybe you'll admire the fact that I won't do pornography. Some people obviously get off on it, but I'm a private girl. You want me to have some skin in the game, I'll do it, but I'll do it as a camgirl."

I could live with taking off my clothes for strangers. It was basically the same as stripping, and I didn't have any prudish hang-ups about that. Obviously, some girls would play with themselves or toys or…whatever, but I was sure I could get away with a certain degree of privacy as long as I milked my sensuality for all it was worth.

Irina's eyes sparkled. "Ah, I was hoping for this."

She snapped her fingers like some kind of Bond villain, and I felt someone step up behind me, a huge someone if the shadow he cast in the bright stage lights was anything to go by.

"My lovely *bruto* will show you where to ready yourself." She waved a hand in the direction of the corridor lined with changing rooms behind me then twisted forward again, already forgetting me. "Richard! Richard, really, if you're about to come I want to see it spray all over their faces. You get one drop on the floor, and I will make you clean it up with your tongue, mmm?"

I slipped out of my chair onto the heels of my fringed boots and turned to look at the man waiting for me.

My fierce inhale of shock choked me, and I doubled over, coughing so hard tears came to my eyes.

A huge hand went thumping down on my back to help me even as Irina shouted at us to be quiet.

"Gotcha," Irina's *bruto* muttered in his deep rumble as he started to escort me to the back.

By the time we hit the doors and moved through to the soundproof hallway, I was recovered enough to pull away from his grip and point at him like some witch casting a curse.

"What the hell are *you* doing here?" I accused.

Lysander Garrison blinked at me, completely nonplussed by my freak out. The only commonality he shared with his sister, Cressida, was their colouring, their rich brown hair, thick and long, and their large, long lashed, brown eyes. Otherwise, Lysander was much as Irina had called him, a brute, an ex-con, and it showed. He was huge across the shoulders and tall, too, every inch of him covered in dense muscle, scars, and tattoos.

Yet there was something soft in his face, something that spoke to the fact he'd once been classically handsome before prison and living hard carved out lines in his tanned skin and hardened those deep, warm eyes.

He had a complicated relationship with his sister just as he did with the club. Having once helped the Nightstalkers MC, a rival club who'd abducted and tortured Cress, he'd also saved Loulou, Loulou's sister Bea, and Harleigh Rose from the same club who'd tried to set their house on fire.

He was a tangle of contrast I had no hope or desire to untangle, especially not now while we were in the den of the viper herself, a place I never would have expected to find him.

"What are you doing here?" I repeated, this time softer.

He shrugged those big shoulders, so rounded with muscle they stretched his grey tee out of shape. "What I'm doin' is nothin' compared to what the fuck you're doin' here. This place is a hellhole, no place for a woman like you."

"You don't know anything about me," I countered.

"No," he snapped, stepping forward to growl low in my face, a whispering roar because we didn't know who might be listening. "But I know my sister's got love for a girl named Lila with flowers on her skin, and I know you're with The Fallen. You getting' tied up in this shit is only gonna lead to bad fuckin' news, and I'm not gonna be the one to deliver more'a that to the club."

"This isn't on you, so don't worry your big, thick head about it," I suggested with a sweet smile and a condescending pat on his corded forearm.

He hesitated, eyeing me like an attack dog ready to launch at the first command. "You worried 'bout what's goin' down here with the girls... don't be. I got it."

"You *got* it?" I asked derisively. "You clearly don't, because women are still getting sucked into this black hole."

"I got it as in I'm workin' on it," he gritted through his teeth. "Nothin' more for you to do here now you know it's covered."

"I don't know shit," I whispered harshly, rounding up to my toes to get in his face. "I don't know you, but what I do know is sketchy as hell. I get Cress loves you and you guys had some reconciliation, but I also know you did the club *and* your sister a serious wrong back in the day. You can't expect me to trust you now. I've got no reason to, and I see no motive for you working with Staff Sergeant Danner and the Venturas other than serving your own agenda."

"You don't know shit, you're right," he seethed, but there was a wealth of self-hatred and grief in his eyes. "But I got more skin in this game than you think. I got somethin' to prove to Cress, and I got people here I care 'bout."

There was a commotion down the hall as a door opened and a young strawberry blonde woman spilled into the corridor, stumbling slightly on her high heels before she righted herself and slammed the door shut behind her.

Instantly, Lysander went on alert, arms at his sides, heavy weight balanced on the balls of his feet.

I looked slowly between him and the girl teetering toward

us, but I didn't recognize her until he growled, "Honey, what'd I tell you?"

The girl looked up at him with glassy eyes and frowned in confusion. "Sander! I dunno, what did you tell me?"

He sighed and stalked toward her, but the moment he reached out to steady her arm, everything about him turned gentle.

"Told ya to stop goin' back to Cisco. Can't help you, you don't help yourself by gettin' clean," he murmured, bending his knees so he was eye level with the smaller, almost delicate girl.

And I realized with a start that *Honey* wasn't an affectionate nickname.

Honey was Honey, King and H.R.'s estranged half-sister, the same one who had gotten tangled up with the Venturas.

My heart clenched at the sight of her, strung out yet still so lovely, looking at her felt like admiring a Monet painting.

"Hey, girl," I said softly, moving over to them. "I'm Lila."

Honey looked over at me with pale brown eyes like sunlight through maple syrup, and I almost caught my breath at how pretty she was, how much she looked like Harleigh Rose, just smaller, more refined.

"Do I know you?" she asked, her words slightly slurred.

I beamed at her. "Not yet, but you will. I work here now, and I have a feeling you, me, and…" I looked up at Lysander, at the way he studied Honey with blatant concern, and I knew he wasn't here to screw anyone over. Regardless of the details, he was in bed with the Venturas for the same reason I was.

To take them down.

"..and Lysander are going to be good friends."

The man in question looked over at me with a heavy knot in his brow. "You're workin' here now?"

I nodded curtly and patted his shoulder. "Better believe it, *bruto*. Now, why don't both of you come inside and help me?"

"This somethin' for the club?"

"Yep."

"What is it?"

I grinned wolfishly and tossed my hair. "I need your help setting up the camera. I'm making my debut as a camgirl today."

Lysander and Honey both blinked at me, the former in shock, the latter drunkenly.

"Fuckin' Fallen MC," he said finally. "I'm startin' to think the women might just be crazier than the men."

I laughed. "You can count on it."

CHAPTER THIRTEEN

Nova

"She's gone."

"She can't be," I blinked, tryin' to wrap my head around the idea of Cressida takin' off. "She wouldn't leave her family without a word."

"She did. Took King's bike and left," Zeus said, starin' at the brothers gathered in church for the first time since he'd gotten outta prison.

Released 'cause his son, King, had set up Staff Sergeant Danner, and his son's wife, Cressida, had helped dig up evidence the bastard cop had hidden that exonerated Zeus.

Fuck, but it was good to see the mammoth man at the head of the table again, wearin' his cut Lou'd polished special so it gleamed in the low light spillin' through the stained-glass window Priest'd installed at the front of the room.

He looked right there.

Buck had tried to take up the mantle, but he wasn't a leader, not really.

King'd done a bang-up job, but the kid wasn't Zeus, and he wouldn't have been without years more experience.

Straight up, there was no one like Zeus Garro, and not one'a us had been spared from feelin' the agony of his incarceration.

It shoulda been a time to celebrate, but too much shit was goin' down, as it always seemed to be, and we had problems to address.

Like Cressida Garro, newly widowed, disappearin' into the fuckin' night.

"I'll find her," I offered.

Priest snorted. "Anyone's gonna find her, it's *me*."

I stared at the redheaded brother, the one who'd been torturin' and killin' our enemies since he was seventeen as if he was born of death and lived to deliver it.

I knew he was right.

"Bat or Kodiak would do a fine job too," Smoke rasped in his ravaged voice, havin' smoked two packs a day for forty years.

This was also true.

Kodiak was the best tracker we had. I'd never seen a man move through nature like him. He claimed his Alutiiq First Nations grandfather had been the best tracker in their community in Alaska, and he'd passed down everythin' he knew.

And Bat, well, Bat was an ex-Marine with so many skills, some of which were straight up terrifyin', that I didn't doubt he'd be able to find Cress.

"No one's goin' lookin'," Zeus said, endin' the conversation.

"Say what?" Boner asked. "We're just gonna let her runaway all sad and alone-like? She'll think we don't give a shit!"

"God forbid," Heckler grumbled sarcastically.

"Shut your mouth," Axe-Man grunted at the asshole.

"Enough." Zeus hit his meaty fist against the table, and we quieted quick. "No one's goin' lookin' 'cause she talked to Lou 'fore she left, and she wants to be alone. Needs time, she said, to grieve and learn to live again. We're gonna give 'er that. She knows she's gotta home with us whenever she wants to head back."

He said it strong and true, unwaverin' as he always was in his role as Prez.

But I knew him enough to see the pain in his silver eyes.

He loved Cress like his own daughter, and her takin' off couldn't have sat well.

Sure as hell didn't with me.

"We got shit goin' down, and if she's not here, maybe it's for the better," Bat suggested. "She doesn't need remindin' that King died to get Z outta prison, and we still got the Venturas to deal with."

"What's the update?" Zeus asked Buck, his VP.

The old timer was still burly as shit, his silver hair bright against his deep tan. He was a good man, and I could sense his relief at bein' back as second-in-command instead of havin' to lead the forces.

"Still got Honey Yves wrapped up with the Venturas, and Javier's ampin' up his diatribe against the club every fuckin' chance he's got," Buck debriefed. "He's tryin' to shift focus from fuckface SS Danner's corruption and incarceration onto us by sayin' the disappearance of some local girls is on *us*."

Zeus's face collapsed into a deep scowl. "Motherfucker."

"I say we just gun the fucker down," Skell declared, slappin' his hand on the table. "He's in public enough. Someone just take one for the team and fuckin' shoot him."

"And this would be why you aren't in charge," Bat said, cuttin' him off with the cold blade of his criticism. "No one's goin' down for the murder of Javier Ventura, or attempted murder. The man is cartel, so there'd be serious fuckin' blow back if we got caught, and even if we were stupid enough to try, he's always surrounded by tight ass security."

"You were a sniper, right, can't ya just get on a rooftop?" Skell continued.

Bat ignored him. "The real problem is, they're tryin to bring the Organized Crime unit up here to look into us. Things could get serious if they do."

"Our shit's tight," Axe-Man said.

"Don't care how tight our shit is, we get the unit up here when we're skirtin' war with the cartel, more than one brother's gonna end up in jail or dead." Zeus's eyes flashed, and his smile went predatory. "Got somethin' in the works with the Venturas, we'll see how it plays out. Javier found a way to track one'a us to the Grouse warehouse, we don't need anythin' else goin' to shit, so keep vigilant and watch for tails."

We weren't about rules. We were a fuckin' outlaw motorcycle club, so we valued freedom and spontaneity more than almost anythin'.

But this was our safety and the safety of our brethren, our families.

No one would say shit against Z's rulin' 'cause we'd already lost too much.

Mute, King, months lost to Zeus in prison.

We'd stay vigilant, travelin' in pairs and packs even though it chafed.

"Good to have ya back, boss," Boner declared after a moment of silence, and then he beat his fists against the solid oak table.

The rest of us followed, thumpin' and hootin' and hollerin' 'cause we'd lost so much, but our Prez was back. And none of us had any doubt he'd lead us to fuckin' victory against the motherfuckers who dared to fuck with us and ours.

Zeus's smile was a grim slash in his beard, but he dipped his chin to his brothers and opened his palms to the sky like some kinda benevolent underworld lord.

"Good to be home, brothers," he declared. "Better we exterminate the vermin darin' to make this place, our fuckin' place, their own. Let's get it done."

There was a roar of consent from around the table, and then the meetin' ended, brothers gettin' up to congregate in the common room or get back to their businesses.

"Hold up, pretty boy," Z ordered mildly.

I stayed seated, wary of his casual tone 'cause Zeus wasn't a casual kinda man.

Somethin' was brewin'.

When the last brother finally closed the door to the chapel behind him, Z angled his head to stare at me, tatted hand in his beard.

"I'm so pretty you just wanted to stare at me a while?" I taunted.

His lips twitched. "Heard you were kissin' a certain Hispanic girl at Eugene's the other night."

"Oh, yeah?" It shouldn't have surprised me he knew. Fuckin' Loulou knew everythin' there was to know about the goin's on of the brothers in the club 'cause we all told her everythin'. She was just that way to us, for us. Our Foxy.

"Yeah."

We stared at each other for a long minute. A stalemate.

"Gotta get to the shop," I declared, makin' to stand.

"Sit your ass down," Zeus demanded then waited as I settled and leveled a glare his way. "Now, we're brothers more than most. You been with me since 'fore I got locked up the first time, and we've been through it all. So don't go thinkin' I'm tryin' to be an asshole."

"Then don't be," I suggested, barin' my teeth in a violent smile.

Zeus's silver bladed eyes pressed into me like the edge of a weapon held to my throat. "Gotta say it, and you were in my position, watchin' a man like you make a play at someone good and pure, you'd say it too."

A man like you.

Yeah, I'd heard that before.

Years of therapy had only solidified what I'd been born knowin'.

I was the black sheep, the dark horse, the animal too beastly for a soul.

Not good enough for shit.

So yeah, I didn't try for much. I was happy with my shop, the reputation I got from sharin' my passion for ink with the masses.

I didn't need more than that and my family and my brothers in cuts.

Love didn't have to factor into my life 'cause I'd learned early it was a trap.

"Don't fuck with Lila, brother," Zeus warned. "You gotta know the girl's had feelin's for ya since she was a girl."

"Oh, yeah? Like Lou did for you?" I dared to point out.

Zeus had saved Loulou from takin' a bullet when she was six years old, and even though they hadn't gotten together until she was a woman, he was the last person who shoulda been holdin' up a caution sign.

His lips flattened. "You think I'm warnin' you off 'cause'a the age difference, you're blind. I'm warnin' ya 'cause you once told me love was for the weak and you'd never do it again. Not after what happened with that bitch, Meredith—"

"Don't say her name," I hissed, hackles raised, the dark animal risin' up my throat so fierce I wanted to howl and snap. "Don't want to hear that name in this sacred fuckin' place."

"Okay, brother," he agreed. "But listen to what I'm sayin', yeah? She's tryin' to move on. Yeah, that Jake is a pansy-ass, but it's her choice. You playin' games with her 'cause you miss havin' her undivided attention? Don't do it. She's been through enough in her life."

She had.

No one knew just how much like I did.

My heart twisted up like a wrung-out dish towel as I expelled a heavy, toxic sigh. I stared down at my hands, at the Suntastic Yellow Sunflower I had inked into the inside of my left wrist that represented the awful night Ellie Davalos had died and Lila's whole life had changed.

I touched the raised inked with my thumb as my heart burned and my throat closed up.

Lila didn't need any more pain, any more mess.

She deserved the best, and yeah, motherfuckin' Jake wasn't that, but I couldn't pretend for a second I was either.

So I needed to move the fuck on from that kiss and the moments that led to it.

But somethin' irreversible had happened when I'd shamed Lila for her crush. She'd pushed me away, sectioned me off into a little box and locked up the lid. We'd still talked, hung out with our families both of blood and leather, but she no longer let me close to her sunflower soul.

And I hadn't realized until she'd put that wedge of intractable space between her and me just how much we'd grown up tangled like twin vines on a wall.

Life felt lopsided without her wit and ramblin', without her hippie spirit spoutin' the joys of vegetarianism and savin' the planet, without her rockin' out to music in the shop as she kept me company while I did bullshit paperwork.

She'd invaded my life so fully, so beautifully, like some kinda mornin' glory I'd planted myself, that I hadn't realized until I'd yanked her out just how much substance she'd given to my life.

And then that kiss.

One kiss changed the course of our friendship for good.

'Cause after that kiss?

I didn't think there was any way I could go back to pretendin' Lila wasn't fuckin' vital to me. 'Cause the feel of her lips on mine was like fresh oxygen after two years of livin' with half a lung.

And now I was addicted to the thought of breathin' free.

"You're not listenin' to me," Zeus noted drily, resigned.

"Nah," I agreed with a lopsided grin. "But when have I ever?"

"You're gonna make a mess'a things," he warned. "Here's hopin' you get your pretty boy head outta your ass 'fore you ruin things for good. 'Cause Lila, she might be your shot at the kinda happy I got with Lou. The kinda happy I carry 'round in my chest like a second heart that beats just for her."

I blinked at him as the image descended.

Lila on the back of my bike, her leather Property of No One jacket swapped out for a new one.

Property of Nova.

And that image? It didn't give me hives like it might've done years ago.

Instead, I felt a flutter like the brush of fuckin' butterfly wings inside my chest.

"Hey, um, boss?" a hang-around I thought we called Chaos said as he peeked his head around the door. "Sorry to interrupt, but Curtains said he just go a ping online 'bout some girl called Lila? Apparently, she's on the Wet Works website gettin' naked on camera."

"What the *fuck*," I roared as I pushed back from the table and stood, stalkin' to the hang-around and pressin' him to the wall with my forearm at his throat. "Bring me Curtains *now*."

CHAPTER FOURTEEN

Lila

I LIVED IN THE BOOTH'S BACKYARD, AND I HAD SINCE I dropped out of university to move back to Entrance. This wasn't because I had money concerns. I made a whack ton in tips at Eugene's, and I'd been making money off of my Flower Child Photogram account for years just for posting about makeup or clothes.

No, I lived in the Booths backyard because I'd missed them when I was in Vancouver at UBC. I'd missed Hudson barging into my room without knocking just because he liked to bug me. I'd missed Milo and Oliver, who had moved out, but only into the rundown heritage house two doors down that they'd converted into a series of condos. Milo commuted to Vancouver every day for his finance job because he, too, couldn't be parted from the family, and Oliver worked for Diogo's thriving commercial fishing company.

Ares was with us at least once a week too, his quiet presence in the house somehow soothing. He was the only person I still spoke Spanish with, though we never it did it in public.

He was almost afraid of his heritage, his words a low Latin whisper he dredged up from deep inside himself. I thought he spoke in our native language more for me than anything else. I liked to hear him read to me from his favourite poets, Pablo Neruda and Federico García Lorca, in the language of Dane's and my own childhood even though it hurt like pressure on a tired muscle.

We all stayed close because that's how we were.

We took turns making dinner most nights, one or the other popping in or out for the last meal of the day, and everyone was there for Sunday dinners.

Molly and Diogo didn't blame me for dropping out of university. Nova had kinda paved the way by dropping out of high school, and they knew me well enough to know I'd find a way to carve out a life for myself with or without a degree.

No, no chastisement from my foster parents.

Instead, when I'd finally packed up all my shit in Vancouver and arrived back at home, exhausted and elated, the entire family had been waiting for me on the front porch with giddy grins on their faces. Hudson had bounded forward to tie a blindfold around my head, and then laughingly, they'd all led me to the backyard.

When they untied the ribbon obscuring my vision, I'd burst into tears.

Because they'd converted the old greenhouse Molly and I kept meaning to utilize into a little house for me.

They kept most of the glass windows in place but replaced the roof, added plumbing, hot water, and electricity. In the end, I had this absolutely adorable green and glass home tucked away amid the flower garden Molly and I had started planting when I was only seven years old.

It was perfect, like something out a fairy tale.

And every time I walked down the cobblestone path to the little cottage, I felt the love my family had for me flare in my heart.

Only, walking back from a long, long day at Wet Works, not even the sight of my house or the Suntastic sunflowers bowing their smiling faces to me in the breeze could remove the frown from my face.

I was exhausted.

Covered in glitter lotion that caused my clothes to stick to my skin like tacky glue, body aching from being on my knees for an hour, contorting in various positions so that the camera could see all of me in all my glory, I was fucking *done*.

Completely drained, I didn't follow the sound of laughing voices through the backdoor to the main house. Instead, I unlocked my door, dropped my leather hobo bag to the ground, and made my way through the dark living space into the small bathroom.

I cranked the shower up to nearly scalding and shed my clothes, throwing them into the wastepaper basket so I'd never have to wear them again.

They felt soiled beyond redemption.

I stepped into the steaming shower and tipped my head under the spray, bracing my arms on the wall so my head could slump between my shoulders.

I stood there for a long time, just letting the water rush over me, cleansing me of the day.

If only the water could purge me of the sight of Honey. Sixteen years old and hooked on drugs, indebted to Irina because she couldn't afford them, locked in the cycle because she was goddamn *sixteen* and didn't have the strength or context or community to know better.

I'd resolved to be her community.

Just one more thing to add to my list, right?

Take down Irina Ventura.

Take down Javier Ventura.

Get Honey Yves out of the life.

As I washed the floral conditioner out of my long locks, I

considered who Zeus and I could enlist from the club to help me. I wasn't naive enough to think I could do it all alone.

Curtains would be the best candidate because of his hacking skills. Dude could do things with a computer I couldn't even comprehend.

I had Lysander for muscle, though, I didn't trust him as far as I could throw him (which wasn't far given I doubted I had the strength to even *lift* him).

I was still puzzling over this when I turned the water off, stepped out of the stall, and started rubbing lotion onto my still damp skin.

So I didn't notice that the light was on in the living room.

I didn't notice that the door to the bathroom was gaping open as if someone had peeked into the room, seen me showering, and perhaps, lingered a little before leaving.

Instead, I moved into the living room briefly, turned down the little hall to my bedroom and changed into a thong and my favourite crop top that read 'Sunflower Soul.'

It was only as I moved back into the living space, stopping to grab a glass from the upper cabinet over my counter looking out over the purple sofa, crate coffee table, and bookshelves that made up the living room, that I noticed a man all in black sitting in the lone chair tucked in the corner.

I screamed before I could catch myself, and the glass slipped from my numb fingers, crashing onto the counter with a tinny *clap* and tinkle. A piece fell onto the floor and cut into my big toe, but I didn't notice the pain because my gaze was locked with the dark, brooding gaze of the man in my velvet chair.

Nova.

"Got a call from Curtains," he growled, actually *growled*, his voice a rumbled, angry rasp. "Seems he's got the whole club locked into some registry. Whenever somethin' new pops up about one'a the members or their families, he gets pinged."

He paused, and the air between us swelled with unbearable pressure, a balloon overfilled to bursting.

"You wanna tell me what he found, or do I gotta remind you?" he asked, his words as slick and ugly as an oil spill.

I blinked at him, completely oblivious to the fact I was barely dressed, so focused on him being in my home after almost two years of avoiding me that I couldn't compute him actually being in my space.

He looked good there.

It was a crazy time to notice such a thing, but that was Nova's beauty for you. It hit you smack between the eyes so you forgot everything inside your head but the colour of those velveteen eyes and that purple red mouth curved and full in the shadow of his dark scruff.

"Lila?" he demanded.

His impatience shouldn't have been hot. It shouldn't have tweaked my nipples into hard points or shot electricity to my core.

"I don't know what you're talking about."

"No?" he asked in a dangerous tone, rolling to his feet so he could stalk toward me, his gait a sinuous swagger. "You don't got any memory of takin' off your clothes for Irina Ventura's fuckin' illegal, fucked up porn business?"

I blinked, shocked that she'd already uploaded the video. I'd thought with editing and everything it would have taken longer.

"Now she's silent," he hissed through his teeth at the same time his body crashed into mine, and I went flying backward.

One long, marble arm snatched out around my lower back to catch me then reel me back to him, slamming our bodies together so hard I gasped.

Then his face was in mine, a dark mask of edgy, barely contained fury.

"You wanna tell me what the *fuck* you think you're doin' workin' for that piece of filth? You know she's got fuckin' *kids*

hooked on drugs, reels them in, hooks them up, and inden-
tures them for life 'cause they don't gotta shot at gettin' clear
of that shit?"

"Yeah, Nova," I breathed because I couldn't drag much
into my lungs with his hard, heavy torso pressed so tight to
mine. "I know."

His lips pulled back over his teeth so he could snarl as he
softly warned, "Yeah, you're a smart girl. Been around long
enough to know the score between us and those cunts. So I
gotta ask myself, why's my Flower Child hooked up with the
likes of Irina Ventura?"

A shiver poured through me, cold and clinging to my
spine. Nova felt it and tugged me even closer, nostrils flaring.

"Couldn't be 'cause you got some fucked up idea in your
head you could help us out by puttin' yourself in the kinda
jam even the club would have a hard time protectin' you
from?"

"It's not fucked up," I argued, finally gathering the threads
of my wit so I could actually defend myself from this overprotective *jerk*. "I've got a real plan."

And then he did something I'd never seen Nova do in the
entire seventeen years I'd known him.

He blew the fuck up.

"Are you fuckin' *nuts*?" he yelled right in my face, features
contorted with rage. "What the *fuck* could you be *thinkin'*
puttin' yourself at risk like that when you got no call to?!"

"No call?" I whispered, so outraged I couldn't breathe
through the crush of anger in my belly. "No call!? My entire
family has been targeted by those assholes for fucking years!
You think I've got no call to want to change that, then it's *you*
who's fucked."

He spun us so abruptly I could only be dragged the three
steps to the other side of the kitchen where he pushed me up
against the fridge and pinned me in the air with his hands on

my wrists, his groin pinned to my elevated hips. I struggled, but I was stuck like a bug in his web.

"You listen to me, and you listen good for once in your goddamn life," he roared. "You are goin' in to that bitch tomorrow, and you're quittin'. No, fuck that, you're e-mailin' her right the fuck now, and you're never gonna see her or that place again. You feel me, Lila?"

"I feel you," I echoed calmly then snarled, "I feel that you're an overbearing asshole who doesn't give one fuck about me unless I'm interfering with his life."

He reeled back, struck through the middle by my accusation as he stepped away from me. I watched as he blinked away the shock then as it sank in.

"You're fuckin' with me," he intoned flatly. "You think I don't give a shit, this bein' why I'm pissed as hell you're involved with those murderin', theivin', scumbags? No, you're right. That makes a fuck ton of sense, Li."

"You're blaming me for getting involved in a situation where my family, The Fallen *and* the Booths, are at risk, and I can help," I argued.

"Help? Other than addin' more work for us, already stretched thin as we are and broken from the loss of King, how the fuck is that helpin'?"

"Irina trusts me," I said, chin to the air. "She knew Ignacio, and she trusts me because I'm his daughter."

Something moved through him, something dark and profound like clouds gathering water for a monsoon.

"You think she's gonna trust you 'cause of your connection to the motherfucker who blew up her operation in Entrance a decade and a half ago? What happened, Li? I thought you were a smart girl."

"I am," I bit off.

"You fuckin' took off your goddamn clothes on camera for a whack ton of creepy as fuck men. That shit is out there now,

Li! Curtains can try to work his magic, but it's out there, and you took that risk without any kinda thought."

"I'd do worse for my family," I shouted, but what I wanted to scream was '*I'd do worse for you!*'

"You're doin' worse to them right now by stickin' your nose in where it doesn't belong. This is club business, Lila, and you got no right to it."

It was my turn to reel back, flattening myself against the fridge so I could get even an inch farther away from him.

Property of no one.

That was me.

At the end of the day, I didn't really belong to anyone.

Not really.

"I can't believe you'd say that," I whispered.

"Can't believe you'd disappoint me like this," he countered, breathing heavily, his entire big torso moving with the effort.

"Don't talk down to me," I shouted at him, shoving the heels of both hands deep into his concrete pectorals. "Don't you dare try to shame me. Love has made people do crazier things, Nova. Just because you don't know a thing about it, doesn't make it untrue."

One of his thick, brown brows arched perfectly into his forehead. "You're fuckin' with me. You got serious fuckin' balls to say I don't know shit about love."

I cranked my chin so high in the air I couldn't maintain eye contact with him. "Yeah *right*."

Nova's gorgeous face split apart with sudden, snarling fury, and then he was moving, lunging toward me so he could wrap a big hand around my throat and shove me up against the fridge again. My breath left in a whisper, and my heart kicked like a wild horse at a barn door.

He was so close, his tobacco and spice intoxicating me, poisoning my body against my mind. All I could see was his tattooed throat, the rich pink hue of the lotus blossom he'd inked onto himself just for Dane, and the blown up black of his eyes threatening to swallow me whole. He leaned closer still, so that his breath was my breath, only I was finding it impossible to breathe.

"You don't get to tell me I don't got love in my heart," he whispered, his voice low and as smooth as a purring wildcat. "You think I got some heart of stone? You think I was un-fuckin'-moved when I held little girl you in my arms as your mum died? Think I didn't about crack in two when Dane, the first brother by choice I ever made, was ripped away from us? You think I wouldn't about *die* if somethin' happened to you? To the girl I swore Dane I'd always protect? To the girl who I used to think knew the heart of me more than anyone else?"

He paused, breath heaving, so hot against my lips it scalded the tender skin. There were tears in my throat, heat building between my legs. I felt like I was about to come apart at the seams.

"You wanna sit on some high fuckin' horse and tell me about my own heart when you clearly know shit all about it, go right ahead, Lila." He released me so abruptly I slid against the smooth enamel of the fridge, knees weak as overcooked noodles, and spilled to the floor.

His face was twisted up, ugly with cruelty. For one second, I thought he would spit on me, shame me with everything he could.

Instead, he sneered and shook his head as he backed away, hands in his pockets. "You're so disappointed in me? For bein' furious, for bein' concerned? Yeah, well, I'm used to that shit. But you? Yeah, Li, I'm fuckin' gutted by my disappointment in you. Let's see how well that sits with you, hmm?"

And then he turned on his booted heel and left.

CHAPTER FIFTEEN

Nova

LATER, SO MUCH LATER IT WAS FLAT BLACK OUTSIDE THE window of my apartment and not a thing was stirrin', not even the racoons, I sat in bed, back to the black headboard, naked but for my boxer briefs, computer on my lap, fingers sweatin' but unmovin' on the keys.

Wet Works website was typed into the search bar, the home page showin' a collection of newly added pornos, the left sidebar the categories available to me, and the right a series of girls one could click on to see them preform a live cam show.

She was there.

Lila.

Listed on the site as *Nina Flores*, a play on Flower Child.

In the screenshot, she was on her knees on a white bed, thighs spread just enough to show a sliver of lace, lavender panties at her sex, the same material strugglin' to cover the twin swells of her caramel breasts. Her hair, the entire thick mass of it, was in disarray, as if she or someone else had been runnin' their hands through it.

Agony burned through me as I stared and fuckin' stared at that thumbnail.

It was too complex a pain to detangle.

I was fucked up over it, disgusted by the risk she'd taken, shamed by the desire I felt like banked fire in my groin, concerned people would find out she'd done this and that they'd humiliate her for it, terrified the Ventura's would catch on to her charade and end her.

That, the last part, was keepin' me up at night.

Couldn't sleep more than an hour, and I was sufferin' for it. The skin under my eyes was so damn bruised with fatigue, it ached, and my body moved slow, so slow I couldn't put up any kinda decent fight against Wrath in the ring or lift any heft in the gym with Bat.

I was driven useless by this.

By her.

By my Li girl bein' so stupid, so damn dumb.

So fuckin' courageous and lovin', so ready to martyr her damn self for others it was as gorgeous as it was horrifyin'.

And there I was for the last hour, starin' at her half-naked on a goddamn porno site.

I tipped my head back and groaned, knowin' it was only a matter of time before I gave in.

A minute later, I clicked on *Nina Flores*.

Immediately, the only video came up, a small counter showin' over 2,000 views in the first three days of it bein' live.

No surprise there.

Lila was a stunner and braced like she was on the bed, her full, dusky mouth parted, tongue peekin' between those lips like a promise, I had no trouble understandin' why it was so popular.

It woulda been easy to tell myself I was watchin' 'cause I

was concerned, 'cause I needed to know exactly what she'd gotten herself into it.

But I didn't.

I could be honest about it if I was gonna fuckin' do it.

I was watchin' Lila 'cause I *wanted* to.

No, more than that.

I wanted *her*.

And seein' her like that, movin' sensuously like a ribbon twistin' in the breeze, curlin' and undulatin' so all us mother-fuckers could watch as she rubbed between her legs over the lace, cupped her breasts and thumbed her nipples that were taffy brown through the sheer material, I groaned again.

This time a sound of defeat.

My hand moved without my conscious promptin' it to the thick swell of my hard cock through the cotton, squeezin' hard.

Lila moved so that her ripe, peachy ass was in the air, wavin' at the camera like red before a bull. Hot hair puffed through my nose as I went animal, turned on so much I could only think of chasin' her down, pinnin' that sweet body to the matteress, buryin' my face in that thick ass, then in what I was sure would be the sweetest pussy known to man.

My hand actually fuckin' shook as I pulled down my boxer briefs enough to tug out my cock, so hard it throbbed an angry, purplish red, the plum head the same ripe colour as the fruit and just as full. I drew my thumb over the precum poolin' in the slit and used it to lube my palm so I could stroke off.

Stroke off as I watched my Flower Child pet her pussy through lace that was turnin' dark with her wetness then finally pull the fabric aside to dive beneath.

There was music playin' in the background, and I recognized it as, fuckin' appropriately, 'Watch Me' by The Phantoms.

And fuck me, but I was watchin' her, eyes glued to every single line of her long, curved, muscular form. It was clear she worked out from the tight bunch of abs barely showin' through the soft skin of her golden stomach and the way she gracefully raised and lowered herself over her fingers, hips rollin' like waves.

She had thick, caramel thighs I wanted to wrap around my head so that all I could taste, all I could breathe and eat to sustain me, was *her*.

That quick, I was ready to blow.

I gritted my teeth and stroked harder, needin' the almost painful friction as penance for my lust.

When I came, I did it strong, spillin' high onto my stomach, cum runnin' into the gutters cut into my abs. I grunted and milked my dick for more, wringin' out every last second of pleasure I could before slammin' the laptop shut and tippin' my head back to close my eyes.

"Fuck," I breathed. "Me."

Years of restraint, of tryin' not to see the woman Lila was bloomin' into, of knowin' I'd never be good enough for her even if I was allowed to look, and I'd finally broke like cheap plastic.

Broke in a way I knew there was no goin' back.

Before I shut off the lamp, I opened the computer and bookmarked the tab, cum coolin' on my stomach, shame curlin' in my gut.

I knew in a way I couldn't shake, I'd watch that goddamn clip again.

If only to stave off the need to watch her do that again, next time in person, my hands the ones in all of that hair, on that lace covered cunt.

I turned off the light, cleaned off my cum, and rolled over in the dark.

But I didn't sleep.

And when mornin' came, sleep deprivation had hatched a plan in my mind I was too tired, too wrung out to question.

So I didn't.

CHAPTER SIXTEEN

Lila

WORKING FOR THE WIFE OF A CARTEL BOSS WAS NOT WHAT I expected.

It was, in innumerable ways, *worse.*

Irina called me at all hours. She wanted what she wanted when she wanted it without question or remorse. I learned that the hard way one night gone midnight when she'd asked me to pick up a man or woman from a local bar and deliver them to her office.

I'd balked.

She wanted me to pick someone up for her to fuck because she was too busy to go find a plaything herself.

It was a bold and awkward request. Made me feel like a fluffer on set getting the men hard and revved to fuck for hours.

But I'd done it.

Driven in the dark, driving rain falling like sheets of

hammered metal to the asphalt all the way down to Vancouver, an hour there and back, to snag Irina a beautiful man.

Later, after I'd dropped the poor, unassuming college student named Trent off at Wet Works, she'd informed me she preferred women.

Just so I knew for next time.

I was already hyperaware of Irina's bisexuality, not only because she made it obvious in the way she leered at some of the girls on set, but because she often hit on me. A fluttering touch at my bare shoulder like a landing butterfly, a kiss in greeting pressed to the corner of my mouth instead of the safety of my cheek. She wanted me, but not enough to take me.

Irina was a woman who enjoyed play in every aspect of her life.

It made her hard to pin down.

I was supposed to work up a schedule for her, a routine that I could give to Curtain (who I'd enlisted) and Axe-Man (who Zeus had drafted) so that we could begin to snoop around the production lot.

As far as I could tell, she didn't have one.

Her marriage with Javier couldn't have been a good one because she was only ever at his side if there was a political event or dinner. Otherwise, she kept to Wet Works and the beautiful Spanish-style home she'd erected at the back of the lot in the forest before the mountains.

She didn't keep anything out in the open in her office, always keeping her phone glued to her long-nailed hand, and she never divulged anything illegal in front of me.

In conclusion, I was nowhere.

Almost two months into a job I hated, a job I'd fought viciously with Nova about, and I had absolutely nothing.

So I was more irritable than normal the Monday following my fight with Nova. Our fight had been on the preceding Wednesday, and we hadn't spoken since.

I tried not to let it bother me, even though I'd taken out my phone to text him no less than three or four times a day.

There was nothing to say that hadn't already been said, no more feelings to hurt that hadn't already been torn apart.

We were at an impasse that had started two years ago when he'd kicked me in the heart and told me to get over my crush, one that had only deepened, maybe irrevocably now that we'd kissed, now that we'd fought so fundamentally over the way we lived our lives.

"You're sulking," Harleigh Rose accused me as we pushed out of the warm, damp room we'd just spent an hour in doing our weekly yoga class. "And you know I hate when you sulk and don't give me the goods. It's the least you could do given I have to put up with this yogi crap once a week just to see you."

I laughed, as she'd meant me to, and bumped her hip with my own as we tugged on our shoes and grabbed our bags.

"You know you secretly love it," I teased.

She snorted then shot me a coy look. "It's hell. But I will say, Lion loves my new-found bendiness."

"Oh, my God," I groaned through my laughter, palming my face. "You seriously can't go an hour without talking about what that man does to you in bed."

She shrugged a shoulder and grinned unrepentantly. "Trust me, if you had a man who made you come until you couldn't remember your own name, you'd talk about it all the time too."

An older woman gasped in horror at H.R., but she only blew her a kiss and tugged me out the doors of the yoga studio and onto Main Street.

"I'm going to tell Loulou that you said that next time you complain about her talking about her sex life with Zeus," I promised.

She narrowed those true-blue eyes at me and scoffed. "You wouldn't dare. Best friends don't snitch."

"A girl's gotta do what a girl's gotta do."

"Bitch," she griped good naturedly as we reached my pale blue VW bug convertible.

"Slut," I returned easily as we got into the car.

She laughed and immediately plugged her phone into the car to play her music. I took a moment to stare at her, feeling twin emotions of soft jealousy and joy that my best friend had found happiness after so long.

She kicked her shoes off and crossed her bare feet on my dash as I pulled into the light traffic.

"So does this sulking have anything to do with Nova?" she guessed. "I'm gonna assume you guys haven't fixed what he broke?"

"You mean my heart?" I asked then instantly regretted it.

I didn't want to be bitter.

It wasn't fair to me, my relationship with him, or to Nova himself.

Our argument the other day had only highlighted that.

It was just, sometimes, it wasn't easy being friends with the person you loved.

Friendships usually operated on the same level, a reciprocity inherent in the contract.

With Nova, I was always too invested, my emotions a lump sum I couldn't parse away no matter how hard I tried to match his call.

"Babe," Harleigh Rose called, pulling my gaze to hers because we were at the one stoplight on Main Street. "I know I've been like sickeningly happy and probably more unavailable than I've ever been since Cricket, but I hope you know, I'm your girl. No matter what."

Her words pulsed like warm light inside my chest, making it impossible to hide the secrets I'd been keeping from her in the dark corners of my mind.

"Nova kissed me," I told her.

Even though I was braced for her indecipherable shout

and the punch she landed on my arm, I still winced when it happened.

"Fuck off!" she cried. "Are you serious right now?"

"As a biker with his Harley," I promised.

"He kissed you? What the hell, Li? You're engaged, does he not get that?"

I winced again. "He did it in front of Jake. He might had goaded him into basically daring us to kiss to prove there was nothing going on between us."

"And?" she gasped, eyes enormous in her head, so round they were comical.

"And…it only proved that Jake's an idiot, Nova's worse, and I've been kidding myself the last two years thinking I could get over him."

That shut her up for a minute, her gaping mouth closed as she averted her eyes to the passing of historic downtown as we drove into the suburbs.

"You know," she murmured, soft and thoughtful. "I always thought you'd end up together. Not because it was the obvious choice, but because there was always this intangible softness between you, even when we were kids. Nova's always been the pretty boy, the affable, unflappable jokester. But around you, he had this depth, like this secret compartment in his personality only you could unlock."

"Pretty," I whispered, meaning to tease her, but failing because I was too moved by her words to joke.

It had always felt that way to me as well. That whatever Nova and I might have been separately, we were something different together. Something more that could have been as beautiful as a wildflower meadow if only he'd let it grow.

"Doesn't matter now," I muttered, fiddling with the engagement ring on my left hand as I palmed the wheel. "I'm marrying Jake."

"Lila…I didn't say anything when you got engaged because I was kinda in the middle of my own shit storm, and I

didn't really know Jake enough to say anything, but c'mon...
you're not going to marry him."

I shot her a look, angered by her assumption only because
it was so accurate, and I wasn't quite ready to give up on the
normal, stable family life marrying Jake represented.

"We're taking a...beat after what happened. I was, no, I
am angry with him for forcing the issue and dredging up stuff
that was in the past. He's been dealing with a lot of stress at
work, so we've only seen each other a few times in the last
month."

And I'd barely noticed, if I was being honest.

I missed the sex, because once I'd discovered it, I found I
had a serious affinity for it. The press of bodies, the slick slide
of hard flesh into soft, wet openings. My own sexuality had
evolved with a rapidity that surprised both Jake and I. I
wanted it constantly, in ways we'd explored and hadn't.

Like all things in my life, I was always looking to push the
boundaries, discover what might be on the other side of the
horizon.

"I'm just saying," H.R. continued, oblivious to my
thoughts as we pulled up in front of the Booth's because my
girl was coming for dinner. "Marriage is serious shit, and
divorce is a reality for way too many people. Just...think
about it."

"Harleigh Rose cautioning me to think before I act?" I
gasped, hand over my heart. "I never thought I'd see the day."

She rolled her eyes at me then laughed as we exited the
car and she started up the stairs to the porch.

"Coming?" she asked when I moved around the side of
the house instead of following her.

"In a second, just going to drop my stuff."

I rounded the house to the backyard and grinned as I
always did when I trailed my hands over the tall, swaying grass
and flat, glossy leaves lining the walkway to my converted
greenhouse.

The smile slid and crashed to the ground when I opened the door to my house and there was nothing inside but my purple sofa, crate coffee table, and empty bookcase. My bag dropped through my numb fingers as I quickly raced to the bedroom then the bathroom and found all of my essential things missing.

What. The. Actual. *Fuck?*

I sprinted out the door and bounded up the stairs through the backdoor of the Booth home. Out of breath, I careened to a halt in the kitchen where my entire family and Harleigh Rose were gathered around the kitchen island facing me with identical expressions of caution mixed with glimmers of amusement.

Only Nova seemed unfazed, the heavy weight of his muscled body leaned up against the counter, his booted feet crossed at the ankles, a smile as sly as a curl of smoke affixed to his beautiful face.

"Who the hell raided my house?" I demanded in a low, cold voice of fury.

I shouldn't have asked the question, not when I already knew the answer.

As one, the family looked over at Nova.

Who clearly didn't care about his personal safety, because he removed the toothpick dangling from the corner of his mouth so he could smile hugely.

"You wanna do somethin' stupid, I'm guessin' I can't stop you short of monitorin' every single step you take, and, Li, love ya, but I gotta fuckin' life to live, and I'm not doin' it chained to your side. So, if you think about it, you asked for this." He opened his tatted hands and shrugged.

"I asked for this? What exactly is *this?*" I seethed.

My family moved around the other side of the island, sensing correctly that I was about to lose it.

"Twenty bucks she goes ape shit," Huds whispered to Milo, who hushed him then tugged his wallet out of his back pocket and retrieved a twenty which he slapped on the counter between them.

I spared a moment to shoot them both an unimpressed glare then set my sights on the asshole in front of me.

"You're movin' in with me," Nova had the audacity to say casually, the way someone might mention a change in the weather. "Correction. You're already all moved in thanks to the family. Oliver wants you to make *maduros* as payment and Ares wants you to take him to Paradise Found for some new books."

My mouth fell open like a fish out of water, moving open and closed as I struggled to find words for the outraged horror threatening to drown me.

Nova continued conversationally. "You gotta shit ton of plants, but I found a way to fit them around the apartment. Your girly ass sofa had to stay, and that ugly as fuck coffee table, but we got the rest of your stuff sorted. Molly packed your lingerie," he added with a wicked grin. "Had to clear out a whole drawer for it in my dresser. Whole lotta lace and garters in there, babe, gotta say I'm surprised."

Harleigh Rose muffled a chuckle poorly behind her hand and leaned into Oliver who wrapped an arm around her and squeezed in camaraderie. Even Ares, my beautiful boy with the somber eyes, grinned minutely.

The fucking traitors.

"You had no right to do that," I started, trying to keep calm in the face of Nova's blatant possessive, overprotective alpha assholery. "You don't own me. You don't decide shit all for me, let alone where I live."

Nova's affability dissolved at the acid of my tone, and his face darkened so suddenly, I almost took a step away from him. Instead, I held my ground as he pushed off the counter, forearms corded and brown beneath his ink as he stalked toward me.

He only stopped when we were toe to toe, and he was

looking down at me from his much greater height. His dark eyes sparkled with intensity, coffee set to scalding as that his moved to my mouth then back up to my eyes. We weren't touching, not quite, but the air between us was molten with heat and buzzing, bumping electrons.

"There's no gettin' outta this, Lila," he said softly, silk over steel. "If I gotta tackle you and drag you outta here like a fuckin' caveman, you are comin' with me. I'll lock up your greenhouse, slash your fuckin' tires so you rely completely on me. 'Cause you don't seem to get somethin' I've been tryin' to teach you all your life. You're my fuckin' family. You wanna put yourself in danger 'cause your too damn brave and too damn stupid and completely, in-fuckin'-sanely loyal, then you do you. But I'll be there to protect you from yourself and the pit of vipers you've put yourself in bed with. I'll be there droppin' you off and pickin' you up, I'll be there sleepin' in the room beside you so if anyone gets any ideas about takin' ya, they'll have to get through me to do it."

He stopped talking, but his eyes didn't stop speaking.

You're mine, they said, *you'll do this because I'll make you.*

"I hate you," I whispered, hot with shame because I was a liar and shaky with rage because I knew there was no getting out of this. And how the hell could I remain immune from his charms if I *lived* with him?

Nova's smile changed, already brittle, it cracked at the edges and went flat. "Sure, Flower Child. Whatever helps you sleep at night."

"For the record," Diogo grunted, "there's no way I'd let you go if I didn't think it was safer with Jonathon than it would be for you here. We're gonna have a talk about why you put yourself at risk without talking to me about it, Li girl, but until then, you're going with him."

"Put five bucks in the jar, Dad," Nova said off-handily, referring to the cookie jar we kept on the counter that everyone paid into when they called him Jonathon instead of Nova.

"I can stay with H.R. and Lion," I countered without breaking eye contact with Nova, daring him to refute the safety of that plan.

"Um…" Harleigh Rose hesitated. "No offense, girl, but Lion and I live in a tiny apartment while the renos are being done at the ranch. I think for the sake of all our relationships, it'd be better you didn't stay with us. I'm not so good at stayin' quiet."

"Ew," Hudson said, wrinkling his nose because he'd grown up with H.R. around, and he considered her like a sister too. "TMI, dude."

"You can't stay with Zeus and Lou either," Ares stated with more authority than any kid should ever have. "They twins've got colic and they don't sleep so good."

Which might have been true, but there was something in the way he slanted Nova a measuring look that said he was rooting for him to win the stand-off.

"You're stayin' with me," Nova cut in intractably. "No one else I trust enough to take care of you."

The words landed like a silken blow, and I hated him for them. Because damn him for loving me like that, *so* much, but platonically. Always platonically.

How could a girl ever be expected to move on from a man who would do anything to keep her safe?

He planted flowers all over my body, inside the cage of my ribs, in the fertile soil of my heart, yet he never noticed how they bloomed just for him.

I looked away, gritting my teeth against the sudden burn of tears in my eyes, trying to call up the anger I'd felt to burn away the oncoming flood.

"I'm not going with you," I told him with a finality he could understand. "There's no way I'm living with you."

"There's no way you're not," he countered simply.

I shoved at his chest, two hands to the white tee, but he wouldn't move.

Instead, he leveraged my weight against me and shifted to the side so I fell forward into the arm he had ready to catch me. Before I could even squawk out a protest, Nova was lowering me to the ground steadily with one bulging arm then kneeling over me, twisting my hands behind my back, pinning a knee in my ass.

"What the hell?" I yelled at him.

"Huds," he said calmly, ignoring my struggles. "Go get me some of Dad's rope."

"Don't you fucking *dare!*" I screeched, thrashing against the floor like a grounded fish. "Get him off me!"

But no one rescued me.

Instead, I heard muffled laughter and Molly's heavy sigh, the same one she'd expelled when we were rowdy children acting out.

Hudson returned quickly, handed off the rope, and Nova made quick work of tying up my hands in tight fisherman's knots I had no hope of escaping from.

"I'm going to fucking kill you for this," I promised.

He chuckled huskily in my ear, patted my ass, then hauled me into his arms as easily as a sack of grain before flipping me up and over his shoulder where he slapped my ass again.

"Fuck, can't think why I haven't done this before," he mused to our family as they snickered and watched me being manhandled. "She's a helluva lot more amenable like this."

"Just don't drop her," Molly called out wearily.

"She weighs like five pounds," Milo said confidently. "He won't drop her."

"Want a call when you get her home and settled in," Diogo warned. "And an update on what the hell you two are wrapped up in right now."

"You'll have some serious hell to pay later," Harleigh Rose noted accurately.

"You better fucking believe it," I shouted. "All of you are officially on my shit list."

"As long as you're alive to have one and Nova can help keep you that way, I don't care," Molly replied with surprising fervor. "Take care of our girl, honey."

Nova's body jerked with his nod, then he started to walk us out the door. "'Til the day I fuckin' die," he promised, and even hanging upside down in a fireman's carry on his shoulder, I felt those words hit home in my heart like yet another strike of Cupid's bow.

I'D ALWAYS LOVED NOVA'S APARTMENT, AND I HATED THAT THE sight of all that exposed brick and black leather and chrome furniture looked even better amid my plants, cool and homey at the same time. It was a massive, open plan space with a loft set back over the living area that contained a small game room complete with dart board, pool table, and a short hall that gave way to two bedrooms. I'd helped him move in years ago, and I both loved and hated that he still had the huge photo of Dane, himself, and me in a place of honour on the wall perpendicular to the TV.

I also hated that he'd kept me tied up on the couch while he moved around the apartment, and then hated, too, that he'd used that time to draw a bath for me with the dried flower bath salts I liked then locked me in there to 'calm the fuck down' so we could have a mature conversation about what was going to happen moving forward.

But I took the bath, letting the rose and lilac soothe me, playing Bishop Briggs on my phone so I could let the lyrics sort my emotions for me.

I felt shook up like a bottle of pop, my emotions fizzing, bursting beneath my skin.

Even though Jake and I had been on a 'break' since the kiss happened, I was still reluctant to let him go. He represented a life way from crime and chaos, a safe future that I felt I *should've* wanted after my upbringing more than I actually wanted it in reality.

Now that I was living with Nova?

I knew the clock on the ticking time bomb of my relationship with Jake was down to its final minutes.

A decision had to be made.

Though sitting in the bath Nova had drawn for me, it was impossible to be objective.

I sighed heavily and drew my black painted, talon shaped fingernails over the swirls in the floral design under my breasts. The blooms grounded me as I recalled their meanings: hyacinth the same blue as Molly's eyes for constancy, the Bachelor's Button at my right hip symbolizing hope in love, the periwinkles intertwined with vines beneath Dane's lotus for sweet remembrance. They were the tapestry of my life and love thus far inked onto my skin, a tangible reminder of everything I held close so that in moments like this, when I felt overwhelmed and flailing, I had a visceral token of who I was and what was really important.

"Feelin' better?" Nova asked as he popped the door open to stick his head into the humid, floral-scented room.

"Nova!" I protested, covering my breasts beneath the spare cover of bubbles. "I'm naked. Get the fuck out."

He ignored me, pushing the door open to reveal his long, toned body. He'd changed into dark grey sweatpants that rode low on his hips, exposing the hard cut of muscle arrowing into either side of his groin and the massive expanse of his fully inked torso complete with a nipple ring decorating his right pectoral.

I choked on my moan and forgot about modesty for a moment. It had been ages since I'd last seen Nova so disrobed, and the sight of him like that lit me on fire, dry kindling doused with gasoline.

He paused in the doorway, letting me look my fill with a cocky grin on his face, before he moved to the toilet, put the lid down, and took a seat, leaning forward on those thickly corded forearms. He cocked his head to the left and a lock of wavy dark hair fell across his broad forehead.

"So," he asked, opening his hands and then clasping them so his silver rings clanged together. "You ready to talk?"

"How about we do this when I'm not naked in the tub?" I asked drily.

"How about we do it now when you're naked in the tub so you can't stalk away from me or slap me when you get riled up?" he suggested. "'Sides, not gonna lie, I'm enjoyin' the view a helluva lot more than I should."

"Don't flirt with me," I snapped, grateful once again that my dark skin didn't hold a blush.

"Why not?" he countered. "I flirt with everyone."

"Exactly," I said. "I'm not everyone, Nova."

"No," he mused, running a hand through the long hair at the top of his head so it stuck up in sexy disarray. "Never thought you were, Flower Child."

We locked eyes then, gazes colliding like two speeding cars so the crash rocked through us both, sending us physically reeling. I was left with only the impact of his words reverberating inside of me, but I had no idea what they meant.

"You're being even more overbearing than normal," I said flippantly, trying to regain my equilibrium. "I know you promised Dane you'd look out for me, but this is a bit much."

"This has got nothin' to do with him."

I blinked, wrapping one arm tighter around my breasts so I could tuck a wet, curling lock of hair back into my bun. Nova's eyes followed the curve of my breasts then the way my hand moved through my hair, his nostrils flaring.

"It's got to do with my safety," I ventured. "Making sure the Booths don't lose more family."

"It's got to do with that, sure," he agreed easily, but his eyes, they churned like restless sea creatures beneath an inky black ocean at night. "But it's got more to do with you and me."

I looked away, unable to hold the intensity of his gaze, and studied the black polish on my toes as they wriggled above the bubbles.

"Li," he called then waited for me to look at him again. "You know you're my best friend, yeah?"

I closed my eyes against the force of feelings that moved through me seeing the sincerity in that handsome face, hearing the vulnerability in his voice.

God, but this man eviscerated me at every turn.

"Yeah, I know," I mumbled. "But you don't see H.R. carting me over her shoulder and forcing me to live with her."

"She might've, she knew what you've been doin'."

"Well, now she has a fucking good idea because of your dramatics," I snapped. "I don't need people knowing what I'm doing with Irina. It puts them in danger, puts *me* in danger, the more people know."

"You think I don't get that?" He leaned forward farther, rocking onto his toes so he could hover over me. "I told them you went snoopin' around, I didn't tell them you were workin' for Irina, and I won't. But we gotta lay down some laws here, Li. Otherwise, I'm lockin' ya up like Rapunzel in an urban tower."

"First," he continued, listing them off on his strong, tatted hand. "I'm workin' this with ya. Don't give a fuck what you think about it. I'm doin' it. Not sure how I'll get close to the bitch yet given I'm solid Fallen, but I'll figure it out so when I gotta have your back I can be there."

I cracked my knuckles, but nodded.

"Second, you and me are spendin' an hour every mornin' at Box n' Burn with Wrath and Bat learnin' how to defend yourself. Like hell I'm lettin' you work at Wet Works when you know fuck all about self-defence."

That was actually a good idea, so I nodded again, feeling stupid for not thinking of that myself.

"Lastly…" His voice went to smoke, and he dropped to his knees beside the bathtub so he could reach over to cup my cheek, bringing our foreheads together so he could speak into the wedge of air between our lips. "You cast aside this space you've put between us. Hurt you two years ago, and not gonna apologize for doin' it 'cause, Li, I got my reasons. There's no part of me worth even an inch of you, and you gotta get that, know it, and forgive me for pointin' it out to you, yeah? You gotta believe I've always got you at my heart, on my mind, thinkin' about what's right for you. And me? I'm not it. But fuck me, that doesn't mean I don't care about you. It'll never mean that."

We breathed the same air for a long moment as I tried to digest his words, failing not to be hurt by them even though it wasn't his intention.

Finally, he pulled away so he could look me in the eye, and I nearly gasped at the beauty of him in the light spilling through the high window, highlighted pink and orange with the descending sun.

"I know you care about me, Nova," I said softly, studying the way the rose gold light gilded his Patrician profile and made him look like a handsome soldier stamped on a Roman coin. "But we both know the way you care isn't enough."

"You'll get over it," he promised, but there was a twist to his lips that said he wasn't sure he believed that.

My own heart flatlined because I sure as hell didn't believe it either.

"Maybe it's not me who needs to get over something," I dared to say, feeling angry and reckless and *done* with Nova and his games.

He knew, god dammit, he knew how I felt. He knew what I wanted, yet he still kept me on the hook just because he couldn't bear to live without me.

There was a knock at the front door, and I stirred, waiting for him to get up to answer it. Instead, he continued to kneel there looking just as frustrated with me as I was with him.

So I took matters in my own hands, determined to prove what he seemed unwilling to understand.

I was no longer the seven-year-old girl who needed his protection.

I was a twenty-four-year-old woman who needed something more, something opaque and carnal like a flower that bloomed only in the warmth and dark of night.

There was another knock at the door.

Watching him carefully, I stood up.

Slowly, like Aphrodite emerging from the waves, bubbles and water, dried petals and foam sluicing down the aggressive curves of my body, caressing me the way Nova never would.

His eyes followed the stream, smoldering against my skin so hot I thought I might burn. They lingered at the swell of my breasts, the tightening peaks of my nipples, sliding down the flat line of my belly to the apex of my thighs where my bare skin was paler than the rest, soft and hairless, clit a hard bud amid my dusky folds.

I could hear the air hiss through his teeth as he took his fill, and I let him.

There was sweat beading on his brow, a muscle pulsing in the hard angle of his jaw.

He looked wrecked by the sight of me, and I gloried in it for another long second before I stepped out of the tub and grabbed a towel. Back to him, ass jiggling as I wiped myself dry, grabbed a Street Ink tee of his hanging on the back of the door, and donned it.

He didn't follow me as I went to the door and pulled it open without checking the peephole.

Like an idiot.

So when the door swung open, I was shocked to see Jake there holding a bouquet of red roses, his suit wrinkled from the drive up from Vancouver.

But he seemed even more shocked to see me, still damp and fragrant from the bath, hair curling half out of my bun, my nipples hard against the fabric of a tee that was clearly not mine.

And then Nova was there, the room gone electric as he entered the living space and swaggered up behind me, no doubt looking smug.

"*Fuck*," I muttered under my breath before Jake dropped the flowers at my feet, turned on his heel, and stormed away.

I made to take after him, but Nova grabbed my arm, halting me to say, "Li, c'mon, he's never been worth it."

I wrenched my arm from his grip and snarled, "He's the only one who's ever wanted to *try* to be worth it."

And then I left Nova and followed after my man.

CHAPTER SEVENTEEN

Nova

SHE DIDN'T SPEAK TO ME FOR A WEEK.

Dropped her off at Wet Works every mornin', picked her up every night 'cause she'd agreed to it, but she didn't say a fuckin' word.

Nothin' like the wrath of a woman wronged.

And yeah, I'd wronged her.

Not by movin' her in without askin'.

Fuck that.

No, by textin' Jake that Li was at my place and she needed to talk to him.

I'd heard the fight through the open kitchen window, leanin' out the black frame to watch as they yelled at each other in the street, smokin' a cig and enjoyin' the show. That's how I knew they'd broken up. That Jake was tired of comin' second to me and the club. And I'd watched as Lila stared after his car, hand to her empty left ring finger, hair caught like a pennant in the wind. I'd seen the cast of her face, filled with mourning.

Probably not my best move, but there was somethin'

growin' under my skin lately, somethin' with roots that went deep and tangled with my gut. Somethin' I was worried about sproutin' through the surface of my skin for all to see.

Somethin' that had to do with Lila and how I felt about her.

'Cause there was a difference now in the feel of her arms wrapped around my waist, her breasts to my back, groin to my ass pressed up against me on my bike. It wasn't like any other girl I'd taken for a ride. I felt responsible for her safety, stirred by the stamp of her on my body, and the whirr of her breath over my neck when we stopped at a light.

I liked wakin' up from my restless sleep knowin' she was there in the apartment, smellin' her flowers, feelin' her mellow, languid presence in the mornin' as she went about makin' up her pretty face and tamin' all that dark, glossy hair.

Hadn't lived with another bein' since I was just eighteen at home with my family, but I found Lila in my space thrillin', like havin' a new TV or buyin' a new bike. I was obsessed with bein' in the apartment if she was gonna be there, eschewin' the clubhouse and Eugene's with the brothers every night to climb the steps from my shop to an apartment that suddenly felt like home after fifteen years of livin' in it.

I felt pussy whipped without even havin' access to the pussy.

Though, watchin' that clip of her actin' as a camgirl, the only one she'd posted, I thought way too much about that too.

How she'd taste if I could put my mouth on her. If I'd get addicted to the scent of her and the feel of those silken folds against my tongue.

I was a man who loved pussy in all forms, but I had a feelin' if I ever got a shot at Lila's, it'd rocket from love to pure obsession.

Never came harder in my life, not with threesomes or kink or any level of fuckery than I did in that week, jerkin' off to that video while Lila herself lay asleep down the hall.

I was a fuckin' perv, but there was no stoppin' me.

The sight of her deep, golden-brown skin naked, inked by my hand, slicked with bath water, and sudsy with lingerin' bubbles as she'd stepped from the tub was the sexiest fuckin' thing I'd ever seen. My mouth went dry and my cock hardened just thinkin' about it.

Somethin' had to give.

But I couldn't just fuck Lila Meadows.

She was my boy's sister, and it didn't matter he was gone 'cause I still couldn't do that to him.

She was my family's lone girl, cherished by every single one'a the Booths.

If I fucked her and inevitably fucked up, that was on me, and my family, blood or not, would let me bear the brunt of their anger for it.

There was no fuckin' Lila anyway. If we came together, I knew in the same way I'd always known how to draw, how to pull from my imagination and create art, that it would lead to love makin'.

And that?

That I couldn't fuckin' do.

As if I needed a reminder, my iPad rattled on the metal tray of tools at my station, draggin' me from my thoughts.

MEREDITH: WE NEED TO TALK.

I blinked at the screen as I squeezed it so tight I thought the metal would warp from the force.

Another buzz.

MEREDITH: WE HAVE THINGS TO WORK OUT, HANDSOME. IT'S BEEN YEARS. IT'S TIME WE FIGURED THIS OUT.

"What the fuck, man!?" Axe-Man hollered as my iPad

went crashin' against the wall, breakin' apart into little glass pieces.

The entire shop paused, tattoo guns quietin', talk stoppin' in its tracks.

Axe-Man, Jae Pil, and Chloe, my artists, all blinked at me, shocked by my outburst.

Wasn't the kinda man who usually had a temper, so it was fair, their concern, but I couldn't handle it just then.

Not with Meredith on my mind.

"Sara, call Marcus, and tell him we're gonna have to reschedule his session," I ordered brusquely, collectin' my cut, helmet, and keys as I passed by her at reception. "I'm out."

"Nova," Axe-Man called, but I only saluted him over my shoulder and got the fuck outta there.

It was early to pick up Lila, but I got on my Harley Davidson FXSTB Night Train and took off with a roar of pipes that took the edge off my bad mood.

Barely.

Of course, fuckin' Meredith would choose today of all days to reach out.

It was Dane's birthday.

He woulda been thirty-six this year if he was still alive.

Usually, I spent the night gettin' drunk alone and findin' a woman or two to entertain me through what was always a sleepless night, but I didn't want to do that this year.

This year, I wanted Lila.

We would celebrate Dane this weekend with the family during Sunday dinner, but I felt the need to do somethin' then with the only person who loved him more than me.

Wet Works was thirty minutes north of downtown Entrance at the edge of the industrial neighborhood that sprawled like a raised hand over the city, fingers of land extendin' into the Faversham Inlet cut into the mountains by the ocean. It was a massive site with dozens of cars parked in

the lot, both scantily clad and normally dressed workers scut-
tling between the buildings.

I swung off my bike, leaned a hip against the seat, and
texted Lila.

Nova: Waitin' on you outside.
Lila: You're early.
Nova: Was in the mood for you.
Lila: I'm busy.
Nova: I'm always in the mood for you, if I'm bein'
fuckin' honest.

The bubbles that indicated she was typin' appeared, disappeared, then appeared again. I tapped my thumb against the
phone impatiently and dug a cigarette outta my back pocket,
stickin' in between my lips without lightin' it just for somethin'
to do.

Lila: What's going on, Nova?
Nova: It's Dane's birthday. Wanna spend the night with
you. Do somethin' special.
Lila: I have my own ritual for today.
Nova: Cool. Doin' it with ya then.
Lila: You aren't invited.
Nova: Tough shit. I'm outside. Comin' in to get you if
you aren't out in ten.

I didn't get a response to that, but I didn't expect one.

So I lit up the smoke, put on my aviators, and tilted my
head to the sun as it set 'cause the rays were warm, the scent
of hot asphalt in my nose familiar, figurin' I may as well enjoy
the moment.

'Cause that was life.

This moment and the next, strung together like beads on a
string worn around the wrist. Some were plastic children's

fare, some glitterin' diamonds or hard stone, but all of them were worth relishin' 'cause I was fuckin' alive.

While some people, the *best* people, were dead.

Or never got a chance at livin'.

I didn't notice I was rubbin' at the tattoo on my left bicep until Lila swung around the side of a buildin', struttin' in her tall heels like she'd been born in them when I knew for a fact she'd grown up barefoot, likin' the feel of the earth beneath her toes.

My hippie girl rock child.

And she looked it today, decked out in a cropped Tom Petty concert tee and frayed jean shorts that exposed the long, carved line of her legs until the tops of her fringed boots, the sweet pink pop of colour from the peonies inked high on the side. Her long, dark hair caught in the fingers of the wind, gleaming with copper highlights in the red gold light of the sun. I remembered how it felt to take that mane in my fist, and my dick kicked at thinkin' 'bout doin' it again.

She was gorgeous that girl, so beautiful in so many ways I wondered if anyone, even me, would ever know the depth of them.

She had a sunflower soul with a heart of gold, a hankerin' for adventure, and a thirst for knowledge. She was raw and earthy, mellow and cataclysmic, sexy and lovin'.

She was the epitome of everythin' I loved in this world.

And it was gettin' hard to remind myself why I shouldn't make her mine.

Then I remembered it was Dane's fuckin' birthday, and I was standin' there with a hardenin' cock pervin' on his little sister.

Lila stopped in front of me, hand to the flare of her hip, one leg kicked out and bronze in the descending light, all sass and flare. "I don't think I've seen you scowl so much in your life as I have the last two months."

'Cause you're drivin' me fuckin' crazy, I almost said.

Instead, I took a last drag of my cig and flipped it to the concrete where I stamped it out with an aggressive twist of my heavy boot.

Lila's sassy expression faltered as she stepped closer and reached up to gently take down my sunglasses.

"Can't ever read your expression if I can't see those velvet eyes," she murmured, touchin' the skin beside left eye, smoothin' out the creases there. "Always smiling, even when you have nothing to smile about."

I snagged her wrist, makin' her jump, but I only pressed my thumb to her pulse as it took off in a sprint, rubbin' the tender skin over it. "Not much worth smilin' about today."

"No," she agreed softly then hesitated, shiftin' from foot to foot in a little shimmy that shouldn't have been hot but was. When she finally looked back up at me, her eyes were more green than brown, glowin' like unearthed emeralds. "I know we're trying to put the past behind us, so...can I hug you?"

Fuck me, but she was sweet.

I felt my mouth curl in a small, genuine smile as I opened my arms and waggled my brows. "Come get it, babe."

She laughed softly then lunged forward to wrap her arms around my neck, press her lush body to mine and hold tight.

She smelled good, like crushed berries and jasmine, earthy and sweet, and she felt even better, like a piece slotted back into place. I put my nose in the glossy sheets of her hair and clutched her hard to me.

"Missed ya," I murmured, 'cause at the end of the day, she was my best friend.

"Missed you," she admitted. "Even though you're a pain in my ass."

"That's what she said," I countered.

She shoved me away, but she was laughin', hair tossed back, eyes alight 'cause I'd set fire to them.

Another of her beauties: she made everyone feel like their best self 'cause she always saw the best in people.

"So you got the ritual. Where we headin'?"

Lila stopped laughin', but her smile stayed, growing warm and sly. "The Wet Lotus strip club."

THE LOTUS WAS FALLEN OWNED AND OPERATED, SO I WAS NO stranger to the velvet booths, blue lights, and mirrored bar, but sittin' there with Lila was a far cry different than lounging around with my brothers and flirtin' with the dancers and bar staff.

Mostly 'cause Lila had insisted we go back to the apartment so she could change and I could drop the bike. We were drinkin' to excess, apparently, so we caught a ride with Axe-Man to The Lotus, and we'd cabs after that. But it was her outfit that set me on edge more than the naked women on stage.

She was wearin' purple.

She'd always favoured the colour, or maybe I had. Either way, along the line it'd become our favourite, and I was used to seein' her in it.

But I'd never seen anythin' like that dress.

All dark lace from the short hem ticklin' her smooth upper thighs to the edge of the flowy sleeves that still revealed her colourful tats through the fabric. It plunged to a point just above her belly button, the lush swell of her breasts shinin', half-exposed in the neon lights, the long spill of her dark hair glowin' black and blue.

When she stood, I could even make out the thin string of her black thong dissectin' the blooms of her hips and ridin' high on her ass.

It was a dress designed explicitly to kill a man's resolve to behave himself.

My fingers twitched on the bar as I watched her watch the dancers, as she shimmied her shoulders to the music.

Feelin' my gaze, she looked over at me and laughed. "You look angry for a guy in a strip club."

Angry? No.

Fuckin' pissed 'cause here I was, tryin' to be an honorable guy for the first time in my fuckin' life, and the personification of temptation was sittin' across from me, completely unaware I'd been half-hard since she emerged from the bathroom at the apartment with big, wavy sex hair and spiked metal high heels.

Now we were at a strip club that pulsed with sex and strobe lights, that practically seduced you into makin' the worse kinda decisions the second you walked in the door and got hypnotized by the beats and the sway of women's hips.

"Can't believe this was your plan. You come here often, Li?" I tried to tease.

This was what Lila wanted to do to celebrate Dane's birthday.

Watch women undress to the heavy beat of pulsatin' music that echoed the throb of blood through your body as more and more clothes were shed.

She grinned at me and moved closer so she didn't have to yell over the music. The air between us was hot, scented with the light musk and bloom of her perfume.

"Dane was twenty-four when he died," she said, hand to my thigh where it burned through the denim like a fuckin' brand. "He was overseas for most of his adult life, and when he was home, he was mostly with me. Every year on his birthday I do something *fun* for him, because he didn't have much of that in his life."

There was logic in that, some rebel girl kinda thinkin' that just illustrated why Lila was the shit. She wasn't offended by nudity or profanity, by the fact that the family of bikers who had adopted her were criminals runnin' by their own set of rules.

She was as free as the wild flowers she loved so much.

My resolve weakened further, a hairline fracture breakin' through to a fault line runnin' the length of my willpower.

I was goin' down fast.

"If you wanna make things fun, Li," I said low, mouth tipped down so I could speak against her ear just to feel her shiver. "We should up the ante."

Her pink tongue peeked between those glossed lips and traced a path over their full curve, mesmerizin' me. "What did you have in mind?"

"Two truths and a lie," I suggested, already flaggin' down the cute blonde server. "A shot for every one you get wrong."

She snorted and tossed that long mane of hair over her shoulder, breasts shiftin' dangerously in the low dress. Under the scent of body oil, beer, and cloying perfume, I caught a hint of Lila's floral scent that went straight to my cock.

"You lie for shit," she decreed with a cat ate the canary smile. "Prepare to get schooled, Nova."

"Oh, Flower Child," I crooned, leanin' close just to see desire blacken her eyes. "You wanna try to school me, I'm all too willin' to sit back and watch you try."

Three hours later, more than fifteen shots deep, tequila in my throat, salt on my tongue, and lime on my breath, I was laughin' so hard I thought I'd bust a gut.

"You are fuckin' with me," I hollered, slappin' the table. "You can't be serious."

"Deadly," she insisted with glitterin' eyes. We were so close, knees slotted together, legs tangled, my arm over the back of the booth, fingers danglin' over the curve of her shoulder, playin' in the ends of her kinked-up hair.

I wanted her closer, sittin' on my lap, preferably naked so I could palm the lush swell of her ass in my palm, but I'd take this.

I'd always liked her too close, even before. There was somethin' about Lila that invited intimacy. She was always knockin' hips, huggin', and kissin' cheeks, but it was more than that. She had the kinda open, non-judgemental aura that drew men and women to her like bees to pollen.

"Seriously, he paid me fifty bucks just to give me a foot massage," Lila laughed her throaty laugh and shrugged. "I was sixteen, and I really wanted a kombucha starter kit, so it seemed like a pretty good deal."

I bent over to grab one of her spike-heeled feet and studied it with mock sobriety. "They are fuckin' sexy."

I looked up at her to find her pink lip between her teeth, her eyes low lidded and sultry. "Worth fifty bucks?"

I grinned, runnin' my hands up her smooth calf to her lower thigh, feeling her shudder under my touch. "Never paid for any of a woman's time or affection, so I don't know the scale, but…I'd probably shell out more for somethin' else."

"What?" she breathed as I rubbed my thumb on the inside of her thigh.

I shook my head, lovin' the feel of her, the play of her mind against mine. It'd always been so easy between us, so intrinsic, that I'd never really thought of takin' our relationship beyond the beauty it already maintained.

But this?

Flirtin' with her in the dark of a bar with my hands on her body, her curves tucked in that mouthwaterin' dress, I wondered how I'd always been so blind to it.

"That's not playin' the game," I murmured, caught up in her like a spider in a web. I grabbed her tattooed hand, the one with the sunflower bloomin' across the back of it, and lifted her fingers as I counted my two truths and a lie. "I'm an ass man, I prefer blondes, and that kiss we had in Eugene's? Best fuckin' kiss I ever had."

I watched Lila's smooth, brown throat move as she swallowed hard then indulged myself by raisin' my hand to trace the line of her neck from the back of her ear to her collarbone just to watch her swallow thickly once more.

She was impossibly responsive, and I was only a man. The effect I seemed to have on her...it was headier than the tequila we'd knocked back, stronger than the hammer fist strike of my pulse in my chest.

I wanted to lay her out and play her body like an instrument just to see what chords would make her sing, how many ways I could make music with her form.

The alcohol had muted the questions I should have been askin' myself.

What happened if we fucked?

Where would we go from there?

What would the brothers think? Our family?

Tequila and lust eroded the chains that bound me to my oath to Dane to protect Lila at all costs.

'Cause gettin' involved with me? The devil in a pair of motorcycle boots?

It would only lead to pain for the both of us.

But as I stared into Lila's gorgeous face, I was reminded how much beauty there was in pain.

Like a tattoo, the beauty was worth the burn.

"The last one, our kiss," she murmured. "That's the lie."

I cocked my head to the side and fully cupped the side of her neck. "Yeah? Final answer?"

She nodded, bottom lip between her teeth again.

I leaned forward until we were breathin' the same air. "If that's your answer, Li, obviously I didn't do it right for ya the first time."

My thumb unhooked that plush lower lip from

between her teeth, and then my mouth was on hers. Instantly, she parted for me, a knife through butter, no hesitation, just delicious fuckin' pliancy. She melted against me as I swept my tongue into the silken heat of her mouth and started to lap at the tequila-sweet taste of her.

My hand moved from the side of her neck to wrap around her throat, and I couldn't resist the urge to lean back to look down at the pretty sight of my skull tatted skin against the purity of her golden throat.

Lips damp, chests heavin' like we'd run a race, I told her, "Like a work of fuckin' art."

Her eyes flared then narrowed, and this time, she kissed me, moldin' her breasts to my chest as she kneeled on the booth and leaned over me for better access.

Her moan rumbled against my tongue, vibratin' through me like the strike of a gong.

And I was done.

A goner to a girl I'd once thought of as a kid.

Only now, she was all woman.

My hands moved over the evidence of her femininity, the lush curve of her ass raised in the air as she bent to me, the sweet shelf of that rounded cheek meetin' the lean muscle of her thigh. I cupped her there, tested the weight of that curve, and groaned to myself.

Hell yeah, I was an ass man, and Lila had the sweetest ass I'd ever touched.

I wanted to test it with my teeth, the stingin' smack of my palm just to feel the bounce back. I wanted to slap my cock between the swells and watch it disappear between the sexy mounds.

Lila's hand found my achin' cock through my jeans and palmed it on a gasp.

"Fuck, you're thick," she breathed, tippin' her forehead against mine so she could look down at her ringed hand on the ridge of my shaft. The sight made us both moan. "I've never held a cock so big."

A primal shudder rattled through my bones, and I nearly fuckin' growled as I pushed her by the sternum onto her back on the booth before followin' her down.

"God," she gasped between the molten press of our mouths meetin'. "I've imagined this so many times, and it was *never* this good."

Somethin' panged in my chest, remindin' me this wasn't a good idea, but I couldn't stop now, not with Lila's hands in my hair tuggin' me close, her legs wrapped tight to my hips like vines.

"Could've been doing this all along," she continued as I placed open mouthed kisses down her throat. "But you were too fucking stubborn to notice I'd grown up."

"Oh, yeah?" I whispered darkly, somethin' dark stirrin' in my belly.

If Lila wanted to play, we could fuckin' play.

She squealed as I carted her into my arms and stepped out of the booth. Felicity, the girl who'd been serving us, gaped as I stalked by her and ordered, "Send a bottle of tequila to the Velvet Room, tell Maja to turn off the cameras in there, and make sure we aren't fuckin' interrupted."

"Nova!" Lila protested, clingin' to me, laughin' even though she was obviously embarrassed.

I grinned wickedly down at her and continued to the private room on the left side of the club. The door was open, the room lit with cool blue lights and throbbin' with the heavy beat of Timbaland's 'Bounce.'

I dropped Lila on the ice blue stage in front of the curved, navy, velvet booth and then took a seat in front of her, legs splayed, palm to my stone hard cock.

She stared at me through her hair, raised on her knees with her hands braced before her. Fuck, but I could've jacked off just to the sight of her like that in that seductive dress.

"You're so desperate to show me what I've been missin'?" I demanded in a low, rough voice I barely fuckin' recognized. "Fine. Take off your clothes, and attempt to impress me."

She hesitated, mouth open in a little moue I wanted to slide my cock through. "Are you serious?"

"As a fuckin' heart attack. You wanna play, Li? We'll play, but I'm the kinda man that sets the rules and expects them to be followed through. I play rough. I play dirty. And I play *hard*. You think you can handle all that, be my guest and fuckin' prove it to me," I ordered, rubbin' my dick through the denim in slow, deliberate strokes that drew her dazed gaze and made her lick her lips.

Part of me wanted to scare her off. To prove to the both of us that she was too good, too pure for the deviant things I wanted to do to her and with her.

Part of me hoped beyond breath that she'd take up the gauntlet I'd thrown down and fuckin' run with it.

Slowly, she moved back to sit with her ass on her heels, tossin' her hair in a black spray of silk over her shoulder.

And then she picked up that gauntlet and fuckin' rocked my goddamn world with it.

I watched with my heart in my throat as she leisurely started to churn her hips back and forth, rockin' to the heavy bass of the song. A hand found its way to her mane of hair, and the other arrowed down her dress to play at the edge of the short hem, gradually makin' its way to the center where she dipped her hand beneath the material and gasped.

"You're so wet for me already, aren't you, Li?" I guessed, drunk enough on booze but more, too intoxicated by the sight of her to speak my mind. "Soaked straight through that little scrap of fabric over your pussy."

"Yes," she hissed, eyes closed, head thrown back as she gyrated, hips rocking like waves, so rhythmic my gaze was hooked inexorably on the pendulum of her body.

"Take of your dress."

Her eyes popped open, but she bit her lush bottom lip and flipped onto her hands and knees, facin' away from me to peel the purple lace up over the inked expanse of her back. A tumble of flowers fell down her spine, stamped by my hand, glowin' in the low light like treasure. Seein' my art on her body made my cock kick and set to leakin' in my jeans.

I unzipped them, tugged out my cock, and squeezed hard at the throbbin' base.

The dress went up and over her head before she threw it to the side of the room, leaned onto her hands, and straightened her legs on those tall heels, ass in the air.

My mouth pooled with salvia as I stared straight at her peachy ass.

She peeked over her shoulder and then flipped back over to face me, huggin' an arm across her breasts.

"Show them to me," I demanded, my voice strikin' out like the lash of a whip.

She shivered, bit her lip, then dropped her arms to the side.

"Fuck," I cursed under my breath as I stared at the full, heavy set of her tits and the gorgeous ink that cupped them the way my hands ached to. "Fuckin' gorgeous."

Her eyes were glued to the sight of my dick in my hand, her tongue peepin' out as if she yearned for a taste. I pulled my cock up and out, displayin' the wide, long length of it to her, feelin' the heat of her gaze stroke up the shaft.

"You like seein' me jack off to the sight of ya?" I growled low. "Betcha wish you could crawl over here and get a taste."

Her chest moved like a billow, workin' hard as she panted after me.

"Can I?" she asked, so fuckin' sweet I throbbed in my palm.

"No," I decided after a brief, cruel pause. "We're drunk, I'm thinkin' we take this slow. No touchin'."

Lila pouted and sittin' as she was, legs spread, panties dark with wet over her sex, hair a mess around her exotic, fuckin' stunnin' face, she looked damn near combustible, so hot my brain threatened to short circuit.

"Lean back, spread your legs, and let me watch you touch that wet cunt," I told her as I eased even farther back in the booth and used my free hand to spread open my jeans to better her view. "You watch me watchin' you."

"Oh, my God," she whispered brokenly as she almost scrambled to get into position, as eager as I was to get her hand on her pussy. "Nova, please."

"Please what, baby?" I asked innocently, even though I could read her desire in her face clear as graffiti tagged to a blank wall.

"Please, touch me," she begged in a pretty, soft voice that wrapped desire around my cock like a silk ribbon.

"No, enjoyin' you like that, writhin' and pantin' after my cock. You ever heard the sayin' patience is a virtue?"

"Virtue is a grace, and Grace is a little girl who wouldn't wash her face," she finished with a scowl.

I laughed, humor movin' through the lust and tangled in a fuckin' heady cocktail that only my Li girl had ever served me.

"Be a good girl and come for me on your fingers," I said. "And we'll see."

And fuck me, but I learned she could take orders well.

Brow knotted, she got to her knees so she could pull her little thong to the side, dippin' two fingers in her sex, and grindin' onto her thumb with the pulse of her hips. Sweat beaded on her crown, sapphire gemstones in the blue lights. I traced the wet roll of it between her perky, swollen breasts down the slope of her belly to the bare skin above her groin.

Unbidden, a drunken thought marked itself on my conscious.

A tattoo.

A small, coral rose to represent passion underscored by the words *read my skin.*

'Cause I understood more in that moment watchin' Lila writhe for me than I ever had before that one'a my skills was *her*.

Knowin' her, readin' her, fuckin' lovin' her even if I'd never done it before like this.

But this was no different.

I could see the tempo of the pulse in her neck, the increasin' tide of her hips crashin' against her hand. I knew she loved the rough abrasion of my voice givin' her orders and the sight of my thick cock weepin' precum over my tight fist.

I knew she could orgasm just from my voice puppeteerin' her to come.

She made a man feel like a fuckin' god, and I wasn't goin' to let her worship be for nothin'.

"Ride that hand for me, gorgeous," I grunted as my fist started flyin' over my shaft. "Let me hear the wet slide of your fingers in that graspin', greedy pussy."

She cursed a string of barely coherent words in Spanish, eyes so heavy lidded they were almost closed, mouth open and damp with her pantin' breath.

"Come for me, Li, show me exactly what I've been missin'," I ordered thickly.

And fuck me, did she *come*.

She broke open on a throaty cry dredged up from the depths of her belly, head tossed back so the long line of her golden throat was exposed. Her hips juddered against her hand, and the wet, sticky noise of her comin' all over her hand could be heard even above the swell of music.

I watched her unravel like a dandelion caught in a heavy breeze and, knowin' I'd done that, I brought her that pleasure and controlled the thrash of that precious pulse, I came too.

I grunted hard as my desire seared down my spine, gripped my balls in an iron vice, and wrung them dry. As I spilled onto my fist, Lila recovered enough to crawl off the stage and kneel at my feet, eyes hot and avid as they track the semen spittin' from the head of my angry, red cock.

She laid her head on the end of my thigh, close enough to watch as I tugged leisurely on my flaggin' dick in the come-down. I put a hand on her silken hair and combed my fingers through it.

We were silent, the air thrummin' with the aftermath of our electric chemistry, heavy with the scent of salt and sex. It wasn't awkward. We were languid with expended lust, sleepy with drunkenness.

And it felt somehow right that Lila should be prone at my knees, her eyes closed as she leaned into my pettin' touch like a cat, a low purr workin' through her throat.

I closed my eyes, tipped my head, back against the booth, and enjoyed the moment, 'cause Lord knew, nothin' this good ever lasted.

CHAPTER EIGHTEEN

Lila

I FELL ASLEEP IN THE CAB ON THE WAY HOME.

Booze had made my body hot and heavy, but the cyclonic orgasm Nova had wrecked me with using just the sound of his voice and the sight of his meaty, club-like cock in his fist made me incoherent and utterly wrung out.

So I didn't notice we were back at his apartment until he was laying me in bed. I murmured sleepily as he sat me up to divest me of my dress, but I stirred to full wakefulness when he sat behind me and gently began to thread my thick hair into a braid.

He remembered.

I always slept with my hair braided because the thick, coarse strands went to frizz if I didn't contain them overnight.

When I was a girl, sometimes when Dane was out with Anne Munn, Nova would do that for me. Braid the thick weave of my hair between his big, surprisingly nimble fingers.

And he was doing it again, propping my drooping back

against his knees so he could make space to cross my long hair.

Tears sprang to my eyes, and I was too tired to control their spill.

I wasn't sure if he knew I was awake, but when he finished, he pressed a kiss to my shoulder, then shifted out to lay me back on the pillows.

I closed my eyes and feigned sleep, too raw from the drink, the sex, and the grief of the day to make sense of my own rioting thoughts.

When he closed the door softly behind him, my eyes sprang open to stare at the glow-in-the-dark paint on the ceiling. Nova had painted a galactic garden like the kind seen on Pandora in the movie, *Avatar*. It was one of my favourite films, and I still remembered Nova surprising me with the design when I was nine and he'd finally gotten around to painting the guest bedroom.

A garden away from home, he'd called it.

Because he always made sure I had a home with him wherever he went.

Tears leaked down my cheeks, caught in the whorls of my ears, and wet the pillow.

I felt washed up on the shore of my own emotions, beaten by the cycle of the crushing waves, waterlogged with tears, panting with a mild panic that lingered even after surviving the worst of it.

Curling up with my legs tucked to my chest like I hadn't slept since I was a girl afraid and alone in Ignacio's house, I wept silently into my knees.

I wept for Dane.

I wept for King.

I wept for the irrefutable, irrevocable fact that I loved a man who might never love me back even though he'd finally noticed me the way I'd always wanted him to.

I was so mired in my own little pity party, I hadn't noticed the door open and close, or the soft tread of heavy weight on bare feet padding to the side of my bed.

Soft, flickering golden light wavered over the bed from behind me as the mattress depressed and a hand landed onto my covered hip.

"Turn over, Flower Child," Nova said quietly into the thick silence.

I hesitated because I didn't want him to see the tears then sniffed and flipped over.

Nova had seen me cry more than anyone else ever had.

I doubted he'd be particularly perturbed by it now.

His eyes were twin dark pools in the night as he stared down at me. Light and shadow played over his face like duelling lovers, making him breathtakingly, almost impossibly beautiful, like an apparition or a god dropped from heaven just to seduce me.

I followed the light to his hands where he held a plate filled with a double stacked cheeseburger, the bun studded with lit candles.

"Can't celebrate Dane's birthday without makin' a wish for him," Nova explained in an intimate, hushed whisper that wound around me like a velvet ribbon. "Didn't think to make his favourite *tres leches* cake until too late, so I figured his favourite burger would make a decent replacement."

A wet sound spilled from my lips, half-laugh, half sob. "From Mo's Fast Food?"

Nova's smile was just a slight curl in his stubbled face. "Of course. Had the cab stop there and ducked into the gas station while they prepped it for the candles."

I touched my fingers to the plate just to make sure I wasn't dreaming. "He'd love this."

"Yeah," Nova agreed. "But I gotta confess, I did it as much for you as him. Know what it's like to walk through this day with a dagger stuffed between your ribs, aimed at your heart. Thought maybe doin' somethin' sweet like this might lessen the pain a bit."

My heart clenched so tightly I worried it would never unfurl. I choked on my breath as it solidified into something hard, immovable in my throat.

"It does," I wheezed past the obstruction.

He nodded then shifted to settle the plate between us. "You ready?"

It took me a moment to understand what he meant, but by then he'd already started.

"*Estas son las mañanitas,*
que cantaba el Rey David,
Hoy por ser día de tu santo,
te las cantamos a ti,
Despierta, Dane, despierta,
mira que ya amaneció,
Ya los pajarillos cantan,
la luna ya se metió."

Nova ran through the verses of Las Mañanitas with ease, his accent perfect because my brother had painstakingly taught him Spanish in their youth.

I didn't join in until the last lines, my voice softer than his purposefully so I could continue to enjoy his raspy lilt.

When we finished, he locked eyes with me in a way that conveyed exactly what to do next.

So I made my wish, and together, we blew out the candles.

"What did you wish for?" he asked in the sudden blackness as the flames snuffed out.

"I can't tell you, it won't come true." Then I hesitated, because I knew it was impossible for my wish to ever come to fruition. "I wished Dane wasn't really dead."

"Babe…" his big hand found my face unerringly in the darkness and pushed back into my hair over my ear to cup my cheek. "If you think I haven't wished different every time I blew out candles on his birthday, you'd be wrong."

I sucked in a shaky breath and leaned into his hand in a silent bid for comfort.

We didn't eat the burger.

Nova placed it on the bedside table, pulled back the covers as I scooted over, then he joined me in bed for the first time in two years.

But just as he had all the other times before, my insomniac fell asleep almost the second he wrapped me up in his heavy limbs, his face tucked into my hair on the pillow, his thick lashed eyes closed.

I laid awake for a lot longer, trailing my hand over the crisp hair on the forearm slung over my chest, staring blankly at the glow-in-the-dark garden he'd painted for me above our heads.

And I wondered how life could get any more complicated.

CHAPTER NINETEEN

Lila

THE MOST ROMANTIC MOMENT OF MY LIFE SO FAR?

The morning after Dane's birthday before Nova was even partially awake, he rolled over in bed, already reaching for me. He tucked me against his hard chest, buried his nose in the crook of my neck, tangled up in my hair and sighed.

He sighed like there was no place on earth so safe and warm as the meeting of our two bodies in this bed.

And then he fell back to sleep, his fragrant, sleep-hot skin heavy against my side.

I memorized everything about that moment. The tap of rain on the wide windowpane, the cool, rough texture of the linen sheets under my back, and the quality of the weak morning light filtering through the clouds like milky honey.

I remembered everything.

And nothing before that moment came close to being so profound, not even when another man got on one knee and proposed to me.

Because what Nova did that morning?

It wasn't studied or planned. It was natural, an extension of feeling he didn't have the wherewithal in sleep to stifle.

It said in ways I might never hear aloud that he loved me.

Not as much, never as much, as I loved him.

But in that moment, it was enough.

I didn't linger in bed even though the sight of his endless inked skin called to me. I wished I had the privilege to lie there and trace it all with my fingers, feel the slight ridge of black outlines, the rise of the scar from his knee surgery in high school.

But I didn't.

There was no way I was going to wait around for him to wake up and realize what he'd done in the drunken dark, lulled by nostalgia and alcohol into doing something he was certain to regret.

So I slipped out of bed, quickly showered, dressed, and got the hell out of there.

It was a Saturday, so normally, I should have been able to avoid him all day, but my phone pinged as I grabbed a tea from Honey Bear Café reminding me I had a tattoo appointment that day.

With Nova.

I bit my lip as I stared at my phone, deliberating whether to cancel, no show, or suck it up and go, preferably with backup.

"Uh-oh," a familiar, husky yet smooth female voice broke through my thoughts. "I recognize that look."

"Uh huh," a lighter, sweeter voice agreed from slightly behind and to my right. "It's that look you all get when you're in the thick of it with an alpha."

I rolled my eyes even as a smile stretched my lips. My arms already opening for a hug, I turned around to greet Loulou Garro and her little sister, Bea. The latter immediately stepped into my embrace, her cloud of pale gold hair sweet as freesia in my nose and just as silken as its petals against my cheek.

"Hey, girl," I said as I gave her a squeeze.

She stepped back to smile widely at me, her eyes huge and so dark a blue they almost looked black from afar. I grinned even bigger when I noticed her white, frilly blouse and super short pink skirt. The girl was nineteen now, but she still dressed like a girly girl in bows, pinks, and lace. It was a stunning contrast to the woman I knew was obsessed with true crime podcasts and horror films.

In comparison, her older sister, Loulou, was as womanly as they came. Her lush curves on her lean form were dramatic, the red pop of her mouth full and well-formed in a face you could've seen in a magazine. She wore a leather jacket with a white sundress and kickass combat boots, barely older than a teenager rockin' her youth, but already a mum to the two biker babies in matching Hephaestus Auto onesies.

"So are you?" Bea demanded as I moved into Loulou to press a kiss on her smooth, tanned cheek then one on each of the babies asleep in the stroller she pushed. "In the thick of it with an alpha?"

She sounded eager, which wasn't exactly a surprise.

We two girls were the hopeless ones in our Fallen biker babe squad. The ones with unrequited love like rose tinted glasses over our eyes.

Only, I loved a man I'd known and (mostly) admired my whole life. Sure, Nova was a manwhore, but he'd never hurt anyone.

Bea, on the other hand, had her girlish heart set on much darker sights.

The club enforcer.

Priest.

He was everything cutting and cruel and criminal.

Bea was everything sweet and sugar and sunshine.

They did *not* make sense, but Bea wouldn't hear it from anyone even when they teased or cajoled.

So I got her hope, but I wouldn't feed into it.

Even if Priest *was* interested in her (which I was fairly sure he was not given I thought he might have been a functioning psychopath), I wouldn't have her with him. He'd suck the light out of her just to brighten his own dark world, and I couldn't imagine what kind of reciprocity there was in that for Bea.

"No, babe," I said with a soft, sad smile. "I'm not in the thick of it."

Bea's full, bubble gum pink mouth turned down at the corners. I tugged on one of her curls then wrapped an arm around her waist to give her a squeeze in silent solidarity.

"That's not what I heard," Loulou said slyly, tossing her thick blonde mane over her shoulder. "A little biker birdie told me they saw you *kissing* a certain inked up playboy at Eugene's a few weeks ago. I tried calling you a few times about it, but I'm still waiting for you to return my call."

I bit my lip sheepishly then laughed at the smugness of the biker queen's face. "I swear to God, the club is worse than a group of old women when it comes to gossiping. Seriously, do they have to tell you everything?"

Lou grinned her sly, feminine grin that spoke to the sheer strength of her charms. She was the most beautiful woman I'd ever known, and thanks to her husband's constant affirmations and attention, she was *definitely* aware of it.

"They don't have to tell me anything…they just know I love keeping their secrets, and a happy Lou is a good Lou to have around."

I laughed, the depth of it warming my belly. I'd forgotten in my drama how good it was just to shoot the shit with my girls. With King's passing and Z getting out of jail, it had been far too long since we'd gotten together for one of our girl's nights at Eugene's or shopping sprees at Hannah's Revved & Ready biker babe boutique.

I vowed to rectify that.

"So," Bea said, jumping lightly on the balls of her Converse sneakered feet. "You're dating Nova now?!"

"No," I snapped then winced. "Sorry, no, I'm not. I just don't want there to be any rumors, okay?"

"But you did break up with Jake," Loulou surmised.

For a girl who was barely an adult, Lou'd always been wise. She was twenty-two years old, a scant two years younger than me, and she had a kickass husband, a club of loyal soldiers in leather who'd die for her, and two twin babies that were cute as hell.

I couldn't fault her for being a little smug and hella perceptive.

"He kind of broke up with me," I admitted. "After Nova conned me into kissing him in front of Jake. It was bad."

Lou laughed. "Only Nova would have the balls to do something like that then have the idiocy not to claim you as his as soon as those ties were severed. I don't know how that man sees straight with his head so far up his own ass."

"Loulou," Bea exclaimed. "Just because you married a man who swears every other word doesn't mean you have to be crude too."

Lou rolled her eyes, but I only smiled because I thought the two of them were hilarious, and I liked the attention off of me.

"You guys okay since the kiss?" Lou asked, bringing us back on track, her eyes pinning me in place so I'd answer her question.

"It's complicated." I shrugged.

Bea and Lou shared a look then they both turned to me with slow moving grins.

"Oh, babe," Lou drawled, "You are *so* in the thick of it."

My phone pinged, and immediately, Bea peeked over my shoulder as I pulled my floral case from my rattan purse to read the text.

Nova: Bad play, Li. I find out you're avoidin' me, your

ASS ISN'T IN MY CHAIR AT STREET INK AT NOON ON THE FUCKIN' NOSE, I'LL TAN YOUR ASS. YOU GET ME?

So apparently Nova wasn't hip on someone *else* doing the walk of shame in the morning before he could wake up.

I sniffed, but Bea's squeal nearly made me drop my phone.

"Oh, my God!" she said, her smile tinged with wickedness, her cheeks stained with peach. "If I wasn't half in love with someone else, I'd probably faint at how hot that text was. Phew, I could feel his intensity *through the phone*. What did you do to deserve that?"

I cracked my knuckles and struggled not to make eye contact with Lou who was staring at me in her voodoo way where I just knew she was reading my thoughts.

"Well," I admitted. "I may have fooled around with Nova last night and then left this morning before he woke up."

They both blinked at me then burst into raucous laughter that had the entire café staring at us in varying degrees of irritation. But we were biker babes, known in Entrance and revered or hated in equal turn, so they left us alone.

When Bea recovered, she wiped a tear from her cheek. "I think you're my hero."

"It's about time someone gave Nova a taste of his own medicine," Loulou said, humor rich in her voice. "And it's about time that person was *you*."

"I'm supposed to get a tattoo in...an hour," I said after checking the pink watch on Bea's pale arm. "I'm not sure how well I'll be able to keep my distance with his hands on my body."

"Do you want distance?" Lou asked, cocking her head. "Last time I checked, you wanted to wear him like a face mask."

"Lou!" Bea cried again, but even she snorted with laughter.

"I'm not going to be some notch on his bed post," I

declared, even though the idea of having Nova's strong, calloused hands on my body made my skin buzz with electric heat. "But I'm not ashamed. So we got drunk and hooked up, big whoop. We can move on from this."

When the girls didn't say anything, I pressed, "Right?"

"*Big whoop?*" Bea shook her head. "He rocked your world, huh?"

I sighed. "I think I came so hard I blacked out, and he didn't even actually lay a finger on me."

Lou nodded sagely. "Seems to be a badass biker talent. Don't worry, babe, we'll go with you to the appointment. I'll drop the babies off with my mum, we'll pick up H.R., and head over there together. He's not going to try dick with all of us there watching."

"Out."

We hadn't just picked up Harleigh Rose.

Cleo and Tayline had also been at the clubhouse, shooting the shit with Axe-Man and Cyclops, so they'd decided to tag along as well.

They weren't even all inside the glass door of Street Ink Tattoo Parlour when Nova's voice lashed out the one hard struck word.

"Out," he repeated, standing by his station to the left of the reception desk, back leaned up against the wall, booted feet and tatted arms crossed, his face set to stone. He looked dangerous, filled with criminal intent and equipped with the means to see it out.

And his eyes, even from a distance, were nothing close to their habitually warm velvet brown.

They were black as banked coals, burning me up as they touched on my face, dragged down my body, then returned to lock with my eyes.

"Nova, is that any way to treat an Old Lady?" Loulou asked sweetly as the girls fanned out in the space.

"Where is everyone?" Cleo asked, looking around the deserted shop with a frown on her sweet face. "I thought you were booked from here to eternity with clients?"

"We are," Nova agreed, pushing off the wall to slowly stalk toward us. "Had Sara reschedule everyone. Shop's closed. That means no old ladies, no hang-arounds, no *anybody* save Lila and me. So *out*."

Tay hopped up on the reception desk and swung her short legs back and forth as she stole a maple candy from the little skull dish and popped it in her mouth. "We won't get in the way. Or do you suddenly have stage fright or something?"

"Awe," Harleigh Rose crooned, "Does the great seducer have trouble preforming?"

"Guys," I warned, seeing the shift in Nova's face, noticing the animal quaking dangerously against the chains that locked him in his gut.

They ignored me.

They were women used to their Old Men, mellowed by love, plenty of orgasms, and mutual respect.

But Nova wasn't anyone's Old Man.

He had a hell of a lot of respect for the club women.

But he was not the kinda guy who brooked an argument when he wanted shit a certain way. He might have been more affable than the average biker, but he was still a hardcore badass, and taking shit shoveled at him by my women when he was already pissed would not end well.

"I'm gonna tell ya one more time," Nova said slow and rough, face darker than I'd ever seen it, his beautiful features cast in granite, his lip practically curled up in a sneer. "Get outta my shop. I got things to discuss with Lila, and I'm not havin' her hide behind you like she's done for the last two fuckin' years."

Lou studied him for a long moment, the leader of our coalition even though I was the one they were all there for. Her face softened, the badass fading into the angelic.

"You got things to say to Lila, you make sure you think before you speak," she advised. "Don't make promises you can't keep."

"Love ya, Lou," he said in a way that seemed like he didn't mean it. "But I'll fuck Lila right here, right now in front of all of you if you don't get outta my sight in the next thirty seconds. You got somethin' to say about my life choices? You wanna stick your nose in my business? Be my guest and critique my fuckin' form."

Lou blinked then turned to face us with her mouth in a little 'o'.

"We're gonna head out," she mouthed at me then whirled her finger in the air, and the girls stepped together into a little group and fled the shop.

Harleigh Rose was the last to leave, whispering with a wink, "Good luck, and use a condom," before she shut the door behind her.

Slowly, the hairs on the back of my neck standing up, my system flooded with adrenaline like prey sensing it's being stalked by a predator, I turned to face Nova again.

He stood in the middle of the shop, arms crossed in a way that made his tatted arms bulge, the muscles beneath his skin like coiled rope. There was an expression on his face, a determination to the set of his jaw and the flare of his nostrils as he breathed like a bull before the sprint, telling me I was in trouble.

Heat arrowed straight down my spine and pooled between my legs.

Because I wanted that, whatever trouble Nova wanted to dole out. I'd take his ire, his frustration, even a degree of violence if it meant he would take it out between my legs.

I had a feeling angry sex with such a man would eviscerate me for good.

"Now what?" I asked, breathless because even the feel of him in the empty store with me was too much for my nervous system, the air stripped of everything but the scent of him, rich with spice and musk and leather.

"Now..." Nova said as he prowled toward me in an aggressive swagger, the right side of his step slightly more exaggerated than the right. It shouldn't have been sexy, but it was, the movement of his broad shoulders, the flex of his muscles through the thin, worn denim of his old jeans.

My mouth went dry, my tongue glued to the roof of my mouth as he stopped in front of me. He slowly lifted a hand so we could both watch as it moved to my chest, flattened to the upper curve of my breasts above the top of my cropped Harley Davidson tank.

"Now," he practically purred, "you're gonna take off this sexy little top and spread yourself out for me in my chair. I'm gonna spend the next hour tattin' the sweet curve of your waist knowin' you're gettin' wet just from the feel of my hands on your skin and my breath bein' close to your pussy. Then, you give me a good answer for why the fuck you left me cold and alone this mornin' like some piss-off one-night stand, I'm gonna peel off those shorts and tend to you with my tongue."

There was a low, heavy pulse in between my legs, growing stronger, weightier with every rough word spoken from Nova's bruised, plum mouth. By the time he finished his tirade, I was swaying into him, unable to find my equilibrium in the force of his gravitational pull.

"I don't think," I cleared my throat because it was as

hoarse as a four pack a day smoker, "I don't think sleeping together again is a good idea."

His thick, dark brow angled high on his forehead. "Yeah? I slide my hand down these tiny denim cutoffs, you sayin' you wouldn't soak my fingers with your wet?"

"I'm saying I don't think it's the *smart* thing to do," I corrected. "I don't want things to get messy."

"Didn't seem worried about gettin' messy last night when you made a mess of your fingers comin' hard just from the sound of my voice," he teased, his mild voice a mockery, his smile so wicked the sight of it hooked into my heart and drew me closer still, even as I fought his pull. "Not that I'm complainin'. The sight of your drenched cunt, you splayed out so wanton and hot, beggin' for my dick...Not gonna lie, Li, never seen a damn thing hotter."

I snorted. "I'm sure."

Instantly, his hand lashed out to pull me close. I smashed into the hard wall of his chest and gasped with the force of it so when he spoke, it was into my open, panting mouth.

"See, this is why we gotta talk before we get to the good stuff. You thinkin' I'm gonna fuck and run is fuckin' *whacked*, Lila."

"Is it?" I hissed, anger sneaking in through the fog of lust clouding my resolve. "Says the man who told me off for wanting him when his dick was still wet with another woman's orgasm? Says the man they call Casanova for a reason? You want to make me feel stupid for expecting the worse when that's all I've ever seen from you?"

"With you?" he demanded, one hand diving into my hair to twist through the strands and pin me with my head angled back, his face looming dark and sexy as the devil above me. "You sayin' I've only ever shown *you* the worst? Or other women? Women who knew the score 'cause I laid it out for them like I'd lay it out for you if you gave me a goddamn chance to do it!"

"So lay it out," I said through gritted teeth.

Because I was tired and scared and the hope I'd nurtured for so many years, a beautiful garden in my chest, was razed and plucked free of petals by the tempest of his hot and cold regard the last few months.

I didn't know what to believe anymore.

My heart had faith, my head held doubt, and my gut was currently occupied with the fire Nova had lit the second he laid those smoldering eyes on me as I entered the shop.

He stared down at me, his eyes burning over my skin as they trailed across my features. I wanted to close my eyes, hide the vulnerability of wistfulness, lust, and love swirling through the green and brown, but I didn't. Instead, I met his gaze boldly and dared him to damn me for my passion.

He didn't.

Instead, his whole countenance gentled. The hand fisted in my hair unclenched and moved to cradle my head in his wide palm, the arm banded at my waist shifted so he could cup my hip and curve me into a hug.

I let myself be moved into the center of his embrace, heard him breathe deeply into my hair as if chasing the scent of me.

And I fought the overpowering urge to cry.

How was it possible that every time I wanted to rage at him, resolved to hate him, determined I would move on from my childhood love and find something new, he drew me back so gently, so coaxingly and inexorably into his orbit that I wondered why I had ever wanted to leave in the first place?

"You gonna stay mad while I ink that fleur-de-lis into your pretty skin?" he murmured, still clutching me close. "Or you gonna be good while I work so I can reward you after?"

A shiver rolled through me, cool and tingling as morning fog across the mountains.

He chuckled darkly into my hair before releasing me. "I'm gonna take that as a yes."

I stumbled slightly as he stepped back then tipped my chin into the air and turned my back on him, walking to his station so I could have a brief moment of privacy to find my balance.

It didn't work.

My nipples were beaded so tightly they ached. For his touch, his mouth, even his eyes on them. Greedy and desperate, my breasts were swollen and throbbing with the hard beat of my pulse.

I could feel the moisture between my thighs as I walked, clenching my teeth against the feel of the seam in my shorts rubbing on my clit as I dropped into the chair.

"Shirt off, babe," Nova reminded me, a rich vein of humor in his voice as he leaned against the half-partition and watched me stretch out in the purple chair. "Need access to all of that skin for what I have planned."

I shivered at the double entendre then bit my lip to keep from squirming under the heat of his gaze as I lifted my cropped tank up and off, revealing my black lace bra.

"Fuck yeah," he growled softly as he moved to the side of the chair and palmed the heavy ridge of his erection through his jeans. "See what you're doin' to me, Li?"

I licked my dry lips. "I'm sure you see naked women in your chair all the time."

"Yeah," he agreed easily, dropping onto his stool and rolling even closer. "None of them were you."

"You've had celebrities in this chair," I argued, staring at the ceiling so I wouldn't have to look at his face and imagine him tattooing popstars and actresses.

"Yeah," he repeated gruffly, as he snapped on his gloves and gently laid the stencil of the design we'd discussed over the left side of my waist, right in the dip before the flare. "*None of them were you.*"

I bit my lip but didn't say anything. If he wanted to flatter me, I'd let him, but I was going to be smart. Or at least, smart enough to know that I was just new, a novelty, and a forbidden one at that, and he would get tired of me just as he tired of all the rest.

It was just a matter of time.

And usually, it didn't take much of that before he moved on.

"Hey," Nova called, pausing as he traced the outline of the tattoo into my skin through the transfer paper. "I got my Flower Child layin' out for me. You're gorgeous, Lila, no doubt about it, but you also got my art inked into your skin, years of beauty you and me created together, stamped all over your tight, sweet curves. You think that doesn't do somethin' powerful to a man, you're fuckin' wrong."

My lip between my teeth, I stared down at him with hooded eyes and tested his words by arching slightly, angling a hand down my stomach to swirl in the flowers already at my hips inching toward the delicate skin near my groin.

Nova's eyes went instantly black, swallowed up with lust so strong I could see the white knuckled grip he had on his tools.

"Fuck yeah," he grunted. "All of that beauty spread out just for me."

Just for me.

And I was—I always had been—just for him.

It only took him eighteen years to notice.

"Why'd you leave this mornin'?" he demanded hoarsely, moving the trace paper back to the table, snapping off his gloves, then tossing them blindly into the bin behind him.

"What are you doing?" I asked as he wheeled to the end of the seat and grabbed my ankles so he could bend my legs back and spread them over the retractable arms of the chair.

When he didn't respond, I let him continue, curious and aroused by the animal look in his eyes, the almost drunk gleam of lust there.

"You answer me, I'm gonna put my mouth on you," he advised, kneeling onto the lower part of the seat and leaning forward so his broad shoulders were notched between my splayed legs.

Reverently, he touched the backs of his knuckles to my denim covered pussy and unerringly traced the swell of my clit.

I groaned, head thrusting back into the seat. "Nova! The door's unlocked."

"Closed sign is up," he muttered distractedly. "Now, answer the damn question so I can put my mouth on your cunt. I've been dyin' to know if you taste as sweet as you smell, like sea salt and flowers."

My legs trembled as I stared down at his dark head over my sex, his big, tattooed shoulders bare beneath the white Street Ink cut-off tee he wore. I wondered woozily if I could come just like that, his eyes on my covered cunt, his fingers pressed just right over the fabric so I'd have to grind my own way to climax.

I wanted that.

I *liked* that.

The idea of working for it.

For him.

Doing that the way I had the night before was without a doubt the hottest experience of my life. I liked pleasing him, working for him as much as for my orgasm, and the thought of doing it again had my pulse racing.

His fingers slid under the edge of my shorts and coasted over the tender skin until they reached the seam of my pussy then dipped into the silken well of wetness there.

He groaned, eyes heavily lidded as he looked up at me. "So fuckin' drenched for me, Li. Why'd you go and leave this mornin' when I was plannin' to wake up and eat you for breakfast?"

"Fuck," I gasped as he brought his damp fingers to his mouth and sucked them, closing his eyes and fucking *humming* as he ate my desire from his skin. "I—I was worried you'd think it was a mistake. We were drinking, and it was an emotional night."

"Most fun I've had in years," he stated as he watched his big hands move to my hips and undo the buttons on my shorts. Then he looked up at me as he ordered, "Legs up."

I hesitated, then raised my hips and legs so he could draw my shorts down and off.

He didn't even bother moving my underwear.

Instead, he played his thick fingers under the edge of my G-string, teasing me, and teasing himself if his throaty rumble was anything to go off of.

"Is that what this is?" I asked, trying to keep my head from spinning off my body. "Fun?"

I had never been so turned on in my life. Not with Jake, not watching Nova fuck that woman at the clubhouse. Never.

My pussy was so swollen it throbbed, and I could feel myself leaking like an overturned jar of honey through my panties and onto the leather seat.

"You're making a mess of me," I said, voice threadbare.

"Yeah," he agreed. "Don't know what this is beyond fuckin' necessary 'cause if I don't get my mouth on you, my cock in you, I think I'll fuckin' die, and that's no joke. But it's more than fun, it's more than gettin' my dick wet to feel good. It's about you and me explorin' somethin' between us that feels like fire."

"That's dangerous," I argued.

"That's *us*," he countered, snapping the strings of my thong with any easy twist of his fingers and tossing them over his shoulder.

There was a dare in his eyes as he lowered his head to my swollen, exposed pussy, and then they closed, his head tipped and his hot mouth sealed over my clit.

I bowed up as he sucked, his tongue swirling, lashing, devastating my nerves within seconds. His arms slid under my raised thighs, folded over my hips, and held me fast to his mouth.

"Hold still so I can eat my fill," he ordered, lips damp against the inside of my thigh.

"I can't," I nearly stuttered, hips quivering even though I was pinned. "Fuck, Nova, I think I'm going to come."

I was on fire with lust and embarrassment, my arm tossed over my forehead so I could close my eyes and pretend I wasn't about to orgasm after only minutes of his tongue on my pussy.

"Love how you taste," he said, nose rubbing against my clit as he spoke. "Sea salt and flowers all the way. Can't keep up, you're drippin' down your thighs so fast. You love bein' played with like this, don't you?"

I whimpered as he punctuated his words with a hard, fast suck at my throbbing clit.

"Yeah," he groaned as he lapped at my slick folds. "Fuckin' gorgeous like this. You wanna come, Li? All you gotta do is tell me how much you love my mouth on this pretty cunt."

I swallowed convulsively, cheeks heating, tummy trembling. I felt like a poorly constructed doll coming apart at the seams, unraveling so fast I couldn't keep up.

"I, Nova, please…"

"Nova, please what?" he demanded, pulling one arm back so he could twist two fingers inside me and press into that tender spot on my front wall that made me see *stars*.

"Nova, Nova," I chanted, arms shooting out so I could clutch his thick hair in my fingers and hold him tight to my crotch. "Fuck, I'm going to come."

"Not until you tell me," he ordered, the words like heavy chains binding me to his will.

"God!" I shouted as he played me higher and higher, as I watched his wet, red mouth move over me. "Nova, I love your mouth on my pussy. Please, *fuck*, make me come for you."

"Okay," he agreed easily, but his words were growled low and deep. "Come for me. Let me eat up all that honey."

My eyes screwed shut as my entire body arched into one long, taut line, a stretched bow about to *snap*. Seconds later, Nova's fingers curled into my cunt, his mouth a hot, silk brand against my clit, and I released, pleasure splitting down my center like a loosened arrow.

I bucked and writhed in the chair, but he kept me pinned as I orgasmed, eating me slower and slower, not stopping throughout the entire climax. Finally, when I was limp and gasping, completely undone, he hummed with pleasure as he licked me clean with his tongue.

"Fuckin' delicious," he praised when he was done, moving up my body to smile at me drunkenly. "Taste yourself," he offered a second before he slanted his mouth over mine and sucked on my tongue.

I absorbed the sweet and salt tang of my cum, the silken glide of Nova's tongue moving in my mouth and trembled. Not because I'd just experienced the sexiest encounter of my life, but because now I knew last night hadn't been an anomaly.

He was it.

My dream man wrapped up in a sinful package.

And he was still completely and utterly forbidden.

CHAPTER TWENTY

Lila

"Done," he announced nearly two hours later, leaning back from my waist to deposit the tattoo gun on the table and peel off his gloves.

He handed me a small mirror so I could see the fresh design just under my ribs.

An indigo fleur-de-lis surrounded by a cluster of the actual flowers stylized in Nova's stark, minimal aesthetic.

A tribute to King, who was not only biker royalty, but as pure of heart as the symbolism of the flower's original meaning.

Every time Nova tattooed me, it was as if he read the words beneath my skin and brought them to the surface. Sometimes it surprised me that he couldn't read my love for him like braille in my flesh because he was so adept at deciphering everything else.

"Gorgeous," I whispered, touching my fingers above the

raw, red-tinged tattoo, careful not to get too close to the design. "It's perfect."

"Been a while since we got some photos for Photogram and the website," Nova suggested as he stood up to stretch out his stiff muscles. I watched his tapered torso bend backward, his chest hard and defined like carved marble beneath his tee. "You up for an impromptu shoot? I'll wrap you up after."

I cracked my knuckles. "Um, do you think that's a good idea?"

Normally, I was naked, or at the very most, in provocative clothes because Nova's brand was freedom.

Free of social mores like puritanism, asceticism, and conservatism.

And I was his muse, his Flower Child.

So I embodied those too.

Nova arched a brow at me as he cleaned his station. "Just had my mouth on your pussy lickin' up your cum like the honey it is. Now you're gonna be shy?"

Flames licked up my neck and cheeks, but somehow, I affected a casual shrug. "Can you blame me? This is…this is new territory for us."

He stared at me for a second, mouth tight, eyes considering, then he moved toward me, not stopping until we were toe to toe. I was so much shorter than him, he had to duck to take my chin in his fingers and tip it up to his face.

"Is it?" he asked quietly. "Feels right in the way art feels right to me. Like I was made to do this."

My heart burned in my chest. I gritted my teeth against the intensity of the hope threatening to raze it to ash.

"Don't lie to me," I begged softly.

"Thinkin' I might've been lyin' to myself for a long fuckin' time," he argued. "Thinkin' I got a taste now for sea salt and flowers that I won't be able to kick anytime soon."

"So what, you want to keep sleeping together? Won't that ruin our friendship?"

"No," Nova confirmed, jaw clamped shut. "Won't let it."

"I don't mind ruining our friendship," I half-joked. "I want to be lovers more."

"We're friends first," Nova said in a voice that brooked no argument.

And it was good, necessary, to hear that. I needed the reminder to ground me when I would float away on this dream. Because he wanted me, it seemed, but that didn't mean he'd stay.

In the history of my life, no one ever had.

"But you want me," I ventured slowly, needing to hear him say it because even after everything that had happened, I still couldn't believe it.

Nova grinned his roguish grin. "Yeah, babe. You make me smile, and you make me horny as hell. It's a potent fuckin' cocktail."

I laughed, a little louder and longer than I should have because I was giddy with relief and joy.

"So we're doing this. This…friends with benefits thing."

"No, Li," Nova corrected. "You know how I feel about labels. Don't gotta put one on us, not when we're so many things I've never been able to find the words for. We both know life's short, we only got one day at a time, the moment we're livin' right now. I'm tellin' you, this minute and the next as far as I care to see, I want this with you." He hauled me tight against his body, my hips pinned to his with the arm banded at my back, my feet dangling off the floor so we were eye to eye. "Give me a shot. Let me make up for all the times I shoulda kissed you and didn't."

I blinked against the urge to swoon hard and nodded. "Yeah, okay."

And when he kissed me, he was smiling, and that smile lasted as I kissed him back, our teeth clicking, our laughter leaking through our joined mouths.

It might have been even better than our first kiss, and our second, because it was *us* just like he'd said this was.

Dangerous and alive and so fun it almost hurt.

Nova set me down and gave my ass a firm slap. "Now, get that sweet ass into the studio."

I'D POSED FOR NOVA A THOUSAND TIMES OVER, BUT THIS, naked except for a thong that read 'Sex & Candy', lights hot on my skin as I bent backward to showcase the tattoos spilling down my entire left side, was utterly different.

I was a bit of an exhibitionist, so I'd always enjoyed modeling for the shop, and a small part of me had even loved touching myself on camera when Irina had blackmailed me into it.

But this was infinitely better.

Because my audience of one was the only person I'd ever wanted to bend, twist, and break open for at their command.

"Arch your back," he demanded, voice frayed with lust as he dropped into a squat to capture the right angle. "Show me the lush curve of that ass."

I twisted and popped my hip so the light caught the spray of pink and purple edged peonies on my hip.

We were in the studio Nova'd built into the back of the shop, a long room filled with rows of windows on three sides and a mirror on the fourth. It was a light box, perfect for the photos he liked to take of me for Photogram, and I was learning, for himself.

"Gonna tack these up in my station," he husked out as he moved closer to run the palm of his rough, padded hand over the curve of my waist before adjusting the angle of it. "Gonna stare at them, bear the strain of my hard dick in my jeans when I do, knowin' my Flower Child gets off on her art as much as I do."

I slid one hand up from my groin, the other down from my throat and let them meet in the middle where they cupped my breasts. Then, leaning forward as if to offer them to him like overripe fruit, I bit my bottom lip and let him take another photo of me.

"I get off on the artist too," I admitted.

He pursed his full mouth, his shadowed jaw an acute angle I wanted to test with my teeth. "You know the difference, Li, between beauty and art?"

"Is there one?" I breathed as he got on his knees in front of me and angled the camera up to my face so he could capture the fullness of my breasts and the detail of the tattoos painted beneath.

He looked good there, his dark hair waving away from his forehead, his tattooed fingers strong on the big camera, body casting a huge, black shadow behind him in the bright studio lights.

"There is. A flower is beautiful as it is, transient, full of colour and life for the time it blooms, but it's simple, shallow even. A flower is just a flower. But *art*? Art is a flower painted so it won't die. A flower on the skin of a woman with depth and texture to her soul? It's the context that gives it beauty," he spoke in a voice like velvet rubbing against my sensitive skin.

He watched his own fingers reach out to run down my thigh as if mesmerized by his inability to censure himself around me.

When he looked up at me, a lock of dark hair fell into his brown eyes, brown as the earth beneath the mountains, rich as the soil I tilled in the yard for my flowers, more beautiful than any others I'd ever gazed into.

"The artist is the tool," he finished, drawing his fingers higher, splaying them out until his entire big hand spanned my whole thigh just beside my pussy. "*You* are the art."

Our gazes locked like magnets, an electric pulse rising between us so strong the hair on the backs of my arms stood on end.

In that moment, I'd never needed anyone as much as I needed him.

Against me, in me, on me.

We reached for each other at the same time. He tugged me down, and I went willingly, landing hard on his torso, legs moving around his hips so I was settled firmly on his lap. One large hand dove into my hair and pinned me so he could plunder my mouth, eating at it with his full lips and wickedly talented tongue.

But I wanted him. Wanted him in a way that moved through me like a storm.

So I grappled with him, rocking my hips to push him onto his back, pinning his hands over his head using the element of surprise to hold him there as I bit into his lower lip and started to work my way down.

His throat was hot and rough with stubble, the skin slightly raised with the whorls and scores of tattoos patterned up his neck into his hairline. I sucked and bit at his throbbing pulse just to feel it beat harder against my tongue.

"*Mi girasol*," Nova groaned as I went lower still, impatiently rucking up his tee to get to the tight tapestry of inked skin over hard, bulging muscle.

I sat back on his thighs to ogle the long expanse of his torso, how it narrowed at his waist and was completely carved as if from rock. I tested the give of his pectorals beneath my nails and flicked the silver barbell through his left nipple just to hear him hiss.

He still had the camera in one hand, and he lifted it as I went lower, snapping a photo of my lips at the ridge of his erection, mouthing him through the fabric. Another *click* as I lowered the zipper with my teeth, and another *click* when I pulled his thick cock into my hand and tested its weight.

"So big," I whispered as wet pooled between my legs. "I wonder if I can get it all in my mouth."

I'd thought of that over the years. Having Nova in my mouth, rocking his world with my tongue, lips, and teeth. I wanted to feel his big, beastly body tremble beneath me.

I wanted to see his resolve, the same resolve that kept him from noticing me as a woman all these years, crumble into dust at our feet.

I wanted to remind him in a way he would never forget that I was a woman now, and I could please him better than anyone else ever could.

So I licked at his leaking crown as I looked up into his heavily lidded eyes, and I asked in a sweet voice, "What do you think, Nova? Do you think I can take this big thing?"

His eyes flashed as he watched me trace the ridge of his head with the tip of my tongue. "You don't try, you'll never know."

I grinned wickedly then opened my lips and braced, sliding his hot length over my tongue straight to the back of my mouth. When he hit my soft palate, I fought the urge to gag and swallowed hard around him.

"Fuckin' Christ, Lila," he rumbled, thighs taut, hips lifted to ease his dick even farther along my throat. "Fuck *yeah*."

Hearing the *click* of the camera shutter again, I moaned around him at the thought of how hot I must look, mouth stuffed with his big dick, hands braced over the ropey muscles arrowing into his sex.

"I'll want a copy of those," I pulled off to say, twisting my hand over his length as I did.

Nova didn't answer because his teeth were sunk into his lower lip, and his head was tilted back on a low, long groan.

"Fuck, you know how to jack me," he praised.

"I want to see you come like this." I gave his head a hard, long suck to punctuate my point, but before I could take him deep again, he was knifing up, pulling me by my armpits up his torso, then flipping us over so he was on top.

His face was savage with desire, dark brows slashing, mouth a wet, red line as he stared into my eyes. "Comin' inside you. Need to feel that sweet, tight heat around my dick."

I shivered as one hand went up into my hair to fist it tight, the sting a pleasant pain, while the other unerringly found the wet well of my pussy beneath my thong. With a quick flick of his fingers, the strings snapped, he peeled the fabric off my sticky sex, and tossed them to the side. He played his thick fingers at my entrance, dipping one then two then three just inside me until I writhed and begged for him almost incoherently.

His dark chuckle wrapped around my throat like a collar. "Look at how wet you are for me. Fuck, I could just play with you like this for hours, slowly stretchin' this tight pussy open for my cock." He paused, eyes burning as he looked up from his fingers inside me to lock with mine. "Never thought I'd see you like this. Now, I have, gotta say, Li, never seen anyone so goddamn stunnin' as you."

"Nova," I protested, feeling the blush in my cheeks even if it couldn't be seen.

I didn't trust his compliments, but then, I'd never trusted anyone's. I'd been taught too well that flattery was a well-heeled tool of manipulation. That beauty was a construct, and I didn't fit well within the frame of it.

His eyes flashed a moment before the hand in my hair

traveled down to my throat, and his fingers wrapped firmly around my neck. He stared at the sight of his hand there, Adam's apple bobbing hard in his throat, then he looked me in the eye to remind me, "You're the art, but I'm the artist. Listen to me when I say you're a goddamn beauty. Hear me when I tell you I've never seen a sight hotter than this, you leakin' to the floor and writhin' so eager for my cock."

A slow, menacing grin transformed his beautiful face into something sinister, so sexy I gasped. "You don't wanna hear it, I'll make ya feel it."

He palmed my entire sex in his big hand, smearing the wet onto his palm so he could then smooth it over his cock, lubing it with my arousal. I watched him polish the head with my moisture and groaned as he fisted the based to tease the tip at my entrance.

"Cock's never been harder in my fuckin' life," he rasped as he watched his cock in his hand slide slowly, achingly into the drenched clasp of my pussy. "Fuck me, like this tight cunt was made for me."

And then he slid home, stretching me open wide and deep so the entire weighted hilt of him was buried inside me.

My head jerked back on a low moan, and my hands scrambled over his shoulders for purchase, needing something to ground myself through the electric storm whipping through my body.

Nova collapsed his weight to an elbow beside my head, tangled the ends of his fingers in my hair, and tugged sharply so I focused my dazed gaze on him.

He looked feral, wholly savage in the bright light of the studio, a spotlight on his primal intensity.

"This," he grunted as he dragged the heavy ridge of his cock to the entrance of my pussy then thrust home in a way that made us both groan and shudder. "This is what we should have been doin' for years. *This* is fuckin' beauty."

"Nova," I called out, needing to say his name, needing it

to anchor me to the moment so I would never forget even a second of the pleasure spiraling through me.

The pleasure of having this big, breathtaking man in my arms, inside my body, in a way I'd never thought in my wildest dreams might really happen.

I clutched at him as a low whine built in my throat. I was already so close to coming, just from the rough, short hair at his groin dragging over my swollen clit, the way his thick cock beat at the tender place inside me that made me forget to breath.

"You're takin' my cock so well," he praised darkly, wrapping his arms around my shoulders to thrust me down on his cock, the tip of it kissing the entrance to my womb in a twin punch of pain and pleasure. "Fuck, takin' all of me in that little pussy."

I tried to tip my head down to look at our connection, wanting to see the width of him sink inside me, to watch our joining like I'd seen so many times in my fantasies.

Before I got the chance, Nova pulled out abruptly and used his large hands to flip me over onto my hands and knees.

I faced the wall of mirrors, staring at my reflection as Nova loomed behind me on his knees. We locked eyes in the mirror, his so dark, so polished with lust they gleamed like chips of obsidian.

"Watch me fuck you," he demanded as he smoothed a hand down my spine, pushing my torso lower so my ass arched high. "Watch how goddamn gorgeous you are takin' my cock."

And then he was pushing inside me again, stealing my breath as he sealed our bodies together. I closed my eyes as sensation exploded through every single atom of my body. I felt like I might die from the overwhelming pleasure, burst into particles and spiral into space.

A sharp *smack* landed on my ass, and then Nova was leaning over me, twining his hand in the long expanse of my hair to use it as reins, holding my head up, urging me back against his ravaging thrusts.

"Watch us," he demanded in a voice abraded with desire. "Watch me fuck you, Li. I want you lookin' at us as I make you come."

So I watched.

I saw the way his beautiful face collapsed into a fierce scowl, dark brows slashing over his eyes as he stared at the way my ass jiggled with each thrust.

I saw the way his inked hand wrapped around my hair, pinning me, *using* me in a way that should have been degrading, but instead, was so hot I felt the smolder of flames burn higher.

I saw my full tits bouncing beneath me, nipples beaded like jewels, and when Nova used his free hand to reach around to pinch my clit, I saw how hard he made me come.

Head thrown back, legs shaking, cunt clenching so hard it almost hurt, I split apart for him. It moved through me physically, but also, almost spiritually, a cleansing, a baptism I'd been waiting for my whole life. This was my god, my church, my religion all wrapped up in one man, and he had complete power over me, my body, and my heart. The wet splash of my cum anointing his cock was loud in the empty, echoing room, punctuated only by my cries for *more, yes, Nova*, fuck *me*.

"That's right, gorgeous, come all over my dick," Nova coaxed roughly as he continued to fuck me through my climax, grunts punctuating every one of his thrusts.

I loved the sound of him, the sight of him coming undone. It made my climax cling to my bones, rattling me, pulsing in my pussy for so long, I thought I might die.

And then he came, punching into me on a series of short, smooth strokes, holding my hips steady so he could drive home. He pulled out just before he released and jacked off violently, his crown a viscous, purple red, the same colour as his mouth held tight in a grimace. I watched intently as cum welled at his tip then rushed over me, spilling and scalding against the skin of my ass.

He watched himself mark me with the look of a satisfied hunter, squeezing every last drop from his fat head until he was utterly spent, and I was covered in him. I waved my ass in the air just to hear him growl at the sight. He startled me when a large hand descended on my butt, and he started to rub his cum into my skin, his gaze so hot on the sight I shuddered, an orgasmic aftershock zipping through me like a current.

"Wear my cum almost as pretty as you wear my art," he murmured as if in a trance. "And don't worry about the lack of a condom, yeah? I get tested every six months and haven't had a woman since the last time, two months ago."

I didn't let myself think too hard about that. About the fact that he hadn't fucked another woman since he kissed me in Eugene's. If I had, I knew my heart would translate the act into some admission of love even though my head knew it was a lie.

Finished with his ministrations, he leaned down to press a surprisingly tender kiss to the dimples on my lower back just above my ass. "Thinkin' you need some ink here so I can see it, feel it, when I hold you down to take my cock again."

Again.

That simple word accompanied by the tender way he stroked over my skin, the way an equestrian might do after riding his horse, stirred me. It wasn't romantic in a traditional way, but nothing about Nova, about the two of us, was.

It was enough to feel the phantom length of him inside my swollen sex, to have his hands on my body gentling me after a rough fuck, to see the way he watched his hands on my skin as if he was drawing his art on me with just his fingertips.

He might not love me the way I loved him, but having him like this was enough.

It would have to be.

CHAPTER TWENTY-ONE

Lila

NOVA WAS GONE THE NEXT MORNING WHEN I WOKE UP, AND I tried not to jump to conclusions when I opened my eyes to see the empty pillow to my right. After the tattoo session yesterday, we'd dressed and continue our day the way we might have two years before when we were still best friends who spent most of our time together. We took a ride up the Sea to Sky Highway, hollering with joy as we took the winding ribbon of road on low corners and bright bursts of speed. He didn't complain when I insisted we stop at Rainbow Falls so we could try to catch a glimpse of the famous prisms of light bursting through the spray of water plummeting from the cliffs. He had even slung an arm over my shoulder, tucking me into his side as he'd done when I was a girl, as he explained that the Greek Goddess, Iris, the messenger of the Olympians, had used rainbows to travel from the sky down to earth. After that, we'd gone back down the mountain and set up shop at Eugene's, drinking some beers, splitting one of their famous burgers, and generally enjoying each other's company before we'd headed back to Nova's place to crash.

And I'd done it in his bed, carried there the moment we

made it through the door and Nova lifted me into his arms so he could practice the art of making out and walking at the same time.

I was sore because he had a thick cock, and he knew how to work it, so I was a swollen, aching mess around him, but I bore that ache with pride and exultation as he took me again and again throughout the night. I loved that he reached for me, that he couldn't seem to get enough of me even after the third time that night when he'd collapsed beside me in a sweaty tangle of inked up limbs, admitting regretfully that he was tapped out. We'd laughed, because he always made me laugh, and that was only part of his magic.

Then we'd slept, Nova wrapped around me as if I was his teddy bear.

So waking up the next morning in an empty bed felt like a betrayal of the progress we'd made, of the perfect day we'd spent that I'd already tucked away like a secret love note into the deepest folds of my heart.

I was glad a moment later when I checked my phone to see three texts from him.

NOVA: CLUB EMERGENCY. BAT'S GONNA TAKE YOU TO WORK, BUT I'LL BE THERE TO PICK YOU UP.
NOVA: PROBABLY WOKE UP HORNY AFTER HAVIN' SWEET ASS DREAMS OF ME, BUT DON'T TOUCH THAT CUNT, LILA, SHE'S MINE.

I smiled so wide it bruised my cheeks as I typed a response.

LILA: I WOKE UP DRY AS THE SAHARA IF YOU MUST KNOW.

He responded twenty minutes later when I was just stepping out of the shower.

Nova: Rose are red
Violets are blue
Don't pretend you aren't wet
Every time I'm around you

I laughed so hard I had to double over to catch my breath, and then I took another moment to wonder if it was possible for my body to withstand this level of happiness for long. Like an overwatered plant, I'd worried I'd die from the excess.

Working quickly because I had to get ready, and I wasn't a low maintenance girl, I dropped the towel, posed in the mirror and snapped a shot of my still glistening body. I attached the photo to the text and wrote:

Lila: Then don't pretend you didn't wake up hard having slept beside this all night.
Nova: Oh, babe, don't think I'm not hard right fuckin' now lookin' at all that's you. Ridin' a Harley with a hard-on is fuckin' uncomfortable, so I'm gonna go think about grandmas knittin' sweaters or some shit before we ride out again. Stay safe, and I'll see ya tonight.
Lila: xoxo

I stared at the hugs and kisses for a long minute after a sent it, regretting my enthusiasm a bit. It was easy to forget myself with Nova, to act as naturally as I usually did.

But everything had changed with the addition of sex to our friendship, and I was already at a distinct power disadvantage.

He was older, significantly more experienced, and the sexiest man in Entrance, if not the entire country.

And he knew I'd once had a crush on him. So I had to be careful.

I was just grateful he didn't know I'd been unconquerably in love with him since I was thirteen.

I needed every advantage I could get in this wicked game we were playing, so I wasn't surprised when I opened the door for Bat, and his eyes went wide with awe.

"Wow, Li, you got a hot breakfast date or somethin'?"

I grinned at him, striking a pose with my hand on my hip and my leg extended in my suede boots. I was rocking a patterned dress with a slit that opened in the front running from mid-thigh to my feet, and what little fabric there was for the top just barely clung to the full rise of my breasts from a strap tied behind my neck. My hair was in messy waves with little braids done up here and there, woven with sprigs of daisies I'd plucked from the little, overrun garden behind Nova's shop.

"Nova's Flower Child, huh?" Bat said after taking another look at me, his eyes shrewd and mouth pressed into a line. "You're bein' careful, yeah?"

"Yeah, Bat," I said with a grin, because I was being as careful as I could be given I'd willing signed up for eventual heartbreak. "Sweet of you to care, though."

"Always," he pledged in that way the brothers had of casually offering their loyalty to their loved ones like it was only natural.

It wasn't natural.

It was sublime.

That was the magic of bikers. They were rough-hewn men, ruled by chaos, and claimed by the road, but for the right people, *their* people, they would lay down their lives with a smile if it meant their loved ones wouldn't suffer.

There was so much power in love like that that, it was no wonder I'd always wanted it for myself.

A bone deep love with its own gravitational pull like Harleigh Rose had with Lion Danner, Cress'd had with King, and Loulou had with Zeus.

My smile suddenly felt wooden on my face, but luckily Bat was already turning to walk down the wrought iron stairs leading to the street where his black and chrome bike was parked.

I almost ran smack into him when he stopped abruptly beside the bike and faced me, his handsome, stern face conflicted.

"Please, don't feel like you have to give me a lecture on Nova," I hastened to say. "I know he's called Casanova for a reason, okay? I'm not totally naïve."

His smile was twisted and sharp like heat warped metal. "Not gonna say shit about it. You do you, girl. God knows I don't have any right to judge. No...what I wanted to say is about your brother, Dane."

Immediately, my heart arrested, caught in the amber trap of his words. "What?" I breathed.

He grimaced and ran a hand through his ink black hair. "I know it was a while back you asked me, but I did end up reachin' out to my buddy at the National Research Council about Dane. He told me they were already actively investigatin' his death."

"What? How can that be after so many years?" My heart was hammering against my ribs, threatening to crack through and fall to the ground like a flailing fish.

"Well, it's unusual, but apparently, they gotta tip that he and a few of the members from his unit who went missin' might be tied up in a sex traffickin' ring they've linked to some ports in Canada."

I blinked at Bat as he split into two then three different people. He reached out to steady me as I wobbled. "Are you saying they suspect Dane is some kind of...villain now? That he didn't die eleven years ago, he just...joined some fucked up terrorist cell?"

Bat sighed heavily and took a firmer grip on my arm to draw me close, hands to my shoulders, knees bent to look me in the eye. Vaguely, I noted how strikingly handsome he was, all that black hair, rich obsidian tattoos, and milky, unblemished skin. He had black eyes so dark I couldn't discern the pupil from the iris.

"I didn't know if I should tell you, but I asked Diogo, and he seemed to think you'd wanna know."

"Yeah," I agreed. "Though, I bet he would have preferred to do it himself."

His lips twitched. "Yeah, but he doesn't have the answers to any questions you might ask. Nothin's concrete, and I don't got much else in the way of info, but I wanted to let you know 'cause he's your brother. Even if he's doin' some fucked up shit, we don't know why. What we do know, what you should focus on, is that he might be *alive*."

I nodded mutely, struck dumb by the development.

Dane could be alive?

Alive and staying away by choice?

Alive and a criminal?

Alive and *alone*.

I had to tell Nova.

He'd know what to make of it all.

"Nova's busy with the club right now," Bat said in that way he had of reading a person's mind. "But you can tell him when he comes to pick up tonight. You wanna skip work, though? Loulou and H.R. are on standby, you need them."

Warmth flooded through my cold veins at the reminder that I had so many people in my life who were willing and happy to have my back.

I rolled up to my toes to press a kiss to Bat's rough stubbled cheek. "Thanks, Bat."

A flush stained his high cheekbones. "Anything for you, you know that."

"You just want free babysitting again," I teased, and my heart was even sort of in it.

He guffawed. "Actually, finally bit the bullet and hired a fuckin' *nanny*. Thinkin' my Old Lady could use a break from the kids."

I sucked in a huge breath and let it out slowly, feeling unbalanced for what felt like the hundredth time in a handful of days.

I'd gotten complacent.

I should have remembered, as Ignacio had taught me so long ago, that things never stayed good long for the Davalos family.

And even though I had another family now, *two*, the Booths and The Fallen, that didn't mean I was truly one of them.

At least, not enough to outrun my blood family's bad luck.

CHAPTER TWENTY-TWO

Lila

Irina was restless.

She was usually a reckless, spontaneous woman who followed her whims even when they were ill-advised, so there was a normal, above-average restless cast to her energy every day.

But today was different.

She'd blown onto set in a tempest of negativity, casting the entire shoot of Baby Makers 2 with the pall of her terrible mood. It was getting late, and I hadn't eaten lunch because Irina had sent me on an errand to get pink fur lined handcuffs when our set had broken. Nova would be there soon, waiting outside for me, and I wouldn't be able to text him that I was running behind because Irina didn't allow us to have phones on set. What should have been a three hours shoot was taking five hours because of her continuously outrageous demands. One of the girls, a sweet young woman by the name of Talia, actually broke down crying while she was giving head just because Irina berated her on the depth of her blow job until the poor girl gagged and sobbed.

It was ugly.

Despicable.

It made my stomach cramp, and the bottle of antacids I kept in my purse for this purpose was now empty because there'd been so many occasions to take them.

Lysander had growled and bristled behind me where he nearly always stood sentry, looking out for me, but also the girls.

He didn't take the time to explain it to me, and I hadn't asked, because frankly, I had enough on my own plate as it was, but somehow, Sander had ended up in the inner circle of the Ventura family.

Irina trusted her *bruto*, and thus, he was the only male in charge of her 'girls', the fifteen or so (depending on the week, and there was some, if not as much as I'd thought, turnover) Irina kept in her stable.

Stable.

Yes, apparently, that was the term for the set-up, a group of women prostituted by a pimp, or in this case, a vicious, woman-hating wife of a cartel boss.

It brought me little to no comfort, though, it was something, that Lysander seemed to genuinely care about the women. He was always putting out some emotional fire, trying to coax them away from further bad life choices like the drug addiction that ran rampant through the operation.

He had a soft spot for Honey.

I wasn't sure if it was the connection to the club they shared or the fact that they'd both been relatively abandoned by it, but there was trust there, thick and tangible as a chain linked between their waists.

So when Honey moved in to do the next take and Irina accused her of being lacklustre, the room filled with static from behind me.

Honey herself didn't seem to care about Irina's censure. Her pretty eyes were dead as fallow earth as she paused, taking off her clothes to join the couple already fornicating on the bed.

"Did you hear me, bitch?" Irina snapped as her phone buzzed with an incoming text.

I watched as something came over Irina's stunning face when she stared down at the screen, something I hadn't seen in the long weeks I'd been working for her.

Fear.

The dark, slick glimmer of it like gasoline spilled inside the dark rims of her eyes.

Knowing there was something that scared Irina, who herself was the scariest person I knew (and I was a biker babe, I knew lots of scary), I was afraid too.

I was so focused on that, at first, I didn't notice Irina get up and stalk across the room. I didn't know what the sharp *crack* of sound meant.

Irina had backhanded Honey across the face, sending her careening to the ground.

Instantly, Lysander was there, gently cradling her small form and carting it into his arms. Honey turned her cheek into his chest and held on, the other a brilliant red from Irina's hand.

"Put the *puta* down, *bruto*," she demanded of Sander.

He did not move an inch. There was a battle cry in his eyes, and I knew it was only a matter of time before it moved to his tongue.

"She's useless now," I said, standing up from my chair with my clipboard in hand, Bluetooth in my ear, in full assistant mode. "We won't be able to cover up the bruise forming in editing."

"Are you volunteering to take her place?" Irina asked me, her voice saccharine.

I swallowed quickly, but bile lingered on the back of my tongue. "I don't look young enough for this scene. Why don't we take a break, and I'll go make some calls, see who I can round up real quick?"

Irina glared at me for a long, eerily intense moment, her eyes racking over me head to toe. She moved to me on the clack of her high heels and stopped when our breasts brushed, so close I could smell the *Bubbaloo Plantano* banana gum she had imported on her breath.

"*Mia hermosa,*" she whispered as she cupped my face. "Such a pretty face you have. I wonder, sometimes, what it might look like reddened by my hand."

"Have I displeased you, Irina?" I asked calmly, even though my heart was hammering so hard in my throat I thought I would choke.

"You?" she asked, surprised. "No, but we all know about the sins of the father, hmm?"

I frowned at her. I was under the distinct impression she had hired me *because* of my connection to Ignacio. A chill swept through me.

"I don't speak to Ignacio anymore," I told her something she already knew.

"Pity. He hid something from me for a very long time ago. I would like it back," she mused as she continued to stroke my cheek. "But I was not referring to Ignacio."

Before I could digest her words, she turned on her heel and eased back into her director's chair, gesturing with a limp hand to the set. "I like this idea. You replace the girl. The contrast between Mary's pale, Irish complexion and your Hispanic looks will be very pleasing."

I was frozen, my body held in the paralysis of my mind as thoughts rocked through me.

This was the worst possible outcome of working for Irina.

Being forced to do as the girls did and get naked, take dick, preform on camera.

For a moment, I was faced with the question I hadn't been willing to ask when I decided to help the club this way.

Was I really willing to trade my body in a bid for their safety?

But then it occurred to me, Irina hadn't divulged any of her criminal tricks or tried to hook me on drugs so that I would stay docile and obedient.

She was betting on the threat of her reputation or her husband's to get me on my knees before her.

I wanted to slam my clipboard across her face, but instead, I laughed a little, just lightly. "I'm not a porn star, *el jefa*," I said, calling her boss. "And I have no plans to start now."

Irina's perfectly manicured eyebrows arched delicately. "*Perdóneme?*"

"I have no plans to start now," I repeated placidly. "What I will do is go to the office and make some calls. If that isn't okay with you then fire me. I hope you don't because I love my job, but even loving it, I won't fuck anyone unless *I* say so."

The air in the studio went flat like stale pop as everyone held their breath.

No one talked to Irina like that.

Not a soul.

She was treated as a cruel goddess, some heathen archetype of beauty and pain that everyone worshipped in fear instead of love.

The odds were good that she would assault me. Or fire me, at the very least.

But I would rather take the back of her hand to my face than take off my clothes because I was weak enough to be coerced.

She stared at me for so long, eyes on mine, that I lost focus, and she blurred like a watercolour painting. It was impossible to read her anyway, so I just concentrated on not throwing up at the idea of what punishment she might dole out.

"Fine, I expect a replacement tomorrow to finish off the scenes," she said finally, on an exhausted sigh as if I had thrown a tantrum. "But, Lila? *Agua que no has de beber, déjala corer*, hmm?"

If you are not going to drink the water, let it flow.

I recognized the saying from Ignacio who was a fan of offering such advice to his lackeys when they got cold feet if the cops started sniffing around.

Don't get involved with something you don't have the stomach for.

In a way, she was right. I had no stomach for the exploitation of youth and women. I had no ability to digest the awful ways Irina conducted her *legal* business, so I knew I would not be able to fathom the depths of her illegal practices.

But wasn't that the point?

Irina was the most villainous woman I'd ever met. Knowing that, knowing her and all the horrific things she did, wasn't it obvious I should get involved because I could? And if I could, perhaps I could end her and her tyranny?

The answer was yes.

One thousand times *yes*.

And this standoff only solidified my righteousness.

So, when Irina blinked her sloe eyes at me then turned back to the set to bark at the actor for losing his erection, I was quick to gather my things and head to the office.

Lysander followed behind me, still carrying Honey.

"Thanks," he grunted before I could disappear into Irina's office.

I looked over my shoulder at him, at the lines beside his eyes and the brackets carved deeply around his unsmiling mouth.

He was a hard man who had lived a hard life, but he still had an inner softness.

And wasn't that what differentiated a monster from a man?

Irina had none of that softness.

I nodded my head at him and smiled gently, feeling a

tenderness for him born of camaraderie against an evil bigger than his sins of the past.

"Take care of her. If you need help, just text me, okay?"

His smile was limited to his mouth, his eyes a flat, hopeless brown. "Tried to get her to quit the drugs 'bout fifty times now."

"I can hear you, you know?" she said drily from the shelter of his arms, peaking through her hair to glare at me. "I'm fine. It's not the first time I've been hit."

Sander growled low in his chest, and I winced.

I only hesitated for a moment before I got closer, gently pushing back the sweaty locks of Honey's beautiful strawberry blonde hair.

"I know what it's like to grow up in a burning building and assume the whole word is alive with flames outside. It makes it so easy to choose the horror you know over the horror you don't. But I'm telling you, Honey, you take one step out of this door, there will be an army of men in leather with their women at their sides ready to shelter you from the burn."

Her eyes filled with tears, and the full set of her mouth trembled before she could purse them flat. When she spoke, her voice was threadbare, the sentiment so worn in her head I'd wondered how many times she'd tread over it before now. "They didn't want me then, they won't want me now."

My chest ached as my ribs shifted to make room for the sheer mass of empathy I felt take root in my heart. I cupped her cheek and leaned close to whisper, as if Lysander wasn't even there.

And in a way, he wasn't.

This was sacredness between women, a safe place for a girl who had been abused in one way or another her whole life.

"I promise you, they won't. The Garros have had a rough go, too, and they're the last people to turn their backs on someone in need. If you let them, they'll help. If you let Sander, you and I both know he'll be there too. If you let me,

I won't abandon you," I swore with a solemnity that made the hall a tomb, my dress a cassock.

Her tears fell then, prettier than I'd ever seen, rolling like crystal down her cheeks to collect in the divots of her sharp collarbones. Lysander adjusted her until she was cozied up to his massive chest even tighter, curling around her like a human shield.

"Got this," he murmured when she turned her head into his pectoral and wept softly. "You focus on what you gotta do for the club."

I nodded at him, gave his concrete forearm a brief squeeze, and ducked into the office.

It had been months of no leads even after being swallowed into the belly of the beast as I was. I'd spoken to Zeus about it, and there was no way Venturas were that clean. He'd explained that there was always a trail, and that Lion Danner, who now ran his own private investigations service, was working that trail from the outside.

I needed to start working harder from the inside.

So I sat down in the tall, white leather desk chair before Irina's computer and painstakingly went through every folder on her desktop, opening every icon, searching through her deleted history, and still nothing.

I tore my fingers through my hair and catalogued everything I knew about Wet Works.

It was, according to speculation from the club, the main front for the Ventura's sex trafficking trade. So where did they keep the girls? Curtains had run a check on every employee associated with the company. All of them had a well traced past, were relatively local, and when approached, stated they were happy (or bound by addiction) to work for the company.

So where were the girls?

And how did they sell them?

Something about that last question triggered an errant thought, a here and gone flash that was forgotten in an instant. Only the urge to check the Wet Works Porn site remained.

I clicked through to the homepage and scoured every single icon and hyperlink.

My eyes blurred in the harsh blue light of the screen, but I refused to give up until something yielded itself.

Ignacio used to say *"El flojo y el mezquino, recorren dos veces el mismo camino,"* which essentially meant the lazy have to do the work twice.

I stayed vigilant, clicking and clacking on the keys, working fast but steady because I knew Irina wouldn't wrap up filming until she had enough footage to salvage the loss of one of her girls.

Finally, in the span of a blink, I clicked on something that triggered the website to go black.

For a moment, I thought she'd caught me. That Irina and her massive bodyguard, Arturo, would burst into the room with guns held high and plant a bullet in my brain where I sat.

No one entered.

A moment later, my hands frozen in a hover over the keyboard, the screen blinked, and a login box popped up, prompting me for a username and password under a simple heading titled 'The Game'. I read the small script below that described 'The Game' as the elite corner of Wet Works Porn, a private club, members only.

The subscription was ten thousand dollars.

A month.

The usual monthly fee for a premium account on Wet Works was thirty dollars.

I gaped at the screen, my skin buzzing, eyes dry as hell, but I didn't blink, worried the image would somehow fade. Keeping my gaze to the screen, I reached into my bag, produced my phone, turned it on without looking, and finally, took a shot of the screen.

LILA: FOUND SOMETHING.

I sent the image and text off to Curtains, Lion, Nova, and Zeus along with the text.

An instant later, my phone buzzed with three responses.

ZEUS: MOTHERFUCKERS. LI, YOU GET OUTTA THERE AND COME TO THE CLUB. WE DEBRIEF AND THEN YOU. ARE. DONE. WITH IRINA VENTURA. YOU HEAR ME?

CURTAINS: ATTA FUCKIN' BABE! NOW COPY THE URL, SEND IT TO ME, AND SEARCH THE USER FOLDER ON HER DESKTOP AGAIN SPECIFICALLY FOR 'THE GAME'. UNLESS SHE'S ENCRYPTED IT, THERE SHOULD BE ANALYTICS STORED THERE.

NOVA: I'M OUTSIDE. YOU DON'T GET YOUR ASS OUT HERE IN TEN MINUTES, I'M COMIN' IN. I MEAN IT, LILA, GET THE FUCK OUTTA THERE.

Evidently, whatever 'The Game' meant, it was *not* good.

I had just done my homework for Curtains, deleted the browser history, and was closing the window when voices sounded outside the door.

"Fuck," I cursed a moment before the door opened, and I dropped to my knees to squeeze beneath the desk.

I probably could have passed off being on Irina's computer somehow, but panicked instinct kicked in and I chose hiding over lies.

It ended up being the best decision I could have made.

At first, I couldn't hear anything over the roar of my pulse and the rush of adrenaline flooding through my system.

And then I did, and I wished I hadn't.

They were speaking in Spanish, which confused me at first because I was too terrified to switch my thoughts over from English.

"Javier, you need to be smart here," someone was saying in a rich, almost rhythmic voice that made my skin break out in goosebumps. "If this ship goes down, you lose your entire fleet. Don't let Irina be the end of you."

"Please, you know I would never let such a thing as my wife get in the way of success," Javier replied with disgust, as if the idea of loving his partner was repugnant. "She has assured me this shipment will more than make up for her past…discrepancies."

There was a pregnant pause and then, "I hope that's the case. My boss is not a man who accepts mistakes. He made allowances for Irina before because I vouched for you given our history, but he nor I will do so again."

"Yes, of course," Javier allowed. "Nor will I. If Irina fails, she knows she is as good as dead."

That could've explained Irina's palpable fear today, but otherwise, I was completely lost to the conversation between the two men. Only, the voice of the first struck a chord with me that reverberated through my bones and made my blood sing.

I could have sworn I knew that voice, or one very similar to it before.

Footsteps padded closer over the carpet, and I held my breath as a pair of dirty combat boots, the utilitarian kind, not the cute, fashionable ones, appeared in my line of sight.

"Should you be here though, Shaytan?" Javier asked silkily, a threat woven into the rich fabric of his voice. "It is dangerous for you and yours to be on Canadian soil. I am surprised you did not want to stay on the boat."

"I fear nothing," the man called Shaytan said as his booted feet moved even closer to me.

I swallowed the rise of bile in my throat as he hesitated before the desk chair then took a seat.

He was a large man dressed all in black, from his military fatigues to the compression shirt on his clearly defined torso. I shrank farther beneath the desk, focused on being as small as possible.

So I didn't notice at first the ink on the back of his dark-skinned hand.

An iris.

The same flower I had tattooed on my inner wrist.

The tattoo Dane and I had Nova inked into our skin as a reminder of Mama, of Ellie, because irises were once placed on the graves of women who needed aid getting to heaven.

I blinked, my heart stopped up in my chest, my breath a forgotten thing like lint caught in the filter of my lungs.

The tattoo remained, small, but profoundly detailed, the purple and yellows still vivid even on the dark skin, even on the back of a hand that always saw the sun.

I tuned back into the conversation in time to hear Javier say, "Irina plans to have the girls in by the end of the month. I will ensure her delivery this time, but the next, she is on her own."

"And you know what that means?" the man with the iris tattoo asked in that soothing, lyrical voice.

A voice I recognized.

A voice I'd known as my first memory before I knew anything else.

A sob bubbled up in my throat that threatened to choke me. I swallowed it down, once, twice, and expelled a small blip of sound from my mouth as I struggled to do so.

But it was enough.

The man in the chair froze, tension in every inch of his massive form, then slowly, he rolled the chair closer to the desk.

I held my breath as he reached behind his back and produced a small gun, adjusting it in his hand so he could lean closer to the table and level it unerringly at my face.

Then he continued speaking to Javier. "Your wife will be dead. Does this bring you no sadness?"

Javier sighed dramatically. "She has been a poor wife since we came up here. Canada has corrupted her. She runs too wild and does not spend enough time on her business. Anyway, there are many lovely women in this town I may choose from. As a powerful businessman and the town mayor, I have my pick of the lot."

"Mmm," the man with the gun to my head said with faux interest. "And do you have your eye on anyone in particular?"

Javier's voice was thick with lust as he chuckled. "Yes, yes, there is someone I have in mind. Perhaps she can be trained to do more than give excellent head."

I squeezed my eyes shut and wished I was anywhere but there listening to two men speak about women as if they were items in a grocery store.

Especially when I suspected one of them might be my long-lost fucking brother.

The gun trained on my head pressed closer, the cold rim of it kissing my forehead.

"Good luck with that. Now, if that's all, I'll wait while you collect the list, and then I'll be out of your way."

Javier agreed, his footsteps moving away as he left the room.

The second the *snick* of the door closed, I was yanked up by a hand in my hair and dragged out from under the desk.

I blinked the tears from my eyes into the sudden brightness from the overhead lights and tried to focus on the man above me.

The fluorescents cast a harsh yellow halo around his head, casting the short pelt of his rough black hair into inky shadow, and his features, always so strong, so proudly carved, into stark, almost menacing relief.

But even the shadows couldn't hide the brilliant, oceanic blue of his eyes.

A sob blossomed like a thorny rose in my throat, abrading the tender insides as it rose and fell out of my mouth with a wet, ragged plop.

"Dane," I whispered through my sudden, cascading tears as I drowned in his unfeeling blue eyes. "Dane, oh, my God."

He blinked at me, those curly eyelashes still as arresting as the day I last saw them. Abruptly, he let go of my hair and fell into a crouch so his face was even closer, the gun still in one hand now casually held between his bent knees.

"*Mi hermana*," he whispered brokenly even though his face was still a perfectly blank slate. "What are you doing here?"

"What are *you* doing here?" I countered, my hands fluttering in the air between us like loosed butterflies from a jar.

I wanted to touch him, hug him, tattoo myself to him permanently so he would never leave again.

But there was a soft menace in his air, as though there was a palpable threat he couldn't curb even if he wanted to.

So I kept my hands to myself even though it killed something inside me to do it.

His full mouth went flat, white with tension. "Javier will be back in a second. I don't have time to explain to you…I—I didn't want you to find out this way."

"That you're alive?"

"That I'm alive," he agreed. "Though I thought you would've known…I sent letters to Ignacio for you. Letters I wrote over the years so you'd know I was alive if I wasn't able to come home."

"I don't speak to Ignacio. I haven't since the last time you made me visit him when I eleven. Dane, what the hell are you wrapped up in?" I asked, searching his face, noticing a scar at his left temple that extended back over his ear and the deep lines beside his eyes that shouldn't have been there at his age.

"I'm coming home," he vowed. "I've been working on it for years, it's just…taken so much more than I thought it would. You can't tell anyone, though, Li. Now that you know, I can try to protect you, maybe even make contact, but the more people who know, the higher risk there is that there is no coming home for me."

"Dane," I said, mostly just because I needed to say his name, because I *could* say his name to his face, something I hadn't been able to do in years. "Explain it to me. I can help. The Booths, they're going to lose it when they see you—"

"You're not gonna tell them," he said, slipping back to the slang he'd used as a kid. "Seriously, Li, promise me."

"I promise," I breathed even though I didn't want to keep such a colossal secret to myself.

I couldn't fathom keeping it from Nova.

He tipped forward to palm my face, his palm ridged with thick callouses, then he planted his lips on my forehead, giving me the sweetest kiss I'd ever known.

"I love you," he said, firing the words at point black range as noise sounded outside the door. "I'm sorry, Li."

And then he lifted the gun, reared an arm back, and hit me across the temple with it.

His name was on my tongue when I passed out, hope turned to ash just as it had all those years ago when I was told that my brother was dead.

CHAPTER TWENTY-THREE

Lila

WHEN I CAME TO, I WAS CRADLED IN UNFAMILIAR ARMS, THE pungent scent of expensive male cologne in my nose and the faintly familiar strains of *Esta Niña Linda* in my ear.

It was one of the Spanish lullabies Ellie used to sing for Dane and I when we were kids.

My eyes snapped open to reveal Javier Ventura looking down at my face with a mixture of awe, disgust, and reverence.

"Ah, she's wakes," he murmured. "I was afraid you might need a trip to the hospital."

I blinked hard, worried I was dreaming a surreal and horrible nightmare. "What happened?"

"You tripped on the edge of the desk and hit your head," he explained calmly, moving the compress I hadn't noticed was on my temple. "When I came in, you were passed out on the ground."

My thoughts were jumbled like a puzzle before completion, but I knew he was lying.

I wasn't clumsy, and I hadn't fallen.

Unbidden, thoughts of Dane rushed back to meet me, and I blinked rapidly as they flipped through my mind's eye.

"Do you remember what you were doing?" Javier asked carefully, eyeing me steadily.

"I needed to make some calls for Irina," I answered, wondering how I could get out of his hold without offending him.

I was shocked and more than a little disturbed that he would try to soothe me at all.

Sensing my discomfort, he opened his arms so I could move away, but he did so with a little smile as if he thought my fear was somehow...cute.

"You work for my wife," he said, half question and answer.

I nodded as I smoothed my clothes and tidied my hair. "Yes. I have for about three months now."

"Ah," he said, looking over my shoulder, lost in thought for several long, awkward seconds. "Yes, I'm surprised she didn't tell me."

A shiver nibbled up my back with viciously sharp teeth. "Why would she? I'm no one."

He laughed lightly, but there was too much shrewdness in his eyes to pass it off as casual. I watched him suspiciously as he rolled to his feet gracefully and adjusted his cufflinks and blazer. He was a handsome man in the way a car salesman was handsome, studied and slick because he knew good looks were powerful. He had the same eyes I did, a warm brown spiked through with green and gold. Only his were narrowed, calculating and suspicious, glittering with dark joy.

"Silly of me to assume you would remember me. I knew your parents."

Of course, he did. Ignacio had been his primary dealer on the coast of B.C. before they expanded their operations.

"Right." I smiled anemically, feeling spread as thin as butter over toast. I needed space to make sense of the last two hours, of Irina's capitulation to my stand-off, Javier's odd intimacy, and Dane.

Mostly Dane.

"You look like her," Javier continued as his eyes swept me head to toe. "As a girl, you looked like your father, but now you're grown, you look very much like Ellie. You have her grace."

No one had ever told me I had grace before. I was a girl inked in flowers who wore cowboy boots and ripped concert tees. I was nothing elegant or graceful, at least not in the traditional sense. But the way Javier said it, as if he was compelled to praise me for it, set my teeth on edge.

"Um, well, thank you. I should go, though, my friend is probably outside waiting for me," I hedged as I moved toward the door.

"Oh, don't worry about Nova Booth. My wife has always been quite taken with him, I'm sure she's only too happy to entertain him."

"Excuse me?" I almost barked.

Irina *and* Nova?

His eyes glittered, elongated like a snake's and just as evil. "Oh, yes, they had a brief tryst some years ago. Irina never quite recovered from it. I wonder…have you?"

My poor, battered heart set a limping gait in my chest, but I stared down Javier with all the hatred I could muster, and it was considerable because this was the man who had framed Zeus and propped up Staff Sergeant Danner's corrupt force which led to King's death. The man who sold women like cattle, drugs like candies, and had no respect for human life other than his own.

"You may have known my parents, Javier, but don't believe for one moment that I am anything like them. They were my blood, not my family, and thank God, I was raised by better than them. Better than *you*," I snapped recklessly, so overloaded with emotion that I had no thought to my safety.

I didn't linger to see how Javier would react to my outburst, so I didn't see the way he flinched slightly at my words. Instead, I pushed out of the office, stalked through the now empty studio, and through the side door out to the parking lot.

Irina was there, her long fingernails on Nova's chest as she flirted shamelessly with him.

Red obscured my vision like a cloak prompting something animal in me that ignited the need to *charge*.

Nova saw me first, stalking toward them with fury engraved on my face, and he grinned.

Grinned.

As if the sight of me aflame with jealousy was amusing and maybe even a little endearing.

It only fueled me further.

It was the proverbial icing on the cake of my supremely shitty day.

"Excuse me, Irina," I seethed as I stepped up to them and attached myself to Nova's side.

Without hesitation, Nova lifted his leather clad arm and tucked me into his side.

Irina's eyes narrowed on us.

"Have you met my boyfriend, Nova?" I asked sweetly even though the words burned on my tongue.

He wasn't my boyfriend. I knew that. But I needed this. I needed someone to believe he was mine and respect it. Even more, I needed Irina and Javier to *fuck off*.

She blinked, her red mouth a little 'o' of surprise. "I wasn't aware the famous Casanova dated anyone."

Nova squeezed my tense shoulder and shot her a lazy smile. "I wasn't until I got my head outta my ass and noticed Lila as more than a friend."

I squashed the happiness that bloomed in my heart under the heavy heel of my mind. He was just playing his part in the charade, and I knew better than to believe his lies.

"If you'll excuse us," I said in that same sugary tone as I started to lead Nova toward his Harley. "We have a dinner to get to."

Irina didn't say anything as we moved away, but I felt her gaze brand itself into the back of my head as I settled onto the bike behind Nova and we took off with a roar of pipes.

I was glad for the silence on the ride back down to Entrance even though it wasn't enough time to make sense of my chaotic thoughts and emotions. I felt exhausted, my heart on tumble dry in my chest as it struggled to sort through everything that had happened.

Nova didn't say a word when we pulled up in front of the Booths house for dinner. Instead, he gently unclipped my helmet, cupped my cheeks as he searched my face for answers, then gently tugged me toward the meadow beside the house. We walked through the thigh-length grass to the center of the wildflower strewn field, and then he pulled us both to the ground, keeping me in the circle of his arms as he did.

"I slept with Irina once, years ago before we even knew who she was. It was the biggest mistake of my life, and I didn't even know it at the time," he started as if we'd been mid-conversation. "Z knows, Bat and Buck too. Otherwise, it's somethin' I keep to myself. Maybe I shoulda told you, but you have this way of lookin' at me sometimes, like I'm the best thing you've ever seen. Not the best looking, 'cause fuck, a helluva lotta people've looked at me like that in my life. Nah, you look at me like I'm the fuckin' *worthiest*, and honestly, Li, I couldn't handle it if anythin' changed that."

It was a good speech, so endearing because it was so *true*.

I thought Nova was the best person on the planet. I thought he was even more beautiful on the inside of that god-like form than he was on the outside.

But it hurt to know he thought I would be so easily moved from my admiration, so I told him so. "You sleeping with Irina wouldn't change that. Nothing short of you disrespecting a loved one would make me think less of you, Jonathon. You've been my hero since the day we met, and you've only proved to be that again and again over the years."

He made a noise in the back of his throat, a kind of helpless grunt as if I'd punched him in the solar plexus.

"My moodiness isn't about you sleeping with Irina, though," I wrinkled my nose as I rolled onto his chest to look down at him. "I had a...rough day. Irina tried to make me take part in one of her shoots, and then Javier came into Irina's office just after I sent you that text about the website. He...he totally creeped me out, to be honest."

"He hit on you?" Nova growled, his body gone to granite beneath me.

"No," I soothed, running a hand down his chest and thrilling in the fact that I was allowed to do that now—touch him— to freely be intimate with him. "It was almost...I don't know. Oddly paternal. I fell and hit my head, he was there holding me when I came to."

Immediately, Nova surged up, cupped my face in one hand, and gently settled me on my back in the grass with the other. He loomed over me, shadowed in the deepening twilight, as he tenderly touched my face.

I hissed when his fingers pressed into the bruise darkening over my ear. A rumble worked itself loose from his chest, but he was acutely careful as he leaned down to plant a kiss there.

It bloomed beneath my skin like a rose, and I knew I'd wear the sensation of his kiss there as an invisible flower behind my ear for the rest of my life.

"Need to take you to get checked out?" he asked as he dropped kisses down my cheek and across my jaw.

"Mmm, you're playing doctor pretty well," I teased as I clutched him tightly to me. "Maybe you should just kiss me better."

He pressed another kiss to my temple. "Like that?"

"No, the pain's actually lower now," I said with mock somberness even though a giggle moved through me.

"Ah, well…" he nodded sagely, but even in the dark I could see the silhouette of his smile. "Why don't you lay back, spread your legs, and let me apologize to you with my tongue?"

There was so much to think about, so many questions without answers, and worries I had to bear alone, that it threatened to overwhelm me. The secret of Dane's existence felt like lead on my tongue, poisoning me, weighing me down. I wanted to tell Nova so badly, I almost felt ill, but I knew divulging the truth would only endanger him. And wasn't keeping Nova safe one of the reasons I'd entered into this situation in the first place?

I sighed deeply, feeling the weight of the day loosen its bonds on my heart and mind as Nova stamped kisses into the skin of my throat, over the peaks of my breasts through the fabric of my dress. He rucked up my skirt to get to my belly, tracing the swirls of my tattoos with his fingers and tongue as he descended farther, to the apex of my thighs.

"Wanna put somethin' here," he said, cheek to my pubic mound, his fingers tickling the thin skin just under and inside my hipbone. "A small coral rose and the words 'read my skin'."

I shivered as if run through by a ghost, because sometimes with Nova, that was how it felt. He understood me so well, all the little things I thought, but didn't have the courage to say, that it seemed he had the ability to stand at the corner of my mind like a specter.

It should have been invasive, but I thought it was exquisite.

"Let's do it," I agreed, combing my fingers through the top of his silken hair. "Whenever you want."

He groaned in answer, lapping at the skin with his tongue then tracing the seam of my groin down to the lips of my sex.

"Fuck me, you taste so sweet," he said as started to eat me, lifting my legs to shift them over his shoulders to give him better access. "Never been addicted to a thing in my fuckin' life, but know I need the taste of this pussy in my mouth every day to sustain me."

God, the thought of that rolled through me like hot air, inflating my oversized heart, firing the love I tried to keep tamed in my chest.

"You can take a taste whenever you need one," I gasped as he drew hot, sucking circles over my clit with his talented mouth. "I wouldn't want you to have to suffer detox."

He laughed against my pussy, the vibrations delicious against my sensitive skin.

"You'll have to endure my shitty ass attitude when the time comes."

And just like that, the hope went out of my chest, punctured by the unwittingly cruel remark.

You dumbass, I wanted to scream at him, *I love you. and if you tried, I know you could love me too!*

"Yeah," I huffed instead as he twisted his fingers inside me in a way that made me squirm. "You think our relationship will survive that?"

"We're still friends now, my mouth on your pussy," he said reasonably before he swirled his tongue at my entrance.

"Friends don't give friends boners," I quipped, tugging hard on his hair so he hissed and surged back up my body. I gripped his iron hard cock through his jeans then made quick work of unzipping them so I could take that hot flesh in my hand. "Admit it, you want me."

His jaw set, hard and intractable, a Booth characteristic that meant he was settling in for the long haul. "Want you, yeah, but want our friendship more."

My nails dug into his shoulders as I wrenched him to the side, rolling him to his back in the long grass, releasing the scent of honeysuckle crushed under his weight. I notched the hot, round tip of his cock at my center and slammed down, crying out as he impaled me.

Nova grunted and flung his arm over his head as I started to move, but I wouldn't have that.

He was hiding, hiding because I *knew* there was something there between us in the shimmering, electric blue of the descending twilight. Something that had nothing to do with friends and barely even anything to do with lovers.

He had planted an entire garden in my heart, across my skin, inside my chest, and whether or not he was willing to admit it to himself, at some point he had to have known what he was doing.

Loving me so hard, I'd had no choice but to grow to love him back.

He might not have had the words to say, the wherewithal to compute it, but it was there, lurking like a monster under the bed at the back of his dark eyes.

Love. Tenderness. The awareness that he'd fall on his own sword if it meant I'd be safe and happy.

"Look at me," I demanded, raking my nails down his chest then hiking up his shirt so I could do it again on his bare skin. "Watch me take you."

It was an echo of our first time together, but this time, I was in control. I was the one cracking open that hard, shiny veneer he wore like a beautiful mask for the world to see so that I could get to the ugly tangle of emotions beneath.

Begrudgingly, he dropped the arm over his face and looked up at me, a muscle ticing in his jaw.

I leaned forward to grab his hands, move them above his head, and twine our fingers together, bringing my face down so I could kiss the pained grimace off his face.

"It's okay to like this," I reminded him. "It's okay to want me more than once, more than twice, maybe even for a long time."

I rocked my hips smoothly, undulating like a boat on the waves, taking him deeply inside my body, then nearly all the way out just to feel the full length of him.

His lids drooped with pleasure and his hips raised, fucking me back as I continued to talk to him.

"Just friends don't look at each other the way we do," I whispered against his damp lips as we breathed the same stuttering breath. "Just friends wouldn't fuck me the way you do, like you can't get enough of my skin against yours, my taste in your mouth. Just friends, Nova? That's not you and me, maybe it never even was."

"Stop talkin'," he growled, eyes flashing angrily to overtake the glimmer of doubt and fear I was almost sure I read there.

"It's okay to love me," I whispered so softly, right into the bowl of his open mouth so he had no choice but to feel the sugary words melt over his tongue.

He growled. "I'm warnin' you. I'll shut you up, and you might not like how I do it."

"Jonathon," I tried to continue, but a second later I was flipped to my back, and Nova's hard weight was on top of me, driving out my air.

"I told you," he said darkly as he thrust brutally inside me again, so hard my nerves sung with pain edged pleasure, "to shut up. Now I'm gonna make you come so hard you don't remember your own goddamn name."

I opened my mouth again to protest, but his fingers were there, driving over my tongue.

"Suck," he ordered, his eyes only pitted shadows beneath his knit brows.

He was so sexy, he eclipsed my thoughts like the sun, swallowing up my manipulations and protests in a single second.

I sucked, I laved, licked, and I pulled on his tatted fingers, watching as his nostrils flared, and his tempo grew ragged.

"You wanna be mine, Li?" he taunted as he fed me his fingers and used his other arm to hike my leg up over his elbow. "Then you show me how well you can take my cock and my cum."

My legs started to shake as he dipped to take one of my nipples between his teeth, abusing it with his bite and the rough lashes of his tongue.

"N-Nova," I stammered around his fingers as everything in my body grew tight enough to snap. "God, Nova, *yes*."

"Fuck, you're so goddamn tight, Li," he panted against my breast then licked my sweat damped neck before leaving a kiss there. "So goddamn tight and so goddamn mine."

"Yes," I cried out as he pulled his fingers away and wrapped them tight around my throat. "Yes, yours, please make me yours."

And he did.

He sunk his teeth into the straining tendons of my neck and sucked so hard I knew he was planting a different kind of bloom there, poppy red beneath my skin.

He hiked my leg even higher and used his other hand to frame our connection, fingers splayed through my wet pussy so he could feel his thick cock churn in and out of my clenching folds.

Finally, he nipped the lobe of my ear before harshly whispering, "Fuckin' mine. You've always been mine."

My climax ripped through me like a knife, so hard it was almost painful. I cried out as it tore down my middle and twisted in my gut, as I spilled open onto Nova's cock and thighs while he continued to beat into me.

He sealed our lips and ate my cries with relish like a hungry hunter, enjoying the way I thrashed around him.

The feel of his cock kicking inside me, spiting hot cum in my still clenching cunt, only drove me higher.

"Oh, my God," I groaned against his mouth. "Oh, my God, I can't stop."

As if I'd dared him, Nova grunted and moved his fingers over my clit, rubbing tight circles into the hard pearl until I shuddered again, climaxing once again even though I wasn't even finished with the first.

My thoughts broke open like fireworks and drifted slowly, slowly back to the ground.

When I came to enough to notice my surroundings, Nova was doing what I hadn't expected.

He was hugging me. He had one hand on the back of my head clasping me to his neck, my forehead over his heavily beating pulse, and the other at my low back, coaxing my limp legs to stay wrapped around him.

Instantly, tears welled over and spilled down my cheeks, watering the flowers beneath me.

"I hope you know, Li," he murmured, stroking a hand down the long line of my hair. "I do love you. It's never gonna be enough, but it's as much as I got in me to give, yeah?"

He paused, sensing perhaps how deeply his words scored through me.

"But it's more than anyone else in the whole fuckin' world, okay?"

I squeezed my eyes shut and nodded into his neck, clasping him to me because even though he was the one to hurt me, he was also the only one I wanted to comfort me.

"'Kay," I agreed, rubbing my nose over his slowing pulse point. "I'm good with that."

His hand still on my hair, he gave my neck a little squeeze, as if he knew I wasn't, but he was grateful to me for saying so.

"You about done?" Molly called out from the half-open screen door on the back porch. "Food's getting cold."

"Oh, my God," I cried out in embarrassment, tilting my head into the crook of Nova's arm where his laugh shook through me.

"Coming now," I shouted after swatting him in the chest.

"Actually, we just did," he teased then threw his head back to laugh uproariously at my shocked expression, his mirth rolling through the flowered meadow for the entire neighborhood to hear.

"I cannot believe they knew we were out here," I moaned

as I pulled away to right my dress. "How fucking embarrassing."

"Hey," Nova said on a chuckle, catching my hands and bringing them up to his lips for a brief kiss on each of my knuckles. "We're grown ass adults. Molly and Diogo aren't gonna say shit. Sure, Milo, Oliver, and Huds will crack some jokes, but c'mon, it's not like you aren't used to their ribbin'. And you know Ares won't say anythin' even though he'll shoot you one of his thousand-yard stares."

"True," I muttered as he stood and offered me a hand up. "Still, I'm not relishing the thought of going in to see my foster family with their son's cum leaking down my thighs."

"Mmm," Nova hummed wickedly, slinging an arm over my shoulder and touching his nose to my hair as he began to lead us inside. "Is it wrong I think that's hot?"

A reluctant laugh spilled from my lips. "One hundred percent wrong, but you wouldn't be you if you weren't."

He winked at me as we ascended the back steps then smiled broadly at his mum as she held the door open for us.

"You have flowers in your hair," she said mildly to her son. "And while I'm sure Lila put them there, I have a feeling she did it in a different way than when you were young."

Nova laughed freely, his grin so wide it was blinding in the honey light spilling out from the house. He ducked down to give her a gentle hug then swaggered into the house, already calling out into the dining room for his brothers.

Molly stilled me with only a tender, maternal look and a soft hand on my arm.

"Never seen him so carefree," Molly whispered, her face infused with love and a gentle understanding that made me want to cry. "Lord knows I want happiness for that boy. But you're my only girl, and there will always be a special place in my heart just for you. I know you have a lot of love to give, Lila, just… just make sure you don't put all of it in one basket, okay?"

I smiled weakly at her as she opened her arm to give me a side hug and lead me into the house that had been my home since I was seven years old.

I didn't tell her it was already too late.

I'd lost my heart to Nova before I'd even known what love was.

CHAPTER TWENTY-FOUR

Nova

IT'D BEEN FUCKIN' AGES SINCE WE'D THROWN A REAL BANGER at the clubhouse, but Z had decided, and rightly, that the club'd been through a shitstorm over the last year, and we needed to cut loose.

When you told a group of bikers and their Old Ladies to cut loose and throw a ragin' party, they fuckin' delivered.

It was craziness, loud and fuckin' chaotic revelry.

The entire lot was strewn with lights the hang-arounds had set up, huge crates filled with ice and stuffed with domestic brews, massive speakers set up between buildin's so the sound of rock drowned out the silence of the deep night.

Some of the brothers from the Quebec City chapter were in town after completin' a long run through the prairies deliverin' guns, and those motherfuckin' Frenchmen were always down for a good time. A few of them had some of the girls dancin' on the picnic tables in front of the clubhouse, and Lila was there, not dancin', but laughin' as Cleo was taken for a spin, and Lion coaxed Harleigh Rose into some kinda country boy two-step.

There were biker bitches everywhere, too, just lookin' for a shot of danger from any of the men in leather who'd give them a taste straight from the source. Normally, I'd be in the thick of that, tangled up in one or two girls 'cause I liked the feel of them, they liked the sight of me, and therefore, I usually got the pick of the litter.

Not tonight.

It wasn't easy stayin' away. I got the pouty looks, the trailin' hands, and whispered invitations, but I stayed free of them.

Lila and I hadn't talked about... exclusivity.

A foreign word, or more like a curse word to the man who'd never slept with a woman more than twice, but one I suddenly found myself repeatin' it at the back of my mind like some kinda spiritual mantra.

I didn't want anyone but Lila.

It was as simple and fuckin' complicated as that.

Especially 'cause I was forced to keep my distance if I didn't want all the Old Ladies and some of the guys on my ass, houndin' me about what was goin' on there.

I had no answers to that question, not even in the privacy of my own mind.

Why'd everyone need labels and sound-bite answers to stupid ass questions?

Life could exist in chaos, and most of the time, it fuckin' well did. That world I operated in just fine.

Why did Lila and I have to change who we were or what we stood for just to make other people more comfortable?

We didn't. I sure as fuck *wouldn't*.

Only...there was a question I caught in the back of Lila's dappled forest eyes sometimes, when I'd turn to see her watchin' me before she could look away, or when I'd wake up and her hand would be playin' over the tattoos on my chest like an archeologist searchin' an ancient text.

She wanted answers too.

"Why're you bein' such a broodin' asshole?" Boner asked,

knockin' his beer into mine so they both sloshed over our hands. "Kendra promised me a blowie if I came over to ask you what the fuck's up."

I arched a brow at him. "You know Kendra'd probably give you head anyway, yeah?"

Boner grinned, his boyish, frat boy looks a deep contrast to the cut and biker swagger he wore like a second skin. "Oh, yeah. But hey, I gotta heart too. Thought I'd check in and make sure you haven't got herpes or some shit keepin' ya benched."

"Jesus fuck, Boner, I don't have goddamn herpes." I rolled my eyes and chuckled 'cause he was a bonehead, but he was always good for a laugh.

"Good." He nodded somberly like he'd been truly worried. "There's plenty of prime pussy here tonight, but you gotta get a jump on it, you don't want those Frenchie mother-fucker's leftovers. Look at 'em! They even got Lila up in there now."

My neck about cramped as I cranked it over my shoulder to check out the scene. Some asshole had cajoled Lila up onto one of the tables with him, and she was laughin' as he spun around then dipped her back, trying to land a kiss on her mouth which she blocked with a raised hand. She wasn't down for the kiss, but she was flirtin' like she had been with the newcomers all night.

Tryin' to prove a point maybe, or more likely, just bein' Lila.

Sweet, outgoin', so easy on the eyes it was hard to pull them off her.

My blood went to poison in my veins.

"Uh, Nova?" Boner called after I slammed my beer into his chest to hold and stalked across the lot.

I ignored him.

Just like I ignored the call of Kendra and her girls as I stalked past them on my way to those tables.

I arrived just as the guy with the handlebar mustache dancin' with *my* Flower Child grabbed her in a tight cinch with her hands behind her back and planted a wet fuckin' kiss on her. When she squirmed, he only redoubled his efforts, lickin' a line from her mouth to her throat where he bit down to hold her still while he gyrated against her.

Rage broke free of the chains in my gut and howled up my throat.

Leanin' into the table, I tagged the asshole's leg and pulled, bringin' him down on his back in a way that shook the table. Lila had the good sense to hop down immediately, but I kept the guy pinned, climbin' onto the table, kneelin' into his chest to pound my fist into his face.

"This is our club, you ask before you stick your dick where it doesn't belong," I growled as I drove my fist into his face again.

No one stopped me.

It might of been the black rage swirlin' around me, but whatever the reason, no one even got close.

"Fuck," the guy groaned, hands up in a weak attempt to defend himself. "What the fuck, man? I asked around, and she ain't anyone's piece."

"You're damn right, she's not," I snarled, droppin' in close to say the words into his bruised up, beaten in face. "She's fuckin' family. You want one of the other girls around here, you damn well ask."

"This ain't a cotillion," he argued. "Just havin' some fun."

"Yeah? Well then, so am I." I grinned into his face, lettin' the beast break through my pretty veneer, then I laid a blow to his cheek, one of my rings splittin' open his skin so red sluiced down his neck. "Sorry I didn't ask fuckin' permission first," I mocked.

"Nova," the soft, feminine voice curled around me like smoke, faintly exotic and heady as grade-A B.C. marijuana.

I shifted enough to look over my shoulder at Lila. She was

watchin' me with big, dark eyes, her breasts swellin' over her low-cut top as she breathed quick, panicked or aroused, I couldn't tell the in the near dark.

"Nova," she repeated. "Don't hurt your hands. He's not worth it."

Her words moved through me in an odd way, pingin' against dead ends and roundin' tight corners until they slotted into a hole in my chest I'd never thought to stop up.

A hole that said I wasn't good enough.

That, at the end of the day, I was good looks and charm, bad choices and fuck ups.

But here was Lila watchin' me beat a man's face in like the monster I was capable of bein', and she wasn't disgusted or angry.

She was fuckin' *concerned*, worried I'd hurt my hands, the tools of my passion and persuasion.

I blinked at her, ignorin' the way the motherfucker beneath my knee moaned and grumbled. Our eyes locked with a near audible click, and everythin' fell away around us. 'Cause it was just that way with us, and it always had been, Lila and me, tucked up in our own world where only our rules applied.

There were no labels there.

Not even any expectations other than one: that we took care of each other.

That was the first, last, and only commandment between us, and Lila was provin' it right there.

A different kinda heat moved through me then, the same flicker of it glintin' in her eyes as she slowly smiled.

And I was done.

So I looked down at the motherfucker who'd put his hands on her and sneered into his face. "You touch a goddamn hair on her hair or the head of any of the other women here ever again without their fuckin' consent, I'll burn your cut with you in it, got it?"

"Got it," he agreed even though his face was mottled red with angry humiliation.

I didn't give a fuck about his feelin's.

I'd be pissed if he laid a finger on any of the women who didn't want it, 'cause that was not the way we ran shit as a club, and there was no way in hell I'd feel remorse for beatin' his ugly mug in for touchin' Li.

Only I was allowed to do that.

I jumped down from the table, jerked my chin up at Z who was watchin' the whole thing with a scowl, ignored the rest of the crowd circled around us, and then ducked to gently hit Lila in the hip with my shoulder before lifting her up, up, over my back.

"Nova!" she screeched as I carted her off toward the clubhouse.

"Lila," I said, calm as fuck. "You flirtin' with that guy to get a rise outta me?"

Silence, just the stomp of my boots up the concrete stairs and the noise of the party inside the clubhouse surrounded us as I stormed a path through the bodies to the hall that led to the bunk rooms.

"Mostly no," she finally ventured, not protestin' me carryin' her anymore.

She was bracin'.

Smart girl.

"Well, congrats, you got one," I growled as I pushed open the door of the first free room I found and slammed it shut behind me.

I dropped her to the bed, let her bounce on the mattress once, then crawled over her, cagin' her beneath my heavy body, securin' her hands over her head.

My voice was a soft rasp as I drew my nose along the length of hers and warned, "You know what happens when naïve little girls play with fuckin' fire, Lila?"

She gasped as I pushed a knee tight to her sex and ground in.

"They get to feel the burn of a real man's wrath," I threatened.

She blinked up at me, a little dazed, a lot aroused, the heady mix of lust and anger scorchin' through me ampin' higher.

I moved quick, liftin' her up and haulin' her over my lap as I took a seat at the edge of the bed and pinned her against my legs.

"Nova," she protested, but there was a shake in her voice that undercut her denial.

She liked bein' over my knee.

"Told you last time you played games with me, leavin' me cold and alone in bed, I'd tan your ass you did it again."

"You can't be serious."

"Fuckin' deadly," I bit out as I kneaded the firm flesh of her ass over her silky dress. "I'm gonna spank this sweet ass until it's cherry red so you feel me for days afterward. Then maybe you won't be so quick to forget the man currently occupyin' your bed."

"Nova," she breathed, but the protest drowned in a heavy moan as I dipped my fingers beneath her skirt and slowly raised it to expose her rounded cheeks.

I palmed one of those cheeks in my hand and squeezed, lovin' the sight of my tatted skin against her golden flesh.

"Now, be a good girl, Li, and hold still while I tattoo your ass red with my palm."

My cock was an iron bar beneath her stomach, and sweat bloomed across my forehead. I was so turned on havin' her in my lap, so prone and trustin' in this new experience, that it swirled through me like fine whiskey. I was drunk on it, on her, and the power she gave me to play with her anyway I wanted.

Smack.

My hand slapped down against her bare skin with a brutal *crack*.

She hiccoughed on her moan, surprised by the way the sting settled in and melted to pleasure.

Smack.

"You have such a sweet ass," I growled as I rubbed the tingle out of her flesh and spanked her again. "So many things I'm gonna do to it, you let me."

A breathy moan leaked from her mouth, and her body, once taut with anticipation, relaxed slightly against my legs.

My girl was so fuckin' dirty.

I swatted her twice on each cheek *hard* so her ass started to glow pink as a neon sign, then I slipped my hand between her legs to test her through her pants.

"Fuck, so fuckin' wet for me already." I slipped my fingers under the edge of her underwear and ran them from her clit up to her asshole. She squirmed as I rubbed my thumb over the crinkled apex, but she did it was a breathy moan that told me she liked it.

"You ever been fucked here, gorgeous?" I asked silkily as I tested my thumb against her pretty, caramel entrance.

"No," she gasped as I drew circles over it and squeezed her ass with my other hand. "But I'd let you."

A rumble erupted through my chest as volcanic lust bubbled low in my gut. "Yeah? You wanna feel me wedge my cock into this little ass?"

She shivered almost violently, and I took a moment to relish the sight of her lush, small form laid out over my legs, hands and feet to the floor bracin' for whatever I wanted to do to her. Her ass was still pink, her sex swollen between her thighs, and glossed like my favourite kinda donut. I wanted to eat her, fuck her, and spank her all at once.

Every time I took her, I wanted more, like some gluttonous beast. I gorged myself on her every night and damn near every mornin', sometimes even in between if we found the time so I didn't get this constant hunger. There was an ache that gnawed through me every hour of the day I wasn't with her.

It woulda been easy to tell myself I was just relishin' a return to our closeness, to havin' her trust and her body beside mine through the all the days of my life.

But I knew no matter how detailed I inked those lies on my body, they would still be fuckin' fabrications.

The truth was, even though my heart was about twice as small as Li's, I still wanted to give every inch of it to her, hopin' beyond hope it'd be enough.

She squirmed on my lap, brinin' me back to the moment, to the sight of her round ass in my lap and my thumb on her little hole.

"A virgin," I mused darkly, lettin' the beast in me come out to play 'cause now I knew my girl liked it. "One day, I'm gonna take you there. I'm gonna claim this ass just like I shoulda claimed your pussy, your mouth, and your very first kiss."

"Yes," she hissed, tossin' her long, dark hair back to stare at me over her shoulder, tiltin' her hips as she did to give me more access. "Please, just stop teasing me. I need you."

"On your knees then," I told her, grabbin' up her thick hair in my fist as she adjusted between my wide knees and instantly reached for my belt. "Get me nice and wet."

The second she wrapped her mouth around me, I started writin' my vows. I'd never had a woman lust so hard after my cock. It was insanely hot to hear the way she moaned as she traced a vein from base to tip, lappin' at the sensitive underside like it was her favourite fuckin' flavour of ice cream. I held her hair away from her face to watch her lose herself in suckin' my dick, red lips wet as she spread them wide to take me deep, makin' me wonder what I might of done in a past life to be so fuckin' lucky.

When I couldn't stand the hot suck of her mouth any

longer, I pulled her back firmly by the hair, grasped her chin, and stole a deep, wet kiss.

Her sweet pink tongue snuck out to chase mine when I pulled back then licked her swollen mouth.

"On the bed," I ordered as I stood up and went into the bathroom to look for some kinda lube.

No way I was takin' a virgin ass without it.

I almost laughed when I reached into the first drawer under the sink and found a half-used jar of the stuff.

Trust my biker brethren to be prepared for that shit.

When I came back into the room, Lila was naked, her hair a dark mess of curls spilled like ink over the white pillows. Her legs were spread, but not far, and I knew without havin' to check any further that my momentary distance had made her shy.

"You think that's enough for me?" I asked in a voice I didn't recognize, low and throaty. "When I told you I was deviant man, what did you think? That you could just spread your legs and I'd step on up? Fuck you vanilla style 'til our teeth ache with the sweetness of it?"

I dipped down over her, fist to the bed, my other palm a heavy weight on her sternum, pressing her to the bed just to illustrate my strength.

"I don't just want your pussy, Lila. I wanna see all the ways I can fill it up and watch it go from pink to red with achy, furious desire. I wanna put my fingers in it when I press my cock into your ass. I wanna lave it with my tongue until you squirm and beg to come in my mouth. You want me to fuck you? I will. But I'll do it bulldozing every inhibition you might have."

Her pupils ate up the hazel of her eyes, leavin' only deep, dark pools of unfiltered desire.

"You ready for that?" I asked roughly as I leaned in to snag her lower lip between my teeth.

Her gasp made me feel like a heathen conquerin' his

maiden spoils…it shouldn't have been so hot, so filthy to think of takin' this girl so much younger and purer than myself in ways both delicious and fuckin' deviant.

But it was.

"Hold your legs back and open for me, I want total access to this pretty pussy and ass," I told her as I moved away to chuck my clothes, watchin' as she immediately obeyed me, her eyes gone to black beneath her thick lashes.

There was somethin' intensely vulnerable about her laying there, legs held back and tremblin' with excitement and nerves. She'd always trusted me, but this was new. I was askin' her to hand over her body as well as her heart and mind. It shouldn't have been such a big thing in comparison to the weight of the other two, the thoughts and soul of a person, but it was.

Lila's body had been a sacred place for the two of us for years, the fertile soil where our flowers grew. A safe place for us to seed the love we had for each other and watch it grow, free of judgements and obstacles. Just our twined emotions as they grew with us in age and changed just as acutely as our bodies, ripenin' and maturin' into somethin' we could no longer ignore.

Bein' able to feel those flowers as they bloomed over her skin, tastin' the peonies at her thighs and the lilies at her pulse points, was like bein' granted access to a pilgrim's place, a holy grail I wanted to kneel and pray before.

So I did, gettin' on my knees in the bed to play my fingers over her wet folds, dippin' in the well, up to her clit and back down to her tight ass.

"Tell me you want me, Li," I said softly as I coated my fingers in the lube and started to press at the rosebud of her ass. "Tell me you want to feel me from the inside out."

She gasped sharply as I breached her then moaned, long and guttural as I started to open her up. "I want you, Nova. I've only ever wanted *you*."

Those words wrapped like a hand around my dick and pulled, wrenchin' a groan that seemed torn from the heart of me. I dipped my head to lap at the cream spillin' from her pussy as I gently coaxed another finger into the tight clasp of her ass.

Every lap of my tongue there, every groan and movement of her body as it flexed and struggled against the crest of climax reduced me to less of a man.

And more of a beast.

By the time I had three fingers inside her, her first orgasm quiverin' under my mouth, slidin' across my tongue, I was gone.

No more thoughts, no more reservations.

She was mine.

And I was hers in the way a wolf is owned by his moon, elementally, fuckin' irrevocably.

As I leaned back to coat my throbbin' cock in oil, hissin' as my hands moved over the over sensitized flesh, I locked eyes with Lila and let her see the deep, dark soul of me. Her gaze burned on my cock as I sat on my heels to present it to her, lettin' her see the thick crown disappear behind the tight cinch of my fist, the pearl of precum offered on the head like a courtesan's gift.

"This is me, Li," I told her, jackin' off slow and controlled, abs tight with the effort not to thrust up into my hand.

Just the sight of her indolent and languid, limbs pliable as warm wax, hair a dark halo around her gorgeous face. It was enough to make my balls tighten and my ass clench with the need to come.

"This is what you do to me," I offered, the only words I really had to give.

My body, my beauty.

Is it enough? I asked, writin' the words I was too chicken-shit to ask in the screens of my eyes for her to decipher.

She pulled her legs back higher and lifted her chin,

meetin' my unspoken challenge. "You're all I've ever wanted. Come take what's yours."

I groaned as I fell onto her, shiftin' her legs before notchin' my cock at the loosened vice of her ass.

"Need your eyes as I fill you up. Need you to watch me take what's mine," I growled as I forced her hands over her head and twined out fingers, then I pressed firmly, gently forging ahead until her tight heat enveloped my cock.

We both moaned, legs shakin' as we adjusted to the burn.

"You're so beautiful," she breathed as I slid forward to the hilt, her voice more air than sound. "You feel so fucking beautiful."

Her lids fluttered as she adjusted to the fullness, and her back arched, her tight nipples brushin' against my pecs.

"Gonna fuck you now, Li," I warned through gritted teeth 'cause there was fire in my gut, and it needed tendin'. "Gonna fuck you nice and hard so you feel me for days."

She whimpered in answer, pressin' her hips tighter to mine as she wrapped those caramel legs around my waist and urged me to rock into that snug embrace.

I drove harder, arrowin' a hand to her wet pussy and easin' a finger inside, thumb to her clit in firm, slow circles. Her eyes went black with lust, blown up by her need for more, for me. She muttered incoherently as I twisted her higher and higher.

"Poor thing," I muttered darkly, thrustin' into her heat, feelin' the squeeze of her all around me, the walls of her ass, her legs wrapped like a ribbon around my waist, her fingers in mine. "Poor Lila, you wanna come for me, don't you? You love bein' filled up with me."

Her eyes squeezed shut, head pressin' back into the pillow so her neck arched and chest raised, breasts callin' to my mouth. I ducked down and bit hard into one nipple. Her ass convulsed around me, and she cried out.

"Come apart for me, Li," I urged, chasin' the heat, needin' us both to go down in flames together. "Come for me, *mi girasol*, and I'll show you just how hard you make me wanna come for you."

"Nova," she shouted hoarsely, her body a strung bow in my hands that I loosened with one rough thrust to the hilt in her ass and a simple twist of my fingers inside her drenched cunt. "Oh, my God, I can't take anymore."

She shook as she came, vibratin' so hard she almost dislodged me. Watchin' her in the throes of passion I'd pulled from her, I felt a surge of primal masculine satisfaction. It thumped in my breastbone like the beat of a war drum to the tune of *mine, mine, mine*, and urged me to conquer her completely, utterly, without remorse.

I pinned her down with my teeth at her neck, tongue to her throbbin' pulse, and groaned as I fucked her through her thrashin' climax then shouted my own war cry as I spilled so hard it hurt once, twice, three times inside her.

Collapsed on her, only a forearm on the bed keepin' my heavy weight from crushin' the small, well-curved lines of her form, Lila did somethin' that surprised me. She locked me up in her limbs, limbs I coulda broken through easy as string, and buried her face in my neck, her lips to my throat.

When I tried to pull out, clean her up and get her comfortable, she squeezed me and didn't let up until I relaxed again.

"Love the feel of you inside me," she murmured sleepily, soft as a kitten curled up against me. "Never wanna let you go."

God, the words scored through me like knives, carvin' up my insides, reducin' the barriers I'd had erected for years to useless scraps of metal. 'Cause I could feel her inside me, too, carbonatin' my blood, wrappin' my heart up in tissue, gifts I felt the sudden urge to box up and leave at her feet.

Take me, I wanted to say to her, but in a different, more profound way than I just had before.

Take me inside you like you're forever inside of me and never fuckin' leave.

But I didn't say any of that. I just held the woman and the girl, my lover and my friend, the cornerstone of what family meant to me, and let those vicious, dangerous thoughts move silently through me. To give them voice wouldn't do anyone any good.

Lila might have thought she loved me, but she couldn't know.

She couldn't know the things Meredith had or she wouldn't love me either.

I'd let someone into that final frontier, that darkest, deepest corner of my soul once before.

The only thing that'd left me with was misery.

And a tattoo on my left bicep for the small life I'd lost 'cause I'd never been worthy of it in the first place.

CHAPTER TWENTY-FIVE

Nova

IT WAS LATE, THE MOON A BELATED THOUGHT IN THE SKY, slowly winkin' out in the dawnin' light of day. The party wasn't over, but it'd mellow like wine left open on the counter. The crowd had thinned out as people hit the hay, went home, or found a quiet place to bang, but there were still people in the common area of the clubhouse even at five a.m.. Boner laid on the pool table with his jeans around his ankles, boxers barely hiked up over his ass, asleep between the legs of one of the biker bitches. Lab-Rat was smokin' a fat blunt with half his body hangin' out the window, the other propped up on top of a speaker spillin' out The Eagles on low.

The rest of us—Bat, Harleigh Rose, Lion Danner, Zeus, Loulou, Cyclops, Tayline, and Priest—all sat collected on the leather couches at the front of the room shootin' the shit when we had somethin' to say, but otherwise just enjoyin' the mellow comedown from a night of carousin'.

Lila sat beside me, not in the circle of my arms like I itched for, but close enough I could feel the warm length of her bare thigh through my jeans and catch a whiff of her floral scent.

I wasn't a man who snuggled or committed public displays of affection, unless you counted sex, 'cause I was a fan of doin' that in public, sure.

Huggin', cuddlin', or any of that shit?

Not for me.

Especially in the aftermath of sex that had rocked me like a hurricane, leavin' me hollowed out and opened up to the elements, too exposed to weather any other kinda storm.

So I sat beside Lila and ignored the way her hand curled palm up on her thigh, a plucked flower outta water too long and dryin' from neglect.

"You hear from Cress?" Harleigh Rose asked sleepily from her place tucked up under Lion's arm.

"Yeah, said she needed more time, but she was feelin' good. Thinkin' she'll wait 'til Harold Danner's caged up for good," Zeus said as he played with the ends of Loulou's pale blonde hair.

"I was going to wait until tomorrow to bring it up," Tayline said after sharin' a look with Cy, who had her tucked up on his lap, strokin' her hair like a kitten. "But I saw a man the other day...a man I remember from years ago when Cy and I first met. Z, you might remember, his name was Greg."

The air in the room went electric.

"Yeah," Z grunted. "Remember him, alright."

Tay nodded, sucked her lower lip between her teeth then released it on a huff of breath. "Yeah, it's hard to forget the face of the man who tried to sell me. So I'm pretty sure I saw him two days ago. He was outside City Hall."

Outside City Hall meant he was talkin' to Javier Ventura.

"They're poachin' local girls now," Lion cut in. "The local PD is in fuckin' disarray now that my father's been outed, and they've got no hope of stoppin' it. I've stepped in to help along with..." he paused, eyes skitterin' over to Lila, "a friend on the inside."

"Problem is, those fuck's are tryin' to land that shit at our door." Zeus dislodged Lou with a kiss to her crown so he could get up and prowl, needin' the space and movement to think 'cause he wasn't the kinda guy who kept still. "There was a fuckin' Vancouver news crew up here today interviewin' that motherfucker, Javier, about the disappearances. Twenty bucks says we know exactly who that asshole pinned it on."

"The Fallen," Cy grunted. "We've had worst shit thrown at us, and none'a it's stuck."

"It's gonna stick this time, we don't get a handle on the problem," Zeus promised darkly, strokin' his beard. "Sent Ransom and Kodiak to do some recon tonight. The party's as good an alibi as anythin', they get busted."

"Where to?" Lion asked.

"Wet Works Production and McNeil," he said, the last referin' to the biggest drug dealer operatin' near Entrance. "Thinkin' he'll have a clue who's gettin' those girls hooked."

"Talia got hooked when she was in high school," Tayline said with a wince. "Warren got a lot of the kids to deal or buy through him. Cress told me she's one of the ones on that list King found at Javier's apartment."

"What list?" Lion demanded. "Dammit, Z, I thought you were keepin' me in the loop on this one?"

Zeus glowered at him. "You're datin' my girl doesn't mean I gotta answer to you or your rules'a righteousness. I do what's best for the club. End'a story."

Lion bared his teeth at the Prez. "I do what's best for this family, 'cause whether you like it or not, I'm part of it now. You don't trust me to do right by the Garros, that's your lack of intelligence, not mine."

Zeus slanted him a sidelong glance as Loulou giggled at the taunt.

"He's got you there, Z," she teased.

"Talia, Honey, and Lila were on the list," Tay offered.

Not so fuckin' helpfully.

I braced as the other women, Loulou and Harleigh Rose, shot open mouth looks of horror at Lila.

My Flower Child?

She tipped her chin into the air and stared them down.

"Why the fuck're you on a list by that monster?" Harleigh Rose demanded.

"Lila," Lou breathed, her huge blue eyes unblinking. "What did you do?"

"Nothing you wouldn't do," Li assured her with an innocent smile. "Promise."

"Fuck that," H.R. shouted, leanin' forward in the couch to point at her friend. "You're my best goddamn girl, what the hell are you up to that I don't know about?"

"She's workin' for Irina Ventura," Zeus admitted, the words expelled like air from bellows.

As if it was a fuckin' relief and an agony to reveal the truth.

"What the *fuck*!?" Loulou and Harleigh Rose exclaimed simultaneously.

Lou sprang out of her seat and slinked toward her much larger husband, her pretty face a mask of outrage. "You thought it was a good idea to send one of our babes into that *place*?" she spat. "And you didn't even tell me." When Z opened his mouth, she rocked up to her toes to press a hand over it and said, "And don't try to tell me it's club business when Lila isn't even a part of the club."

"King was gone, I was still inside," he admitted gruffly when Lou pulled her hand away. "Wasn't the best decision."

"Okay, fuck this," Lila snapped, standin' up to address the room. "I may not be anyone's Old Lady or blood relative, but I *am* a member of this family because you made me one. I've been with you through the last few years of chaos, and if you think I don't have a right to help when my family's in trouble, it's you all who are fucked in the head."

She sucked in a deep breath, her little chest heavin'. "And

just so you know, I did have a plan, and it's finally starting to work. Because of little ol' me, property of no one, we know how Irina's selling her girls. So you got a problem with what I'm doing, you lay it at my feet. Not Z's and not Nova's. I am responsible for my own actions. *Me.*"

There was a clotted silence as everyone stared at Lila in the aftermath of her uncharacteristic tirade.

Finally, a slow clap erupted from the corner.

"Atta girl," Cy said as he beat his meaty hands together. "Fuck yeah."

I knew Lila would've blushed if she could, her cheeks swellin' with an embarrassed smile she tried to bite off. She turned to me, eyes big, as if askin' me why she'd had a moment of drama.

I winked at her, 'cause damn, seein' her passion for the people I loved, the people I'd always wanted her to have, too, was a thing of serious beauty.

"Come here," I said quiet, just for her.

'Cause in that moment, I didn't fuckin' care about the looks or the words of censure Lou or H.R. might fire at me. I just wanted to comfort my Li girl.

She smiled then, small and genuine, then sat down beside me again, this time so close, I had to raise my arm to let her settle underneath.

Fuck, but she felt good there. She always had.

"Li, it isn't about you not being family or something stupid like that," Harleigh Rose argued, but her spirit wasn't in it. Instead, she looked worried and vulnerable with it. Lion reached out to rub at her back as she tried to find the words. "It's just, we've lost a lot of loved ones lately, and we wouldn't survive losing you too."

"I get that," Lila agreed, shooting a reassuring look at her best friend. "But sometimes you have to do dangerous things because they're the right things. I think you know a little bit about that, babe."

H.R. sighed gustily and slumped back against Lion, who chuckled and kissed her hair. "Yeah, yeah, pot meet kettle, both of us are black."

A sound like rushin' wind roared nearby, overtakin' our laughter.

There was a squeal of tires as disturbin' as a pig at its own slaughter outside the clubhouse and then a horrible *thwunk* as somethin' heavy dropped to the pavement.

We were on our feet in an instant.

"Stay here," Z barked to the women as he, Lion, and me filed after one another to the front door, hands on our weapons.

"Watch 'em," Zeus ordered Priest as the rest of us pushed through the front door out onto the lot.

There wasn't much out there but long, liquid shadows and the bright yellow splotches of light spillin' down from the motion sensor prompted spotlights.

But we could see it.

A body layin' in a pool of black that looked like leakin' motor oil in the night.

We knew it was blood before we even got close.

We didn't know who it was or if he was alive until we loomed over him.

"*Fuck!*" Zeus bellowed as he dropped to a crouch beside our beaten prospect, Ransom, and checked for his pulse.

There was blood everywhere, bubblin' up from a stab wound in his side, crusted over his entire face, and still leakin' from the multitude of abrasions and splits in his swollen flesh from landed punches and the cutting edge of brass knuckles.

He was fucked up so badly, if we hadn't known the kid so well, the short pelt of dark hair, the long, hawkish nose, and the tattoo of a ram on the inside of his bicep, we wouldn't have been able to identify him.

"Easy," Bat ordered as he and Lion started to lift Ransom who let out a gurgled moan. "Easy, brother. We got you."

The seventeen-year-old prospect groaned again then seemed to pass out as we lugged him into the clubhouse. The girls were huddled in a corner with Priest standin' before them, two guns trained at the door, the dead look in his eye said he'd kill the entire population of Entrance if they tried to enter with the intention of harm.

"Oh, my God, no," Loulou gasped as they watched us carefully carry the kid to a pool table.

Lila and H.R. hopped up immediately. My girl grabbed a blanket off the couch and rushed over to lay it out before we placed Ransom on the felt, and Harleigh Rose ducked behind the bar to grab the first aid kit.

"I got this," she told us with absolute authority as she swept me aside and opened the kit on the side of the table. "Li, go get me some hot water and clean cloth, yeah?"

Lila nodded, dashin' off before H.R. was even finished speakin'.

"What the fuck?" I muttered as I noticed somethin' peekin' out from under Ransom's back. "Hey, help me roll him a bit."

Bat appeared beside me, and together we lifted him enough for me to see what it was.

A sheet of blood-drenched paper was *nailed* to Ransom's back through his plain black prospect's cut.

> *Spy on me again, and I'll start felling The Fallen one*
>   *by one.*
> *Xx,*
> *Irina*

AFTER READIN' THE SCRIPT ALOUD, I LOOKED UP AT THE PALE

faces surroundin' our fallen prospect, each one of them impassioned with fury and grief.

No one fucked with ours and got away with it.

Fuckin' no one.

Violence radiated off of Zeus from beside me. He looked forty feet tall under the low ceilin' of the clubhouse, big as some kinda mythical beast and just as fuckin' scary.

The sight of him so filled with wrath only roused the same beast within me, an alpha wolf howlin' to his brethren. I felt it stir, yawnin' wide, sharp jaws open in preparation to stir, hunt, and fuckin' ravage whoever did this to our guy.

"Call up the chapter," Zeus said, his words rumblin' like thunder through the quiet room. "Church starts in thirty minutes, and everyone better fuckin' be there."

"Good, now unless you're going to help me, *back off*," Harleigh Rose ordered as her deft hands flew over Ransom's wrecked form. "I need to stop the bleeding now."

"Can we take him to the hospital?" Loulou asked, lookin' pale as she reached down to hold Ransom's hand, comfortin' him even though he was unconscious.

"We should," Lion cut in, his cop instinct's kickin' in. "There's no way The Fallen could feel any fallout from the cops 'cause one of your own men got jumped, and he needs serious attention. Let Rosie and I take him in, get him settled, and you can coral the troops to visit in the morning."

"It is the mornin'," I said as I caught sight of a flashin' light out the window and went to investigate. "And the cops're already here."

CHAPTER TWENTY-SIX

Lila

I DIDN'T NOTICE HER RIGHT AWAY.

I would later wish I had.

There were cops crawling all over The Fallen compound, a search warrant in their possession that allowed them to do so because they had reasonable cause to believe the club had kidnapped or was harbouring two local women who had gone missing in the last two weeks.

Talia and a woman named Melissa.

As soon as they'd stated Talia's name, a new cop on the force (most of them were new because more than half of the old guard had been corrupt officers under Staff Sergeant Danner's thumb) stepped forward to tell Tayline she was being taken in for questioning.

Cyclops stood calmly by her side as the officer approached, his entire manner subdued, even lethargic.

But as soon as the male cop reached for Tay, Cy's massive fist landed a sickening blow to the smaller man's jaw. The cop swayed for half a second, the momentum and force rendering him dumb, before he crumpled to the ground.

Four more cops were on Cy in a heartbeat, but their attempts to pin the giant men were as comical as the Lilliputians trying to rope down Gulliver. He tossed them off his back, roaring that he wouldn't let them take Tay.

I slid closer to wrap an arm around Tayline's shoulder and hugged her close so I could say, "Talia works at Wet Works Production. She's hooked on drugs, and I think she's living with one of Javier's dealers...I can get the address if they push you for it."

She nodded, her delicate face pale as a paper heart. I'd never seen spunky, hilarious Tay so subdued, but she seemed almost terrified, stale memories playing out behind her eyes.

"It'll be okay," I assured her. "I bet Mr. White will beat you to the station."

"He should really ask for a raise," she murmured just to watch me smile.

I bumped her with my hip.

"Cy," she called as her man finally got corralled to a cop car. "I'll see you at the station, Mr. Big."

The smile he shot her was sweet and intimate, a love note tucked into the craggy planes of his face, before a cop shoved him into the car, and he snapped at his hand like a feral animal.

Tay giggled.

That was when I noticed her.

The lone woman in the group of invaders.

She stood off to the side, half obscured in shadow at the edge of the clubhouse. There was just enough light, a fat wedge of yellow, that fell across her face to see she was older, middle-aged, for sure. At first, I thought maybe she was a new detective, in her pencil skirt and kitten heels she looked the part, but then she shifted back, and I saw someone emerge out of the shadows.

Nova.

He stalked her backward until she hit the chain link fence,

then moved closer still, caging her in with a hand clutched through the metal.

A shiver of omnipotent foreboding slithered down my spine like a snake in the grass.

I moved away from Tay, away from Lion working the cops for info, away from Zeus standing sentry at the door, watching the police in a way that was meant to scare them, and *did* if the way they kept dropping things and stuttering was any indication.

Lion, Bat, and Harleigh Rose had snuck out the back with Ransom, carting him into the boat they kept moored on the dock so they could head into the dark, unencumbered by the police.

I forgot about them all.

There was only the feeling deep in my stomach, like shifting plates beneath the earth, that told me Nova needed me.

So I went.

As I drew closer, I heard the woman's voice, cultured and smooth, slow moving as her injected lips formed the words. It was the voice of a woman who cared what people thought of her eloquence and manner. The voice of a woman with very different priorities than me.

"Well, handsome boy, you should have returned my calls," she said, leaning forward into Nova's face.

From where I stood just behind them, it looked for a moment like they were kissing.

Nausea crashed in to me like a sixteen-wheeler, rocking pain through every surface of my body.

Why hadn't it ever occurred to me that Nova might cheat?

Was it even cheating?

We had no definition, no rules. He was a biker man. I was a hippie biker babe. Life was too short to spend time sorting everything into boxes and labels.

Life was for the living, and recently, I'd been living my dream.

I didn't want to ruin it with rumination, digging myself into holes I'd never get out of.

So no labels.

No exclusivity. No rules.

Suddenly, I felt terribly young, ridiculously inexperienced. I was twenty-four, but I'd only ever been with two men. The nuances of dating and sex were written in a language foreign to me, in a book I'd never thought to pick up.

I had been expecting it to be easy. I loved him, and in his own way, he loved me. We respected each other. Shouldn't that have been enough?

How foolish of me to think it would be. Was anything enough for the ever-hungry human heart?

"Last time I saw you, told you I didn't wanna see your face ever again, let alone talk to ya," Nova growled.

His voice ripped across my skin like torn Velcro.

I had never heard him so incensed, so viciously disgusted.

I hesitated, swallowing the sour at the back of my tongue so I could focus on the conversation.

"You were so young then," the woman said condescendingly, smiling the way a librarian might at a stubborn boy who refused to read, as if it was only a matter of time before she persuaded him otherwise. "I told you then, I'd always love you."

"You didn't love me," he barked, but oh, I could hear the pain in that roughly torn sound, as if he'd yanked it straight out of his heart, still bleeding, still beating.

The woman pursed her lips together. "Really, Jonathon, you're being juvenile. You were a *boy*, there was no way I was going to leave my husband for you."

"You were pregnant with my fuckin' kid," Nova snarled, shaking the fence with a violent rattle.

My heart stopped.

The woman sighed. "It was barely even alive. I got it taken care of early."

A sound worked itself loose in Nova's chest, something animal and full of mourning like a bear separated from its cub.

Oh, my God.

I closed my eyes as the information passed through me, a metaphorical knife through my chest.

"Wasn't just your choice to make." His voice was stripped of anger now, almost hollow, the words falling flat to the ground between them. "Shoulda told me."

"I *did.* Why do you always have to get caught up on this? We were happy together, weren't we?" she crooned, reaching up to touch his cheek.

Nova jerked away, almost stumbling backward. "I would've been worthy of that kid. You gave me the chance, I would've fuckin' proved it to you every goddamn day. But you *robbed me,*" his voice cracked from the pressure of pain rising in his gut.

Something toxic twisted on the woman's pretty face. "You're pathetic. It was nothing. An abortion. People have them all the time. And come on, sweetheart, you and I both know you had nothing to offer a child. A high school drop out? A man-boy with nothing to show for himself but his looks? I made the only choice I could have. You would be a horrible parent, sweetie. Even now," she gestured to the cops on the compound, the squares of flashing blue, red, and white lights shifting like disco lights over the lot. "A criminal? I thought our sessions would've helped you find the right path, but I was right to think you were always hotter than you were clever. Now that I'm consulting with the EPD, I'm sure this won't be the last time I see you involved with the police."

Nova didn't say anything for a long moment, but the set of his broad shoulders was rigid, overloaded with the weight of his pain like Atlas bent beneath the crush of the entire world.

I stepped forward out of the shadows and placed a gentle hand on his back.

Instantly, he tensed, a low growl in his throat like a startled beast. Then, sensing me maybe, he relaxed back against my hand and looked over his shoulder for me.

His face was scarred with old pain, dark eyes haunted, breath a careful metronome that told me he was struggling hard to keep himself under control.

"*¿Estás bien?*" I asked softly, because the bitch didn't need to know what we spoke of.

Are you okay?

"*Ni siquiera cerca,*" he replied gruffly.

Not even close.

My chest constricted like a python around my heart as I stared up into his gorgeous, agonized face and wondered how long Nova had been carrying the weight of this trauma alone.

"Excuse me, we were having a private conversation," the bitch interrupted cattily.

Slowly, I turned to her.

Blonde hair tucked into a ritzy chignon, jewels at her ears, wrists, and throat, a silk blouse opened just a little too deep at her breasts.

Something niggled at the back of my mind, a loose thread caught in the wind.

I tugged at it and gasped when it unraveled.

I knew this woman.

I remembered her in glimpses and snatches of childhood recall.

Dropping Nova off at his therapist's house after one too many fights at school and the incident of Ellie's death. Molly thought he could use help for his insomnia, his reckless decision making, and carousing.

He'd gone for *years* to the woman.

Dr. Meredith Canterbury.

It occurred to me, like a slap across my face, that Meredith might have been planting a garden, too, much like the one Nova had grown in my heart. Only, hers was a garden of self-hate, strewn with doubt and self-flagellation.

Had she been telling Nova for years that he wasn't good enough?

Anger bubbled up in my gut, spitting up my throat to burn lava hot across my tongue.

Meredith took me in, eyes narrowed as they slid over my tattoos, my cropped peasant blouse and tiny, ripped shorts, I knew exactly what she thought of me.

She assumed, because I had ink and a sense of style that didn't cost me an arm and a leg for a simple *tee*, that I was trash, lesser than her in every way. She didn't care about what was in my head or my heart or in what direction my moral compass swung.

I was pinned in her mind by her skewed judgement, tacked to the wall by her contempt and immediate disregard.

"I'm sorry, the situation I walked in on didn't seem like a conversation," I said conversationally, baring my teeth in a grin that looked more like a grimace. "In fact, if I didn't know better, I would say it was a confession."

She sneered at me, eyes narrowed on the place I touched Nova. "You have no right to interfere. Leave us alone."

"Oh, I have the right," I practically purred as I stalked forward.

She hesitated at the warning sign on my face then hastily stepped back, flattening herself to the chain link fence. I didn't stop moving until I was in her face, caging her in the way Nova had just done. My lips were a whisper from hers, her blown open eyes the only thing I could see. The fear in them made my heart palpitate with savage joy.

I wanted her to be afraid of me.

I wanted her to suffer.

"I have the right because I'm that man's family. I have the right because the man you just accused of being worthless fucking raised me. He gave me a family when I had *nothing*. It seems like you were lucky enough to have the same option, yet you *blew it*. That's on you. Not Nova. But you being here? You coming to this place that's our home and laying this bullshit at his feet? There's no call for that. There's no hope for you. You murdered that when you made the decision to take family away from a man whose family is everything to him."

I wrapped my fingers around her throat, felt her pulse fluttering like a caged bird beneath my hand, and sneered. "I'm going to have a chat with him, and if I find out you've been putting this fucking garbage in his head since he was a teenager entrusted to your care, I'm going to have one of the brothers find you. And when he's found you, after he's done playing with you himself, I'm going to be there, and I'm going to make sure this pretty face I'm sure you love so much isn't so pretty when I leave. You get me?"

"You're filth," she spat. "Jonathon, get this trash off of me."

I reared back, bringing her with me by the hand on her neck, then crashed her back into the fence. She gasped and choked, hands ripping at mine on her neck, but I was strong.

I ran every week, practiced yoga, and learned to kickbox at the club's new gym. I could hold my own against this bitch, even if she was taller than me.

"You obviously didn't hear me," I growled at her, letting the heat of my anger infuse every inch of me, feeling almost supersonic, superhuman with hate. "You're going to leave here and never contact Nova again. I hear you even so much as looked into him, and lady, I have my ways of knowing that, I'm going to let The Fallen loose on you. Trust me, they'll relish the chance to show a grade-A bitch a taste of her own medicine. You get me?"

Meredith struggled, but I only squeezed tighter. "I asked, do you *get* me?"

"Lila," Nova murmured from behind me, stepping close so I could feel the wall of his heat at my back. "Let her go."

I didn't.

"Flower Child," he coaxed softly, a hand moving the hair off my shoulder so he could press a surprisingly soft kiss there. "My little badass. Come away from her."

Firmly, gently, he pried me away from Meredith and tucked me under his arm, the limb a heavy weight barring me from attacking as much as it provided me comfort.

"You heard her, Mere," Nova ordered flatly. "Get the fuck outta here before I let her loose on you again. She's small, but trust me, she has claws."

Meredith looked between us, a hand rubbing at her throat, doubt, humiliation, and of all things, *hope*, working behind her eyes. "Jonathon... I think we got off on the wrong foot. I just wanted to talk to you, see if we couldn't reconcile. Tim...Tim and I broke up, and—"

I lunged forward so quickly, Nova couldn't restrain me, and I slapped Meredith hard across the face. "It's you who's not fucking worthy of this man. Now, I'm going to give you one last chance to get the hell out of here, or I'm going to chase you down and show you a good time with my fists."

She blinked at me, hatred curling her lips like burning paper, but then she looked back at Nova, and her face softened, just briefly, but enough to show that maybe, in her own twisted way, she did have genuine feelings for him.

"You should control this piece of trash," she dared to tell him.

And then, I wasn't in her face anymore.

Nova was, his big body inflated further with quivering fury. When he spoke, his voice was pure smoke, black with carcinogenic hate. "You speak one more word against my girl... I don't hurt women, Mere, but I might make an exception for *you*. Now get the *fuck* outta here."

Him she listened to.

After one brief, lip trembling moment staring up into the gorgeous face she would never see again, she took off, walking back to one of the cop cars, brushing off an officer who tried to speak with her.

Suddenly, there was too much space between Nova and me. Echoing acres of it that seemed insurmountable. We stood inches apart, but I'd never felt so far from him, not even in the two years we'd struggled to get over my crush.

He sighed heavily and linked his fingers through the fence again, letting his head fall between his shoulders.

"She made it seem like nothin'," he murmured. "Wasn't nothin'. She was pregnant for nearly four months when she decided to end it. Didn't tell me 'til it was done. Texted me to say she was pregnant, left enough of a pause for that to settle happily, then told me it was over."

He rolled his head from side to side as if to work out the kinks in his spine, the trauma he wore under his skin. "Went out the next day and got my first tattoo." His hand disengaged from the fence to clasp his bicep then dropped back down. "A heartbeat breakin' down to nothin' with the date underneath."

I knew the tattoo. He'd shown up at the house with his sleeves rolled up, gauze and plastic taped over the hard swell of his arm, a sad, satisfied smile on his mouth.

He'd only been nineteen.

Nineteen, used and abused by his therapist, and a father for only as long as it took to receive the message that he would no longer be one.

I only hesitated for a moment before I went to him, pressing up against the long line of his back, fitting myself to him like tailored body armor. I hugged him like that, arms around his lean waist, cheek to his smooth cut. I hugged him so hard, I felt the bones in his spine creak, but I didn't let up.

I needed him to feel the overwhelming amount of love I had for him in my heart. I needed him to know the words Meredith had planted inside him, the ones that had so obviously taken root and flourished in the darkest depths of his psyche, were *wrong*.

"What she did was wrong," I murmured. "It was ultimately her choice, obviously, but that doesn't mean she handled it with any heart or grace. I'm so sorry you lost your baby, but you have to know, that's not ever going to be your only opportunity to have one. What she said about you not being worthy of a child is based on her baggage, her garbage personality, not anything about the quality of yours."

He was silent still, so unmoving I felt I was hugging a statue.

"A pretty package with nothing inside the box is temporary. It's not beauty, it's a *lie*," I said softly, fiercely. "You are not that, Nova. You are the most handsome man anyone in your life has ever known because every single inch of you on the inside is flawless. I've spent years learning you. Loving you. I've traced the path of your personality as you've grown and changed, mapped the roads of your spirit and the valley of your heart so well I would know them with my eyes closed. So trust me, please, when I tell you, the least important of all your many gifts is your pretty face. You could be scarred tomorrow, I could go blind the next day, and I would still think you are the most dazzling soul I've ever known."

He turned so swiftly I gasped, hands under my pits to lift me up and press me against the fence, his body plastered to mine.

And then he kissed me.

He kissed me without warning, without doubt, without even a shred of regard to who might be watching. He kissed me like he couldn't help himself, and he didn't even want to try. Like the only option for him in that moment was me. Like I was the very air he needed to breathe, and he wouldn't survive a moment more without my oxygen.

I angled my head for him, giving his tongue deeper access,

and wrapped myself around his like vines, giving myself over to the totality of his need.

He moaned as he kissed me, a staggering sound of need that made my toes curl and my heart flip over, tumble, and right itself in my chest.

"I want you," he muttered harshly against my lips. "I fuckin' need you."

"Take me," I offered, uncaring that we were outside, that around the corner cops patrolled and brothers rolled in for church.

I just needed to give to him in that moment. I needed to stop up that awful hole in his chest where missing and grief sat and throbbed.

His breath was ragged as he cupped my face entirely in his big hands, his eyes dark as a starless night as he stared at me, into me, through me.

"I don't deserve you," he said achingly. "I never could."

I put my hands over his on my face and spoke the truest thing I'd ever pulled up from my heart, a lovely bouquet of honesty. "You could tell me every dark thing you've ever done, every terrible thought you've ever had, and I'd still love you. The bad we've done doesn't make us inherently bad people, Nova. It makes us human. It's the good we've done that matters. And you? Everything good in *my* life was planted there by you. How could I not love you for that?"

His exhale moved over my face, baptising me with his sorrow, with his hope that what I'd said was right. He shifted his hands to tip my head up and bring his lips down on mine for an achingly tender kiss that was more about intimacy than lust.

I wanted the moment to be about him, to show him I was there for him, but I'd just laid my soul bare, and I needed something, *anything*, to shore up the walls I felt crumbling down into ruin around my heart.

"Do you…" I sucked in a deep breath and forced myself to look into his eyes. "Do you feel anything like that for me?"

A groan tore through him, and he tattooed his forehead to mine, the velvet black of his eyes my entire universe. "Fuck, Lila, I feel goddamn *everything* for you."

He didn't kiss me after that.

Instead, he carefully wrapped himself around my body as if I was precious, fragile, and he was my shield and my comfort, tending to me and protecting me in equal measure. We stood there for a long time in the quiet as the cop cars finally rolled out, and the tidal swell of Harley pipes grew louder, more frequent as The Fallen brothers convened for church.

We stood there until the door of the clubhouse closed, and I knew church was in session.

Only then did Nova stir, like a bear from some deep hibernation. He didn't release me as he stretched and groaned into wakefulness, he just pressed me deeper into his bowed body as if I was a piece of him he didn't want to break.

"Get some sleep in a bunk room, yeah?" he offered wearily, a tired smile on his face as he tucked my hair behind my ear. "If you wake up, hang out until this gets done, and I'll take us home."

Take us home.

God, but those words were lovely.

I nodded, letting his eyes rake over me as he pulled away, jerked his chin up, then turned around to walk back into the clubhouse.

A heavy sigh fell from my lips as I closed my eyes and leaned back against the fence.

"Hold up," Nova said, back suddenly, his arms wrenching me to him so he could seal my mouth in a furious kiss, running his tongue over my teeth, my tongue, the inside of my cheek, claiming every inch of me.

When we broke apart, his smile was bigger, genuine and

warm with his usual charm. The sun was breaking over the horizon, spilling white gold light over the lot, the gilt limning Nova's face. He was just straight-up, unfiltered gorgeous. From the thick waves of his dark locks glinting with threads of copper and gold, to the way his eyes caught the shine of the new day and reflected it back at me.

"Thank you," he said, holding my hand as he started walking backward. "Thanks for bein' my person."

"Anytime," I said light-heartedly as our fingers unclasped and we lost eye contact as he rounded the corner.

Then, to myself I whispered, "Every day of my life."

CHAPTER TWENTY-SEVEN

Lila

THE EARLY MORNING AIR WAS ALREADY MELTING, WARMING like butter in a pan as the sun rose over the craggy peaks of the tall, snow-capped mountains and spilled onto the valley where Entrance was nestled amid the thick carpet of old growth trees and the narrow fingers of cliff lines that descended steeply into the sea.

My feet churned through the milky fog still clinging to the forest floor of Wolf Creek Provincial Park as I ran through the trees. I hadn't been able to sleep after the drama-filled night. Tay and Cyclops were at the PD with Zeus and the club lawyer, Mr. White, while Lion, Harleigh Rose, Bat, and a few other brothers were at the hospital with Ransom. He had three broken ribs, multiple contusions, a severe concussion, and a stab wound that just missed his right kidney.

Life was not easy, and it seemed to me, the only way it could go from here was down. We needed to take down the Venturas, to end Irina for touching a hair on a Fallen head, and then maybe, we could taste peace.

For now, I chased after it during my bi-weekly jog. I'd had

my gym bag in my trunk, and I'd snuck out after feigning sleep for a couple of hours.

There was music in my ears–Wild Horses by Bishop Briggs—morning dew and sweat glistening on my skin, and the deep, fragrant scent of pine, cedar and musk-sweet earth in my nose.

This, running through nature, brushing my hand over bark, trailing it through long grass, was my happy place.

This was why, even in the darkest moments of the last two years when I'd wondered if I'd ever get over Nova, if I'd ever be able to commit to Jake and move down to Vancouver, I'd never wanted to live anywhere but Entrance.

Mine was a wild, curious soul, so I loved to travel, and I had a bucket list of destinations the length of my five-foot four frame. But this was home.

As I ran, my mind clear as the lake sprawling out to my left, the detritus on the bottom magnified as though looking through glass, I knew it wasn't just the natural beauty of the place that made it home.

It was, of course, the people.

Growing up, I'd never thought a person needed a community.

Ignacio had taught us to be suspicious of strangers, of kindness and connection.

It was blood over everything. Blood first, blood last, blood always.

But I'd learned differently in the years since he'd disappeared from my life.

It wasn't blood.

It was *family*, first, last, and always.

It was my girl Harleigh Rose, my biker babes, and their men.

It was Hudson with his goofiness and elastic expression, Milo with his sharp mind and twitching lips, and Oliver with his intense manner but quick, rapid-fire laugh.

Molly and Diogo, the only real parents I'd ever known, and Zeus who had stepped up like some kind of magnet, calling me to him and his just because I was Nova's.

And Nova.

It was Nova more than anyone else.

Nova had defined my sense of home since I'd seen him gangly and beautiful stepping from that minivan across the street from the structure I'd slept in.

I could've moved to the other side of the planet, never seeing him again in person, just painted in exquisite brush strokes in my mind's eye, and still, I knew he would always be the home my heart was settled in.

Sleeping with him had done nothing but solidify the dream I'd constructed the moment he told me I needed something to wish for, something that was my own.

If Nova had planted a garden in my heart all these years without stopping to smell the flowers, he was tending to them now, watering the growths, shaping the topiaries into something even more exquisite, even more precious to me.

There was no hope now that I'd ever recover from the magic of his love.

To weed it out would kill me, hollow me in a way I'd never be myself again.

And I was okay with that, I thought, as I moved through the forest and watched my own heavy breath bloom in front of me.

Even living only a moment of this dream with Nova was worth a lifetime of heartbreak.

Being there for him last night after the party had only cemented my love for him, my desire to see him safe and loved even if it meant I'd be alone for the rest of my life, too busy tending to him to look for someone to tend to myself.

And I was an optimist. Maybe one day, years and years from now, I'd be able to glue the broken porcelain of my heart back together with the melted down memories of my friends and family over the course of my life.

I was rich with those, and I could survive on that.

Or maybe, the small mad hope I'd nursed all my life burst forth to think, one day he'd grow to be in love with me too. It might take time. God knew, I understood that even more now after the party and meeting the bitch Meredith than I ever had before.

But time I had. These feelings weren't going anywhere anytime soon, so I could wait and water, pray and garden, hoping that one day his love for me would bloom into more too.

My heart still pumped a lopsided beat as I pushed hard, sprinting through the densest part of the forest before I curved back toward the clubhouse.

My pulse beat so hard in my ears, I almost didn't hear it.

But I did because whoever it was fucked up when I broke into a sprint.

They broke into one behind me.

If you paid attention, the forest offered no lies.

The birds called through the trees, the deer crunched over leaves as they plodded from meadow to meadow, and even the plants rustled in the breeze.

Now, it offered me the rattling of branches pushed to the side, the hard, crisp crush of undergrowth beneath heavy feet.

Someone was following me.

No, they had been following me, but they'd now given up their secrecy to *chase* me.

Immediately, panic rushed through my system, revved my engine even higher, and I exploded into a fierce sprint. My headphones ripped from my ears, torn away by the wind as I tore through it, but I was glad for it because I needed to hear.

They were close, just a few yards off me even though when I twisted my head to look briefly behind me, I couldn't see them through the trees.

Briefly, I thought about slowing down to pull my phone out of the pocket of my spandex shorts to call Nova, Zeus, *someone* to come help.

But I was in the middle of nowhere with a predator on my tail. What were they going to do to help me?

I was on my own.

So I swerved off the running path into the ferns and moss-covered rock terrain and hoped I would be able to lose him or her in the dense bush.

There was a rough, pained curse from behind me.

A man.

Immediately, I wondered if it might be Dane coming back to try to connect with me, but just as quickly, I abandoned that thought. He would never chase me without calling out that it was him.

I had no idea who might want to stalk me and no idea what they would hope to accomplish by capturing me.

And I wasn't eager to find out.

"You run, it'll only cause more trouble," a rough, out of breath voice shouted, too close behind me.

I stumbled slightly, caught off balance by looking over my shoulder, and I fell hard in the dirt, my shoulder tearing over the hard edge of a rock.

He was on me in a second.

I felt the hand grab my ankle and kicked at it, but he held fast. Flipping to my back so I could see my attacker, I was shocked by the sight of him.

Grizzled and weathered as only a biker can be after years of sun exposure and riding free in the wind, the face that look down on me was the same face I recognized from the night Ellie died.

It was the man who had come to take us away.

He opened his mouth to say something, but I used the leg in his arms as leverage and kicked up with the other one, striking him in the face with the heel of my foot. Immediately, he grunted, letting go of my other foot as he staggered back, blood pouring from his nose or mouth.

I didn't stop to check.

Lurching to my feet, hopping slightly on a twisted ankle, I took off.

My breath exploded from my mouth as I pushed myself even faster, ducking around trees and leaping over stones almost recklessly. One wrong step and it would have been over.

But I knew this forest like the back of my tattooed hand. I'd spend countless days in it as a girl playing with Dane to get away from the house and then even more hours running through its trails as a woman. When the forest breathed, I breathed, and I had a small, perhaps silly sense, that she was going to help me out of this situation.

I ran for so long, my legs threatened to give out, and my ears buzzed with my erratic, stomping heartbeat.

Finally, I made it to the falls.

The loud rush of water pouring into the basin canceled out any hope I had of hearing those predatory footsteps, but I didn't need to anymore.

Instead, I raced on tiptoes through the shallow edge of the pool until I was adjacent with the cliff face, and then I slipped along it until I reached the thundering veil of water. I sucked in a deep breath and dove through the edge of the plummeting river, landing on my hands and knees in the cave on the other side.

I wouldn't be seen from there, obscured by the opaque, spitting sheets of water, but I also couldn't see what lay on the other side.

My phone was dead, waterlogged with only the hope of a rice bath to bring back its functionality. So I waited.

I waited until my teeth chattered in my mouth, my spine wobbling with cold and fatigue. Until my fingers went white and wrinkled and my pulse nose-dived to a sluggish speed.

When I finally crept out of the fall, the sun had dramatically changed position, presumably sometime after noon when I had left before ten in the morning.

There was no one in sight.

A small, scared part of me wanted to burrow deeper in the cave and stay there another full day. I had no weapons or recourse against a man with skill and a gun, if he had one. It would have been easier to hide.

But I pictured Nova going to his room at the compound and seeing me gone, my wallet left on the bedside table beside my car keys.

He'd freak out when I didn't return in a timely manner.

Then the club would freak out.

And the Booths.

I wrapped my arms around my shivering torso and took off back through the forest. Tears ran down my cheeks unchecked, but it felt good to shed them. It felt as if I'd been scared for so long, of what might happen to my family and friends, what *had* happened to Dane, and now the sheer terror I'd experience myself... it was the straw that broke the camel's back.

When I finally found the path that led back to the industrial neighborhood north of the city, I turned west and walked along the water, holding the stitch in my side until I hit the high, chain link fence of The Fallen compound.

I could see activity through the fence, brothers getting on motorbikes, Zeus bellowing something to someone inside the clubhouse while Bat emerged from Hephaestus Auto carrying a gun.

The gates were open, so I made my way slowly up the drive and stopped just at the mouth beyond the gate.

"Hey," I called weakly, then tried again. "Hey!"

As one, the men stopped mobilizing and looked at me.

"Nova!" Zeus shouted into the open door of the brick clubhouse. "She's here."

A second later, Nova was in the doorframe, his hair a rioting mess, his face taut with strain.

"Flower Child," he mouthed, and a second later, he was pushing off the door and sprinting in his motorcycle boots and heavy leather cut directly to me.

I gasped as he caught me up in his arms, cradling the back of my head and holding me up with an arm under my ass. He smelled like home, spicy smoke and leather. I dragged deep lungfuls of his fragrance into my chest and focused on not breaking down.

"What the fuck happened?" he barked, already carrying me into the clubhouse.

Loulou met us at the door with a blanket and tucked it around my shoulders when Nova sat us both in the first couch by the door. I thanked her with a shaky smile and accepted her kiss on my crown.

Then, I told the collected brothers what happened, feeling Nova get tenser than an uncomfortable plastic chair beneath me.

When I was done, Zeus immediately stood up and growled, "Meetin', church, fuckin' *now*. Get the brothers back I sent off already. Fuckin' *fuck*, this ends now. If we gotta storm that fuckin' production lot, we will."

There was a collective grumble and grunt of assent. Most of the men shot me sweet little smiles as they followed orders and moved toward their sacred meeting room at the left side of the clubhouse, but Zeus himself stalked toward me and crouched his huge frame at my feet.

His face was filled with so much fury, it was hard not to feel frightened when one of his big, scared hands reached out to gently touch my face.

"We got you," he told me quietly. "We're gonna handle this now, yeah? You did good, Li, gettin' that info for Curtains. But we can take shit from 'ere on out. You never shoulda been involved. Fuckin' regret sanctionin' this shit...I was in a bad place with King's passin', but fuck, that's no excuse."

I put my hand over his on my cheek and mustered a genuine smile for him. "It's the best excuse and probably the only one that would have allowed you to let me do this. I would've anyway, Z, but I'm glad I didn't have to do it behind your back."

His smile was soft, blurred at the edges with sadness. "Brave girl, ya got, Nova."

"Don't I know it," he responded woodenly. "Meetcha in there in a minute, boss man."

There was something in his voice, something toxic, that Z seemed to notice, too, because he looked over my shoulder at his brother for a long moment before he sighed loudly, clapped my thigh, and left for church.

"Lou, give us a second, will ya?" Nova asked.

Loulou bit her lip as she looked between us, pity in her expression when it lingered on me.

And I knew.

Just as Z and Lou had.

Nova wasn't just freaking out. He was breaking, tearing off the piece of me he harboured in his chest, readying to give it back to me.

I didn't notice Lou leaving, but I didn't have to because Nova spoke as soon as she did.

"This ends now," he intoned like some automated speaker at the end of a 1-800 number.

I twisted to look at him then, struggling to stay on his lap when he firmly settled me at his side.

"What does?" I demanded even though I knew.

"You workin' for Irina," he began, stopping to take a few deep breaths. "You puttin' yourself at risk for this club. You nearly getting' fuckin' abducted 'cause of *me*."

"It wasn't because of you," I retorted sharply, wanting to slap him. "It was because there are some crazy ass people in the world, and some of them happen to want to take down this club."

"*This club* you think you have to protect 'cause of me," he bit off each word and spat it out with contempt, his face a gorgeous mask of indifference.

The mask he always tried to hide behind.

"You think you'd be willin' to do what you're doin' if I wasn't around?" he argued before I could reply. "You wouldn't even *know* these people if it wasn't for me. I'm the one brought you around here thinkin' it'd be good you had family, not carin' what kinda family I bought you."

"You bought me the best family there is," I cried out, shedding the blanket because suddenly I was hot with anger, the fabric like needles against my flesh.

"They got Mute killed, King killed, Z in jail so he missed the first months of his babies bein' alive," he said flatly.

"The club did shit all to buy that! The Fallen gave Mute and Ares a home like they gave me. They made King into the kinda guy who'd take a bullet to save his family, and they gave Zeus *Lou*. You think they would've crossed paths if it wasn't for the First Light Church shooting?" I waited for my words to sink in then fell across the couch to take his apathetic face in my hands. "Ignacio was always spouting these stupid sayings, but this one, *"no hay mal que por bien no venga,"* means there is no bad from which good doesn't come. Nova, you cannot blame this on the club or on you. If you do, then you have to balance it with the fact that you've both brought me untold beauty over the years. So much more than the ugly. Why can't you see that?"

"You're askin' me to do that while you got dirt and blood on your skin after bein' run down like a fuckin' *animal* 'cause of your connection to the club?"

"It could have been because of Ignacio," I shouted, stranded on the hot sand of my anger looking at the tsunami wave of pain gathering to bear down on me and tear every shred of my recent happiness to smithereens. "Nova, listen to me, do not do this to us."

He didn't look at me, eyes fixed to a spot on the counter, jaw wired shut.

I climbed back onto his lap and cupped his handsome face in my hands so he would have to look at me. If he was going to end this, *us*, I wasn't going to make it easy on him.

"I am *not* Meredith. I don't think the only thing you have to offer the world are your good looks. You are the kindest, loveliest, most misunderstood soul I know, and it breaks my fucking heart because the person who misunderstands you the most is *you*."

I pressed my forehead to his, hoping for some mysticism, some connection at the third eye that would open his mind to what I was saying, what gift I was so desperate to give him.

"Whenever I think of home, it's you," I told him, plucking at the flowers in my heart, pulling up the grass and roots so he might see the beauty and depth of my love for him. "You're my closest link to Dane, you're a Booth and a Fallen man. But…it's more than that. It's like clean laundry and sleeping in our own bed after vacation. It's like loving someone because you were born loving them, like your parents or siblings, but more. You're more than my family, you're more than my best friend. You're the choice I want to make every single day, to live to the fullest and love the hardest."

My impassioned words drew lines of pain on every inch of his face, more vivid than his tattoos, so stark I wanted to comfort him even as he broke my heart.

He opened his mouth, and knowing the words that would tumble out, I kissed them off his tongue, swallowing the bitter poison so I wouldn't have to hear them spoken.

I didn't stop, even when he tried to pull back, even when he would have protested.

I kissed him with everything I had, and when his heart kicked at mine through our pressed chests and I felt the growing ridge of him in his jeans, I asked for one last thing before he broke my heart.

One last memory to take with me into the dark.

"I need you," I whispered into his mouth. "Please, give me this. One last time."

"Lila, no," he insisted, but there was panic in his eyes, and his hands still clutched me close. "Don't."

"If you care about me at all," I almost cried, "you'll give me this one last time."

He looked down into his lap, hair shifting over his forehead, shoulders rounding.

It wasn't fair, what I was asking, maybe, but I wouldn't let go without a fight.

And when he looked back up at me, his heart was in his eyes, and I knew I'd won the battle even if I lost the war.

He collected me up in his arms like an abundance of flowers, gently, reverently, nose to my hair to breath deep as he walked us back down the hall to his bunk room and laid me down.

We took our time, softly peeling back clothes, tracing valleys with fingers, kissing peaks with open mouths and wet, lashing tongues. He worshipped me, his hands on my body as reverent as a servant tending his vassal.

We didn't speak, we didn't even moan.

We were all heavy, feathering breaths and the slide of slick skin against skin.

When he notched himself at my entrance, he locked eyes with me, hands with me, legs with me and pushed through to the hilt. I watched the way desire played out in his eyes and squeezed mine shut to sear the image into my memory.

And when I came, a climax that washed through me like warm water as he made love to me, I cried.

He kissed the tears off my cheeks, licked them from the corner of my mouth, and sighed into my mouth as he released inside me.

Wrecked, ruined by his body and his love even if he refused to call it that, I fell almost immediately into the arms of sleep, exhausted by the day and by him.

"I hope you dream of me," his voice whispered as he held me close, still inside me and all around me, tight like he couldn't bring himself to let go. "I hope you never stop."

CHAPTER TWENTY-EIGHT

Nova

LILA LAY BESIDE ME, LOST TO THE WORLD IN AN EXHAUSTED slumber, dreams racin' behind her lids in a way that told me her fears had followed her into sleep. I felt her perfection move through me like a religious experience, the way a zealot might feel after a long, hard pilgrimage lookin' on his final destination, his place of peace and worship.

And I hesitated.

I hesitated 'cause I was willingly cuttin' out the best part of my life and what felt like the best part of myself by endin' this thing with her.

I wanted it, her beside me in bed every mornin', the scent of flowers in my nose as I buried my face in all that hair. But I couldn't shake the feelin' that I'd been doin' her some grave wrong. That bein' shackled to me would only bring her down, anchor her in a way she'd never get full light.

She wanted me, she fuckin' *loved* me, and I could see it shinin' in her eyes whenever she looked at me. I wondered how long she'd been lookin' that way, how long I'd been blind to her 'cause of her age and our circumstances.

Pain ripped through me.

'Cause I realized I'd been plantin' flowers across her skin and a garden in her heart for years, and I'd never known how badly that must've hurt her until I realized that same garden, planted by her hand, existed in me.

I loved her.

Not the warm, gentle affection of a man for a little girl, not even the solid, intricately woven rope of affection tyin' a brother to a sister.

I loved her in all the complicated ways a flower thrives in a garden. I loved the way she tended to me like I was somethin' precious and not monstrous. I loved the way she wore blooms in her hair and inked into her skin 'cause she spoke the language of flowers better than the language of men, and she'd always been so in sync with her surroundin's. I loved the way she turned her face up to me as if seekin' sunlight, needin' the warmth of my praise and presence to grow and thrive.

It was a heady fuckin' thing, bein' someone's sunshine, their rain, their entire ecosystem.

But it was dangerous too.

'Cause I would raze that all to the ground with one wrong move, one of my stupid mistakes.

And it would be gone, laid to waste forever.

This was better, rippin' out the weeds of romanticism I'd been so stupid to sow in her heart. The other stuff, with time, would survive.

We'd always be family, and eventually, we'd get back to our friendship.

Two years hadn't ruined us, what was a few more in an effort to heal her heart and give her the chance to win someone better?

I sat on the edge of the bed, dressed, boots tied, hands in my hair 'cause I couldn't shake this feelin' I was bein' a fuckin' dumbass for endin' it even though I *knew* it was right.

"Sneaking out?" she whispered.

I looked over my shoulder at her, the sheet clingin' to the curve of her hip, the flowers I'd inked on her back vivid against her dark skin and the white covers. My fingers twitched to trace them.

"Nothin' about this is easy, Li," I admitted. "I feel like I'm hurtin' you if I do, hurtin' you if I don't. I'm just tryin' to find the best option here. You might not believe it, but I'm tryin' to do what's best for you."

She blinked up at me, those wide, long lashed eyes that had stared up at me for years, so trustin' and lovin' were now shuttered, guarded against me.

My heart rattled against the cage of my ribs, strugglin' to get out.

To get to her.

"I know you think you aren't good enough. I know you've always had that kernel of doubt about yourself because you were different, and growing up, people told you that made you bad. I know Meredith solidified that for you. But I want you to think it about it like this," she took a deep breath, and I braced for her words. "You saying your not worthy enough? It's like me saying the same just because Ignacio is my father, and I have his blood. I choose every day to be better than what he gave me, Nova, even though he'll always be a part of me. You could make the choice to be better than what you think you are, for me, if you wanted."

She had a way of sayin' someone's name like that. The same way she said the names of flower varieties, as if each word itself was a novel, and she was tryin' to convey a summary of the entire thing in one word.

I'd memorized the way she said *Nova*, as if it was the great novel ever written. As if it was a sacred text she'd studied, runnin' her hands over the pages until they went cotton smooth with use and lovin'.

I *wanted* to be that for her, to try for her, to love her better every day, but how selfish would it be to keep her in this life of mine?

Lou and Z had been separated for months by prison, Cressida had lost her King.

Wouldn't I just be condemning Li to a similar fate somewhere down the line?

"You know, Nova, I've loved you all my life. Since the day I first saw you across the street stepping out of that minivan, I thought you were the most beautiful thing I'd ever seen." She laughed softly, and I thought I'd never heard a laugh so full of grief and mourning. "But for a pretty boy, you have an ugly heart."

"Lila," I started, but my voice was wrong, strangulated by the cobra of emotion twined around my throat, squeezin' the life outta me. "Don't say that. Not you. I'd fuckin' rip out my own heart to see you safe, to see one fuckin' smile on your face."

She was so fuckin' lovely in her despair, tragic in a romantic way like Juliet before her Romeo. Of course, even my Flower Child made heartbreak look pretty.

"That's just it. You could make me smile every day for the rest of my life so easily. All I've ever wanted was your love."

"I love you," I said instantly, but the words fell flat and heavy when they should have soared, hollow and cheap as a children's toy dropped to the floor.

"Not enough," she declared with a sad kind of triumph as if I'd put her outta her misery in some horrific way.

As if she'd just been waitin' for me to disappoint her all along.

"Not enough," she repeated softly. "Not enough to even *try*."

I watched her with my heart in my goddamn throat as she got up, naked and glorious as a nymph crossin' my path, and went to the bathroom. Before she closed the door, she turned to me and said, "I hope you're gone when I come back. And you should know, this time? I'm not waiting for you."

CHAPTER TWENTY-NINE

Lila

"*HOLA, MI HERMOSA.*"

I blinked as I held the phone to my ear, sitting in my car outside of Nova's apartment where I'd just collected my essentials so I could go back to my cottage at the Booth's.

Axe-Man was already at the house, my assigned biker for the day until everything settled and the brothers could construct a plan to get at Irina. Until then, the club was on lockdown, and because I refused to be on the compound at the same time as Nova, Axe-Man was my shadow.

My phone had rung with an unknown number, and I hadn't thought before answering it. I never put contacts into my phone, so I was always getting calls like that.

I hadn't expected Irina to call.

Not after she found Ransom snooping around.

I'd just assumed, as the rest of the club had, that she had guessed I was a traitor because of my ties to Nova and therefore the club.

I wasn't planning on going back to Wet Works, or ever seeing Irina again if I could help it.

"I can hear you breathing, pretty girl," Irina crooned through the speaker. "I know you are scared, *si*? You are scared because you know who I am, you know *what* I am, and you know I do not tolerate spies. Do you think I will have you killed, *chica*?"

I didn't say anything. Instead, I scrambled to slot my keys into the car and started the engine.

"I won't kill you," she promised sweetly. "I can restrain myself. Did you see the sexy little boy I left alive at your doorstep? I didn't kill him. And I won't kill you, Lila Davalos. You are too valuable, you see. Don't worry, I have bigger plans for you."

I hung up as the sound of her laughter filled my car, releasing the emergency break as I made to pull out.

My phone rang again.

I was going to ignore it, but then something made me check the number.

It was different than the one before.

Hesitantly, I answered, not speaking, just accepting the call.

"Lila?" Dane's voice exploded through the phone. "Lila, where are you?"

"Dane," I breathed, relief sluicing through me. Part of me had thought seeing him at Wet Works had only been a dream. "Oh, my God, I'm so glad you called."

"Where are you?" he hissed in a rough, low whisper as static sounded over the line. "Are you somewhere safe?"

"I'm in my car," I told him with a frown. "Just heading to the Booths'."

"Don't," he ordered, panic carbonating his words so they fizzed and popped. "Get to Jonathon, get to a police station, get anywhere safe."

"Why?"

"Irina's coming for you. You're on her manifest."

"Manifest?" I asked, my entire body growing cold. "What do you mean?"

"You're on the list of women she's selling to the people I work for," he snapped. "The exchange is happening tonight, so if she doesn't already have you, she's coming."

My heart crashed against a wall of sheer panic then tumbled upright into a sprint.

Over the roar of blood in my ears, there was a soft *rap* of knuckles against my driver's side window.

I startled, a scream ripping from my throat as the door to my car was torn open, and I was dragged from it by my hair by Arturo, Irina's right-hand man. I struggled, thrashing and kicking out, turning my head to bite savagely into his wrist, the hot, copper tang of blood flooding into my mouth.

My phone dropped to the ground, Dane's voice a tinny wail from the speaker as Arturo reared back and landed his elbow at the back of my neck.

The next second, everything went black.

CHAPTER THIRTY

Nova

WE WERE IN THE MIDDLE OF CHURCH WHEN THE PHONES started blowin' up in the bucket we kept for them outside of the room.

No one moved to answer them.

We were deep in conversations about how to storm Irina's house at the base of the mountains behind Wet Works Production so we could hold her for ransom against Javier or just fuckin' end her like she deserved.

It was only when the front door busted open with a rip and a thunderous clap, that we surged to our feet as a unit, reachin' for the weapons we all had tagged at our hips.

A second later, the door to the chapel burst open, and a huge man stood in the frame, face broke open with horror, chest heavin' as he panted.

"Lysander Garrison," Zeus grumbled darkly, already stalkin' forward with his gun raised to the man's chest. "What the fuck are you doin' in my house?"

"They took 'em," Lysander huffed out, completely ignorin' Zeus, his eyes goin' wild as they searched the men then pinned on me. "They took the girls. They got Honey, Talia...all of them. Even Lila."

Everythin' in me turned to stone as he spoke, forebodin' coursin' through me like quick dry cement and then, when he said the name of my Flower Child, it struck me hard as a hammer blow and I went crackin' right down the middle.

Zeus dropped his gun, pulled out his phone, and dialled a number as he said, "Tell me the facts. How'd you know this? Where did they take 'em?"

Sander licked his chapped lips and sucked in a deep breath. "Went to pick up Honey, she was gone. Went to Wet Works lot, it was empty except for basic security and a girl dead from an O.D. on set. I don't got much, I usually work with Javier's men, but he put me on loan to Irina to watch over her operation. He didn't trust her lately not to fuck up."

"Fuck," Zeus cursed before tunin' in to his phone. "Lion, yeah, we got a serious fuckin' situation. The Ventura motherfuckers got Honey and Lila."

"You work for Javier fuckin' Ventura?" I asked soft, so soft 'cause my lungs couldn't pull in breath, and I didn't have much air left.

My mind had short circuited with enraged horror. I was just instinct, the beast in my gut unchained and dominant, operatin' on sheer intuition.

"You work for that motherfucker?" I asked again. Seethin', I suddenly jerked outta my seat to grab the large man by the throat, poundin' him into the wall of the chapel so hard the paneling bent to the shape of him.

Lysander let me manhandle him, his eyes almost dead but for the panic corrodin' the edges of his grim face. "Been workin' for him for 'bout a year."

"He's workin' with me," Lion said through the speaker

phone of Z's cell. "He's been undercover with the Venturas for months."

"And you didn't think to fuckin' tell us that shit?" Zeus growled.

"No," Lion said firmly. "You and Sander have too much history. You don't trust him, and I get that, but *I* do. I'm comin' down now, don't kill him until I get there, and we can sort a plan of action."

Zeus hung up, but I didn't let go of Lysander. Instead, I breathed like a stuck bull and tried not to pound in his face.

"You knew this could happen," I accused in a hissin' breath as the snake coiled around my heart constricted tighter. "Just like you didn't protect your sister when you should've, you didn't protect those women."

"What do you think I'm tryna do now?" he countered quietly, firmly. "Why do you think I'm workin' for that fucker in the first place? 'Cause I like takin' orders from a psychopath? I'm doin' this to make things right after all the wrong I did."

"You can start by tellin' me where the fuck I can find Irina Ventura," I offered with a nasty smile, pressin' hard against his windpipe.

"You don't wanna go there, man. Woman's mean as a viper. She'll kill any Fallen man she sees soon as you get in her sights."

"Not me," I promised darkly, mind racin', pulse poundin' so hard I nearly choked on it in my throat. "Every villain's got a fuckin' weakness, and Irina's is her cunt."

I CUT THE ENGINE OF MY HARLEY AT THE END OF HER driveway, takin' in the massive, honeyed yellow mansion with the terracotta roof lookin' straight from her homeland. As I pulled of my helmet, I noticed the men on both sides of the house with guns trained on me and the man on the second story with his rifle pointed at my head through a cracked open window.

I was casual as I swung off my bike and ambled over to the front door to ring the bell, actin' unfazed when a huge motherfucker with a face as ugly as a swine's ass answered the call.

"Lookin' for Irina," I offered with a cocky grin, leanin' against the doorframe as if I had all the time in the world to wait for the bitch. "She in?"

"*Guapo.*"

I looked over the man's shoulder as Irina descended a sweepin' marble staircase clad in a skin-tight, white dress done up from breasts to toe with a single zipper.

Bile surged up my throat and coated the back of my tongue, but I swallowed it back as I shoved my helmet into the doorman's chest and pushed past him to grin wickedly at Irina as I slowly check her out.

"Lookin' gorgeous, Irina," I told her as she took her last step and accepted my offered hand. I tugged her closer, watchin' her face closely 'cause I was playin' the most dangerous game of my life, and I needed every single fuckin' clue I could get.

"I thought you weren't interested in my beauty anymore?" she asked lightly as she studied me with the slanted eyes of a snake. "I thought you were being a good boy, not dabbling with the wicked witch set against your precious club."

"I've always been more of a bad boy at heart," I said with

a wink as I ran a single finger down her neck then slowly wrapped it with one hand.

Hated doin' it knowin' how much Lila'd loved it, my hand collared around her pretty neck, the sight of my tats the prettiest necklace she'd ever wear.

But Irina loved the danger of bein' with me almost more than she loved my good looks.

So I gave that to her and watched her lids lower, heavy with arousal.

"Well, well," she purred, cantin' her hips into mine. "This is suspicious timing, *guapo*, given I just sent one of your young boys home after a lovely beating from my men, but who am I to resist temptation?"

"Roberto," she called to the behemoth at the door. "Check Señor Booth for weapons."

I kept an easy grin nailed between my cheeks even though the effort cost me as the man stepped forward to pat me down aggressively. When he was done, he nodded curtly, and Irina clapped with glee.

"Oh, you really are here to play," she cried. "And there are so many things I've thought to do to you over the years, handsome. So. Many. Things."

"Lead the way," I offered as I moved toward her and dipped down to kiss her neck.

She smelled of banana candy and expensive, cloying perfume. The fragrance clogged up my nose and made me want to puke on her designer shoes.

Instead, I let her twine her fingers with mine and lead me back up the stairs, presumably to her bedroom.

Roberto followed us, his steps heavy with his weight against the stairs.

He remained outside the door, the bulge of a weapon under his jacket as he crossed his arms and stood sentry for his boss while she took me into the room.

That would complicate things.

But he was large, slow. I was a big man, but I could move, and I trained to emphasize that quickness.

He wouldn't be an obstacle for long.

Irina locked the door and pushed me roughly onto the bed before climbin' on top of me, pinnin' my hips to the mattress as she leaned forward to stroke my torso through my thin, white tee.

"So handsome," she murmured, transfixed by the sight of her hands on my body. "I am already so wet thinking of the ways we will play."

I sunk my hands in her thick hair and whispered low, filthy things as she worked her way down my body, lulling her into a false sense'a security.

My beauty had always been the source of my shame, as if bein' a pretty boy meant I had nothin' more to give than my handsome face.

I'd let those thoughts corrode my confidence, throw off the balance of my self-worth, so I believed in the worst instead of the best.

I'd believed I had nothin' to offer a soul but the perfection of my smile and the elegance of my art on their flesh.

How fuckin' stupid of me not to have seen how my face could be a tool like any other. A tool used by the weight of my intellect, the power of my loyalty, and the reckless bravery in my heart to protect the family I loved and secretly believed I wasn't good enough to be a part of.

It was ironic, I thought with a little smile as I lay there bein' falsely seduced by a woman who underestimated me, that I would turn the whip I'd used to self-flagellate myself for years on the woman who prized beauty over morality enough to sell women into slavery.

Her lips trailed a line of bitter kisses along the top of my waistband, and I decided she was lulled enough.

So I snapped forward, hauled her up my body, and flipped

her onto the bed, high against the pillows so I could be close to the nightstand.

'Cause there was a vase there, pink and ugly as fuck, but porcelain.

My weapon.

"You wanna feel all of my beauty?" I growled as I pressed my hips into hers on a slow roll, keepin' them there so I'd be able to stay her hips.

"*Si*," she panted, hands movin' over my bare torso, legs curlin' over my hips so she could gyrate against me.

My stomach rolled with acid, but I pulled up the thought of Lila housed somewhere dark, dank, and alone, scared outta her mind thinkin' she might be lost forever.

And anger burned clean through the disgust, leavin' only resolve.

"I'll show you every inch of beauty I got to give," I pledged to Irina, claimin' her seekin' lips in a kiss as I reached out carefully for the lamp.

The moment it was in my grip, dark, monstrous joy surged through me, and I gave the beast it's head.

Mouth a prison on hers, body an anchor, I raised the lamp, jerked it free of the plug, and in the moment before she gained awareness of anythin' beyond her desire, I shifted my head away and brought the heavy porcelain lamp crashin' down on her face.

Her scream tore through the air as her nose crunched under the pressure, and blood bubbled from her nostrils, floodin' past her open mouth and chokin' off the sound.

I wrapped my hand around her throat again and shoved her viciously against the headboard so her entire body rattled.

"Listen to me carefully, Irina," I seethed, fingers crampin' in their hold on her, anger threatenin' to drive me from a place I wouldn't be able to come back from. "You're gonna tell me where your men took those girls you're plannin' to sell. You're gonna tell me in the next thirty seconds, or I'm gonna use a piece of this pretty little lamp to slit your throat. You feel me?"

She gargled as she tried to breathe through her nose, gaspin' as I squeezed tighter when she didn't immediately answer.

There was a knock on the door, Roberto checkin' to see if everythin' was alright.

I ignored him, leanin' closer to Irina's gaspin' face to threaten one last time. "You got eighteen seconds now, bitch, I suggest you get talkin'."

Roberto knocked on the door again, louder this time. Again, I ignored him. I had time enough to deal with him when I was finished with Irina.

"You're a dead man," she vowed wetly, spittin' into my face so her bloody salvia ran down my chin.

"I'm a dead man anyway I don't find the woman you're tryin' to take from me," I growled. "Now tell me what I want to hear, or you die in your own bed."

A few seconds later, the sound of pipes roared up the drive like a rush of wind, and then the air peppered with gunshots. There was a loud crash as the door busted open downstairs, followed by shouts of Spanish and more gunfire, then the clomp of motorcycle boots up the stairs.

By the time Bat and Zeus appeared in the doorframe, I was done with both Irina and Roberto.

Zeus looked down at Roberto lyin' on the floor with a bullet blown straight through his chest, eyes unseeing' as they looked up at him, then over to me.

"You get what we need?" he asked mildly as he took in the sight of me sittin' on the end of the bed tuggin' my blood-stained tee back on while Irina sagged in the bed behind me, unconscious, tied to the headboard with strips of her high thread count sheets.

She had a thick gash across her face from the tip of one side of her forehead to the end of the opposite cheek.

I'd wanted to murder her.

Slaughter her not once, but twice, thrice, fuckin' again and again like some cruel god punishin' the worst of the worst in Tarturus with eternal punishment.

Only the thought of Lila, the thought of tryin' to be worthy of her, held me back from the dark edge.

So I didn't murder the bitch, and I wouldn't let the club kill her.

Instead, I carved up her pretty face so good, Priest would've been proud, and I took the thing she valued the most.

Her goddamn beauty.

Then, I called the cops 'cause I knew there was no worse fate for Irina than rottin' unseen and alone in some dank prison cell.

"Yeah, boss," I grunted as I stood up and tagged my cut from where Irina had shucked it on the floor. "I got what we needed. They're in Vancouver harbour."

I stopped to pull out my phone as it vibrated and noted I had thirteen missed calls from the same unknown number.

Flippin' it open, I followed the brothers outta the house, steppin' over the dead bodies with ease, and stated, "What's up?"

The ghost of a man I hadn't seen in a decade came over the speaker, his voice like a bullet in my ear.

"Jon, I got a plan to help get Lila."

CHAPTER THIRTY-ONE

Lila

I WAS IN A MOAT FILLED WITH SNAKES. THEY WRITHED IN THE cold, inch-deep sludge and pressed up against my numb skin, seeking whatever heat they could find in the icy darkness. I'd stopped screaming a long time ago and now only the soft hiss of breath and the occasional splash interrupted the silence.

Powerful sedatives still muddled my blood, and together they churned sluggishly through my veins, clouding my thoughts. Mostly, when I opened my eyes, the left submerged halfway in brackish water, the snakes were menacing, their bodies flashing silver in the occasional light spilling in from some crack on the left side of the room. But increasingly, I realized the bodies were humans, women, naked and stewing like prunes in the bowel of some huge ship.

My thoughts rolled fruitlessly like a marble spinning in an empty bowl.

Time passed strangely, though, some part of me knew that I couldn't have been there for more than a day or two max. The slurp of sucking lips roused me to the idea of drinking the slimy water I lay in, and a few times I puckered my lips, held my breath and pulled some into my mouth, straight down my gullet. It left a metallic taste like blood and a thick film on my tongue, which wasn't really surprising. One of the women beside me had a long, thin slice across her belly that wept occasionally in thin red streams.

I had never pictured hell this way, hadn't figured it would be a pit of naked, stinking, bleeding women submerged in slime, but now that it was my reality, I could hardly imagine anything worse. I wasn't sure how many of us were still alive. Honestly, I wasn't even sure I was.

As the hours passed, my mind cleared enough to know what had happened.

Irina had taken me.

And now, I was in some kind of ship or container housed with dozens of other women she planned to sell into sexual slavery.

I squeezed my eyes shut as the horror of it hit me like a thousand cuts. It would have been so easy to lie there in the muck and cry, wishing for a different end, thinking about the fact that I didn't get to say goodbye to anyone I loved.

That the last thing I'd told Nova was that he was a pretty boy with an ugly heart.

A sob exploded from my throat, punctuating the mostly silent space.

I tried to breathe through the pain, to wiggle against the bonds that tied my hands behind my back and my feet tight together, but it took forever to dull my panic enough to really *think*.

And the first thought I had was Honey.

If Irina had taken the girls from Wet Works, it stood to reason the estranged half-sister of the Garro family would be there.

"Honey," I croaked, the word like a knife down my sore, dry throat. "Honey?"

There was a little whimper and then, "Lila?"

Oh, my God.

"Honey, are you okay? Are you hurt?" I called out.

"No…but I think the girl I'm laying beside is dead," she whispered brokenly. "They gave her something, some drug, and she was already so high on crank…I felt her overdose beside me. I-I can smell her."

"Fuck," I breathed, unable to imagine laying beside I dying woman, submerged in her filth. "Okay, okay. Do we know how many of us are in here?"

There was a loud sniff then a meek voice said, "I think twenty?"

I recognized her voice. "Talia?"

"Yeah," she replied on a little sob. "They must have dosed me wrong because I remember how they took me. Irina had about six of us on set in the wet room for an orgy scene. Instead of filming, someone threw something in the room that made us pass out and then some men came in to collect us."

The wet room. We used it for shower scenes and water-sport play. I hadn't ever had to assist Irina with a film in there, and I'd been grateful.

I was sickened by her use of it and wondered just how many times she'd done that.

"The rest were already here when we arrived," Talia continued. "They, they've been here a while I think."

If the smell was anything to go by, she was correct.

"Lila?" Honey called, sounding even younger than her sixteen years, so vulnerable I wanted to weep for her. "Are we going to get out of this?"

I dragged in a deep, rancid breath and struggled to tap into the hope I could always find in my chest. Hope that Nova would come, that he would arrive on his stead of chrome with his knights in leather and vanquish every single obstacle in his path to get to me.

To save me.

As he'd done throughout my entire life.

But laying in that filth, feeling the cracks in that hope from the hammer-like blow of Nova's decision to our end our relationship, I couldn't believe we would ever be found.

"I don't know," I said softly instead. "Let's hope someone finds us, but if they don't, we need to think of a plan for ourselves."

"It's useless," another voice pitched in. "I've read the stats before, once we've been taken it's like a one in one hundred chance of us being found."

"I've always liked impossible odds," I joked half-heartedly, because we were mired in a pit of despair and we didn't need any more.

And so, even though there was no hope in the dank blackness, a dozen girls and I dreamed of our escape.

An indeterminable amount of time later, when my eyes were closed and the bodies were all completely still, light flared across the room after a soft *shush* of air was released. The glow hurt my eyes even from behind their closed lids, but I wasn't willing to forsake an opportunity to figure out where I was.

I cracked open a lid, finding a dark silhouette in the doorframe and another peering in from outside.

"Smells like shit in here." The man's voice was rough and muffled in my water-soaked ears, but I yearned for the sound of it.

If we wanted to escape, we needed someone first to come down here.

"Just grab her, asshole." The other grunted from the doorway. "He hates it when we keep 'em waiting."

The first man splashed into the water as he took a step down from the door ledge, a flashlight in his hand so he could check the faces of the women as he quickly trudged his way over to my corner. I wasn't always in the same spot, somehow the women and their undulating bodies had moved enough to transplant me from beside the door to the farthest reaches of the room. I had been grateful when they first opened the door, but my distance didn't seem to deter the man. He ignored the gasps and sobs as he stepped on the limbs and organs in his way, and when he reached me, he wrenched my arms from my sockets as he hauled me to my feet. I headbutted him in the chin, drawing a curse from him before he backhanded me so hard, stars burst through my vision. He caught my body as it swayed then threw my boneless mass over his shoulder, laughing at my tiny scream.

The harsh light in the hallway stabbed my corneas, and I squeezed my eyes shut on a low moan. My head lolled against the back of the man carrying me, jarring me in and out of consciousness.

"Ah, Greg," Javier's voice called out from somewhere in the room we ended up in. "*Gracias*. Put her in the chair, please."

He dropped me in a deep leather chair, jostling my sore bones so much I cried out. When I righted myself, my eyes snagged on Javier sitting like a commander in what looked like a boat captain's office, maps tacked to the wall behind him, instruments piled on the desk before her. He was watching me, eyes tagging every single imperfection on my skin like a body scanner even though his face remained implacable.

When Javier next spoke, his voice was soft, sweet in a way that chilled me. "Greg, did you hit this woman?"

Greg shifted on his feet beside me as I lolled my head against the seat back to watch him. He was tall and lanky as if he'd never quite grown into his body, and he shifted nervously from a lifetime of working for people who were cruel in their disappointment.

"Yes, boss," he admitted, wringing his hand. "She acted up when I tried to get her."

"Ah," Javier nodded sagely as if he was at peace with the explanation.

One moment, he was seated behind a desk strewn with

nautical equipment, and the next he was standing, his arm raised to level a gun at Greg.

The sharp *crack* of a discharged gun rattled through my eardrums.

A moment later, Greg, mouth open in horror, fell at my feet like a sack of rocks. A red ribbon of blood poured from the hole in his forehead, curling to the floor beneath him.

I blinked up at Javier in shock.

He smiled kindly at me, almost paternal in his affection, as he dropped the hot gun to the table and rounded it to lean on the front and stare at me.

"I'm sorry he hit you," he said softly. "I'm sorry you're here at all."

The leftover drugs in my system and the impact of being without food or water for so long left my brain underpowered to deal with the overwhelming nature of the situation. I wanted to cry, curl up in the fetal position, and wait for Nova to come save me.

Only, I had no idea where I was or how long I'd been there.

And I knew there wasn't much hope for that.

That it was up to me to get through this.

So I sat straighter in my chair and addressed him. "If you were really sorry, I wouldn't be here at all."

His smile was almost proud as he responded in Spanish. "Yes, yes, too true. Which is why I plan to let you leave."

I gaped at him, prompting him to release a self-satisfied chuckle.

He was a dramatic man who enjoyed his power.

He was loving this.

"Why would you let me go?" I demanded as there was a knock at the door.

"Come in," Javier called.

"Boss, just wanted to let you know the cops found your wife trussed up and beaten in her room at home. You want one'a them to bring her in?" The voice was familiar, a shiver racing up my spine.

Javier went from jovial, jocular uncle to cruel drug lord in a heartbeat. I watched as he sucked on his teeth and cracked his neck, as if the urge to attack someone was in his blood and hard to beat.

"Yes," he agreed after gathering control of himself. "Have her brought here."

"She's already en route, should be ten minutes until the boat gets here."

"Oh, Piston," Javier called before the door shut. "Come here. It's been a while since you saw Ellie's daughter, hasn't it?"

I froze, my heartbeat stopping, my breath arrested in my throat.

There was a soft thud as feet crossed the carpet, and then the man was in front of me, smiling through his beard.

It was the biker.

The one who had tried to take Ellie and I away when I was six, the one who had chased me through the forest days ago.

I shrank back into my chair away from him before I could curb the impulse.

Javier laughed as he clapped the leather clad biker on the back in friendly comradery. "Thank you, Piston, that's enough for now."

Piston nodded, hesitating as he looked me over again, then plodded out the door.

"What the fuck?" I breathed as Javier just stood there smiling at me.

He clapped his hands together. "Yes, excellent question. You see, *abejita*, I once knew your mother very well. So well, in fact, that when she decided she could no longer stand your father, I sent Piston to bring her to me."

Oh, my God.

I couldn't breathe as his words punctured deeply into my mind, wounding memories I'd never relished and somehow making them worse.

"You see," he drawled slowly as he pushed off the desk and dropped into a crouch before me, pinching his slacks so he could squat comfortably. "I once found your mother extraordinarily attractive, Lila. I still remember when she served me pancakes at that little diner." His eyes lost focus as they trained on the memory. "She had your smile, and it tempted me to take her the moment she trained it on me. I am not a man to deny myself," he said with a self-deprecating grin, opening his palms as if in surrender to it. "So I took her. And I had her for eight wonderful years whenever I came to Entrance, until your beast of a father murdered her."

His eyes flashed dark, and his hand was at my face so quickly I flinched, thinking he would strike me.

He didn't.

Instead, he cupped my cheek in his smooth hand and stared at me nostalgically. "I called her my dark beauty...did you know, sweet Lila, that is exactly what your name means?"

Nausea rolled through me. I leaned away from Javier, curling over my rebellious stomach to vomit all over the side of the chair. My head swam as I expelled the small, remaining amount of nutrients I had in my belly, and when I righted myself, sour still clung to the back of my tongue.

"Hmm," Javier hummed in mild disgust as I retched. "Don't worry, I'll have that cleaned up."

There was a shrill cry from outside the room, feminine and outraged, and then Piston was shoving open the door, pushing a bleeding, mutilated Irina into the room so hard she stumbled and fell to her knees.

She looked up at Javier through her hair, eyes crazed, split open face held shut with butterfly bandages and still seeping blood. "Javier, that *hijo de puta* scarred me!"

"I can see this," Javier noted calmly.

So could I. The sight of her beauty torn diagonally down the middle by a ragged wound made something dark and gleeful flare in my chest.

From my position, I could see the way Javier leaned back against the desk, his fingers curling around the gun he'd discharged earlier.

"We must kill every single one of those men," she shrieked, moving her hands through her hair, trying to right it. "I will make an appointment with a plastic surgeon in Mexico and convalesce down there while you clean up the club. I do not want to spend one more moment in this horrible country."

"No," he agreed softly. "Irina? Did you not see we have a guest? I believe you invited her yourself."

Irina paused for a long moment then slowly turned to look at me, half hidden in the huge chair. Her face blanched so deeply she looked like she might keel over into a faint.

"Javier," she started, scrambling to get to her feet.

"Stay down!" he snapped, his mild veneer cracking as he stalked forward to loom over his wife. "Do not act innocent when you know what you did. You hired Lila as a tool to use against me, Irina, and you know how I feel when you try to manipulate me."

"I, I didn't, I just—" her words cut off with a gurgle as her reached down to grab her throat and haul her half into the air.

"You did," he snarled. "You are pathetic. You think I would not know you tried to use Ellie and her daughter against me? You think if you bring me pain, it will bring you power?"

He let her go, watching as she crumpled to the ground before he spat on her face.

Then, he moved back slightly, just two steps, and pulled the gun he'd put in his waistband free so he could point it straight down at his wife.

"My wife," he purred. "It will only bring you death."

And then he pulled the trigger.

I screamed as Irina's head exploded, the sound like a burst watermelon, pieces of gore flying everywhere.

That was why, I realized as I gagged behind my hand, Javier had stepped away.

To avoid getting blood on his suit.

"Hush, hush," he soothed me as he put the gun down and moved forward to stroke my hair even when I flinched and gagged again. "She will not bother you again."

"What do you want with me?" I demanded before I gagged again. "What am I to you?"

He studied me then, somber and considering me for so long, I worried that I'd pushed too far and he would use that gun on me too.

"I have lost children before," he explained slowly. "It is the bane of a man of power to watch the vulnerable in his car be exploited or killed. I… I would not have that happen to the daughter of the woman I once loved."

"So you're actually going to let me go?" I ventured.

He smiled sadly then went alert as boots stomped over the deck above and shouts erupted.

"This was not my ship that is sinking," he explained cryptically. "I am merely cleaning up my wife's mess. I have a feeling it is I who must leave now, not you. But, *mi abejita*," he paused to stroke his hand down my hair again. "I will see you again soon."

I wasn't surprised when he reared back with a regretful smile to backhand me across the face on the very same cheek Greg had struck.

And when I fainted, I was somewhat relieved.

"LILA."

I was dreaming.

In that dream, Dane was sitting beside me in the flower meadow beside the Booths'. He was picking flowers, a massive armful so tall, I could barely see his face.

"Lila," he called, even though I was there beside him, happy to sit in the grass with him and never leave. "Lila!"

My eyes popped open, the light assaulting my corneas so violently I gagged again, bending over someone's arm as they held me to relieve my stomach of the acid churning through it.

A big, rough hand held my hair back until I was done then helped me right myself.

"Is this one of them?" A thickly accented voice demanded.

We were above deck on a massive freighter just outside of the inner harbour in Vancouver. It was twilight, the shadows long enough to obscure the details of the shipping containers housed on deck. But I could see enough to make out the tall, thick man standing with four armed guards and the group of grimy, damp women clustered together before them.

"She is," the person holding me said in answer to the question.

I jerked in his arms to stare up at Dane, his eyes pale and glowing in the muted light. He gave me a little squeeze as he set me on my feet.

"Ah, this is the one I remember from her video," the other

man, clearly in charge, stated as he strolled forward to check me over. "The one I might keep for myself."

The men chuckled darkly.

But that was it.

I was done.

Overwhelmed with disgust and hatred, tired and hopeless, I didn't care if they killed me where I stood.

I was tired of being objectified.

I wasn't this man's property or Javier's or Ellie's or Ignacio's.

I was my own.

So I collected the bare amount of spit I had on my tongue and hurled it at his feet.

Beside me, Dane sighed a split second before the asshole sex trafficker shouted something in a language I didn't recognize and raised a gun between my eyes.

"No," Dane said, stepping forward with his weapon to press it against the man's temple. "That's my sister."

The man looked at him, so shocked it would have been comical in any other situation. "Shaytan, you will not kill me."

A gun fired, but it wasn't Dane's, and the man fell to the floor at my feet.

I looked up to see Nova, Zeus, Bat, and Axe-Man with weapons drawn, running across the deck, a ladder thrown over the side of the ship.

I only had one moment to lock eyes with Nova across the stern before all hell broke loose.

I ducked as bullets started flying, moving toward the girls who were screaming and crying, looking for shelter.

"Come on," I yelled, catching sight of Honey's strawberry blonde hair.

I ducked behind one of the massive shipping containers, dragging the girls with me by blindly reaching for their hands. Honey was there, and she launched herself at me, crying and holding me so tightly it hurt.

I looked up to see Nova, Zeus, Bat, and Axe-Man with weapons drawn, running across the deck a ladder thrown over the side of the ship.

I only had one moment to lock eyes with Nova across the stern and then all hell broke loose.

I ducked as bullets started flying, moving toward the girls who were screaming and crying, looking for shelter.

"Come on," I yelled, catching sight of Honey's strawberry blonde hair.

I ducked behind one of the massive shipping containers, dragging girls with me by blindly reaching for their hands. Honey was there, and she launched herself at me, crying and holding me so tightly it hurt.

"This is so fucked up," she yelled in my ear.

I patted her back, then moved her away, back into the press of women huddling together beside me. "It's okay, The Fallen are here."

Honey's dark eyes flashed and her mouth went flat. I realized I'd never seen her so sober, but I was still surprised when she spat on the ground at her feet and said, "Fucking Fallen men."

My frown quickly transformed to a gasp when strong hands pulled me away from the girls and an arm wrapped around my throat.

A moment later, something cold pressed to my temple.

"I'm getting out of here," someone hissed in my ear. "And you're the ticket, aren't you, pretty thing?"

I tried to rear back in the way Bat has taught me, thrusting my head into my attacker's nose, but he shifted me to the side so I missed. Which was okay, because Bat had also taught me what to do in that case. Using the space his maneuver had given me I brought my forearm up and angled my elbow in a downward thrust that connected beautifully with the man's groin.

He collapsed behind me.

I spun around too fast, panicked breath exploding through my lips, head spinning with adrenaline and exhaustion.

As I stumbled, someone caught me.

He smelled of spices and leather.

Instantly, I burst into tears as Nova wrapped me up against his body in a tight, desperate hug that hurt as much as it comforted, and then he pushed me away so quickly I couldn't protest.

"Got you, Li girl," Zeus soothed in a rough whisper as he caught me and held me close.

I settled almost instantly in the protection his huge arms, but mostly because my eyes were transfixed on Nova.

He'd bent to the remaining sex trafficker, lifted him with a hand fisted in his bullet proof vest and then hammered a bone crunching punch to his right cheekbone. His silver rings cut three long gashes in the cheek, blood fanning through the air against Nova's face.

He didn't care.

If anything, it seemed to spur him on.

I watched in a trance as Nova beat the man to a bloody pulp systematically, ruthlessly. Sitting on his hips, pinning him to the floor of the freighter as The Fallen spoke softly to the traumatized girls behind me, Nova killed a man with his bare hands.

Just for threatening me.

When he was finished, he stood and turned to face us. There was blood dripping from his fists, in his hair, and on his feral, savagely handsome face.

The anger in his eyes scorched a hole through my chest that was cauterized the moment he stepped forward, hands open in benediction, face collapsed in sweet, aching relief.

"Lila," he croaked, and then I was in his arms.

I didn't care about the blood, the violence, the fact that this man had just murder another in front of me.

Bloodshed and violence were a part of The Fallen, Nova

was a part of that and he? He was a part of me. I couldn't judge him for doing what I wished I could have done.

Because I would kill them too.

All of them.

Irina, Javier, Piston, and the rest of their crew, the rest of the men on the boat bent on selling female flesh.

I was glad they were dead and gone.

I was proud that The Fallen had done it.

And *Dane*.

I pulled away from Nova's fierce hug just long enough to whisper Dane's name.

"Yeah," he responded hoarsely, dipping his head down to press his forehead against mine. "He's alive, Li. Fuckin' beautiful asshole is alive."

I nodded as my legs wobbled and tears ran scalding down my cheeks. I was too dehydrated to waste moisture on crying, but I couldn't seem to stop.

"*Mi hermana*," Dane called softly from behind me as if summoned like the devil by his name.

Nova didn't release me, but he turned me in the circle of his arms so I could face my brother.

The second he did, Dane surged toward me, covered in sweat and blood, tears already streaming, and he hugged me.

He hugged us both.

My eyes clamped shut with the force of my sobs as I collapsed between the two men I'd loved since I was a girl and let them carry my entire weight. They only pressed closer, Dane's hands in my hair, on my neck, eyes scouring my face like a cartographer mapping lands before he forgot what they looked like.

I didn't do the same.

I didn't care what Dane looked like, how he smelled, different or the same.

I only cared that he was in my arms after so many years, loving me still as I loved him the same. All I needed to do was press my cheek to the hard muscle over his chest, my hand to his neck over his thrumming pulse, and listen to the sound of his heartbeat.

All around us, women wept with relief as The Fallen coaxed them down the ladder into boats waiting below to take them to safety.

But I stood there for a long time, shaking like a leaf, but pinned between the two bodies that had always kept me anchored and safe.

It was all worth it, in that moment.

The fear, the trauma, the heartache.

To have saved those girls, protected my family, and finally, fucking finally, have Dane back in my life.

CHAPTER THIRTY-TWO

Lila

I DIDN'T LEAVE THE BOOTHS' FOR TWO WEEKS.

Mostly because they didn't want me out of their sight. Diogo even took time off work to stay home with Molly and me. He taught me how to make my favourite vegetarian Portuguese dishes like *caldo verde* and *pastéis de feijão* in exchange for lessons on how to make Ellie's *maduras*. Milo and Oliver insisted on working out with me in their makeshift garage weight room, so that I'd be stronger if anyone ever tried to fuck with me again. Hudson and Ares didn't leave my side at all. Between Hudson's constant jokes and cheer, and Ares peaceful aura and spoken poetry, I was distracted from the trauma of the past few weeks from the time I woke up until the time Molly put me to bed.

Dane had made me promise I would stay safe, locked up in the Booths house like some princess in a tower while he worked through whatever it was he had to do with the military in order to finally come back home to Entrance for good. And I was absolutely *not* going to break the first promise I made to my brother after years apart even though I was going stir crazy.

I also stayed because of the club.

They wanted me safe at home while the police investigated Irina's sex trafficking ring and Dane's boss's operation out of the Middle East. They didn't want me disturbed or interviewed by the many camera crews rolling through town, and they wanted me accounted for at all times.

There was always a brother in leather at the Booths' house.

Almost every single one of them took up rotation, for their own peace of mind and for mine, I thought. Boner always made sure he was there for dinner because he loved Diogo's grub, Bat and Cy dropped by to keep up my self-defence training, and Axe-Man sat with me in the garden while I worked, handing me tools or weeding with me when I asked him to. He was a quiet man who liked quiet things, so I enjoyed his company in the chaotic, over stuffed house.

Nova didn't visit.

After holding me on the freighter and the entire trip home on one of Diogo's fishing boats he'd lent the club for the operation, Nova had gone with me to the hospital in Vancouver so I could get checked out. He'd held my hand, eyes to me every single second as if he was afraid I'd disappear, and then ironically, when we'd separated so the doctors could give me a CT scan to check for a possible concussion, he'd disappeared himself. I'd asked the Booths about it as soon as I noticed him gone, but Hudson had distracted me by arriving with a bottle of my favourite kombucha and a burger brought all the way down the mountain from Eugene's.

What I didn't realize until the last day of that second week, was that no one would *let* Nova visit.

Harleigh Rose explained it to me while we were out in the garden that day, her head tipped to the sunshine, the new, gleaming engagement ring on her hand twinkling in the light.

"He's paying his penance," she told me.

"What?"

She sighed, lowering her aviators to give me a look. "Babe, he broke your heart. Everyone's fuckin' pissed. Oliver actually fought with him about it. You should see his shiner, it's a real beauty."

I gaped at her. "What? How has no one told me this?"

She shrugged. "Um, maybe because you were just stalked through the woods, abducted, and almost sold into a lifelong career of sexual slavery? Or the fact that your long-lost brother is alive, helped save you, and he's moving back to Entrance?"

I shut my mouth with an audible click. "Yeah, there's stuff going on, but there always is with the club. That doesn't mean I don't want to see Nova."

Or that it hadn't hurt, thinking he didn't want to see me, that even after almost losing me he was so wholly unaffected by it.

"Oh, babe, it's not that he didn't want to come see you," she said with a beleaguered sigh. "You should look at yourself right now. So filled with hope... girl, I don't want to get your hopes up, but he's come to the house every day since you've been here. That's why he and Oliver fought, he tried to duck around them, and Oliver wouldn't allow it. You know how boys solve conflict."

My heart had been cold in my chest since the morning after the party at the clubhouse, like something used up and left out to dry.

But hearing that, it stirred and began to unthaw.

"I want to see him," I demanded. "Next time he's here. I want to see him."

She pursed her lips then looked up over my shoulder and laughed. "Your wish is my command."

My pulse roared in my ears as I hesitated then turned over on the blanket in the grass to look at the house.

Nova stood by the side of the porch, staring at me like I was an eclipse, some rare and mesmerizing event he would miss if he so much as blinked.

The sight of him illuminated by the noon day sun, every inch of his long, broad form highlighted in gold, his hair cast to copper and his eyes deep, dark pools trained unerringly on me... he was the most beautiful thing I'd ever seen, and I knew that would never change.

"Jonathon," I whispered, so soft even I barely heard the sound, but he flinched all the way across the yard as if I'd breathed the word into his ear.

He was wearing a plain black tee that clung to the quilted muscles in his chest and shoulders, highlighting the sheer strength he possessed, and contrasting the vivid colour of the ink penned from his fingertips to the lower half of his hairline.

"Wanted to see you," he said simply, opening his hands to the sky like he'd been helpless to resist and was asking for forgiveness.

A laugh shot from my lips, a burst of disbelief and relief.

"Well then," I said, gesturing to the blanket.

Harleigh Rose shifted, rolling to her feet. "I'll just... check out the greenhouse for a second. See if it's ready for Dane."

We didn't watch her walk off. Instead, I tracked him as he swaggered across the lawn, his eyes pinned to mine the entire time, even as he gracefully collapsed onto the blanket beside me.

I didn't know what to say. Everything I felt defied words, the gravity of hope that still clung to my heart, the stubbornest of weeds, the gratitude I wanted to express that he'd searched for me and found me, the love I had, always, glowing so bright in my chest I worried it would give me away, as bright as a second sun.

"How're you feelin'?" he asked then cleared his throat of hoarseness. "I've been comin' round to see you, but the family's pretty pissed at me."

"I just heard. I hope you know, I wouldn't, I would never want to keep you away." And I wouldn't, not ever. I'd tried that before, to cleave him from my life as much as I could in those two years I'd been with Jake, but it had only strengthened the bond between Nova and me like a tested muscle growing strong under the strain.

"I know."

We lapsed back into silence. I looked everywhere but at him, unable to bear the sight of the black stubble on his square jaw, the intensity of his velvet gaze even when his left eye was still faintly purple from Oliver's fist. Instead, I watched the flowers bow in the breeze, their bright faces unwavering smiles.

I smiled back.

"You know, when I can't sleep at night, I still play that game," Nova said, his voice low and intimate, like incense in a small room, warming me, perfuming the suddenly small space between us with memories. "Amaryllis, Bluebells, Calla Lilies... usually, by the time I get to Suntastic Yellow Sunflowers, I'm mostly asleep."

I hummed, because I couldn't open my mouth or a sob would spill out.

"It's not the game that lulls me to sleep, though, Li," he admitted hoarsely, leaning forward to cup my face feather-light in one palm. "It's the thought of you. The thought of you curled up in your bed as a little girl, so fuckin' afraid 'til I got onto the bed with you, as if you trusted me to keep you safe no matter what. The thought of you with lopsided braids in your hair at the skate park talkin' trash too young 'cause Dane and I taught you *los tres Caballeros* didn't take shit from no one."

He sucked in a deep breath and watched as his hand traveled down my cheek to wrap whisper soft around my neck, his thumb rubbing back and forth over my thrumming pulse.

"It's hard for me to express exactly how I feel about you,

Li, 'cause I've never felt this way about anyone or anythin' before. It's like askin' a blind man to describe the colour blue. So forgive me if I don't do this justice, it's the best I can do, and a wise woman once told me it's the effort that counts."

He smiled, and it was a new expression, one I'd never imagined on Nova's gorgeous, arrogant features. Small, almost shy, and not quite realized like a bloom still tightly budded.

"I did you wrong, and I've been doin' you wrong a long time by forcin' our relationship into a box it no longer fit into. We grew outta that kinda friendship into somethin' more a long fuckin' time ago, but I was too chicken shit, too much of a dumbass to see it. I kept sayin' I wouldn't ever be worthy of you, and honest to Christ, I gotta say, not sure there's a person on the planet worthy of the kinda love you have to give, but... I'm gonna fight for it. To deserve it. To get it back, even if I broke it to pieces when I ended things."

His jaw set in that stubborn Booth way, a muscle jumping, eyebrows thick black slashes across his face, but still his touch on my throat remained achingly gentle.

"I'm gonna fight for you," he repeated. "The way I fought for you as a girl. I'm sorry as fuck I ever stopped, and I swear to God, I won't again."

I stared at him, at the ferocity of his expression, at the delicateness of his touch, at the beauty of his face cracked open with vulnerability just for me.

And I forgave him.

Just that easy, just that much.

Because he was Jonathon Booth, and whether he realized it or not, he'd been fighting for me all along. His only mistake was in thinking he should be fighting to find me better than him when he was the only answer all along.

Still, it wouldn't do to let him off the hook so easily.

And I wasn't sure, even though hope throbbed like a second heartbeat in my chest, if he truly loved me back.

He hadn't said it, even though the look in his eyes might have said otherwise.

"Okay," I said slowly, just to watch him squirm. "You can try to make it up to me."

He blinked at me then stole my breath as a gorgeous grin curled his purple red mouth. "Yeah?"

"I guess," I said with a one shouldered shrug. "You can try."

"Oh," he said, that grin going rogue, his eyes sparkling again, my Nova back in full force as relief edged out that uncharacteristic shyness. "I'm charming as fuck, so I'm not sure you stand a chance."

"Arrogant, much?" I quirked an eyebrow, swallowing my laughter.

"Hey, you win some, you lose some… it's just," he paused dramatically, leaning back onto his hands so his entire broad, muscled chest was on display for me. My eyes snagged on the ring in his left nipple showing through the fabric, and my mouth watered. "I always win."

I laughed, letting the sweet rush of relief spread through me like a river through parched earth. I soaked up his goodness, the feel of his smiling eyes on my skin, and let myself luxuriate in his presence after two weeks apart, after thinking we might never recover.

How silly of me, I thought then as we smiled at each other like two kids with crushes on the playground, giddy and shy with our newfound feelings. How silly of me to doubt our bond for even one second.

"Nova," Milo called from the porch. "What'd I tell you about bothering Li, huh?"

"Don't make me come down there," Oliver warned as he cracked his knuckles ominously.

I laughed again, so filled with lightness I felt I might drift away.

"I'm gonna go," Nova said. "But I'll be back tomorrow.

And the next day. And probably every day until you get sick of me."

"You are *very* annoying," I teased.

"You love me just the same," he said simply, not cruel, not mocking my feelings, just acknowledging them in that way he had of stripping the truth to the bone so it was just plain fact.

I shrugged, unwilling to give him anything else.

I noticed Harleigh Rose out of the corner of my eye, hesitating before walking back toward us.

"I'll see you," I said.

Nova lingered a moment then got up on his knees to lean over and kiss my forehead. I felt the burst of sensation on my skin like an electric shock.

"See ya, Flower Child," he said, rocking to his boots and winking at me as he backed away then swung forward to leave the yard.

"You didn't see it, did you?" Harleigh Rose asked as she flopped to the blanket again.

I yanked my eyes from his retreating back. I'd always loved to watch him move, smooth and rolling, a slight hiccough in his swagger on the right side from where he'd torn his ACL doing dumbass tricks at the skate park with Dane. He didn't have a limp now, he had fully recovered ages ago, but I knew he kept that hiccough gait because the girls had loved it.

"Sorry?" I asked, still distracted by the impression of him caught on the inside of my lids like black spots from looking into the sun.

"You didn't see it," she confirmed with an awed shake of her head. "But I did."

I rolled my eyes. "You're always so damned dramatic."

"Fuck off. I saw it with my own eyes, otherwise I would never have believed it."

"Believed what?"

"He just looked at you like you were a flower that bloomed just for him."

"Shut up," I ordered as my heart jumped up and down in my chest. I pressed my hand there, hating the way it jarred. "Don't say that."

"I'm sorry," she said, but there was a growing twinkle in her eye. "But it's true. That man? He loves you, Li. As in, he's in love with you."

I collapsed to the blanket beside her and rolled into her body, shoving my face in the rose-scented hair at her neck so I could whisper, "I hope so."

CHAPTER THIRTY-THREE

Lila

THE NEXT DAY WHEN I WOKE UP THERE WAS A PACKAGE ON my bed.

There was no note, only a purple heart drawn in his modern, minimalist style on the brown wrapping paper.

I knew immediately it was from Nova.

I tore the paper apart like a child with a gift on Christmas morning then rent the box clean in half so that the tissue wrapped item fell into my lap.

My hands shook as I opened it, because somehow, I knew what it was before I even pushed back the tissue and my hands encounter cool, glossy leather.

A biker babe jacket.

Like the *Property of No One* jacket Harleigh Rose had got me one birthday when I was a teenager.

This one was gorgeous, perfectly tailored, a leather belt wrapped around the waist that would cinch me in and emphasis my curves.

But that wasn't why I loved it.

I flipped it over with my eyes closed, my heart in my throat beating so strong I couldn't breathe.

My fingers ran over the back, touching silken stitching and the rough texture of a patch.

When I opened my eyes, tears leaked out.

Property of Nova was sewn into the back on two rockers, an upper and lower punctuated with a flower in the middle.

A sob bubbled in my chest and spilled onto the duvet as I hugged the jacket to my chest the way I wanted to hug Nova.

Later, after breakfast, I got the first text message.

NOVA: A HISTORY OF US IN PICTURES.

And then they came, one every hour for the rest of the day.

The graffiti image of *los tres Caballeros* on the back of Eugene's bar.

A photo of the blueberries at the Summerland farm I'd first fostered at.

The selfie of Dane and Nova they'd sent me minutes before picking me up, their faces so young and bright with joy.

Another of the three of us at the skatepark, me between the two teenage guys holding my skateboard in the air like a trophy.

The image we'd graffitied together for Dane on the side of Street Ink Tattoo Parlour, then the lotus blossoms we both had tattooed on our bodies.

My first tattoo.

There were photos of us pressed cheek to cheek, wet with rain and smiling so huge you could count every one of our teeth as we posed in front of the Algarve coast on our Portugal trip on a rare bad weather day. I remembered how Nova had forced us all to go to the beach anyway, even in the driving rain, and how much fun we'd had playing in the waves, laughing as we were soaked through to the bone.

So many photos, so many visual reminders of the tapestry we had created together, two lives into one.

When the last one came through that evening after dinner, when I was just giving up hope of Nova arriving in person, it made me want to cry and smile at the same time.

Nova: ADMIT IT, WE LOOK DAMN GOOD TOGETHER. SIX, SIXTEEN, TWENTY-SIX, SIXTY-TWO…WE'LL LOOK GOOD TOGETHER FOR THE REST OF OUR LIVES.

"Lila," Molly's voice startled me so badly I dropped the phone to the couch and looked guilty despite the fact I didn't really have anything to be guilty about.

She laughed softly, those hydrangea blue eyes crinkling as she sat beside me on the couch, pressing our knees together.

"You don't need to look so ashamed. I'm a mother of four men, so trust me, nothing shocks me anymore."

I bit my lip, staring down at my knuckles as I cracked them. "Not even Nova and me?"

"Honey," she said, lips trembling as she pressed them together in a bid not to laugh at me. Her hands reached for both of my mine, and she rubbed them absently in that maternal way she had of instantly providing comfort. "I've known about you and Nova since before *you* and *Nova* knew about it."

I huffed out a laugh and collapsed back against the leather couch. "You and everyone else in Entrance."

"Probably," she agreed easily, making me laugh again.

"I love him," I admitted, and it felt so good to say aloud. "I love him so much sometimes it feels like an invasive species inside my chest."

"He can be that way," she said, teasing me and him both before she sobered and slid closer to tuck my hair behind my ear and cup my cheek. "Lila, my sweet girl, you are more precious to this family than I could ever hope to express. I hope you know that. I hope we've been able to show that—"

"You have!" I cried out, horrified she might think otherwise. "I owe this family everything."

Molly's sweet, open face shuttered like a prison on lockdown. "No. You do not owe us anything. You've repaid us every day you've lived in this home with your kindness, you spirit, and your huge heart. We all love you and have our own special relationships with you just like in any family. But Nova, well..." She smiled softly, secretly as she thought of her eldest son. "He always believed he wasn't good enough for the happiness he was born into. He believed that he hadn't suffered strife, he wasn't tested enough, so he threw himself recklessly into every new experience, any bad idea, just to collect scars like most boys collect baseball cards. It was Dane and you that gave him a purpose, that made him feel like a better person just for loving you, for giving you two the opportunity to enjoy the fruits of his life too."

She stroked my hair again, smiling at me the way one woman smiles at another in a secret, feminine confidence. "If that was the foundation of his love for you, you can imagine how difficult it might have been for him to realize that he was in love with you too. Over the years, I think we all saw it, even sweet, oblivious Hudson, but we left it alone, hoping you two would work it out. It's taken a little longer than I thought, but I hope now you are."

"We are, I think," I murmured, looking at my phone, letting the warmth of those photos overtake me again.

"Since you turned sixteen, you've always looked at each other just a little too long to be just friends," Molly divulged with a low chuckle. "I still remember the first time Diogo noticed. He was not too pleased with his eldest son. But he gets it, we all do. Sometimes two people become so entangled in one another that they have no choice but to fall in love."

"It's still a choice, though," I insisted. "And I choose him."

There was a knock at the door then, and I shot to my feet,

startling Molly and making her laugh again. I straightened my new leather jacket and my purple boho dress then struck a pose for my foster mum.

"Good?"

Her smile was slow and sweet. "Always, but yes, very good."

I beamed at her then practically floated to the door.

When I opened it, I frowned at Nova mockingly. "Lost your key?"

He grinned as my eyes raked over every inch of him. His tee was a brilliant white, heightening his tan, his ink, the brightness of his teeth and the whites of his eyes, and he wore new jeans, dark with a faint crease still down the middle thigh from being folded at the store.

"No, this is a date. I knocked all proper and shit," he declared proudly.

"Well, bravo," I teased then tried to look behind his back. "What do you have back there?"

"Oh," he frowned then leaned close. "Give me a kiss first. Nothin's ever free."

I laughed and darted forward to press a kiss to his cheek.

"Not what I was thinkin', but I'll take it," he said churlishly.

I laughed and absently, I wondered if I'd ever been so giddy, so absolutely filled with positive anticipation and hope.

I gasped when he brought his hands around his front holding two massive fistfuls of sunflowers.

Suntastic Yellow Sunflowers.

I looked at him over the top of the blooms as wet hit the back of my eyes, and my nose started to sting. "You're going to make me cry, and I have makeup on."

"Don't cry, we got shit to do," he ordered, handing Molly the flowers as she came up behind me. "Hey, Mum. How many vases do you think you have?"

She frowned at him. "Um, a normal amount."

He nodded, a little grin tucked up on the left side of his mouth. "Huh, well get Milo, Oliver, and Hudson over here, you might need help with the rest of Lila's flowers."

We watched as he gestured to the street, and then we both gasped at what we saw there.

My little blue VW bug had all the windows rolled down, flowers exploding out of every opening like an overstuffed doll.

Nova laughed, a fully bodied, rich sound that rang through the air and made me smile even though I wanted to burst into tears. He grabbed my hand and urged me down the stairs toward the car. I bent to the flowers instantly, running my hands over the blooms, shoving my nose in the fragrant collection of freesias, roses, sunflowers, lilies, and more.

When I pulled away, I stared at Nova, almost afraid to touch him in case this was a dream.

He noticed.

"You still too mad at me to come over here where you belong?" he questioned.

I shook my head.

"Got pollen on your nose," he chuckled, reaching out to rub it off with his thumb.

"Please don't do this," I said on an explosive rush. "Please don't tease me with the fairy-tale you told me you would never give me if you don't really mean it. I... I honestly don't think I could stand it."

Every trace of humour drained out of Nova's face, and when he stepped forward, he looked more serious than I'd ever seen him. He bent until we were eye level then framed my face with his hands.

"Hey," he murmured. "I know I'm an asshole, but I would *never* do that. Let's go, yeah? I got two more things to show ya, and then we can talk."

"We're takin' off," he hollered at Molly as his brothers crowded around her on the porch. "Deal with this shit, yeah?"

Moly laughed, but his brothers grumbled.

"You fuck this up again, I'll give you another shiner," Oliver yelled as we moved to Nova's Harley and got on.

Nova flipped him the bird as he revved the engine and peeled out onto the road.

I pressed my chest to his back, my legs tight to his outer thighs, and lifted my arms into the air to yell, "Fuck yeah!"

His chuckle moved through me as we took a corner and led us down to Main Street. I wasn't surprised when we stopped at Street Ink Tattoo Parlour. So much of our relationship had taken place there, it seemed fitting he would want to have our talk within its walls.

He led me through the dark shop, not turning on any lights except for the one at his station. I sat on the edge of his tattoo chair as he readied his tools.

"Am I getting another tattoo?" I asked, a smile in my voice because it was just like him to design something for me on a whim, and just like me to immediately, sight unseen, want it inked on my body.

Nova was one of the best tattoo artists on the west coast, and usually his designs went for a pretty penny, so I considered myself lucky I got the family discount.

"Not quite." I watched as he printed a design on Thermafax paper, unable to make out what he'd drawn. "Wanna try somethin' different today."

I frowned as he rolled the tray close to the chair and handed me the paper. A simple but beautiful purple barbed wire heart with the initials JB + LM stared back at me.

When I looked up at him, he was taking off his tee, tugging it from the back of his neck in that way men did that I'd never understood but thought was insanely hot.

"Nova?" I asked quietly, afraid to disturb whatever was happening between us.

Then he was shirtless, the tapestry of ink on his torso moving with the flex and roll of his densely muscled chest. My mouth went dry as he hopped up on the tattoo chair and pulled me between his legs.

"Want you to tattoo it right here," he said, thumping one of the only remaining bare sections of skin on his chest, just below the lotus bloom inked at the base of his throat. "Been keepin' it empty for a long time now, waitin' for somethin' as important as Dane to ink there so me and everyone can see it all the time no matter what I wear." He paused, lifting those deep brown eyes with black streaks like the ink on the wood grain of the Booth's kitchen table up to me, the fans of his lashes so thick and long they looked almost unreal. "This seemed right, given the circumstances."

My brows cut high on my forehead. "Circumstances?"

"Yeah." He nodded, framing my hips in his hands, his fingertips expanding all the way to my back, his thumbs anchored on my hipbones in a way that made me feel feminine and small as much as it made me feel possessed and taken. "The circumstance bein' us spendin' the rest of our lives together."

A strangled mewl burst through my slack lips as hope overinflated my heart and made it soar up into my throat.

Nova's hands flexed on my hips, but he continued. "Not sayin' it's always gonna be a breeze, you bein' with me, me tryin' to be the kinda man worthy of the woman you are, the best kinda woman I'll ever fuckin' know, but you got patience, and me? I got time. That is, you wanna spend the rest of our life with me too."

I opened my mouth to respond when he grinned wickedly and shrugged. "I mean, you'd be crazy not to wanna spend the rest of your life with all of this goodness, but I'm tryna be a gentleman here, so I felt I should give ya the option."

I tried to say something again when he tugged me closer and nipped my bottom lip. "I should mention, that was total bullshit. There really isn't an option. I'll make you mine no matter what. Like I said, I'm not the kinda man who loses."

I burst out laughing, sinking my hands into his hair to pull tight in a bid to shut him up. Then, still chuckling, lips to his, I said, "There was never an option. I've been yours since you told me I needed a dream for myself. I dreamed that one day I'd be a Booth, but over the years I realized I didn't just want to be a Booth, I wanted to be yours."

Nova grabbed my hand and pressed it to the middle of his chest. "You've been that since I first inked you. Now I want your ink on my body too."

"I don't know the first thing about tattooing, what if I mess up?" The idea of screwing with his gorgeous body almost gave me hives.

But I also loved the gesture, that he wanted not only a tat that represented me, but one done by my own hand. It was sweet and possessive in the way only Nova could be.

He snorted. "Babe, I've been tattooing since I was eighteen, and I still mess up, everyone does. Anythin' can be fixed."

"You're not really inspiring confidence," I muttered.

He laughed and while still laughing, he kissed me. A moment later there was nothing left to smile about because we were making out, his hand on my ass, mine in his hair, our tongues tangled together, warm and silken.

"I want it in *your* writing. Your mark on me. I'll coach you through it," he offered huskily when we broke apart. "I'm a good teacher. Remember how well I taught ya to take me in your virgin ass?"

"Nova!" I protested even as I laughed. "Fuck, you're outrageous."

He grinned shamelessly. "I got some outrageous ideas of how I wanna celebrate afterward, and they all involve a fuckuva lot less clothes. Actually, why wait? Lose the dress."

Before I could move, he was bunching the fabric in his hands and lifting it off me. I obliged by raising my arms.

A low growl rumbled through Nova's chest as he ran his hands over my mostly naked flesh. I grinned, a feminine smugness tucked into the expression because I'd come prepared.

Dark purple satin lined with black lace, the bra a demi cup that lifted my breasts into sinful swells, the thong cut high over my hips.

Nova dipped his head to my breastbone and pressed a kiss to the top of each breast. "Fuck me, thinkin' about all the things I'm gonna do to your fuckin' sinful body makes me feel like an animal. Wanna take you in the shop, our bed, the meadow, on my bike… anywhere with a flat surface and a fuckin' modicum of privacy."

I tipped my head back to moan as he sucked hard at one nipple through the satin then startled when his hand smacked down on my ass.

"Let's get to work," he growled, dragging the table of tools closer then laying back with his hands behind his head, arms flexed in a way that made my mouth water. "Come sit on my hips so you can feel how fuckin' hard you make me as you ink me."

I swallowed thickly as I straddled his narrow waist and followed his instructions. I started by placing the tracing paper in the valley above his mountainous pectorals, following the design with a special skin pen so the barbed wire heart and stylized initials were replicated perfectly on his golden skin. I'd held a tattoo gun before, years ago when I'd expressed curiosity about it during one of my first sessions, so I was prepared for the violent buzz of it in my hand, but learning about how to dip the inks was specific and nerve wracking.

Nova remained calm throughout, as if I was just getting ready to shave him instead of inking something permanent into his flesh.

The muscle flexed beneath my hand as I pressed the gun to him, but I braced on the chair and bent so close I ws nearly lying on him to make sure I followed the lines just right.

There was a palpable tension in the room, an electric heat in the air like the atmosphere before a storm rolls in. It made me squirm slightly over the crest of Nova's half-rigid cock.

"Be still," he ordered, roughly. "Or we'll both ruin the tatt 'cause I'll be inside you, fuckin' you up and down my cock in a way you can't keep that hand steady."

A shiver zipped up my spine. "It's just so sexy, my hands on you, this big, beautiful body all laid out for me like this. Getting to put something on your skin you're going to see every day that reminds you of me."

"Got that wrong, Li. I'm not puttin' it there as a reminder to me. Every thought I got in my head finds its way back to you, like the ocean always rollin' back into the shore. Don't need a reminder so much as I want you to know the love I got for you is more permanent than any ink. I want you to know I wear your heart proud as fuck in my chest."

Tears pricked like hot needles at the backs of my eyes. I tried to blink them away, concentrating on the left arch of the barbed heart.

"Hey, Li, don't cry, my gorgeous girl," Nova crooned softly.

"I've just loved you for so long," I whispered past the obstruction in my throat. "Hoped for so long. It's hard to digest the fact that the love I've had sitting in my chest for years is finally yours. Honestly, I thought it would always be the perfect gift ungiven."

A soft, broken sound of grief vibrated his chest under the tattoo gun.

I didn't look up into his eyes, those eyes that always read my thoughts and wrecked my emotions. I was too shook up, like a can of upended soda, and I was afraid too much more would make me burst open.

As if sensing my need to focus, to settle, Nova stayed quiet, a hush, contemplative silent overtaking him until, fifteen minutes later, I finished the flourish on the 'B' of the design.

"I'm done," I whispered, leaning back to survey the art. "Actually, I don't think I did a bad job."

"It's perfect," he said assuredly, even though I hadn't handed him the mirror to confirm it. "Now, come here."

He curled up, abs popping in his torso like stacked boxes, to cup my face and pull me in for a deep, wet kiss I felt in my toes. The chemistry that had lingered mostly dormant in the air flared to life around us like flame, licking up my thighs, settling in my core like banked coals.

Careful of his tender new tatt, I curled around him, hands in his hair fisting to pull him even closer.

I moaned around the hot slide of his tongue then gasped as his big palm slid down my spine, molding every vertebra before roughly grabbing my ass. He ground me against the swell of his cock, undulating my hip until I moved to his rhythm.

Something sparked inside me at that possessive, aggressive touch that sent the fire blazing even higher.

I fumbled as I reached down to undo Nova's belt and jeans, sighing as his hot length fell into my hand, nearly scalding my skin it was so hot.

"Need you inside me," I panted as I lifted just enough to notch his head at my already drenched entrance, pull aside my panties, and then impale myself on his thick shaft.

We both groan together, long and long in perfect harmony.

The feel of him deep inside of me was so invasive, so over-whelming in both size and beauty. It was a struggle to all of him, but I loved the stretch, the way my muscles melted around him after a few thundering heartbeats.

I loved that I felt every thick ridge and vein of him rub against my front wall on each inward thrust and that angled as

I was with my hips canted back, my wet clit rubbing against the coarse hair on his groin, a rough, delish brush of sensation each time.

"Fuck, the sight'a you taken my cock like that," Nova said as he clasped my hips and forced me to churn harder. "Alla that beauty takin' my dick like you can't get enough."

One of his hands arrowed in from my hip over my pubic bone where his hand pressed firmly in a way that heightened the feel of him inside. His thumb dipped lower and stroked at my exposed clit.

I tossed my head back as I reared up, unlatching from his hair to score my nails over his shoulders.

"Fuck yeah, look at you," he growled. "So fuckin' gorgeous and all fuckin' mine."

I gasped as he built the fire higher at my clit. My hips bucked, the wet slide of his cock and the ragged pulls of our breath the only sounds in the shop.

"Look at me," Nova demanded, reaching up to clasp my lower jaw in his hand. "Watch me as you take my cock. Gonna make you come so hard the sweet clasp'a your pussy's gonna milk me dry."

Heat seared down my spine and pooled between my legs as the wet slapped of our flesh increased.

I looked down at Nova, so beautiful even in the harsh artificial light. The crown of his hair was dampened with sweat, his pulse pounding at the side of his tattoo throat. I couldn't stop looking at that long, strong column of flesh thinking about that heart that finally beat for me. So, I wrapped my own hand around it as his was wound around mine, just holding, not pressing, just to feel him alive and aching for me beneath my palm.

"My Lila," he grunted as I ground down and spasmed around him, so close I could feel the ache in my womb as it clenched tight. "Wanna feel you drench my cock with your cum."

His words razed through me like a forest fire, leaving my thoughts in ash, my inhibitions dust on the wind. I tipped my head to the ceiling as I cried out; pleasure tearing through me from my pussy, my belly, up my throat, so heavy and bursting, so all consuming I couldn't contain it all within me so I shouted.

I shouted the name of the man who was all I'd ever wanted.

I shouted it like a victorious war cry because finally, after years of fighting for him, hoping for him, he was mine.

Nova jacked up to curl his other hand around my head and bring my lips to his. He ate my cry off his tongue with a hungry, heathen moan that illustrated just how triumphant he felt at making me his too. I felt the kick of his cock inside me and then the sudden flood of warmth as he claimed me with his cum.

His hands moved over me as I drifted slowly down from my climax, the way a coach might massage an athlete after a vigorous trail. I felt feline and soft under his strong pants, arching into his thumbs as they rubbed over my breasts firmly, easing the swollen tissue, then up over my shoulder, flexing gloriously into my hair.

I groaned again, this time a replete, shuddering sound like an engine out of gas.

He chuckled lightly and kiss my temple where my head lay tucked against his neck and shoulder.

"I knew," he murmured, as if continuing a conversation we had just abandoned. "I knew about the barbed wire heart you hid in the graffiti outside the shop. At first, thought it'd be kinda funny to hide messages in the art I inked on your body too. A tongue-in-cheek kinda humor only for me. Over the years, I spent hours thinkin' about what I'd hide next." His fingers skittered over the peonies on my thigh, swirling over the blooms. "Hid a quote by Nabokov just here, the words makin' up the edge of the petals. 'she always nursed a small, mad hope,'" he quoted softly, and I felt my heart clench so painfully I wondered if it might burst.

"You knew," I accused in a hushed voice, as if we were in a museum of memories and loud noise might get us kicked out. "You knew how I felt."

He grinned and shrugged a shoulder that was quilted with muscle and stamped with a demonic cupid. "I knew we had a connection, somethin' special. That you might think it was romantic 'cause you were young."

I hit him. "Look who ended up wrong in the end."

His chuckle was heady as pot smoke curling between us, going straight to my head. "Maybe."

"What else?" I asked, leaning back to give him access to my entire front. "What other secrets did you hide?"

"The butterfly here." He pressed a kiss to the purple butterfly on my right hip then licked down the line of the bone through my skin so I squirmed. "There's really two, one hidden just behind and to the left of the first. One butterfly symbolizes strength through struggle, which you obviously know, but two?" His nose brushed over the delicate skin making me shiver. "Two means two souls together in love."

"I just got that one last year," I breathed, turned on by his touch, wrecked by his words.

"I loved you last year," Nova told me with such raw honesty I flinched. "I've loved you since the day you stole my skateboard and bailed tryin' to do a kickflip trick. Just somewhere along the line, probably around the time I tattooed this," his palm slid up my belly to cover the lotus between my breasts, "that love changed, grew petals and turned into somethin' a helluva lot bigger than brotherly affection."

I pressed my hand over his on my sternum and blinked away the tears in my eyes.

"I love you too," I said simply, maybe stupidly because of course, he already knew.

"I know," he said, eyes warm like sunlight on tree bark. "Your love's been the backbone'a my life for a long time now."

Then he kissed me, hand splayed over my heart, lips clinging to mine, tongue plundering, and I felt flowers bloom in my chest just as I had every time he looked me, touched me, loved me in anyway over the years.

But this time I knew, Nova would never let the garden he planted in my soul go untended ever again.

EPILOGUE

Lila

THERE WAS NO SOFT DENOUEMENT AFTER THE ARREST OF IRINA Ventura's higher-level staff at Wet Works Production. News crews camped out in Entrance for a month, stalking Javier for answers about his missing wife. Of course, he found a way to spin it, because he was not just some thug in a suit. Javier was smart and psychotic, he had an edge over the rest of us because he was willing to go places none of The Fallen would even consider entering. Including lying about his wife being set up by her co-workers to take the fall for the sex-trafficking ring we'd busted.

Still, there seemed to be a détente between the club and the cartel. I wondered sometimes, late at night when I couldn't sleep from the trauma cluttering my thoughts, if that détente had anything to do with me. If, perhaps, there was some kernel of truth to Irina's heinous claims.

That maybe Javier and Ellie had been lovers for a very, very long time.

But it was a thought Nova wouldn't let me entertain. Even if he was sleeping, which he did a lot of now that I spent every night in his bed, he stirred, woken by the energy rolling off me like an incoming storm off the ocean. He'd roll into me, settle that sweet, heavy weight between my legs and do things with his tongue that always made me forget everything, even my own name.

Then there was Dane.

He was back.

Back in Entrance, back in our lives, but *not*.

Bat told me it was severe PTSD from his time as a prisoner of war in Afghanistan, that it was natural he would struggle to adjust to civilian life, that he himself had struggled for years.

And was still struggling even now.

It made me weep more than I was proud of to see Dane sit at family dinners like a mute automaton, no more alive in spirit than he had been as a ghost at our table for all the years he was missing. He didn't want to hang out with Nova or me, he didn't want to explore Entrance or meet the new people in our lives. He just wanted to sleep or lay on the couch catching up on years of TV he hadn't seen.

He didn't want to talk about what happened, his time as a POW, or how he'd enlisted to help take down the sex trafficking ring with ties to the city he'd been held hostage in. We didn't know much more than what his superior officer had told us when he'd arrived to drop Dane off one day.

But at least he was home.

He said he didn't want help, but I didn't really care anymore what he wanted. It had been two months since the incident at the port, and I was desperate to have my brother back.

So I enlisted the only two people I knew might help.

Bat arrived at the Booths' house looking handsome and grim, clad all in black, his lips like a pale, twisted scar between his cheeks. He greeted with me with a kiss on the cheek then didn't pull back immediately.

I looked up into his eyes, so dark they seemed purely black, and blinked.

"It's not the kinda thing takes an hour chat with a fellow ex-vet to fix," he murmured, squeezing my bicep gently. "But however long you need me, you got me. I'm here for him 'cause I'm here for you and Nova."

Ah, that biker magic.

I smiled tremulously at him and moved aside to let him enter my old greenhouse where we'd set up Dane upon his return.

Zeus didn't say a word when he pulled up on his Harley, tucked his helmet under his arm, and came at me. He just scooped me half into the air in a one-armed hug then set me down, jerking his chin up at me as he ducked into the little door of the house.

I badly wanted to sit with them as they talked to Dane, but I knew it was better to give him space, so I turned back to the task at hand. Molly had kept up most of the garden after I moved out, but she couldn't control the weeds in my wild-flower garden at the side of the greenhouse, so I was on my knees in the dirt, arms filthy up to my elbows.

"He's going to be okay someday," Ares called from the back porch.

I shielded my eyes from the sun to look over at him as he walked down the steps along the path to my side and sat in the dirt. His handsome face had filled out in the two years he'd lived with The Fallen, his frame finally getting bigger, broad so it seemed he might grow into a tall man after all.

"Oh, yeah?" I asked, smiling at him even though I wanted a hug because I knew he didn't like to be touched. "I admire your faith."

"It's not faith," he argued with that strange intensity a preteen boy shouldn't possess. "I know it because I lived it. The memories never go away, but sometimes, if we're lucky enough, we can bury them six feet down with new ones, better ones."

I blinked at him. "You clearly spent too much time with King."

He grinned broadly, and it transformed his somber features into something utterly charming. "Yeah, I know. Can I help you dig?"

"Do you know what you're doing?"

"No." He shrugged then smiled a small, impish smile that reminded me he was only ten. "But how hard can it be? Even squirrels do it."

I laughed as we settled in, shoulder to shoulder sometimes, the deliberate press of his body into mine his silent way of offering me comfort while I waited to see how the meeting with Dane went.

I didn't expect it, but I wasn't surprised when it came sometime later.

The crash of something breaking against a wall.

I froze as shouts echoed through the house, unsure if I should stay where I was or go help.

There was another fierce cry, and I flew into the house, dirt kicking up behind me as I careened through the front door and stopped just inside the living room.

A vase lay broken at the base of the wall by the TV, wet flowers glistening in the debris. The crate coffee table was overturned and broken in pieces on one side where Bat sat amid the splinters, a cut in the cheek facing me.

He was holding my brother.

And Dane?

He was crying.

No, sobbing. Great, heaving sobs that wracked his massive frame so violently, he shuddered.

My heart stopped, the fist of furious sadness wrapped so tightly around it I wondered if I might have an embolism.

Wide eyed, I looked at Zeus who was watching the scene grimly with arms crossed over his chest. He caught my eye and sighed as he tromped through the wreckage on heavy boots and took my shoulder in his hand.

"Leave us for a while, yeah? We'll get 'im sorted," he said softly as he lead me gently back out the door.

"I should be here," I protested, aching to go to Dane and wrap him up in my arms.

"No," he argued. "This is the man who raised you, he wouldn't want you to see him like this which is why he hadn't had a breakdown yet. Let 'im be, Li girl, and I'll call you when he's through it, yeah? Trust me."

I stared up at the patriarch of the best-found family I'd ever known with tears in my eyes because I was so struck by the beauty of his heart, I almost couldn't breathe.

"You're going to help me fix him, aren't you?" I wheezed through the tears. "Just like you helped Mute and Ares and me?"

"Hey now," he said in his monstrous voice, rough and deep with eyes as soft as cotton. "I didn't do dick. Just got to watch as all'a ya found your own way."

I nodded, muted by my tears and gratefulness. I rose on my tiptoes to plant a kiss on the edge of his bearded jaw and cast one last look over his shoulder at my brother, still cradled in the firm hold of Bat's unwavering arms, before I left.

It was one of the hardest things I'd ever done, which was saying a lot given the events of the last six months, but I was glad I did it.

I was even happier when, a year later, I got to watch Dane

patch into The Fallen, and then some time after that, when I got to attend his wedding.

After years of taking care of me, of giving me the Booths and a better life, it was finally my turn to offer up my family, The Fallen, to Dane, and know that I was giving him a better life too.

TWO MONTHS LATER

"HEY ALL!" I SHOUTED AS I SWUNG THROUGH THE DOOR OF Street Ink Tattoo Parlour to pick up my man for lunch.

No one greeted me.

Sara wasn't behind the reception. Jae Pil, Axe-Man, and Chelsea were gone.

There was only Nova, sitting back in his own tattoo chair with his hands behind his head as if he was just waiting for me to walk on over and service him.

I grinned, dropping my purse to the reception desk as I made my way to him.

"Hey, handsome." I leaned over him to speak against his lips then kissed him deeply, drinking in the taste of him like a woman's first drink out of the desert. "Where is everyone?"

He didn't answer. Instead, he pulled me closer, fisting a hand in the back of my hair to pin me against his lips. I groaned as the silken slide of his tongue parted my mouth and dove inside. My body melted against him instantly, growing liquid and languid as instant lust poured through me like hot water.

When he finally pulled away, I couldn't peel my heavy lids open at first.

His smoky chuckle wafted over my tingling lips, and when I looked at him, he was smiling so beautifully, it literally made it hard to breathe.

"That was some greeting," I murmured, holding onto his wrists to keep from wobbling on my weakened knees. "What's going on?"

"I got somethin' I wanna show you," he said with that roguish grin.

I groaned. "Babe, I've seen it, I love it, I know it's big."

He threw his head back and laughed, that rich, warm sound wrapping me up tight in its hold. When he recovered, he stamped a kiss on my mouth still flavoured with his mirth.

"Somethin' new," he quantified as he started to lead me out of the shop.

I watched the way our feet fell in tandem as we walked, such a little synchronicity that stood for so much more. In the weeks since we'd ended Irina's operation, Nova and I had only grown closer.

I didn't think it was possible to love him more than I did, but it happened every single day. We sunk deeper into our relationship, making room for each other and our shared dreams. We talked late at night in the hours before sleep and after fucking about where we would travel, the things we would do, and the family we might one day have.

The look in Nova's eyes when we spoke about family moved through me like an earthquake every time. I knew he wanted a baby with me more than anything, not only because of that look, but the way he pressed his cheek to my belly sometimes and drew circles on my hips, as if he was just waiting for a time when he could plant a baby in there and watch it grow inside me.

I didn't need marriage or stability, the white picket fence and 2.5 kids I used to think I needed in order to feel normal, to feel safe. With Nova, I'd learned how to love life exactly the way it came, because seeing the world at his side, through his eyes, made me eager for any and everything each day had to offer. Even the most ordinary of things was made exemplary through the prism of his love.

So I wasn't expecting to round the corner of Street Ink, into the alley we'd once graffitied with a tribute to Dane, to see the entire brick wall filled with colourful, magnificent art.

And I wasn't expecting that those images, the plethora of flowers, the skateboard in one corner, the music notes spiraling into the sky, to surround a central image that was at least twelve feet tall.

An image of *me*.

Every detail was there, the shine and heft of my thick hair as it slid over my tattooed shoulders, the way my eyes creased underneath when I smiled, and the exact form of my mouth coloured a pale, dusky pink.

Above it all, in sloping, incredibly cool graffiti were the words, 'Nova's Flower Child'.

And below it all, the words, 'Marry me'.

I gasped, both hands flying to my wide-open mouth as if to catch the shock spilling out my body.

When I looked over at Nova, he was on his knees below me, that wicked, roguish grin cutting into his gorgeous face.

"Meant what I said about the rest of our lives," he began, eyes shining so bright I had to blink at the beauty of him. "Wanna make you mine in every way I can even though I know nothin' in the world can shake you from my side. I'm gonna be your best friend, your family, and the lover who rocks your fuckin' world," I laughed through the sob stuck in my throat, "for the rest of our time on this earth. But I'm still gonna ask you, Lila Meadows, to make both of our dreams come true by bein' my wife and officially becomin' a Booth."

I was crying so hard I couldn't see him through the flood in my eyes, but I still launched myself into his arms and peppered his face with kisses as I chanted, "Yes, yes, yes."

He laughed then, a bright, loud burst of sound like birdsong erupting through trees. I pulled back so I could blink away the wet and watch him, the beauty of his tattooed throat, his thick, kinky, dark hair in my hands, his mouth moving with the sounds of joy I'd given him.

And when he tipped down his head to smile at me, I kissed the laughter right off his lips.

Thank you so much for reading INKED IN LIES!

DMW (The Fallen Men, #6) is coming next autumn!

Curious about what happens when King and Cressida return?
Stay tuned for a Christmas novella coming December 2020!

If you want to stay up to date on news about new releases and bonus content join my reader's group or subscribe to my newsletter!

Need to vent?
Join the Inked in Lies Spoiler Room!

If you loved reading about the angsty age-gap between Lila and Nova, you will love The Fallen MC's President, Zeus Garro's taboo love story! Discover what happens when the Prez of The Fallen MC saves the life of the mayor's daughter and their lives become entangled for good...

A Top 40 Amazon Bestseller...

"Taboo, breathtaking, and scorching hot! I freaking loved WELCOME TO THE DARK SIDE."—Skye Warren, *New York Times* bestselling author

One-Click WELCOME TO THE DARK SIDE now!

Turn the page for an excerpt...

Welcome to the Dark Side (The Fallen Men, Book #2)
Excerpt

I was a good girl.
I ate my vegetables, volunteered at the local autism centre and sat in the
front pew of church every Sunday.
Then, I got cancer.
What the hell kind of reward was that for a boring life well lived?
I was a seventeen-year-old paradigm of virtue and I was tired of it.
So, when I finally ran into the man I'd been writing to since he saved my
life as a little girl and he offered to show me the dark side of life before I
left it for good, I said yes.
Only, I didn't know that Zeus Garro was the President of The Fallen
MC and when you made a deal with a man who is worse than the devil,
there was no going back...
A standalone in The Fallen Men Series.

Prologue.

WELCOME TO THE DARK SIDE
EXCERPT

I was too young to realize what the *pop* meant.

It sounded to my childish ears like a giant popping a massive wad of bubble gum.

Not like a bullet releasing from a chamber, heralding the sharp burst of pain that would follow when it smacked and then ripped through my shoulder.

Also, I was in the parking lot of First Light Church. It was my haven not only because it was a church and that was the original purpose of such places, but also because my grandpa was the pastor, my grandmother ran the after-school programs, and my father was the mayor so it was just as much his stage as his parents'.

A seven-year-old girl just does not expect to be shot in the parking lot of a church, holding the hand of her mother on one side and her father on the other, her grandparents waving from the open door as parents picked up their young children from after-school care.

Besides, I was unusually mesmerized by the sight of a man driving slowly by the entrance to the church parking lot. He rode a great growling beast that was so enormous it looked at my childish eyes like a silver and black backed dragon. Only the man wasn't wearing shining armour the way I thought he should have been. Instead, he wore a tight long-sleeved shirt under a heavy leather vest with a big picture of a fiery skull and tattered wings on the back of it. What kind of knight rode a mechanical dragon in a leather vest?

My little girl brain was too young to comprehend the complexities of the answer but my heart, though small, knew without context what kind of brotherhood that man would be in and it yearned for him.

Even at seven, I harboured a black rebel soul bound in velvet bows and Bible verse.

As if sensing my gaze, my thoughts, the biker turned to look at me, his face cruel with anger. I shivered and as his gaze settled on mine those shots rang out in a staccato beat that perfectly matched the cadence of my suddenly overworked heart.

Pop. Pop. Pop.

Everything from there happened as it did in action movies, with rapid bursts of sound and movement that swirled into a violent cacophony. I remembered only three things from the shooting that would go down in history as one of the worst incidents of gang violence in the town and province's history.

One.

My father flying to the ground quick as a flash, his hand wrenched from mine so that he could cover his own head. My mother screaming like a howler monkey but frozen to the spot, her hand paralyzed over mine.

Useless.

Two.

Men in black leather vests flooded the concrete like a murder of ravens, their hands filled with smoking metal that rattled off round after round of *pop, pop, pop*. Some of them rode bikes like my mystery biker but most of them were on foot, suddenly appearing from behind cars, around buildings.

More of them came roaring down the road behind the man I'd been watching, flying blurs of silver, green and black.

They were everywhere.

But these first two observations were merely vague impressions because I had eyes for only one person.

The third thing I remembered was him, Zeus Garro, locking eyes with me across the parking lot a split second before chaos erupted. Our gazes collided like the meeting of two planets, the ensuing bedlam a natural offshoot of the collision. It was only because I was watching him that I saw the horror distort his features and knew something bad was going to happen.

Someone grabbed me from behind, hauled me into the air with their hands under my pits. They were tall because I remember dangling like an ornament from his hold, small but significant with meaning. He was using me and even then, I knew it.

I twisted to try to kick him in the torso with the hard heel of my Mary Jane's and he must have assumed I'd be frozen in fright because my little shoe connected with a soft place that immediately loosened his grip.

Before I could fully drop to the ground, I was running and I was running toward him. The man on the great silver and black beast who had somehow heralded the massacre going down in blood and smoke all around me.

His bike lay discarded on its side behind him and he was standing straight and so tall he seemed to my young mind like a great giant, a beast from another planet or the deep jungle, something that killed for sport as well as survival. And he was doing it now, killing men like it was nothing but one of those awful, violent video games my cousin Clyde liked to play. In one hand he held a wicked curved blade already lacquered with blood from the two men who lay fallen at his feet while the other held a smoking gun that, under other circumstances, I might have thought was a pretty toy.

I took this in as I ran toward him, focused on him so I wouldn't notice the *pop*, the screams and wet slaps of bodies hitting the pavement. So I wouldn't taste the metallic residue of gun powder on my tongue or feel the splatter of blood that rained down on me as I passed one man being gutted savagely by another.

Somehow, if I could just get to *him*, everything would be okay.

He watched me come to him. Not with his eyes, because he was busy killing bad guys and shouting short, gruff orders to the guys wearing the same uniform as him but there was something in the way his great big body leaned toward me, shifted on his feet so that he was always orientated my way, that made me feel sure he was looking out for me even as I came for him.

He was just a stone's throw away, but it seemed to take forever for my short legs to move me across the asphalt and when I was only halfway there, his expression changed.

I knew without knowing that the man I'd kicked in his soft place was up again and probably angry. The hairs on the back of my neck stood on end and a fierce shiver ripped down my spine like tearing Velcro. I didn't realize it at the time, but I started to scream just as the police sirens started to wail a few blocks away.

My biker man roared, a violent noise that rent the air in two and made some of the people closest to him pause even in the middle of fighting. Then he was moving, and I remember thinking that for such a tall man, he moved *fast* because within the span of a breath, he was in front of me reaching out a hand to pull me closer...

A moment too late.

Because in that second when his tattooed hands clutched me to his chest and he tried to throw us to the ground, spiraling in a desperate attempt to act as human body armour to my tiny form, a *POP* so much louder than the rest exploded on the air and excruciating pain tore through my left shoulder, just inches from my adrenaline-filled heart.

We landed, and the agonizing pain burned brighter as my shoulder hit the pavement and my biker man rolled fully on top of me with a pained grunt.

I blinked through the tears welling up in my eyes, trying to breathe, trying to *live* through the pain radiating like a nuclear blast site through my chest. All I saw was him. His arm covered my head, one hand over my ear as he pulled back just enough to look down into my face.

That was what I remember most, that third thing, Zeus Garro's silver eyes as they stared down at me in a church parking lot filled with blood and smoke, screams and whimpers, but those eyes an oasis of calm that lulled my flagging heart into a steadier beat.

"I got you, little girl," he said in a voice as rough and deep as any monster's, while he held me as if he were a guardian angel. "I got you."

I clutched a tiny fist into his blood-soaked shirt and stared into the eyes of my guardian monster until I lost consciousness.

Sometimes now, I wonder if I would have done anything differently even if I had known how that bullet would tear through my small body, breaking bones and tender young flesh, irrevocably changing the course of my life forever.

Always, the answer is no.

Because it brought me to him.

Or rather, him to me.

Get it now for FREE on Kindle Unlimited!

THANKS ETC.

I wrote this book during an odd time. A pandemic was raging around the world, economies suffered, and racial issues in America reached new highs of horror that gave birth to a revived social justice movement. Amid so much chaos and sorrow, I had a supremely difficult time taking my mind off the important issues in my reality. Happily, Nova and Lila saved my days, tugging me into the beloved world of The Fallen to give me an escape from everyday negativities, and I hope as you read this book, it does the same for you.

Nova Booth is a complicated hero, and therefore, no surprise, one of my favourites. Charming, gorgeous, and sociable, he seems on the surface to be exactly what he represents: easy-going, untested, and beautiful in every way. I love that Lila brings out his depth, the over-the-top possessive, growling, brooding man we never see with anyone else. He's kind of the opposite of my normal biker, who is gruff on the exterior but sweet within. Nova is deceptive, a prettily wrapped package hiding a nuclear reactor.

Unrequited love is one of the worst, most hopeless feelings a human can experience. It makes you feel as if you have this beautiful treasure in your chest that no one wants to see. I hope Lila's angst resonated with you, but I hope more that, her choices made sense to you. It is incredibly hard to cleave two entangled hearts like hers and Nova's, but I believe she was right to have faith in him and in their love.

On a serious note, sex trafficking is a very real issue that still impacts the lives of a disastrous amount of people internationally. Both men and women exploit youth by getting them hooked on drugs, offering them love and/or money, and then slowly introduce them to sexual slavery. It is a horrible reality that lingers at the edges of society and often doesn't get enough attention.

If you are a victim or suspect someone needs help, please reach out to Canada's national human trafficking hotline at 1-833-900-1010 or the hotline for your country of residence.

Now, on to the good stuff, because thanking the people who make my dream job possible is like the icing on the cake of having published another novel.

Allaa, my love, thank you for being my twin, my rock, and my sounding board. Even though words are my livelihood and my passion, I cannot find ones adequate enough to express my love and appreciation for you.

To my #dirtysoulsister Michelle Clay. We are kindred souls, and with you, I feel utterly myself and 100% supported. I admire and aspire to you as a woman, and I am so incredibly grateful to have your love in my life.

Annette, my sweet love, your optimism and light bring joy to my every day. Thank you for taking care of me, for looking out for me, and for always stepping up. I love you so much sometimes it makes me want to cry.

To Ella, the Chanel to my Coco. We've been through a lot together, and I look forward to years of more laughter, chaos, and sisterhood. Thank you for being a safe harbour and someone I can always trust.

Bre, I am so glad we finally took the plunge and started to work together! Thank you for being so receptive, encouraging, and most of all, kind. You make my chaotic life much more efficient, and I am so grateful for that.

Ashlee, my Slytherin, my graphic magician, my friend. You make me laugh, you make me weep horny tears over the graphics you make me, and you always make me feel loved and supported.

Kim from Kim BookJunkie Editing, thank you for harnessing the calamity of my manuscript and taming it into something clear, concise, and grammatically correct! You are a Godsend, and I'm so grateful you are my editor.

Jenn from Social Butterfly PR, I am so glad we finally got to work together. Your expertise, management, and just straight up charm completely wow me and made this release my best yet. Thank you so much for everything you do!

Najla Qamber from Najla Qamber Designs, as always, you deserve thanks for putting up with my last-minute demands for your gorgeous graphics and for making me the most stunning covers. I can't imagine working with anyone else, and I wouldn't want to.

To Nova's Naughty Review Team, thank you so much for being my cheerleaders. Being an author is a lonely pursuit sometimes, and it's hard not to be paranoid about your own abilities as a writer, but you guys always give me so much love and support! Thank you for shouting about my books!

Giana's Darlings, you are the best reader's group on the planet and my safe, little happy place on the Internet. I love talking with you all about books, boys, and real-life problems. It's like having my own personal girl squad, and that's pretty freaking cool.

I have so many friends in this amazing community that I cannot possibly pay tribute to all of them, but I have to give special thanks to Sarah Green for making me laugh every single day and Parker S. Huntington for always being my sounding board and guru. This community is filled with so many outstanding authors and truly amazing women, so I consider myself blessed to be a part of it.

There are countless bloggers who made this release shine like the North Star in a sky filled with innumerable book releases, and I'm so grateful to each and every one of you. My most special thanks has to go to Jessica @peacelovebooksxo, Lisa @book_ish_life, Emilie @gianadarlingfans, @krysthereader and @kerilovesbooks for always sharing and supporting my posts.

To my sister, Grace, thank you for always believing in me. From the beginning, you were one of the only voices that encouraged me to follow my dreams, and I am so damn glad you did.

To my Armie. I miss the days of lulling you to sleep with the sound of my clacking keys, but even separated, you still inspire me to be my best self and produce my best work. Thank you for being the best friend I always dreamed of. You mean everything to me.

Fiona and Lauren, you are two massive supports and joys in my life. It constantly astounds me how supportive you two are. Your encouragement and love buoys me even when I'm drowning in stress, doubt, and deadlines.

My Albie, you've been my best friend since middle school, and I cherish every single moment we've spent together over the years. You've helped me grow into the person I am today, and I love you so much more than I could ever hope to relay.

Finally, to the Love of My Life. Amid all the chaos of the last six months—a global pandemic, job instability, canceled plans and trips—your love was the constant that got me through. Thank you for believing in me even when I don't, for supporting me when I forget to take care of my needs, and for making the choice to love me passionately and fiercely every single day.

ABOUT GIANA DARLING

Giana Darling is a *USA Today*, *Wall Street Journal*, Top 40 Best Selling Canadian romance writer who specializes in the taboo and angsty side of love and romance. She currently lives in beautiful British Columbia where she spends time riding on the back of her man's bike, baking pies, and reading snuggled up with her cat, Persephone.

Join my Reader's Group
Subscribe to my Newsletter
Follow me on IG @gianadarlingauthor
Like me on Facebook
Follow me on Goodreads
Follow me on BookBub
Follow me on Pinterest

OTHER BOOKS BY GIANA DARLING

The Evolution of Sin Trilogy

Giselle Moore is running away from her past in France for a new life in America, but before she moves to New York City, she takes a holiday on the beaches of Mexico and meets a sinful, enigmatic French businessman, Sinclair, who awakens submissive desires and changes her life forever.

The Affair

The Secret

The Consequence

The Evolution Of Sin Trilogy Boxset

The Fallen Men Series

The Fallen Men are a series of interconnected, standalone, erotic MC romances that each feature age gap love stories between dirty-talking, Alpha males and the strong, sassy women who win their hearts.

Lessons in Corruption

Welcome to the Dark Side

Good Gone Bad

After the Fall

Inked in Lies

A Fallen Men Companion Book of Poetry:
King of Iron Hearts

The Enslaved Duet

The Enslaved Duet is a dark romance duology about an eighteen-year old Italian fashion model, Cosima Lombardi, who is sold by her indebted father to a British Earl who's nefarious plans for her include more than just sexual slavery... Their epic tale spans across Italy, England, Scotland, and the USA across a five-year period that sees them endure murder, separation, and a web of infinite lies.

Enthralled (The Enslaved Duet #1)
Enamoured (The Enslaved Duet, #2)

The Elite Seven Series
Sloth (The Elite Seven Series, #7)

Coming Soon:
AhiL (Dante's Book)
DMW (The Fallen Men, #6)

CPSIA information can be obtained
at www.ICGtesting.com
Printed in the USA
BVHW032211161022
649599BV00016B/82